A SPIRITED MOUNT

Meridene guided the plodding mare toward Revas. Dressed in tight-fitting trunk hose and a quilted leather jerkin, he looked like a gentle man, rather than a warrior eager to command all of the Highlands.

Grasping her waist, he set her on the ground. "You enjoyed the ride?"

The casual question fired her temper. "Twasn't a ride, but a crawl. I'd like a better horse."

"You prefer a stallion, perhaps?"

No wonder the people of Elginshire sought his counsel; his easy manner could melt the coldest heart. But not hers. "Is he spirited?"

"He's been known to ride throughout the night and never lose his wind or break his stride."

Innocent though she was, Meridene knew he wasn't talking about horses. "Does he take well to the bit?"

Banked passion smoldered in his eyes. With hands equally suited to wielding a broadsword or coddling a child, he cupped her face. When his lips were only a breath away, he whispered, "Your stallion has a soft and willing mouth."

She'd come too far to retreat, but heaven help her, she feared losing her heart. "You're trying to trick me."

"Nay, Meridene. I'm trying to love you."

Turn the page to discover praise for
ARNETTE LAMB's other magnificent tales. . . .

CHIEFTAIN

"Powerful, emotionally intense, sexually charged, *Chieftain* typifies Arnette Lamb's storytelling talents."

—*Romantic Times*

"As readers have come to expect of Arnette Lamb, *Chieftain* is an excellently written and powerfully moving Medieval romance novel. . . . All-in-all, another superb read from the pen of a master storyteller."

—*Affaire de Coeur*

BORDER BRIDE

"*Border Bride* is vintage Arnette Lamb. This irresistible tale warms your heart, tickles your funny bone, and delights your senses."

—*Romantic Times*

"The incredibly talented Arnette Lamb weaves a fascinating tale that incorporates Scottish history into an emotionally moving and realistic love story."

—*Affaire de Coeur*

"Arnette Lamb's *Border Bride* is not light, but deep and sensuous. It shows the emotional effect on a child denied love, and the danger of child's play. It's sexually stimulating and very fast-paced. Its theme is love heals the human heart. You will bask in its afterglow."

—*Rendezvous*

BORDER LORD

"All that a historical romance should be: fast-paced, funny and hot-blooded. . . . *Border Lord* is one of the best of the year."

"*Border Lord* is stupendous! Arnette Lamb has a tremendous gift for writing genuine, warm, humorous, sensual love stories. Treat yourself. . . ."

"What a warm and witty tale Ms. Lamb has spun!"

"A twisting, turning maze of laughter and love. This is Lamb at her heartwarming best."

"An excellent tale of high adventure. . . . Ms. Lamb has written a choice story filled with humor and a special understanding of human motivation and love."

Books by Arnette Lamb

Highland Rogue
The Betrothal
Border Lord
Border Bride
Chieftain
Maiden of Inverness

Published by POCKET BOOKS

ARNETTE LAMB

MAIDEN of INVERNESS

POCKET BOOKS

New York   London   Toronto   Sydney   Tokyo   Singapore

This book is a work of fiction. Names, characters, places and incidents are products of the author's imagination or are used fictitiously. Any resemblance to actual events or locales or persons, living or dead, is entirely coincidental.

An *Original* Publication of POCKET BOOKS

POCKET BOOKS, a division of Simon & Schuster Inc.
1230 Avenue of the Americas, New York, NY 10020

ISBN: 0-671-88220-1

First Pocket Books printing March 1995

10 9 8 7 6 5 4 3 2 1

POCKET and colophon are registered trademarks of Simon & Schuster Inc.

Cover art by Lee MacLeod; stepback art by Lina Levy

Printed in the U.S.A.

For my sister,
Carol Lamb Seacat,
in whose hands a Ping five iron
becomes a deadly weapon

Special thanks to Alice Shields for her creative input and support, to Christina Dodd for her expertise, and to Pat Stech for her eye for detail.

MAIDEN of INVERNESS

PROLOGUE

Auldcairn Castle
Scottish Highlands
Early fall, 1296

"Bring the butcher's lad to me!"

The angry voice behind the closed door belonged to Edward Plantagenet, the first of that name to claim the throne of England, and the last, pray God, to covet the crown of Scotland.

Sweat beading his brow, his stomach churning, Revas Macduff locked his knees to keep from running. But to where? English knights lined the hallway and filled the common room below. Welshmen patrolled the castle battlements, deadly longbows at the ready.

"Fetch him, Brodie!"

A hand clasped Revas's shoulder. "Go on, lad," said Brodie, the sheriff of Elgin. "By the cross, he's had his fill of killing our kinsmen this day."

Revas hoped it was so, for he could not die. His father needed him. There was no one else to sharpen the butchering knives or care for the horse or fetch water from the well.

Turning, he looked up at Kenneth Brodie. Fatigue

rimmed the sheriff's eyes, and dirt streaked his kindly face. His hair still bore the imprint of a helmet. Without his chain of office, his tunic looked plain and his shoulders the breadth of an ordinary man.

Revas's fear turned to impotent rage, for Kenneth Brodie was a fair man with little patience for those who broke the law, and less for those who ignored the poor. He'd been stripped of his power, but his life had been spared.

Revas's own fate was uncertain. "Why has the English king summoned me?"

"I know not, Revas, but the steward heard him asking after the common lads of Elginshire. In with you, and address him as 'Your Majesty.'" Leaning down, the sheriff whispered, "But remember, the king is but a man with loyalties and debts, same as you."

The sheriff's words echoed in Revas's ears, but when the door opened, his courage shriveled.

Wearing chain mail, leather trews, and war boots with golden spurs, the king of England sat on a bench near a table strewn with rolls of parchment. Some folks said that he cast a long shadow over Scotland. Revas understood why.

Looking up, the king glared. Revas fought a shiver at the coldness in those blue eyes.

"Are you the butcher's lad?"

Remembering to speak slowly so his voice wouldn't break, Revas said, "His son, Your Majesty."

With a gauntlet and a dirk, the king spread out a map roll and weighted the edges. One corner of the parchment curled around the fingers of the blood-stained battle glove, but the weight held.

"How old are you?"

"Three and ten, Your Majesty."

"Brawny for your age, eh? Or do you lie?"

Revas did lie, on occasion. If his father miswielded his crutch and accidentally toppled the water bucket,

Revas swore he'd left the pail in the way. He also lied when he came home with a bloodied lip, not from a fall, as he told his father, but from fighting with the chandler's son, who claimed Revas's father had cut off his own leg and sold it for a mutton shank. Yes, Revas lied, but only when necessary.

The king rose. "Answer me, lad."

Intimidated by the English monarch's towering form, Revas glanced at the rich furnishings; yet his interest strayed from luxurious tapestries and tallow candles to the man who had vanquished the mighty Highland clans.

Swallowing back a lump the size of a gull's egg, he said, "Nay, Your Majesty. I'm a good lad and true; ask anyone."

The king began to pace. Rushes crunched beneath his heavy foot gear. "Do you aspire to greatness, Revas Macduff?"

"I honor my father, Your Majesty."

"'Tis said you are of common stock."

"Common?" The word came out as a squeak. Revas cleared his throat. "I haven't a title, or spurs, or golden bands of war, Your Majesty."

"But you've enough Scots pride to fill what's left of Wales."

He made it sound like an insult. Revas could think of no polite reply.

"Know you why I summoned you here?"

"Nay, Your Majesty."

"Do you read?"

What an odd question. A butcher's son had no need of a clerk's skill. It was a low prank the king played, robbing a lad of his dignity. Royalty ought to behave better. But what could Revas do besides girdle his pride and bide his time? King Edward of England would grow bored and move on to other sport. Father had said so. Revas was too smart to be lulled into a trap, even a royal one. "Nay, Your Majesty. I do not read."

"Just so. Well, Revas Macduff, it suits me to give you a wife and see you wed this day."

Revas jerked back, his mind a mass of confusion. Was the king daft? "A wife?"

"And this castle, too. Think you can govern here?"

The wrong answer could mean further humiliation. "But what of Sheriff Brodie?"

"He will advise you, until you are old enough to hold this keep for me. What say you?"

Revas blurted, "Cutberth Macgillivray is the king of the Highlands. He will rally the clans of Chapling. They will storm these castle walls."

The king made a fist and pounded the table so hard, the weights bounced off the map, and it snapped back into a roll. "Then I shall hammer the clans of Chapling as easily as I conquered Elginshire. Chapling," he scoffed. "Putting a name to unity will not make Macgillivray a king. The throne of the Highlands is pure ceremony, bestowed at the hands of green-eyed women."

A fearful Revas took two steps toward the hall door.

"Stay." As quickly as it had come, the king's anger fled. "And meet your bride."

He left a gawking Revas and went to a side door. Opening it, the king said, "Come, lass."

A ladies' maid with carrot-colored hair tucked beneath a coif marched into the room. She was bonny in her own way. She was also old enough to have given birth to Revas. He couldn't wed her. Surely it would be a sin.

She curtsied, then looked back into the doorway. A moment later, a young girl stepped forward.

Dumbstruck, Revas watched Meridene Macgillivray, the grand princess of the Highland folk, move toward him. Kings and queens and their get came and

4

went, but since the sixth century, when Saint Columba brought Christianity to the Scots, her clan, in every generation, had bred a raven-haired, green-eyed daughter. *The Maiden of Inverness.*

Revered and cherished by the Scots, she, and only she, could crown her husband king of the Highlands.

But she was only eight years old. And she was a princess. Revas couldn't marry her. Astounded, he glanced at the king.

"Comely, isn't she?" He winked. "Or should I say she's a bonny lass?"

Revas thought the term had been coined expressly for Meridene Macgillivray. She wore a bloodred surcoat over a bliaud of white fabric so sheer that he could see her skinny arms beneath. A border of five-petal flowers, the device of the Maiden, ringed the garment at her wrists and neck. Tied at her waist was a tartan sash, the bright red, blue, and green plaid worn only by the royal family of the Highlands. Her husband would one day don that special tartan.

According to the old wives, the Maiden sported a halo that shimmered with heavenly light. Not today. Meridene Macgillivray looked as if she would vomit her supper. Agony dazed her bright green eyes, and her fair complexion paled with illness. A bruise discolored the side of her face. Had the brutish king beaten her?

She raised a small hand to the discoloration on her cheek; then she blinked in fatigue.

Revas knew that if she didn't sit down soon, she'd fall in a heap. No, he corrected, when this lass swooned she'd wilt gracefully, like a feather drifting to the floor.

He had to help her. He moved forward and, with practiced ease, pretended to step on something sharp. Yelping, he hobbled to cradle a foot.

"Have you no shoes, lad?" said the king.

"Nay, Your Majesty." Still watching her closely and willing her to understand his ploy, Revas said, "I mean, yes, I have shoes, but only for church."

"Not an audience with your king," came the rueful murmur.

When she swayed, Revas said, "May we sit, Your Majesty?"

With a pained smile, the king waved toward a bench. "We'll all sit."

The king took the only chair. Revas helped her to the bench, then sat beside her.

"Thank you," came her soft whisper. "I fear I'll disgrace myself."

"Nay. I'll help you."

"You're very kind."

She smelled of new linen washed in costly soap. She was just a girl, and some brute had beaten her. Revas wished he were older and skilled with a broadsword. He'd drag the bully into the yard and whack him to pieces.

"Have you nothing to say to *me*, Macduff?" asked the king.

Revas couldn't resist looking at her again. Her black-as-night hair trailed down her back and pooled on the bench. Upon her marriage, she would wear a coronet of rowan leaves. Upon her wedding day, the lass of the Macgillivrays would demand her father's sword. With the ceremonial weapon, she would dub her husband king of the Highlands.

"Do words escape you?" said the king of England.

"Nay, Your Majesty." He caught the king's gaze. "But the Maiden is betrothed to the earl of Moray's heir, and her father wants an alliance with them."

Sighing, Edward Plantagenet scratched his gray beard. "That match ill serves my plans for the future of Scotland. Marriage between the two of you pleases me greatly."

"Nay!" wailed the red-haired serving woman.

"Out!"

At the king's command, she blanched, then fumbled with the latch before dashing from the room.

"Wretched, ignorant Scots," he murmured.

"But I cannot be king of the Highlands," Revas confessed. "I'm but a butcher's son."

"Precisely." The king leered, as if proud of himself. "You will wed this lass posthaste."

Hadn't he noticed the Maiden's distress? "She's hurt, Your Majesty."

"Of course she's hurt," he bellowed, loud enough for the bishop in Nairn to hear. "Her wretched father beat her rather than see her wed to you. What say you, Revas Macduff, to that bit of deviltry?"

Small pearly teeth covered her bottom lip. Her flat chest quivered with sobs she struggled to control. Yet she held her chin high and her back stiff. *The Maiden of Inverness*. Here. Seated so close to Revas Macduff, he could feel her warmth.

Awe filled him, and years of loyalty to the ruling Macgillivrays colored his opinion. "But her father's the king of the Highlands."

The English king shot to his feet. The Maiden rose, too, but her footing was unsteady. Revas jumped up and took her arm.

"Cutberth Macgillivray is the king of nothing." Plantagenet's blue eyes widened, and making a fist, the king laid it across his own chest. "I rule here now, and if the dead you see are not proof enough, by Saint George, I'll strike the battle again."

The elders believed that England could lay claim to Scotland until the sea swallowed the land, but they'd never govern the Highlands. Revas thought of the blood-soaked battlefield, an hour's ride away. Closer, evidence of England's might was everywhere to see— bodies of clansmen had been piled high and even now awaited the torch; severed heads of a dozen clan chiefs stood on pikes at the city gates.

Revas shuddered at the waste of human life and Scottish dignity. Did the Maiden feel it too? So closed was her expression, he could not tell. Where were her clansmen?

"Where is her father?" he asked.

"In retreat," growled the king. "Where all good cowards go. Now. I return to England today, but I command you to take this lass to wife and hold this castle for me."

The notion of Revas Macduff wedding the legendary Maiden of Inverness was wild beyond belief. Governing Auldcairn Castle didn't bear considering. He said the first thought that came to mind. "But she's as weak as a lamb."

Chuckling, Edward Plantagenet said, "And you're as pure as she is, I'll wager. Are there no willing wenches in Elginshire? Or are you too green yet to mount one and give her your all?"

The blow to his manhood was more than Revas could bear. He puffed out his chest. "I could've had the carter's daughter."

A girlish gasp of embarrassment followed his artless admission.

The king scoffed. "Perhaps I should have chosen the carter's son to wed this girl. He would have done as well."

"Revas," she whispered. "You must not let him goad you into rebellion."

The king laughed and reached for a goblet of ale. "Mayhap there's a banked fire in you, butcher's son." He held up the cup in a mock salute; then he marched from the room. The door closed behind him, but his booming voice rang clear. "Summon a priest. The Maiden of Inverness will wed the butcher's son."

Laughter erupted in the hall.

Overwrought, Revas took her hand. It felt cold and small and soft. "I beg your forgiveness, Maiden."

"'Twasn't your fault, Revas."

Although weak, her voice sounded like a spring breeze stirring the rowan trees. She looked up at him, her green gaze open, kind. Lovely didn't begin to describe her delicate features. From birth, she'd been pampered and tutored. She'd never slept on a soggy bed or tried to light a fire with damp wood and hope.

She eyed his worn tunic and mended hose. "We're pawns, you know."

"Pawns?"

"In wedding me to you, the English king ends the legend of the Maiden of Inverness. A butcher's son cannot rule the Highlands."

She seemed so mature. And defeated. He had to brighten her spirits. "But your mother could have another daughter."

Tears pooled in her eyes. "She'll have no more children. I fear she regrets giving birth to me."

Revas felt his heart break. "Oh, nay. You're too bonny. Surely she worships you. Everyone else in the Highlands does."

A sad smile lifted the corners of her mouth. "You're so innocent, Revas Macduff."

He did feel like a child. Odd, for he was five years her senior, and a lad, too. He grasped a manly subject. "Your father eluded the English king."

"Eluded?" She shook her head. "'Tis true that he retreated to the safety of the Black Isle."

"Then how did you fall prey to the king?"

Her chin quivered. "My father and mother gave me to him."

Revas could think of no fitting reply to the heartless act, so he asked about her home, her friends, and her favorite pastimes. She spoke freely until the side door opened, and a smallish man entered. He wore a short black surcoat, but he did not carry himself like a servant. In his hand he held a tankard.

In the blink of an eye, she assumed a queenly air. "Thomas, what do you here? If the English king sees you—"

"Shush!" The man came forward, his glinty eyes casting furtive glances from Revas to the door. "I've brought you a reviving drink, Lady Meridene."

"Why did Moira not bring it?"

He shoved the mug into her hand. "She's at other duties. Important duties. Here. 'Tis your favorite, barley water. Drink."

The Maiden hesitated. Revas knew he should say something, but what?

Nudging her arm, the man said, "Moira's readying your escape. You'll need your strength for the journey home. You do wish to go home, do you not, my lady? Your mother sore misses you and awaits your return."

Her gaze searched Revas's face, as if she sought reassurance. What could he say? That she should give up her birthright to wed a common lad?

"Lady Meridene," wheedled the man called Thomas. "Think of the Highland people—of your brothers, Robert and William. They await you. Refresh yourself, so I can take you home."

Hope glimmered in her eyes. "William. He loves me well." She drank and coughed.

Voices sounded in the hall.

The man Thomas glanced toward the door. "Worry not, Lady Meridene. The English devils will suffer defeat. Your sire has sworn 'tis so." Then he scurried from the room.

Staring into the mug, she said, "Will you betray Thomas and me?"

For as long as tales had been told, the romantic legend of the Maiden had been passed from generation to generation. It must continue; Revas would lay down his life to make it so. "On my honor, nay. Not even should they burn out my eyes."

A pained expression pinched her face. She licked

her lips, then set the tankard atop the table. "Where do you live?"

Pleasant conversation was the last thing he expected of her now. But then, she'd been trained in the gentle ways of nobility. Revas had been reared in poverty. "I live aback the butcher's stall. But the king said he would give me this keep. If you stay, I will learn to protect you. I'll become a soldier."

"Have you a sword?"

"Nay, but my sire will give me his."

"I've never met a butcher. Is your father a goodly man?"

Family pride swelled Revas's chest. "As braw as the king, except—"

The door flew open. In marched the king, the priest, and the sheriff.

"Come," said Edward of England. "The church is in readiness."

In the time it took to skin a hare, documents were signed and properties transferred. With each activity, the Maiden grew weaker. Kneeling beside Revas in the chapel, she murmured the words, but her voice held little conviction, and she wavered so often, he had to put an arm around her waist to steady her. He accepted the stewardship of Auldcairn Castle, but his thoughts stayed with the girl beside him. Just as the priest made the sign of the cross, she wilted and fell into Revas's arms.

Bracing himself, he held her. Her face blanched as white as death, and her black hair trailed to the floor. Her delicate, white hand lay faceup on the stones, lifeless.

"Maiden?" Revas entreated.

When she moaned, he looked imploringly at the king.

"What's amiss?" Edward leaned close and sniffed her breath. "By the swans, she's been poisoned."

He scooped her into his arms and returned to the

castle. In the lord's chamber, he glared at Revas. "I'll feed you to the hounds for this, Macduff."

She reached for the king's arm, her fingers pale against his colorful tunic. "Blame not Macduff. 'Twas my father's man, Thomas." Her gaze darted to the side door. "In there."

Sheriff Brodie flung the door open, but stopped. The red-haired woman lay in a pool of blood, her throat slashed. "He's gone, Your Majesty. I swear we did not know he was here."

Although his face had reddened with anger, the king spoke softly. "Mark me well, Meridene of Inverness, I'll house you in a place where these Scottish monsters will never find you."

"Monsters." Her voice broke, and she closed her eyes.

"Aye, lass," said the king. "Every man with a drop of Scottish blood."

Frantic, Revas shook her gently. "Rouse yourself, Lady Meridene."

She gasped, clutched her stomach, and doubled over.

"Curse unto hell the men who make war on children." Rigid with anger, the king yelled for his guards to fetch his surgeon.

"Fare you well, Revas Macduff."

At the sound of his name, Revas looked down.

She looked forlorn and frail and close to death, and he was a lowly butcher's son. He'd been given this keep and this important girl. But he was too young to defend either. Tears of confusion blurred his vision. He searched for words to comfort her. "You won't die."

"Nay. I had but a swallow. I'll rally."

She had been betrayed by her family. But now she belonged to Revas, and she would live. His spirits soared.

Lamely he promised, "All will be well, you'll see."

She looked toward the king, who was conversing with the priest and Sheriff Brodie. Reaching into her sash, she withdrew a book. "Here, you must hide this or return it to my mother."

"What is it?"

"'Tis the Covenant of the Maiden. It must not fall into enemy hands."

Larger than his hand and still warm from her skin, the book had wooden bindings illuminated with ancient symbols. Revas slipped it into his tunic. "I shall guard it and you with my life."

A tear fell from her thick black eyelashes and trailed over her cheek. "Only the English king can keep me safe from Scottish monsters."

His spirits plummeted. She belonged to Revas Macduff. The priest had said so. Papers had been signed. Her family had tried to kill her, and King Edward thought they would try again. Now he was taking her to a place of safety.

"I cannot protect you now, but I'll learn a warrior's skill. I'll come for you, my lady," he pledged. "When I'm older, I'll come for you."

"Oh, Revas, did you not hear the king's threat? You'll never find me. What happened today was not a real marriage. I only spoke the vows because a king commanded me."

Determination beat like a harvest drum within Revas. The priest had said the words before God. The Maiden of Inverness belonged to Revas Macduff.

Suddenly he had a man's duty and a husband's vow to fulfill. "I swear on the soul of every Macduff who walked his land before me, I'll come for you."

CHAPTER

1

Scarborough Abbey
North Yorkshire, England
Thirteen years later

"Awaken!"

The whispered command pulled Meridene from a sound sleep. A man's callused hand covered her mouth. His thumb and index finger pressed at her nostrils, almost blocking off the air.

For a groggy moment, she thought of her father. His harsh words, his bruising fist, his indifference to a child who craved his love.

Drawing on that memory, she fought back her fear and squinted to see the face of the man hovering over her. He appeared a huge shadow surrounded by gloom. Frantic, she bit down. He grunted and withdrew his hand.

"Be silent," he hissed. "Or you'll endanger the others."

She filled her lungs to scream. But for whom? For Ana, the Scottish heiress of nine and ten, who occupied the next chamber? No, not Ana. Could she call for the old caretaker who needed a crutch to walk from the garden to the granary? No, not him. Sister

15

Margaret had left yesterday for Fairhope Tower in the Debatable Lands and taken the guardsmen with her. There was no one to challenge this intruder except Meridene, and she would fight.

"Stand away, you wretched cur."

"Shush!"

Flailing her arms, she struck out at the darkness and felt a moment's gratification when she landed a solid blow.

He cursed and pinned her arms at her sides, then rolled her, trapping her in the bed linens. A soft woollen cloth was slipped over her head and secured around her neck. Lifting her off the mattress, he swung her into the air and over his shoulder.

Trussed up like a doomed goose, her head spinning, she was jostled and jolted with every step he took. But to where? Where was he taking her, and why?

She twisted, trying to free her arms. When that failed, she kicked and squirmed. He did not care. His grip was strong, but not bruisingly so. If he planned to ravish her, he intended to do it elsewhere and at his leisure.

But why her? She was of no value. The legend of the Maiden was a forgotten custom—even Meridene knew little of her birthright.

Comelier girls resided at the abbey, wealthy maidens from established families with coin to pay a ransom and lands to attract a suitor.

Then the truth dawned, and Meridene didn't know whether to laugh or cry. This brigand had mistaken her for one of the moneyed heiresses who called Scarborough Abbey home. She had to explain that he had erred. Then she'd laugh in his face.

Sweat dampened her skin, and she gulped for air. Knowing she'd suffocate if she continued to fight, Meridene grew still and listened. She heard only the muffled sound of his breathing.

Heartbeats later she heard the familiar creaking of the postern gate. Then she was lifted again, onto the back of a snorting, prancing horse. A hand pressed her down. The animal lunged into motion.

As soon as the churl reached his destination, she would inform him of his blunder. Whatever profit he expected for his villainy would go unpaid, for no one would ransom Meridene Macgillivray. The notion was laughable. The people of Scotland had forsaken her.

Her benefactor, Edward I of England, was dead. His son and heir, Edward II, either did not know of her existence or did not care, for he hadn't continued her support. Now she earned her keep by the prick of a needle and the stroke of a quill.

She longed to prick this ruffian from gullet to navel, and if he did not return her immediately, she would.

An eternity later, she smelled the sea. The horse stopped. Again she was hoisted into the air and carried. Bootheels sounded on planking. Gulls screamed into the night.

After a shorter walk down a stairway, she was lowered onto something soft. Pray God it wasn't a mattress. Pray God he did not try to ravish her before she could explain.

The gentle rocking motion confirmed their location: a ship. Heart pounding, she rolled free of the blankets and ripped the cloth from her head.

He'd brought her to a small cabin.

He.

Her abductor stood with his back to her. No wonder he had carried her with such ease; he stood as tall and as broad as a century oak. He wore a long black robe and boots that were tooled with ancient Scottish symbols. As a child, Meridene had learned to draw those same designs.

The past rose in her mind—images of a young man,

17

a barefoot lad who had carried himself like a prince and made promises to match.

An utterly unthinkable sensation swept over her.

Turning up the lantern flame, he faced her. "Meridene."

She gasped in surprise. Those deep brown eyes, flaring brows, and arrestingly handsome features could belong to only one man: her husband, Revas Macduff.

Her head grew light, and she hugged herself to stave off a shudder.

He swept off the robe, and his striking red, blue, and green tartan plaid told her something else, equally unthinkable: The butcher's son had declared himself king of the Highlands, and he'd come for his queen.

Wishing it weren't so, and determined to play no part in Scottish politics, she easily summoned indifference. "You've sworn to unite the clans. You challenge my father for the Highland crown."

Lamplight sparkled on his fair hair, turning the strands the hues of sunlight. "Aye. Most of the clans have forsaken him. He has beggared his people to buy a mercenary army."

Scottish meant deceit, treachery, and a landscape littered with corpses. Scottish meant terrified young maidens could be beaten and abandoned, then poisoned by their father's servant. Only the sheltering English abbey had offered Meridene safety and a respite from the memories of her blighted Scottish heritage. The abbey had offered food and warmth and surcease from the starvation and cold that was the lot of Scottish women and children whose men cared only for their own selfish purposes.

Her stomach turned sour. "How entirely Scottish of my father."

"'Tis unfair for you to scorn us all for his crimes."

The burr in his commanding voice reinforced sad memories of Scottish monsters who had ruled her

18

childhood. Guards outside every door. Armed soldiers escorting her even to chapel.

She shivered, but not from the cold, for a brazier radiated heat throughout the close cabin. She could not remember the last time she had thought of her father, and the nightmares had ceased years ago. "My father can buy a legion of tartars for all it matters to me."

Her husband moved to the fire and warmed his hands. The only time she'd seen Revas Macduff, he'd been gangly and unkempt. Charmingly chivalrous, he had braved the wrath of Edward I to spare her dignity.

"You must not fear your father. He will not hurt you again."

Had war and the promise of power vanquished the thoughtful lad she had been forced to wed so many years ago? Probably so, and for that misdeed she felt a fresh surge of anger. As surely as the church trained up priests, Scotland turned innocent lads into fighting men. It was only one of the many reasons she despised her homeland. She might have pitied Revas his circumstances, were she not so distraught by her own.

With effort, she controlled her fear. "How did you find me?"

"A message from a concerned friend."

She'd been estranged from Scotland for so long that Meridene had been certain they'd forgotten her and the tradition that bound her to the people. Some villain had revealed her whereabouts. "Friend? I suspect 'twas a fellow kidnapper."

"Would you have come willingly?"

The absurdity made her smile. "Of course, but not until I had grown fins and scales and acquired a taste for seawater."

Caught off guard, he stared in shock, his lips slightly parted, his eyes alight with confusion. "'Tis no small matter, Meridene."

"Not to you, perhaps."

19

"I vowed I would come for you." He crossed his arms over his chest, revealing a pair of gold bands at his wrists.

She hadn't for a moment believed his promise, but considering his powerful size and commanding presence, he had taken the boyish pledge to heart. "When did you acquire the war bracelets?"

His jaw tightened and he stared at her chin. "I was but five and ten."

Two years after he'd wed her, Revas Macduff had become a blooded soldier. Yet beneath the manly exterior, she could see the lad who'd sworn to suffer the perils of hell rather than betray her.

Damn him for spoiling the sweet memory. Damn him for thinking a marriage between children was real. Damn her for falling prey to him. Scotsmen had been the bane of her youth; they would not pollute her future. Especially not Revas Macduff.

"You sound apologetic for killing your first man."

Tugging on the sleeves of his jerkin, he covered the bands of manhood. "I confess that I would rather build than destroy, a view common to many Highlanders today."

Highlanders. Meridene's stomach roiled. They were all brutish men who had beaten her and cast her out. The tragic turn of events saddened her, but her heart and mind had long since abandoned her homeland. As an orphan in England, she'd tried to forget her brutish people and the father who'd sent a man to poison her.

"What are you?" she challenged. "A reluctant Highland warrior turned gentle farmer? Do not expect me to believe that."

He winced at her angry tone, then adjusted his sword belt. "Did you think I would forswear my vows to you?"

In declaring himself a contender to the Highland throne and returning Meridene to Scotland, he had outsmarted the other Highland chieftains and the now dead English king who had spirited her to safety in England. Against all odds Revas Macduff had risen to glory.

He was doomed to bask in it alone.

"I gave you little thought, Revas. Yours was a youth's promise made to the Maiden of Inverness, who was suffering the effects of poison. I release you from your vow."

"But I do not wish to be released from my vow."

Go gently, she told herself—be reasonable and try to make him understand. "While I'm certain you believe your cause is just, I will not go back to Scotland."

As if he were questioning her refusal to take honey with bread, he casually asked, "Why not?"

She gritted her teeth and tried to look away. She could not. "I feel nothing but hatred for the Highlands."

"What of your duty?"

Years of estrangement from a people who wanted her for nothing more than ceremony strengthened her will. One handsome and enterprising Scotsman would not bend it. "Duty? I was forsaken."

"Never, Meridene, have you been forsaken by me."

Had he turned zealot? That possibility frightened her. He was at ease in her company—comfortable, even after taking her against her will. He was easy to look upon—his face well made, his body strong, and his brown eyes alive with character.

She wanted none of it. "You should not have bothered. My life is in England. I thrive there."

He nodded in sad commiseration, and his overlong hair raked his shoulders. "Ana said you believed 'twas so."

Startled at his familiarity toward the girl, Meridene grew fearful for her friend. Ana had only been at the abbey for a few months. A quiet, shy girl, she followed

21

Meridene like a cat after the fish cart. Ana was innocent. "What have you done with her?"

"Her kinsman is settling her in another cabin."

"Her kinsman? You cannot know Ana or any of her clan. They are Sutherlands."

He grew pensive and stared at her bare feet for so long, Meridene thought he would not reply. He seemed unaccustomed to explaining himself, another trait common among Scottish chieftains.

At length he said, "A man makes friends."

A sense of unrealness swept over her. If he shared a camaraderie with the Sutherlands, whose land lay far to the north, Revas had done more than challenge her father. He had alienated the Macgillivrays from the other Highland clans. A powerful move. "A Macduff does not usually befriend a Sutherland. They have been enemies for hundreds of years."

Confidence poured from him. "*This* Macduff does."

He could make alliances until Gabriel again blew his horn, but Revas Macduff would never wear the Highland crown, not without her, and therein lay her strength. "I care not if the pope calls you companion. I will not go with you."

His direct gaze pinned her. "Your life in England is over, Meridene." The ship began to move. "We sail for Elginshire."

She dashed for the door. He caught her short of her goal. Held against him, she pummeled his chest and bit her lip to hold back tears. He smelled of wool freshened with dried heather, a scent that conjured sad memories of her childhood.

She would not go back.

"Stop fighting me, Meridene."

"I hate you and all of the others."

His hands were gentle on her back, as if he were comforting an ailing child. "You'll find the people changed."

Surprised by the lull in her defenses, she stepped

out of his embrace. "I care not if they have sprouted haloes and mastered the harp."

If determination had an essence, it thrived in the countenance of Revas Macduff. His eyes gleamed honesty, and his hands lay open in earnest entreaty. "They are good people, who believe that you will change their lives. I believe it, too."

She felt his will, tried to push it away, yet it clung to her defenses like lichen to damp rock. He held himself with the easy grace of one born to rule and bound to conquer.

Still, her heart was a desert where Scotland was concerned. "Then disappointment awaits you."

"Because I'm a hapless butcher's son who once groveled before an English king?"

Those were her words, spoken in confidence to a woman she'd considered a friend. The extent of his intrusion into her life dawned on Meridene. "Ana is your spy."

Pride wreathed his handsome features, and he suddenly appeared too large for the small cabin. "Her father is my liege man."

The mighty Sutherlands had gone so far as to swear fealty to Revas Macduff? The notion defied logic and tradition. Clans often united for a common goal. But when the objective was met, they closed ranks around their individual chieftains. Swearing fealty constituted a permanent alliance, and were the Sutherlands to align themselves with anyone, they would bend a knee to her father, the king of the Highlands. Not Revas Macduff.

The direction of her train of thought disconcerted her as much as the man. "I want no part in Scotland's future."

"Resign yourself. We're going home."

"You are going home."

A knock sounded at the door. He opened it, and Meridene watched in dismay as two subalterns carried in her loom, her writing materials, and her books. Revas spoke quietly to the men. Next they brought a finely made trunk into the cabin.

When they left, Revas eyed her nightrail. "Your new wardrobe, my lady. I'm certain you'll want to dress yourself in something fitting and warm. If you will recall, the Highlands are cool this time of year."

She became aware of her own state of undress. He was not bothered in the least that she wore a sleeping gown. Rather he appeared disinterested, for he spoke of honoring vows while he practiced abduction. That troubled her more. "You blackhearted, selfish monster."

He sighed, and his expression softened, giving her an unexpected glimpse of the vulnerable lad she remembered. "Shall I be cruel to you?" he entreated. "Must I lock you in and play the tyrant?"

As a lad, he'd been the only Scottish male to look beyond the legend of the Maiden and see the frightened girl beneath. But the kind lad had become an ambitious and charming man.

She balled her fists. "No doubt you've mastered that tyranny."

"What's this? Pettiness from the Maiden of Inverness? It doesn't suit you." He gave her a rakish smile. "I'm actually a lambkin at heart."

She laughed at that, for he looked as formidable as the king he aspired to be. He'd get no crown from her; her father would wear it until the stars fell into the sea. "You have no heart. Why else would you keep me against my will?"

He straddled the trunk and toyed with the brass latch. The comfortable pose belied his intentions. "Because you are my wife and duty-bound to serve the people of the Highlands."

Her anger turned to hostile rage. "Without so much as a by-your-leave, you expect me to march up to my father and, with all of Clan Macgillivray as witness, demand that he relinquish his throne to you and yield his ceremonial sword to me?"

"Only if I can wield it." He stiffened his arms, and his bulging muscles strained the seams of his jerkin. "I assure you that I have spent the last thirteen years preparing for that very event."

More than battle prowess was necessary to successfully rule the Highland clans. He'd need patience, fairness, and a plan for the future. She doubted he had any of those. What kidnapper could? "Your preparations are in vain."

"The women of Elginshire will support you when you claim the sword of Chapling."

Chapling. It was an old word meaning unity, and the man who wore the Highland crown also assumed the chieftainship of Clan Chapling.

Baffled, Meridene rubbed her temples. "The women of Elginshire? What have they to do with the crown of the Highlands?"

"They will accompany you to Inverness and stand behind you when you demand the sword from your father. 'Tis a pilgrimage they long to make."

Pilgrimage? The word sparked an old and complex memory, but the image was too vague to recall in its entirety. One aspect, however, stood out sharply, and as always, it involved one man: her father. "Oh, no, for I will never set foot on my father's land. Not for you, not even for the promise of paradise."

"You dishonor the women who have sworn to share your quest."

The women. A band of strangers who expected her to demand the crown of the Highlands from her father, then bestow it on Revas Macduff. Not for a place at the right hand of God would she face the father who had tried to kill her rather than see her wed to a man not of his choosing. A monster. Scotland teemed with such beasts.

As if he'd read her thoughts, Revas said, "Your

father will not foul so much as the air you breathe. On that you have my word of honor."

His useless chivalry angered her more than his selfish assumptions. "The devil with Scottish honor."

Revas wanted to shake her and curse her for abandoning her birthright. Deep in his heart, he had harbored the hope that she would willingly come home to Scotland and seek her destiny. He'd underestimated the depth of her feelings and deluded himself about his own. He would do neither again.

"Resign yourself, Meridene."

"Delude *yourself*, Revas."

He had imagined what it would be like to hear her speak his name, but his expectation had not included scorn, for the Maiden should be beyond petulance. He had thought to woo her—a prideful mistake on his part. "Given time, you'll see the right of it."

"Given time, I will wreck your household." She rose and moved so close that her gown brushed his knees. "I will turn maid against bootboy. I will insult the cook until she leaves in disgust. I will publicly accuse your steward of thievery." Her pretty nostrils flared and even her hair quivered with the rage she could not control. "When I'm done, you'll beg me to leave Scotland."

By the sacred stone, she was bold, and her formidable passion drew him like wind to sail. His servants would follow the Maiden of Inverness into the fires of hell. He'd spent years making it so. She couldn't possibly disrupt his household. The notion was laughable.

"Spare yourself the trouble, Revas. Take me back to the abbey now."

Excitement thrummed through him at the prospect of harnessing her passion. But first, he had to get her attention. "Very well." She relaxed until he added, "I will return you to the abbey . . . when our first child is old enough to travel. I'll even accompany you myself."

"You're mad." She pointed a slender, unadorned finger toward the door. "Get out."

She looked so formidable, so set in her ways. Since the moment she'd ripped off the hood and bed linens, Revas had been stunned by the changes in his bride. As a child, she'd been fairylike in her girlish beauty, but the years had transformed a princess into a queen. Gone were her freckles and inquisitive stares, replaced by flawless skin and a forthright manner.

She'd give him sons to slay the dragons of injustice. She'd give him a daughter to carry on the most romantic of Scottish legends. With luck, she'd give him years of companionship and help him shoulder the burdens of his office. He wanted all of those things, and he wanted them from her.

"Stop gawking at me and get out."

It would take more than harsh words to deter him. "A husband is entitled to look at his wife." For effect, he added, "And more."

She swallowed and licked her lips, her eyes glittering with alarm. "Will you ravish me?"

That brought him up short. "You think I will force you?"

She scanned the cabin, then gave him a look rife with irony. "Force seems to be your way."

He fought back a smile at her clever logic. Lord, he'd enjoy trading barbs with her and wooing her back into the Scottish fold. "Do not despair. I will ravish you well and often, once you take the sword of Chapling from your father and give it to me."

She relaxed and pitched her waist-length hair over her shoulder. "Your chivalry has a base purpose. You will not exercise your husbandly rights now, because the Maiden must be pure of body and spirit when she demands the sword from her father and passes it to her husband."

She spoke of the Maiden as someone else. He'd change that, too. For now, he was grateful that she had at last broached the subject of her duty. "Do not forget that you must also be *pure* of heart."

Her gaze sharpened. "How do you know so much about the traditions required of the Maiden?"

He had committed to memory every tenet of the Covenent of the Maiden. Should he tell her that he had taken seriously her long-ago plea that he protect the sacred book? Perhaps later. For now, he would mince words. "'Tis a trait any man would desire in his wife."

She drew back, leaving the air scented with the very English and detestable smell of honeysuckle. "You'll get nothing from me."

"Aye, I will. You'll give me the sword of Chapling." And he'd bathe her in heather.

She studied him, from the mussed strands of his hair to the symbols of rank that adorned his wrists and war boots. A knowing grin gave her a siren's appeal. "Were you my only choice of mates, Revas Macduff, I would willingly go to my grave an innocent."

He'd been too bold, but he knew no other way, and he could not retreat now. "I *am* your choice of husbands until you go to your grave."

"Pity your mother did not go to *her* grave virtuous."

Laughter threatened to burst from him. "Alas, my maiden bride," he said, "I expect we'll manage well enough. Your cutting wit promises to enlighten the loneliest of my nights."

"Be careful, my daring husband, lest you bleed to death in your sleep."

Inwardly he winced at the verbal blow. "'Twill be enjoyable, seeing you yield to the lure of the Highlands."

"I'd sooner drag a dung cart through a bog." Chin high, shoulders squared, she moved around him and opened the door. "Now get out."

Past achieving a graceful exit, Revas stepped into

the companionway. She could not escape him now. "Rest well, Maiden."

"Maiden?" She snatched up his cloak and threw it at him. "I'm no virgin."

Struck dumb, Revas watched as she slammed the door and threw the bolt.

Not a virgin. A denial roared inside him, and his fingers crushed the fabric of his cloak. She had to be innocent. She'd been bred into a code of feminine honor as old as Saint Columba. For centuries the women of her clan had shaped the destiny of the Highlands. Like her mother, some of the Maidens had failed in their marriages and chosen poor husbands. Like her namesake, other Maidens had prospered. It was all written in the Covenant. She knew the rules, the risks, and the rewards. So did he. And when the book was passed to their daughter, Revas would see Meridene add her page to the chronicle and, with God's help, name her husband a truehearted king of the Highlands.

It had to be.

He had devoted his life to righting the wrongs of her father, Cutberth Macgillivray, and winning a kingdom to lay at her feet. Was the daughter as treacherous as the sire?

The unfairness drained Revas as no battle had, for the success of his life's work rested, not on his ability to lead and thrive, but on one woman's virtue.

"Do you believe her?"

Turning, Revas saw John Sutherland rise from the bottom rung of the companionway steps, a lantern in his hand, a sheen of sea spray in his graying hair.

Hope forced Revas to say, "Nay. She's a maiden to her soul."

"Maidenhead or no, 'tis a blessing she's already wed to you, for I know a dozen Sutherland chieftains who'd trade their father's best sporran for a chance to tame her heart." He pushed to his feet. "By the stone, Revas, she is comely."

Revas had expected other men to covet his wife for her beauty, but not for her spirit. The fact that she was the Maiden of Inverness was enough to inspire a man to possess her. But she belonged to Revas Macduff. "She has a fire in her."

Sutherland laughed so hard, he almost dropped the lantern. "You've a gift of understatement even our sovereign, Robert Bruce, would envy. She's a bonfire of defiance."

Revas had no intention of putting out her fire; the Highlanders needed her spirit. Especially now when autonomy from England had become an attainable goal.

Meridene needed the people, too; she just didn't know it yet. He had a plan to change her mind and win her heart. She'd left him no choice but to kidnap her; his informant, Ana, had told him Meridene would not come willingly.

"How fares Ana?"

Shaking his head, Sutherland blew out an exhausted breath. "She saw you carry your wife aboard and recalled your promise to treat Lady Meridene kindly."

Revas battled back guilt. The cog pitched and he braced his arm on the bulkhead until the ship crested a wave. "She's not to fret, John. Meridene is unharmed, and what I did 'twas for the best."

"Aye, you've an obligation to the people and a duty to your wife."

Revas was beginning to think that winning a kingdom might prove easier than swaying his wife. "Would that she were a wee bit biddable."

Sutherland nodded in sage agreement. "What of your promise to Bruce?"

Robert Bruce, the king of Scotland, knew and

approved of Revas's plan to bring Meridene home, as long as she was willing, and Revas had assured him she was. If not, Bruce expected Revas to take the throne of the Highlands by force from Cutberth Macgillivray.

The grim alternative depressed Revas. By reverting to the old ways and declaring war on his dissenters, he could only hope to rule the Highlands by force. The solution was unthinkable, for in returning to the warlike past, he risked losing the peaceful future.

Frustrated with his choices, he headed up the companionway stairs. "Is Randolph's ship still in sight?"

Sutherland followed, holding the lantern high to light their way. "Aye, a dozen ships' lengths off the starboard bow."

Randolph was the younger brother of Drummond Macqueen, a former chieftain who'd recently received a pardon from English captivity. Drummond's wife had been raised with Meridene at Scarborough Abbey. At Christmas last, Drummond had sent his brother, Randolph, with a message for Revas. In the note, he revealed where Revas could find Meridene and explained that she wanted nothing to do with her husband or Scotland.

Then Revas had sent Ana Sutherland to Scarborough Abbey to verify the story.

At the top of the stairs, Revas threw open the hatch. The night wind whistled across the deck, and he drew on his cloak to ward off the chill.

"Shall I hail Randolph's ship?" Sutherland asked.

Revas spotted the vessel, riding the waves hard by. "Aye. He's to take a message to Bruce."

"A message? But the king expects to *see* the Maiden. He said as much when we left the parliament at Saint Andrews."

Never had Revas lied to his sovereign. Through

Robert Bruce, Scotland would break the bonds of English dominion. The Maiden was an integral part of that plan.

Skirting the truth was his best choice. "Have Randolph tell him that the voyage has visited ill humors on my wife."

Sutherland clucked his tongue. "'Tis partly true."

And wholly unfortunate for Revas Macduff. "Send my regrets and invite the king to Auldcairn Castle for Midsummer's Eve."

"Two months? 'Tis wise, Revas, for 'twill give you time to tame her."

"Worry not, friend, for she'll better accept her circumstances on the morrow."

But she didn't.

CHAPTER

2

When Meridene emerged from the companionway, she gave Revas a cold stare, then sought solitude near the bow. He deserved her anger. He intended to combat it with kindness and reason. But now he was momentarily content to simply admire her.

She'd donned the warmest of the cloaks he'd provided, an ankle-length garment of miniver, fashioned with the tanned hides turned inside out. The hides had been worked to suppleness, then dyed a pale leaf green and further embellished with a border of interlocking cinquefoils, the device of the Maiden. The color complemented her forest-hued eyes, and the soft fur accentuated the delicacy of her skin.

She'd braided her glorious black hair and coiled it at the nape of her neck. When a gust of wind whipped around her, she drew up the hood of the cloak and continued to stare at the horizon. Standing just so, she looked like a queen ready to bless a fleet, rather than a wife eager to desert her vows.

Since pledging his troth to her, he'd dedicated every waking hour to unifying Scotland. In contrast, she'd made a vocation of loathing it. Even in her dreams, she cursed her homeland, and when the visions grew too horrid, she cried out in her sleep for help.

Last night she'd awakened him with her screams, but a bolted door had prevented him from comforting her. Soon he'd lie beside her, and when those dark dreams visited her, he'd hold her in his arms and face the demons with her. In their waking hours, he'd bind her to the Highlands again and teach her to love the people who awaited her return.

His heart ached for the young Maiden who'd been so mistreated that she hated her country. Revas prayed that he could make her feel safe, for he believed her hatred stemmed from that fear.

With a tenderness that was bittersweet, he admitted that he revered her, too, and overmuch, for he grew distressed to see her so unhappy at the thought of returning home. She had a right, he was certain, for her memories were painful and her experiences ghastly. His abduction must seem horrid to her in the extreme.

Life had been cruel to his beautiful Scottish princess, and while he could not undo the past, he could assure her future. At his side, she would prosper, and in return, she would ease his loneliness and help him achieve his destiny. She'd reign over the Highlands with the skill of the first Maiden, her namesake. Matching the prowess of that woman's mate promised a challenge that Revas welcomed. Oh, yes. They were in for a merry time, he thought with a smile.

When he'd looked his fill, he approached her. Taking her arm, he said, "Good day, my lady."

She jerked out of his grasp. "Worry not that I contemplate jumping into the sea. I will not forfeit my life for Scotland."

Resigned that he'd made no progress, Revas started again. "For what, then, will you risk your life?"

She turned her face to the wind, her eyes glittering like emeralds in the sun. "For the chance to return to England."

"Achieving your destiny and returning to England are different sides of the same coin."

Her delicate brows arched in confusion, and she tilted her head to the side. "You've become a Highland philosopher. How singular."

The insult bounced off Revas like pebbles hurled at a battle shield. Reminding her of her duty had produced drastic results. He must guide her, steer her gently, then lead her where she truly wanted to go. "Nay. 'Tis only that I had not expected you to deprive yourself of volition. I expected more intelligence."

On a half laugh, she scoffed. "You'll make a fine king of the Highlands. The people deserve a trickster like you."

He grinned, but his mind was a tangle of doubts. He had truly thought flattery would draw her out. A foolish error on his part. "Does that mean you'll get me the sword?"

"No. But I relish seeing you delude yourself."

Be patient, he told himself. She was justified in her anger, and he faced certain defeat in challenging her again. Tricking her was something else altogether. "I anticipate a much more rewarding association with you."

She gave him a withering glare. "Then you have a perverse imagination."

Sensing that she tiptoed close to his verbal trap, he threw out the bait. "Because I ask that you weigh your options?"

Peering over the side, she followed the progress of a family of seals. "Weigh my options? I cannot, for they were not of my choosing."

"Options seldom are, else we'd never have the supreme joy of facing a quandary."

She peered up at him, her interest seriously engaged. He'd forfeit his favorite retreat to Sheriff Brodie for a conversational reply from her.

"Do you embrace strife, Revas?"

Good-bye, hunting lodge, he thought, and said what was in his heart. "I'd rather embrace you."

She blushed, and he held her gaze, even when she would have looked away. Come out and play, Meridene, he silently willed her.

"No."

At least she hadn't said never. He must be making progress.

Ready to give back to her, he relaxed. "I've forgotten the question."

The fur lining of her cape fluttered around her face, the snowy miniver a perfect foil for her jet eyelashes. She almost smiled. "You were trying without success to get me to weigh my options."

He wanted to whoop with joy. He'd led her exactly where he wanted her to go. "Scotland is an option."

She stiffened. "An unacceptable one."

"How do you know? You haven't set foot in the Highlands in thirteen years."

She touched her breastbone. "And I have thrived."

She had, indeed. Now he intended to see her prosper. "Do you possess a mount, Meridene?"

Confusion lent an earthy aspect to her regal beauty. "Yes."

"Did you select the horse yourself?"

"Of course." She stared up at the lookout. "It did not fall out of the sky."

"If I told you a fine mare was available for purchase, if I sang her praises and extolled her virtues, would you not be curious to judge for yourself? Or would you reject the beast out of hand?"

She faced him squarely. "If you recommended the beast, I would reject it out of hand."

With regret, he admitted the small defeat. But he'd never been accused of cowardice. "Your mind is narrow."

She huffed. "Your ploy is obvious."

Suddenly enjoying himself again, he leaned against a water barrel. "Enlighten me, then, as to my ploy."

"'Tis simple. Now that you've taken me captive, you will ignore the cruelty of your actions. You will take me to your home and wait me out. You think to woo me with your charm and enthrall me with your masculine appeal."

He couldn't help saying, "So you think I am appealing?"

On a half laugh, she said, "I'm angry, Revas, not blind."

He savored the compliment, for he instinctively knew she would not often praise him. Not until she fell in love with him. "Do you remember the last time we saw each other?"

"Certainly. You barged into my room and took me against my will."

Tried patience nicked at his decorum. "Before that time."

"Yes. I was eight years old and straining to keep from retching on the king of England."

His heart went out to that valiant girl, but if he showed any weakness, the mature woman would take advantage. He must find a balance between both. "I understand. I expected the king to hang me before sunset."

Her eyes drifted out of focus. "You did?"

"Aye. I even forgot to wear my shoes."

Her expression softened. "My apologies. I didn't see—I hadn't—"

"Thought about what I was feeling that day?"

"No. I was too ill and beset with worry for myself."

"Have you thought of it since?"

"Not in a very long time."

She had, though, and he took that small gift to heart. "You pledged your troth to me. The people of Elginshire witnessed the ceremony."

"They matter not. What of the people in England whom I call friends?"

"Invite them to visit us at our home."

Stubbornness had her in its grip. "I do not wish to be your wife."

"I do not wish to grow old, either," he said reasonably. "But I cannot stop the clock of time."

She gave him a quelling look that probably sent servants scurrying for cover. "Age cannot be annulled. Our marriage can."

Dissolving the marriage was out of the question. "We were chosen for each other."

She tugged at her gloves. "You want a legend, Revas."

He couldn't resist laying a hand on her shoulder. "I want you, Meridene."

Glancing at his fingers, she murmured, "You are eager to become a husband and father?"

The subject of children was a dangerous one and best generalized for now. "'Tis a man's duty to God."

A knowing smile curled her lips. "But first you must take up the sword of Chapling."

Chapling. It was an ancient term, perfectly chosen by the first Maiden of Inverness to symbolize the unity her marriage wrought. The sword had been her gift to her husband. The details of their blessed lives were chronicled in the Covenant. As always, the sentiment made Revas's chest grow tight. "Aye. I will take up the sword and uphold the legend—"

"Aha! I said as much. 'Tis not me you want, but a prophecy."

That took the wind from his sails.

"Do not apologize," she went on. "'Tis a meaningless symbol. What would prevent me from demanding the sword and giving it to you in exchange for passage back to England?"

His own ambition, Revas thought. He could rule the Highlands without the ceremonial sword in his scabbard and the Maiden at his side, but he'd have to conquer Clan Macgillivray first. He wanted unity through peace, and he could not achieve it without her. "I'll tell you what prevents you from demanding your birthright: fear and loathing of your father."

Said plainly, his truthful comment had the desired effect: She dropped the facade of indifference. Earnestly she said, "You think you know so much, Revas."

"About you, yes."

"You would not settle for the sword." She moved around the barrel and out of his reach. "You would seek to bind me to a land I abhor. You want children of me."

She had artfully dodged the emotional perils and the very real danger that existed between father and daughter, a skill she'd had thirteen years to master. Only in her sleep did she become that frightened little girl. "'Tis cruel to deny a man children."

Her interest engaged, she pressed on. "Truly, Revas. How badly do you want the sword?"

More than air to breathe, his soul cried. But he guarded the thought. They were conversing civilly; it was a start. "How badly do you wish to return to England?"

Her force of will was palpable. "Enough to continue bartering with you until God stands as witness to this futile exchange."

Formidable. There was that word again. The too apt description of her inner strength made him rethink his strategy. Were he to strike a bargain with her, he ran the risk of losing and having to honor it. "You plan to await the Second Coming."

She set her jaw. "Yes, and the Third Coming."

In the face of her implacable determination, he aborted his original plan. The irony of his predicament gripped him, and after years spent preparing to welcome her home, he must now compel. She had said the people were doomed to disappointment. A woefully poor description; they would be crushed, for he had gone to drastic measures to make a place for her in the hearts and lives of the people of Elginshire.

The brisk April wind fluttered her cloak, and the damp air made ringlets of the wisps of hair that framed her face. The climate suited her well.

"'Twould appear," she trilled, "that we have, as you say, the supreme joy of facing our first quandary."

He added witty to her list of attributes. "Have you everything you need?"

"How gracious of you to inquire after my needs. Before I answer, you should tell me how long you intend to keep me."

He couldn't help but growl, "Leave off, Meridene."

She blinked in feigned confusion and pulled off her gloves. "Oh, but I'll gladly leave you to your life, should you leave me to mine."

Damn Cutberth Macgillivray for his cruel treatment of her. Damn her father for turning her against all Scots. Damn Revas Macduff for living up to her low expectations. "You take pleasure in being stubborn."

A grin played about her pretty mouth. "You are too quick for me, Revas. I'm but a country girl."

He laughed. "And I'm chancellor of England."

She laughed, too, and he wanted to embrace her.

"When will we arrive?" she asked.

"In a few days—as the weather allows."

"Good. That should give me ample time."

He grew still and cautious. "Time to what?"

She reached up and laid her hands against his cheeks. Her palms were icy cold, yet her eyes shone with warmth. He could fall into that alluring gaze and follow where she led.

"'Twill give me time," she whispered, "to plan your downfall."

With that she left him there, the breeze ruffling his hair, her words rattling his composure.

Two days later, the ship docked at dawn at the seaport of Elgin's End. Meridene dawdled in her cabin, busying her hands with folding and refolding the fine garments Revas had provided. Her eye was drawn to a rose-colored surcoat embroidered with golden thistles at the hem and neck. The garment fitted her perfectly, as did the contrasting bliaud of dark red linen. Even the shoes, gloves, and under-clothing had been fashioned precisely for her.

Ana must have supplied him with the particulars.

Feeling betrayed, Meridene slammed the lid on the trunk, walked to the bulkhead, and peered through the small opening. An endless, churning sea filled her vision.

Since they'd sailed past Aberdeen, she'd grown apprehensive, as if a drum in her chest were beating out a rhythm of foreboding. For the hundredth time she wondered how she could free herself from Revas Macduff. The promise of an eight-year-old girl shouldn't hold sway, not when she'd been ill and confused and coerced into pledging her troth. The law should free her from any obligation. If not, the church must surely annul the unconsummated marriage.

Unconsummated. Therein lay her escape. She had stayed alone in this cabin during the voyage and searched for a means of thwarting him. Prejudice had colored her thinking; now the truth shone clear. Revas's influence could not extend to the church. She would seek refuge in the clergy. They would shelter her and appeal to the pope on her behalf. The new King Edward might be persuaded to endorse her cause for an annulment. It was said he had forbidden the clans to unite.

Her fear ebbed and her heart soared.

A scratching noise on the door interrupted her euphoria.

"Who is it?"

"'Tis Ana, my lady."

The informer. Meridene tried to summon dislike for the girl, but in her heart she knew that Ana had simply followed the dictates of her own father and Revas Macduff. With only a little imagination she could picture him cajoling the impressionable girl. Thirteen years ago, he had done the same to another child, a girl whose father had tried to kill her.

Meridene opened the door.

Her pretty features pulled into a worried frown, Ana stepped into the room. She wore a cloak of heavy black wool lined with the subtle tartan of the Sutherlands, a rich pattern of green, black, red, and white. Her fair hair was mussed, her skin chafed from the wind.

"I suppose you hate me."

"I cannot hate a stranger, Ana, and that is what you are to me."

Her pert chin puckered with determination. "I only pretended because 'twas necessary."

The admission that she'd feigned a friendship saddened Meridene. She'd had few friends in her life, and her oldest and closest companions, Clare and Johanna Benison, had been taken from her—one by death, the other by marriage. Like Ana, the other wealthy heiresses at the abbey were all younger than Meridene and prone to seek her out as mentor rather than friend. "You've done your part, Ana."

She made a fist of her gloved hand. "I would give my life for Highland unity."

Meridene almost laughed. "You err in thinking I will do the same."

"But you were born to it."

"While commendable, your enthusiasm ignites not one spark of loyalty in me. Quite the contrary; I envy you, for England is my home. So do not embarrass yourself by belaboring the point."

Ana touched the symbols on Meridene's new cloak. "You have forgotten how important you are to us."

"To *us?*"

"Aye, to the Highlanders. With you at his side, Revas will bring peace to all of the people above the line."

The Highland line. A demarcation uncharted on any map, yet etched deeply into the hearts of the Scots. Once her father had ruled the clans from the Frasers in the East to the Macleans in Inverness. Revas Macduff had expanded the territory to include this Sutherland woman and her kin in the Western Highlands.

The extent of his domain was staggering. How much did he know about Meridene? "I confided in you, Ana. Did you tell him all of my secrets?"

She stiffened with umbrage. "You'll know the answer soon enough."

Would he give freely of himself to Meridene? Would he cherish her above all else, including Scotland? The obvious answer depressed her, and discussing her private hopes again with Ana served no purpose.

In dismissal, she said, "You have discharged your duty with aplomb, Lady Ana. Fare you well, and God preserve your precious Highland line."

Like a dog after a flea, Ana refused to leave it alone.

"Revas has worked for too long to bring accord to the clans. Why do you hate him so and disparage your own people? They've done you no harm."

No longer the biddable girl eager to follow in Meridene's footsteps, Ana Sutherland was now a self-assured young woman bent on furthering a cause. Meridene didn't care; she wanted no part of a people who poisoned their children, then discarded them like old cloaks. "You know precisely why I despise Scotland, and you repeated my every word to Revas Macduff."

Her eyes pleaded. "He has a goodly heart."

"Then *you* worship him!"

"A score of women want him," Ana taunted.

"So he's a Highland rogue. I'm delighted to know that there's enough of him to please a mere twenty women."

"He wants only you. The English have swayed you otherwise."

"The English *saved* me. The Maiden is no more."

"But you belong to us."

Meridene gave up the fight; Ana would never understand. "Farewell."

Tears filled her eyes. "You don't deserve to be the Maiden of Inverness."

"I couldn't agree with you more. Perhaps you will take up the burden?"

"Burden?" Ana sighed and turned to leave. "You're selfish and cruel, Meridene."

Meridene had thought herself immune to verbal blows, but Ana's parting words stung. Had her life unfolded as it should, Meridene would have gladly fulfilled her duties. She would have wed her father's choice of husband and ruled as her mother and her kinswomen before her. Politics, not her own wants and needs, had determined the course of her life.

How could people hold one female responsible for the acts of the powerful king of England? She had been a child when the king forced her to wed. She couldn't pick up her life now—as if she'd simply been away on holiday for thirteen years. The politics of Scotland was a dangerous web of intrigue, spun by men. Legends like that of the Maiden were romantic tales, completely out of tune with the social climate of the day. Men ruled. And that, as Sister Margaret liked to say, was that.

On the heels of that thought, another doubt crept into Meridene's mind. Had Sister Margaret known of Revas's plan to kidnap Meridene? No, for the kind nun had been more like a mother than a spiritual advisor. She would not condone such villainy, even if a lawful husband had committed it.

Feeling better, Meridene gathered the brush and comb and other personal items Revas had provided. Just as she donned the beautiful new cloak, he came to fetch her.

Once on deck, she scanned the scenery. Patches of snow glistened in the shadows, and the hearty bushes near the waterline were still winter-naked. Dozens of fishing boats bobbed at their moorings in the shallow water; others were upended on the beach, their hulls in various stages of repair. Wattle-and-daub houses dotted the shore, and fishing nets were strung between the dwellings, effectively connecting the residents with the commerce of the village.

Ugly memories of another arrival years ago at this place intruded, but Meridene pushed them back; she must not let that dreadful occasion dull her spirit. She would stand up for herself. Someone here would help her.

Behind her, she heard Revas saying his farewells to Ana and her father. As soon as the cargo of iron and salt was unloaded, the ship would take the Sutherlands home to Drumcardle in the Western Highlands.

Eager to disembark and find the church, Meridene made her way down the gangplank. Moments later, Revas followed.

Watching him stroll toward her, she understood why twenty women wanted him. Not that she cared a sour apple. But she was honest enough to admit that he cut a fine figure, especially dressed as he was in a rust-colored tunic and tight-fitting hose. The tooled boots made his legs look inordinately long and perfectly suited his easy gait.

Arms swinging, the wind ruffling his golden hair, he surveyed his kingdom with the eyes of a man accustomed to rule. When his gaze rested on Meridene, she couldn't stifle a burst of pride for the butcher's son who'd risen to glory.

"Have I dirt on my face?" he asked.

Flippantly she said, "I hadn't noticed. I was too busy thinking that you have deceit in your heart."

His eyebrows flared wickedly. "To be sure, I am beset with wickedness, but it lies in my mind. One night soon I'll share it with you."

Night? He was speaking of ravishment. She wondered when he'd find the time, considering he kept so many women. "You needn't bother. Ana told me."

"Told you what?"

"All I need to know about you."

He shrugged, but he was curious. "Shall we?"

A snaggletoothed lad wearing a squire's tunic approached, leading a golden stallion and a piebald mare. Eyes agog, the boy stared at Meridene. His gaze never left her, even when he bowed from the waist.

Melancholy swept over her. Her mother had always drawn awe-filled glances and gestures of obeisance. Not in years had she thought of the woman who stood by and let an English king snatch her eight-year-old daughter from the nursery and thrust her into danger.

In parting, her mother had put the Covenant of the

Maiden in Meridene's hands. She had always known the book and the responsibility would fall to her; Meridene had been schooled for that very task. Since the day she'd learned to read and cipher, she had begged her mother to let her read the book. But that was forbidden until her wedding day. She had heard the tales of her forebears, but she had not been allowed to read the stories for herself.

"Pray God King Edward protects you, my child," her mother had said. "You'll find only heartache at the hands of Highlanders."

Meridene closed her eyes against a pain that was as fresh as that day so long ago. Not only had her mother forsaken her, but by withholding the Covenant until the day the king took Meridene away, Eleanor had seen to it that Meridene learned little of her forebears. Privacy had been impossible, and when the king had stopped for the night, no one had bothered to give her a light to read by.

After the short journey to Elginshire, Meridene had pledged her troth and yielded the book to Revas for safekeeping. She hadn't read the chronicles of her grandmothers. She'd been cheated of their experiences and deprived of their good counsel.

"Are you well?" Revas asked. "Would you prefer to ride in a cart?"

His solicitous tone burned like salt on a fresh wound. Meridene stared at the horses and grumbled, "I don't suppose I have to ask which mount is mine."

His brown eyes twinkled with glee. "Can you control the stallion?"

She sensed that he wasn't talking about the horse, but himself. Eager to snuff out his masculine fire, she withdrew her dagger. "With this, I can make him a gelding."

Although tightly leashed, his resolve shone through. "He might have something to say about that."

"Yes. I expect him to cry . . . *Ouch.*"

Interest narrowed his eyes. "My compliments, my lady, and I wonder why you did not choose the red gown."

He referred to the most striking and costly gown in the trunk—a dress of red velvet trimmed in gold. Under different circumstances she would have cherished the garment.

"The color better suits your mood," he added.

"Mourning perfectly suits my mood."

Into the battle of wills, the young squire asked, "Is she truly the Maiden?"

Revas gave her a pointed glance, then cuffed the lad's head. "In the flesh."

The boy handed over the reins and raced off shouting, "'Tis the Maiden. 'Tis the Maiden come home with our laird."

"A Macduff! A Macduff!" someone shouted.

Others in the small seaside village picked up the chant. Voices young and old, hoarse and lyrical, called out for their laird, their future king. In answer to their time-honored salute, Revas waved his arms.

He looked happy to be home, and the contrast between her feelings and his made Meridene want to scream.

Over the din, he said, "We suffered a harsh winter."

"You will suffer a harsher spring."

Pulling a face, he feigned fright. "At your dainty hands?"

"Mock me if it suits you. 'Twill go the worse for you."

He sighed in fake resolve. "Then perhaps I should surrender to you now."

The notion that so powerful a man would yield made her smile. She sheathed her dirk and kept her opinion to herself.

Grasping her waist, he lifted her onto the mare, but

did not release her. "Perhaps I should grovel at your feet, Meridene, and beg you to share . . . uh . . . spare my wretched life."

Her humor vanished. His grip was too strong, his authority too intimidating, and he played with words like a child with a new top. "Perhaps you should hold your tongue."

Softly he said, "I'd rather hold you."

"You *are* holding me."

His grin was wolfish, and the look in his eye turned keen with awareness. "When I take you into my arms, you will know the meaning of the word. Until then, I will content myself with introducing you to your home and your subjects, my lady."

Seated on the mare, Meridene had to look down on him. She liked the vantage point, for it gave her a sense of power over so formidable a man. "I, on the other hand, shall content myself with enjoying your downfall."

He winked, then mounted the prancing stallion and led the way to the road.

Meridene fumed. Like a beast nearing the safety of his lair, he grew confident. Let him wallow in it for now. Soon enough she would disabuse him of his despotic assumptions. She would seek refuge in the church. Then she would flee this godforsaken land of monsters.

With the bannerman in the lead carrying a pennon emblazoned with the rampant lion of Macduff, they retraced the path she had traveled so many years ago.

A well-worn road cut through a forest of bare hardwoods, and an occasional larch and wayward cedar gave the land its color. Up ahead, the road forked, and another dark memory beckoned. Her mind's eye traveled back in time. The golden lion on the fluttering pennon became a broom pod on a field of red and white. The man beside her became a

Plantagenet warrior king, and she was once again a fearful child.

Following the dictates of the past, she guided the mare to the right arm of the fork.

"Not the old road," she heard someone say.

Old road. Old memory. Her mind retreated further back. She stood in the common room of Kilbarton Castle, her father's estate. She had pleaded with him, begged him not to let the king of England take her away. Her father slapped her so hard, she tumbled to the floor. Her cheek throbbed. He cursed her, shamed her for her birthright and the power she would one day wield. Towering over her, he wished her dead.

Cringing in childish fear, she begged her mother to intervene.

Her pleas fell on deaf ears.

"Meridene?"

Revas Macduff. Not a barefoot butcher's son, but a skilled warrior, who had returned her to a land of nightmares and cruel memories.

"What's wrong, Meridene?"

He guided his stallion abreast of her slower mount. She heaved a shaky breath and blinked back tears.

"You're afraid," he said, wonderment lacing his words.

Through a veil of sadness, she said, "Leave me be."

He scooped her up and sat her before him on the stallion. Too distracted to fight, she stared at the barren forest and felt just as lifeless.

Men had taken her future and stolen her chance to have a husband of her choosing and children of her own. With greed and power as their tools, Scotsmen had sentenced her to exile. Yet she had embraced the safety of England—only to have it yanked away at the hands of yet another Scot. This Scot. The Highlander, Revas Macduff.

Her husband.

"What are you thinking, Meridene?"

His soothing tone drew her from the painful reverie, and she felt enveloped in a cocoon of warmth. When had she laid her head on his shoulder? She couldn't recall. When had she slipped an arm around his waist? She didn't know.

The quilted velvet of his tunic cushioned her cheek, and his hands caressed her back and her shoulders.

"Please tell me what burdens you so."

Spoken in a whisper, the entreaty went straight to her heart. Her tears began to fall, and she burrowed closer, seeking warmth and a wealth of unattainable goals.

"You undo me with your sorrow, dear Meridene."

Dear Meridene. Would that it were true. Girlish dreams of a loving husband and beautiful children faded. The years ahead unfolded, and her life became a bottomless well of clan loyalties, clan feuds, and clan ceremonies. Guards following her everywhere. A child who always observed, rather than participated.

A searing pain squeezed her chest.

"Tell me."

Gathering her composure, she sniffled. "You're despotic."

He patted her back and guided the horse away from their escort. "Aye."

"You're thoughtless, same as all Highlanders."

His lips touched her temple, then her cheek. She shifted on his lap. His powerful thighs tensed.

"I am the same as *these* Highlanders," he murmured.

"That's no defense."

"Nay, no defense at all."

"Why are you being so agreeable?"

He gave her a brief, fierce hug, then leaned back

51

until their eyes met. His gaze was warm, and one side of his mouth curled in a self-effacing grin. "Because I forgot that you were a terrified child when last you visited my home." With a gauntleted hand, he brushed away her tears. "'Tis natural for you to recall that time and quake in fear."

Her better judgment sounded a warning. He was a Scot, and worse, a Highlander. He shouldn't be so nice, not unless he had a purpose. That he'd read her so easily troubled Meridene more than his winsome smile.

Miffed at her girlish reaction, she drew back. "I did not quake."

His gaze never left hers. "Nay, you did not. You yielded sweetly, and for that I am grateful."

Yield? Her defenses rose. "I'll be a toothless crone before I yield to you, Revas Macduff."

His grin broadened. "Perish that first thought. You're far too bonny to ever turn cronish."

Pretty words rolled off his tongue like stones in a landslide. Twenty women wanted him. Twenty women were welcome to him. Did he desire them all as well? "Save your roguish words."

All agreeable and confident male, he nodded. "'Tis a bargain made, then. You keep an open mind, and I'll resist the urge to flatter you."

He didn't know it, but she wouldn't be here long enough to make a pact with him. Sanctuary of the church awaited her. "Ha! Spoken like a true Highlander. I'll make no bargain with you."

His smile turned bittersweet. "You already have. Thirteen years ago, you gave yourself into my keeping."

He was a sloth to bring that up. "'Twas the king of England who did the giving. I had no choice."

Using only his legs, he guided the stallion back onto the road. "Then I give you one now. You may act the shrew and shame yourself before these people, or you can honor your forebears."

They had reached the crest of a hill. "People?" she said. "What people?"

"Those people."

She turned, and the sight before her robbed her of breath.

CHAPTER

3

Hundreds of people lined the road leading to Auldcairn Castle. Farmers doffed their caps and jabbed the sky with hoes and rakes. Women waved their kerchiefs and dabbed at teary eyes. Children hopped and squealed and scrambled for the best view. Carts had been moved to the rough edge of the lane, and cattle and sheep had been left to their grazing.

Pride filled Revas. In sad contrast, the Scotswoman sitting sideways before him on the horse held herself as still as a post. The show of elation was for her, and she cared not a whit. Disappointment dragged at him, for he had hoped this rousing welcome would begin to thaw her cold heart.

The hood of the cloak shielded her face, which was turned toward the throng. Pray she did not punish them unjustly; her quarrel was with a king and a butcher's son.

A girl of about six dashed onto the road, a bundle of pink frost lilies in her hand. Revas slowed the horse

54

and leaned to the side, hoping Meridene would take the flowers.

Praise Saint Columba, she did, saying, "My thanks to you."

The girl beamed and raced back to her family.

A lad came forward next and presented Meridene with a palm-size bowl. Carved into the rim were cinquefoils, the device of the Maiden.

"You honor me, sir," she said to the boy.

"Aye," he chirped, rocking on his heels and twisting his mended tunic. "Every Sabbath and twice on Hogmanay."

"Well . . ." She searched for words. "You are a goodly lad."

He bowed, then dashed to his father's side.

Honoring the Maiden of Inverness was a practice as old as the celebration of Harvest Eve. Why did she not remember and address the lad's devotion?

Holding the blossoms to her nose, she whispered, "I hate you for this, Revas Macduff."

The need to protect his people overwhelmed him. "Is there no room in your heart for love freely given?"

"Freely? You are wrong. Their adoration comes at a price."

How could she barter over so precious a commodity? "What price?"

"The loss of my home, my peaceful life. My friends."

"These people are innocent in their praise. You will make new friends of them."

Fathers lifted their sons for a better view. Mothers helped their babes wave. It was the same welcome her namesake had received hundreds of years ago upon arrival at her husband's home. Did Meridene not see the significance? The details were precisely recorded in the Covenant—the flowers, the bowl, and the other gifts to come.

She said nothing, save quiet curses for him, until the twin square towers of Auldcairn Castle loomed in the southern sky.

"I remember only one structure. When did you build— I withdraw the question. I have nothing to say to you."

"Aye, you do. You're curious, and I'm eager to oblige your inquisitive nature."

Pushing back the hood of the cloak, she glared up at him. "Then tell me which cave you call home."

Pollen dusted her nose, and he wondered what she'd do if he kissed the pretty smudge away. Amused at both the answer and her retort, he adjusted his hold on the reins so that his arms surrounded her fully. "I built the second tower to celebrate the death of Edward the First. There's a third tower, but 'tis not so tall. You cannot see it from here."

"What poor soul does it honor?"

He tried to contain his laughter, but he failed. "You."

Her head came up, slamming into his chin. A promise of retaliation glittered in her eyes. "I want no dwelling here."

Of course she did; the book of the Maiden prescribed it. Why did she deny a major stipulation? "It must be."

"Because you say so?"

"Nay. 'Tis written in the Convenant. You cannot accuse me of depriving you of your due."

"The Covenant," she replied, as if the word were unfamiliar. "You read the book."

Thinking she referred to his common beginnings, he took great pleasure in saying, "'Tis true I once was illiterate, but at ten and four I mastered the skill. Do you doubt my ability?"

She looked surprised, as if she'd taken bitters when she wanted sweets. "Nay, I believe you've had years to study the Covenant. The accommodations will better allow me to absent myself from you."

Revas intended to devote himself to her. One day soon she'd throw flower pennies to the people of Elginshire and kisses to him. "Impossible, Meridene, for I will escort you to church."

"Church." Like the mist off the moor, her confusion vanished. A brilliant smile followed. "Oh, I would so love to meet the priest."

That piqued Revas's curiosity, but he'd gained ground. He would hold his position for now. At all events, the priest would support his cause; Father Thomas had been instrumental in the preparations. Scotland's clergy wanted and worked for autonomy as fiercely as laymen did. When the pope excommunicated Robert Bruce, the clergy had rallied behind Scotland's king.

Amid a squealing of wheels and a rattling of chains, the castle gates opened. With Kenneth Brodie in the lead, a dozen mounted guards burst onto the road and cantered toward Revas. This special troop sported sons of chieftains from most of the ruling Highland clans. Leslie rode beside Forbes. Grant served with Murray. The absence of a Macgillivray represented Revas's greatest disappointment and his most trying challenge.

Meridene would change that. She would influence the lives of more Highlanders than any of her predecessors. Like London to the English, Elgin would become the open city of the Scots. She just didn't know it yet.

"Your army has arrived," she said, leaning away from him.

And your destiny beckons, he thought.

The guard slowed. Brodie doffed his crested helmet and dropped his chin to his chest in a quick salute. His chain of office chinked with the movement. "Lady Meridene and sir."

Revas forbade his men to call him lord. He did not aspire to nobility; he wanted to lead. Their worship was better and rightfully bestowed on Meridene. Revas asked only for their respect and loyalty.

"Do I know you, Sheriff?" she asked.

Discomfited, Brodie replaced his helmet. "'Twas many years ago and you were—"

"A prisoner," she said. "As I am today."

Revas decided that her generosity ended with children bearing gifts. She had not acknowledged any of the men who rode with Brodie, and from their eager looks, they all wanted to strut their manly wares before her.

When Brodie sent him an inquisitive glare, Revas shook his head. He would explain, but later and in private. "My lady wishes to visit the church straightaway."

"'Tis Wednesday," Brodie said, guiding his stallion away from Leslie's moody mare. "Father Thomas has gone to Nairn."

"When will he return?"

She had spent years among the clergy. Still, she was overeager in her devotion. Revas hoped she did not harbor queer notions of the church. He knew men whose wives were unnaturally fond of prayer. Maclaren's woman had an altar in every room, even the buttery. As a result, the nursery was empty. That wouldn't happen in Auldcairn Castle.

"On Friday," Revas said.

Satisfied, she sat straight. "Then you may take me to my apartments."

She said the last with emphasis on the separation the word implied. Her defiance was understandable. Revas was in no hurry. He had years to explore her mind and win her heart.

Nodding to Brodie, he kicked the stallion into motion. The guard moved to flank them. When they picked up speed, Revas tightened his hold on Meridene. When they reached a gallop, she held on to him.

The freshly mortared curtain wall that ringed the vast outer bailey played perch to a horde of moor hens and noisy gulls. The birds took flight when the sentries moved along the wall toward the narrow opening.

In the inner bailey, sheep scattered and cattle bellowed. A horn blared as the horses thundered into the castle yard. The guardsmen on the wall sent up a familiar greeting. "A Macduff! A Macduff."

If Meridene heard that name once more today, she'd shriek like a madwoman. She felt crushed beneath the weight of so much adulation and loyalty. Could she truly be the only person who opposed Revas Macduff? No. Not in the Highlands, for there was always strife up here. Accord reigned now. But tomorrow or next week one clan would slight another. Male pride would bristle. Grown men would act like stiff-legged dogs circling with hackles raised. War would commence. Prosperity would cease. Mothers, wives, and daughters would grow sallow-faced and brokenhearted. Fathers, husbands, and brothers would justify their destruction with talk of might and right and the law of the clan. Daughters would be sacrificed to the enemy.

Praise be to God her role here was that of visiting spectator.

The twin towers soared into the sky. The fishtail slits in the stone that usually housed eagle-eyed bowmen now served as vantage points for the curious. To her amazement, Meridene estimated two hundred people milled in the castle yard proper. She saw the very wall where, years before, severed heads of men had rested on pikes. Today, pennons of Macduff and dozens of other clans fluttered in the breeze. One flag caught her eye: Macqueen.

Now she knew how Revas had found her; her best friend, Johanna, had revealed the information to her husband, Drummond Macqueen. He had passed along her whereabouts to Revas. The logical conclusion disheartened Meridene, and she longed to see her childhood friend again. Out of love for her nephew, the ever brave Johanna had assumed her sister's identity and embarked on a fulfilling life. For that, Meridene envied her; her own future looked bleak.

Between the two square towers of Auldcairn Castle stood a small, round structure with costly glass in the windows and a ring of rowans planted in the yard. Cartwright and cooper flanked the smithy, and an impressive barrack and armory butted the castle's defense wall. In a patch of hard-packed earth, the quintain stood idle and deceptively harmless.

Looking east, Meridene at last spotted the church, wedged between the carpenter and the weaving shed.

Sanctuary awaited her there, and the knowledge calmed her.

Following the bannerman, Revas guided the horse around the well and stopped at the doors of the keep. On the steps, the castle staff stood like soldiers at attention. The maids were neat and composed, the men tidy and serious. Had Revas taken to heart her threat to disrupt his staff? Could she carry it out? Yes, given cause.

Holding her against his chest, he dismounted in one smooth movement. She felt like a feather pillow moved from here to there, so easily did he carry her. The louse.

She hadn't looked at him since their exchange about the church; she feared he'd see through her plan to seek out the priest and request an annulment. But even if he did suspect, she'd wager her best loom that he'd put aside his quarrel long enough to introduce her to the servants. He wanted her here. Showing support for her to the staff was the first duty of a husband to his wife.

Wife. The word inspired a wealth of maidenly

dreams. Not in months had she been beset with longing for a mate and a home of her own. Now she must rid herself of both.

On Friday she'd go to the priest and set in motion her plan to break her ties with Revas Macduff. Now she would bide her time.

He waited until she fluffed out her skirt; then he took her arm and escorted her to a man of about fifty. As befitting his age, he wore a long woollen robe tied with a leather thong at his waist.

"Lady Meridene, may I present our steward, Sim Grant."

With great dignity, he bowed from the waist. "I yield to you the accounting, my lady, and my father's pouch." He held out a sporran. Made of an ancient badger pelt, it sported no golden tassels or brooches of silver. His sire had been a common man.

When she did not take the precious offering, Sim grew insistent. "Should you find my accounting unfairly derived, you must keep my father's purse." He looked away, emotion choking off his speech.

It was his prized possession, and this tidy stranger was giving it to her. "Why?"

"To dispense justice, as the Maiden will."

The Maiden. Surely Revas Macduff or the burly sheriff meted out justice here. Unless this Sim referred to some tenet set down in the Covenant? Revas knew them all. The sloth. She couldn't accuse the steward until she read the Covenant. She wanted no part of the traditions, and what did she care if Sim Grant cheated Revas Macduff? She hoped the man beggared him.

She took the pouch and placed the wooden bowl inside. Then she handed Sim the flowers. "I'm certain you've performed your office fairly. Please put these in water."

Next came the cooks. "Sibeal and Conal Montfichet."

They were as different as night and day. Sibeal was twice her husband's size, and fair to the point of sallow.

"Montfichet?" Meridene said, curious about the name.

A slight man, Conal had cropped his black hair unusually short; yet his beard was as thick as a sheep's pelt. "Aye, my lady. From the East, we are."

"From Nairn," Sibeal put in.

"We came here when our city was burned in the fall of thirteen and seven."

His wife huddled inside her shawl. "'Twas in October."

"'Twas unimportant jabbering."

"Only because you did not think to say it."

Bickering came easily to the pair. Meridene knew well that kind of friendship. She and Johanna Benison had spent hours goading each other and years learning to forgive. Johanna, the friend who was now wife to Drummond Macqueen, the beast who had revealed Meridene's whereabouts to Revas Macduff.

She gave her husband an appraising glance. "I'm surprised that Bruce would come into your domain and make havoc."

His eyes narrowed, as if he were wondering how to answer. At length he said, "At the time I did not answer to Robert Bruce."

Taken aback, she almost dropped the steward's sporran. "You were a rebel chieftain?"

"Aye. I made a request of Bruce. He refused and commanded me to do what I could not. When I refused, he put my lands to sword and flame. With your father, he vanquished Nairn."

That surprised her, for her father had seldom made alliances with lowland Scots. But since her move to England, Robert I had been crowned king of all Scots. "What did you request of Bruce?"

Revas tossed his cape over his shoulder and hitched

up his sword belt. "As he is our sovereign lord, and you were nowhere to be found, I asked him for the sword of Chapling. He refused—in anger."

Meridene tensed. Her suspicions were borne out. Revas didn't want her; he wanted the sword, had tried to claim it before. Had he bothered to look for her prior to that time? Oh, blast it, she silently cursed. "What did Bruce ask of you?"

Grinning, he slid a glance at Sheriff Brodie. "He commanded me to bend a knee to your father."

Huffs of disgust spread through the guardsmen. But Meridene took heart from the statement. If Robert Bruce was against Revas taking up the sword of Chapling, surely he would help her escape Scotland.

"Bruce still ruminates on that frolic," boasted one of the guardsmen. "Cutberth'll see a bended knee." He pointed to his own knee. "I'll break his head on it."

The hoots of approval grew so loud that Revas raised a hand to quiet them. The outspoken man focused his undisguised attention on Meridene.

A darkly handsome youth, the stranger carried himself with a pride unique to Highlanders. His cocky stance and ingrained self-assurance reminded her of her older brothers. But this man had spoken in contempt of her father. She couldn't agree with him more.

"Who are you?" she asked him, noticing that his wrists were bare while all of the other men wore golden bracelets of war.

He swept an impressive bow. "Summerlad Macqueen."

"Drummond's youngest brother," Revas said by way of explanation. "And he's very glad you've come."

"Lady Clare speaks well of you, my lady," Summerlad said.

That he called Drummond's wife Clare was of great

interest to Meridene, for it answered a question that had puzzled her since Drummond's unexpected release from the Tower of London. Johanna, the woman who now lived with Drummond, had kept secret her true identity from the people of Elginshire.

Surrounded by so much male power, Meridene felt small and helpless in a land of strangers. She turned away and pretended interest in the third tower.

"Does it suit you?" Revas said.

If he could generalize on important subjects, so could she. "'Tis a place any wife would favor."

"Since I have only the one wife, I assume you speak from the heart."

With so many witnesses, she carefully phrased her retort. "'Tis safe to say that you always know when I am speaking from the heart, my lord."

His eyes turned hard and sharp as flint, and he drew her near his horse and out of earshot of the others. With quick, angry motions, he unbuckled his money pouch. "Revas suits me well."

She tapped him on the shoulder. When he turned, she rose on tiptoes. "England suits *me* well."

As if she'd asked for a pinch of salt, he loudly said, "Oh, very well, Meridene." Then the blackheart tossed the bag to Sim, pulled her into his arms, and kissed her!

Before she could push him away, he grasped her tighter and whispered, "Be gentle, my brave one, and have a care. You're poorly armed for this battle."

"Are you threatening me?" she said, her nose very close to his.

"Nay. I'm promising. Should you snip at me again, with these men as witness, I'll throw you over my shoulder and carry you away. I've done so before." He gave her a blinding smile. "Then, my spritely Maiden, the battle will commence."

She had no business challenging him in front of his men; she knew better, but years had passed since she'd learned her lesson and fallen prey to that bit of Highland protocol. "A battle you think you will win someday."

"Winsome?" He spoke in a melodious tone, one intended to convey intimacy. "You flatter me well."

Meridene fumed. "Not I, and stop twisting my words. Never would I find you appealing."

"I'm certain 'twas what you said."

"And I'm certain 'twas one of the twenty women you keep who said it."

The guardsmen grumbled among themselves; she had spoken too loudly.

"A score of women?" Revas drew back and stared, his dark eyes wide with alarm. "Who told you that?"

"Never you mind." A glance over her shoulder proved wise, for the men were inching closer. "I'd like to go inside now."

"Your happiness is my quest."

To a stranger, the pledge sounded sincere, but she knew him for a blackheart.

He turned to the sheriff. "See that the gate is greased. It sounds like a rusted siege engine. And have a man ride hotfoot to the ship. He's to speed the luggage cart along."

"Aye." The sheriff marched off, shouting orders. The guardsmen followed like goslings after a goose.

Revas dismissed the servants. "Come, Meridene."

Although cordially said, his words conveyed an order. Despotic was too kind a description for him. Her mind harkened back to the subject of Robert Bruce. Was he friend or foe? Determined to learn the answer, she followed Revas into the keep.

A walk-through hearth separated common room from dining hall. Above the stone cavern and carved in the smooth rock were the words "Community of the Realm," an ancient and long-unanswered cry for Scottish unity.

The motto was newly carved, for even as a girl, she

would have remembered seeing the daring statement openly displayed. She looked at Revas, so comfortable in his role as benevolent lord, so constant in his bid to keep her. She wished him well in his certain disappointment. Still, she couldn't quell a sense of happiness at what he, a butcher's son, had accomplished here in a mere thirteen years.

The rounded walls were studded with heraldic battle shields. The symbolic Gordon buck stood beside the eagle of Clan Munro. Macpherson's regal cat shared a space next to the mighty sword of Clan Gunn. And reigning over them all was the rampant lion of Macduff.

"Did you ever think to see such a gathering of Highland goodwill?" he said.

"No, and I do not expect it to thrive."

His smile faded and his eyes grew distant. Her remark had hurt him, and she almost begged his pardon. But encouraging false hopes was surely the poorer service.

"Do you care for ale or herbal wine?" he asked. "Sibeal Montfichet brews a popular drink from weeds and stems and berries."

Should she excuse herself? The sight of so much Highland armor hanging about ought to have frightened her. It did the opposite. For the first time since leaving England, Meridene felt safe, and that awful pounding in her chest had ceased.

Knowing she would soon return to Scarborough, she chose to keep Revas's company for a time. "I prefer barley water, but if you have none, the wine will do."

"See that Montfichet keeps a ready supply of barley water for my lady."

"Aye," said Sim. "I'll send the kitchen lad to the granary straightaway."

Revas nodded to the steward, who pivoted sharply

and marched off, his shoes making little sound on the flagged floor.

"Tell me what happened between you and Robert Bruce."

"We made peace. He's anxious to meet you."

Would the crowned king of all Scotland condone Revas's villainy? Probably so, if they were allies. The knowledge was a setback, but Meridene had other options. "Then by all means, summon your sovereign lord."

"'Tis done. He comes at Midsummer's Eve."

Meridene rejoiced. Robert Bruce would go wanting if he sought an audience with Meridene Macgillivray. June would find her knee-deep in good English clover.

"Delightful," she said, for lack of anything else.

"I know what you're thinking, Meridene. The answer is yes, he favors your return to the fold."

The need to correct him fell prey to the notion of savoring a victory later. "Splendid."

He took a chest from a high shelf on the wall. From the box he withdrew a chatelaine's belt. "For you."

Finely worked interlocking chains of gold and silver formed the symbol of feminine authority. Even her mother's had not been so fine. "I'll not don it."

"Aye, you will."

If he suspected she planned to escape, he could try to prevent it. So she relented, took the chain, and fastened it around her waist. "It has the feel of a chastity belt."

"What know you of chastity belts?"

Two years ago, a Kentish girl had arrived at the abbey wearing one of the ghastly devices. By separate messenger, the key had been delivered. For amusement, Meridene had borrowed the key, and she and the others had tried on the belt. Later, Sister Margaret had ordered the blacksmith to fashion the contraption into a handsome trivet. "I know enough."

From a gaming table near the hearth, he picked up a pair of dice and rolled them in his palm. "Shall I commission you one?"

"Do and I will fling it in your leering face."

He *tsked* in reprimand and let the dice fall back onto the table. "I seldom leer."

"How pleasant of you to reveal so much of yourself."

"Do you often encounter forthright men?"

"Of late, no. I seem destined to keep the company of cowards and kidnappers."

He walked to the table and returned with the ring of castle keys. "Should you sweeten your tongue, you will fare better here."

"Are you, a butcher's son, commanding me?"

"Nay." He hooked the heavy ring onto her belt. "As your husband, I am advising you."

With the added weight, the chain slipped low on her hips. "I'll never obey."

Revas noticed, and moved to adjust the belt. "Because my father was a butcher?"

She stepped out of reach. "No. Because his son is a blackhearted monster."

He touched his chest, and his eyes gleamed with mock innocence. "But I'm a lambkin."

She chortled. He'd said that foolishness before.

"If you're so gentle, why did you kidnap me, rather than woo me with your tender mercies?"

He paced, his hands clasped behind him, his mind brewing God only knew what mischief. Would he never grow angry? Lord, she'd walk back to England if he would show his true self.

Expecting more verbal trickery, she took the lead. "I suppose you'd prefer that I fall into your arms and shower you with affection."

As if daring her, he held his arms wide. On a man of lesser stature, the yielding pose would have looked foolish. But Revas Macduff was too well made, and he knew it. Against her will, she found herself admiring him, his trim waist and powerful legs, his broad shoulders and winsome ways.

Winsome. Her interest waned and she regretted the bold words.

When she did not move, he lifted a brow in disdain. "'Tis as I thought, but you're too much the coward. I doubt you've ever had a passionate thought." Shaking a finger at her, he sagely added, "'Tis the English who have spoiled you for romance."

"How dare you aspire to decipher my thoughts." He knew her not at all. "What would a Highlander know about the needs of a woman's heart?"

Deep in contemplation, he strolled toward her, stopping an arm's length away. "Any Scotsman worth his salt will tell you that your skin is supple enough to make a man go begging for the touch of your hand. Your smile is a treasure that rivals a saint's ransom in gold."

The sweet words washed over her. He took her hand and brought it to his nose. "Except that you smell of leather and horse."

She froze, trapped between umbrage and laughter. When he winked, the latter won. Chuckling, she went to the table and washed her hands in the basin. The soap was scented with heather. A memory flashed in her mind.

A very long time ago, she had frolicked in a field of heather so tall, she couldn't see over the tops of the plants. How young had she been? Three or four, she was certain, for at six she'd shot up in height like a larch in the sun.

Revas handed her a cloth. "What makes you smile?"

A happy thought, which was odd; she seldom recalled her childhood with fondness. It wouldn't do to make a practice of it now or to share the details with him.

She looked for an answer to his question and found it in the return of Sim. "I smile at the thought of tasting Mrs. Montfichet's brew. I should like to savor it while I bathe."

His knowing expression said he wasn't fooled, but he had the good manners to let the matter drop and hand her the goblet of wine. "This way."

He led her down a narrow and well-lighted hall to an iron-studded door. Carved deeply into the wood was a cinquefoil.

She couldn't hold back a sarcastic reply. "You have an odd penchant for that flower."

He cocked one eyebrow, but his expression reeked of tolerance, not disdain. "For more than the flower, Meridene. You have my sacred oath on that."

"You can take your sacred oath and weave it into a tartan for all I care."

Not in the least bothered by her angry words, he unlatched the door and pushed it open. "Your apartments."

Momentarily stunned at the beauty of the room, Meridene ignored the three serving girls who stood quietly against a wall. This was the small dwelling situated between the two square towers, the one with the rowans planted out front. She had admired it from the yard.

Recently constructed, the solar contained costly glass, and before the windows lay a fine carpet. Upon it sat baskets of yarn and precious silken thread. Her loom would perfectly suit that sunny spot.

Off to the right stood an enormous bed, its canopy soaring to the ceiling. The hangings were made of dark green velvet and tied back with golden cords. The mattresss bore a matching coverlet embroidered with one golden cinquefoil in the center. Two stone braziers, as large as rain barrels, sent an inviting warmth throughout the cozy chamber.

The room verily screamed an invitation. Unable to refuse, Meridene stepped inside. No rushes littered the room; small woollen tapestries were scattered on the flagged floor.

Behind an open door, a buttery contained an assortment of wines, a keg of ale, and mugs enough to serve a small banquet. Her mother had entertained her father in a room that looked and smelled just so. The linens on her mother's bed had been blue, but fashioned the same as these drapings.

But how had Revas known?

The book. The blasted Covenant of the Maiden. The sloth had not only read the book, but he'd furnished the room according to the descriptions written by her forebears.

Descriptions Meridene had not been allowed to read. Why had her mother withheld the book? Like most children, Meridene had been confined to the nursery, except for special occasions. At those times the talk always centered around clan loyalties or an impending English invasion. In the beginning, she had been too young to understand, and just when she'd begun to grasp the subject, she'd been sacrificed to the enemy and forgotten in England.

"Will it suit you, my lady?"

It was a foolish question, for the room was grand enough for a princess—a peaceful place that encouraged her to cast off her worries and languish here.

She looked up at him, and the anxious expression in his eyes gave her pause. He'd gone to great lengths to prepare a place for her, and now he expected her to thank him. She'd dreamed of a different life in a land where men didn't make war over a herd of cattle or a drunken boast.

But for a reason she did not understand, Meridene couldn't disappoint him. "'Tis beautiful."

He smiled, and she again thought of a chivalrous lad who had braved a mighty Plantagenet on her behalf.

I expected the king to hang me before sunset.

Watching him now, she knew in her heart that an army of kings couldn't harm this Revas Macduff, yet a cruelty from her on the matter of this room would bring him low. "Thank you," she said, knowing she'd regret it.

He put his hand on her shoulder and turned her to face the waiting servants. Two of the girls were of an age, probably twelve years old. The third was considerably older, probably twenty. All three wore matching yellow smocks over white bliauds.

"Your handmaidens," he said.

Meridene's mother had had three such servants, as every Maiden did. From the age of five until she'd been cast out of Scotland, Meridene had served her mother in all three capacities. The positions and duties were legend. Revas had discovered that in the book as well.

Sentimentality choked her, and she had no weapons against the longing of a daughter for a mother who had forsaken her.

"Meet Lisabeth," he said, "the keeper of your quills."

With an effort that was suddenly new, Meridene staved off the old yearning.

The girl with brown hair and hazel eyes fidgeted with excitement at being presented first. The other girls, a tall redhead and one as fair as summer wheat, stared at their hands.

So endearing was their disappointment, Meridene put aside her own discomfort. "All of you, come forward at once."

Revas continued. "This carrot-haired lass is Serena, tender of the rowans. She is especially glad you have come. She's eager to marry that young buck, Summerlad Macqueen."

The older girl blushed, causing a clash of colors between complexion and hair. "Welcome, my lady."

Mother's handmaidens had always ended their service on their twelfth birthday. Obviously that was not written in the book, for Serena was far beyond that age. Or was it written? Meridene wanted desperately to know.

"And this fair lass is Ellen, keeper of the bath, which was, I believe, your immediate request."

Ellen curtsied, and her blue eyes darted from Meridene to an open door off to the right. Meridene could see that the room contained an overlarge tub, drying cloths, and an extravagant looking glass as big as a beef platter.

Understanding the girl's quandary, Meridene said, "You may fetch the hot water, Ellen."

Her small shoulders slumped with relief, and she hurried out of the solar, her long blond hair flying behind her.

"Is such luxury your doing, Revas?" Meridene asked.

"I suppose. But the giving of a bath was begun by the husband of your tenth grandmother back. She was one of the Marys. She described it in the Covenant." He shook his head as if remembering a fondness. "An endearing soul, that Mary—according to her account."

Shocked, Meridene almost challenged his explanation. The Covenant contained advice and rules for governance, not individual chronicles. Or did it? Her mother hadn't said so. Had she omitted the information?

Meridene didn't know, and the mere fact that she was curious about the contents of the book bothered her more than the knowledge that Revas planned to keep her. Her ties with Scotland had been broken over a decade ago. She belonged in England. Bother the wretched book!

"Have you duties for Lisabeth and Serena?" Revas asked.

Meridene grasped the respite from her troubling thoughts. "Yes. Lisabeth, you are to watch for the arrival of my trunk. When it comes, put away my writing things. And, Serena, you are to supervise the setting up of the loom. I'd like it there, by the windows."

"In a trice," the older and braver girl, Serena, said. "My father is a fine and prosperous weaver. I'm the veriest expert at tending a loom."

"When do you find time to keep the rowans?" Meridene asked.

"They require no keeping now. They're as barren as an Englishman's soul."

Behind her, Meridene heard Revas sputter with laughter. She couldn't help saying, "That may be true, Serena. But do you know what the English say about the Highlanders?"

Her chin came up. "Nothing good, I'm sure."

"They say," Meridene began, casting her voice toward Revas, "if you want to tame a Scot, you must capture him young."

Serena looked like she'd swallowed a thistle.

Revas leaned close. "The English also make a habit of capturing Scottish princesses and turning them against their kin. But we catch them, and then we make them ours again."

She whirled around and came nose to chin with him. "You'll run afoul of reason should you think that, Revas."

His mouth was but a whisper away from hers. "Did they tame you, Meridene? Or have they left that pleasure to me?"

She swallowed a lump of apprehension. "Pleasure?"

His gaze roamed her face, inspecting and admiring

what he saw. "Aye. Pleasure of the most rewarding kind."

Twenty women had fallen victim to his masculine charm, and Meridene understood why. Her own heart thumped loudly, and she couldn't help wondering how his mouth would feel on hers. Twenty women knew. Did he also imprison them with his alluring eyes?

He gazed past Meridene, and with the smallest movement of his head, he indicated the door. She heard the girls leave, but her mind whirled with inappropriate questions about Revas Macduff. She couldn't turn away from him.

He rested his arms on her shoulders, but she didn't notice the weight. "Close your eyes, Meridene, and give me a kiss."

He had called her a coward on the field of romance. Proving him wrong while satisfying her own curiosity posed a challenge. The daring look in his eye sparkled with a friendly invitation she would not refuse. Her eyes drifted shut, and in the next instant his mouth touched hers, softly, then melting closer and moving in slow, deliberate circles.

Did all women feel this dizzying, floating yearning? If so, she certainly understood why the fishwife in Scarborough always wore a smile the morning after her husband came home from the sea. Meridene intended to explore the practice and come away from it with the knowledge she had been denied.

His lips parted and enlightenment followed, for his mouth tasted as sweet and as welcome as a warm drink on a cold winter night. Relief relaxed her to her toes, and when she swayed, his hands gripped her, steadying her, drawing her into the cradle of his chest and arms. Against her breast, his heart beat loud and constant, and his breath wafted against her cheek.

Pleasurable visions began to dance in her head—a joyous spring morn and a breakneck ride on a swift mount through a meadow of wildflowers. She imagined the wind whipping her hair and heard the drumming of hooves in her ears. Her idle fingers touched the velvet of his jerkin and felt the rippling of muscles beneath.

He groaned deep in his chest, and the demeanor of the kiss changed. He grew insistent, his tongue nudging her lips apart, his hands playing across her buttocks, kneading gently.

The intimacy alarmed her. Did he have ravishment on his mind? She pulled back and asked him.

His eyes were glassy, and he shook his head as if he'd been awakened from a sound sleep.

"Were you trying to ravish me?" she repeated.

He blew out his breath and stared at the bed. "Not today." His gaze slid back to her. "You *are* a virgin, Meridene Macgillivray. On the ship you claimed otherwise just to spite me. That was your first kiss."

Indignation made her bristle. "'Twas my first kiss from one of your kind."

Pride held him still. "My kind?"

"Yes." He liked his own words so much, she threw a few in his face. "A man who smells of leather and horse."

She might have told him he was the finest lord in Christendom, so complete was his relief. Breaking into a grin, he gave her a quick kiss on the cheek. "Enjoy your bath, Meridene. I'll come back for you at eight o'clock."

"I will not answer your knock."

Strolling toward the door, Revas tamped back the desire that clawed at his loins. "Then I'll use my key."

But as he ducked beneath the dainty portal, he saw

Kenneth Brodie standing in the hall, a bundle of rolled parchments in his hand, an anxious look in his eyes.

"There's trouble, Revas," he said.

More than you know, Revas thought, and made his way to his own chamber with Brodie close behind.

CHAPTER

4

"Give me the last of the messages, Brodie, and I pray you have not saved the worst till the end." Revas took the remaining bite of his apple, pitched the core out the window, and reached for an orange.

His friend and mentor pushed back from the small trestle table. "Angus has called his young Munro home."

The Munro youth was one of dozens of lads who fostered with Revas. While teaching them to wield a sword and mace, and govern fairly, Revas enjoyed alliances with their fathers. Angus Munro's land lay due west of Inverness and shared a border with Cutberth Macgillivray. If Munro now wanted his heir back under his wing, it could mean only one thing: Cutberth was brewing trouble in the Highlands. No wonder Brodie looked so haggard. But they'd been through hell once and purgatory a dozen times with Meridene's father.

Meridene. Here. In the flesh. At home. At last. For

years, Revas had imagined precisely that. In his randy youth, he'd envisioned himself getting a strapping son on her even before the wedding feast was done. His gallant days had inspired poetry to her goodly heart and enchanting eyes. Yet now when he considered a life with Meridene, he thought of the binding ties of children and cozy evenings before a fire. He'd have them and his helpmate, but only after she fell in love with him and lost her heart to Scotland. A challenge that rivaled uniting the Highland clans. A challenge he accepted without hesitation.

"Revas, are you not concerned that Munro has called his son home?"

Yanking himself from his favorite pastime, Revas plunged into the exhausting and dangerous realm of politics. "Is that why you sent young Munro after the luggage cart?"

"He needed time alone to think about the summons before seeing you."

Spoken plainly, the simple words conveyed a wealth of honesty. Revas replied in kind. "I will not influence his decision."

"Not apurpose."

Brodie looked weary, and Revas couldn't hold a bad thought. Meridene had come home. His goal was within reach, and he wanted to dance atop the curtain wall and shout his glee like a half-wit on May Day. Brodie ought to smile, too, and since achieving goals had become the order of the day, Revas took up the challenge of improving his friend's somber mood.

"I suppose 'tis too much to hope that Munro's sister is getting married and our young friend must return home to stand as witness to her unexpected nuptials."

The weariness faded from Brodie's august expression. "Aye, 'tis too much to suppose."

Revas tossed the orange from one hand to the other. "Then perhaps his priestly uncle is being canonized."

Real humor twinkled in the sheriff's eyes. "Not unless the church is ready to face a revolt by our priestly Thomas."

Revas plunged onward. "Has a pretty maid offered for the hand of our young Munro?"

Brodie did laugh, but he shook his head, as if fighting it all the way. "Nay."

"Has our pretty maid presented young Munro with a son?"

Yielding, the sheriff slapped his thigh. "You're a devil, Revas Macduff. And although I'm like as not to regret saying it, 'tis good to have you home." He surveyed the tray of fruit and cheese and hacked off a chunk of the latter. "Alas, *your* pretty maid doesn't share your enthusiasm."

An understatement, thought Revas, and his mood turned melancholy. If missteps were victories in battle, his skill rivaled that of the Holy Roman Emperor, the greatest swordsman of the day. "Aye, my friend. She is hesitant."

"The sword of Chapling holds no interest for her?"

Revas's mood darkened. He surveyed his private chamber and paused at the sight of his empty bed. If he closed his eyes, he could see her there, languishing naked on the coverlet, her glorious black hair fanning the red velvet, her enchanting eyes beckoning him to celebrate their love.

"Revas!"

He jumped like a caught thief.

"You're smitten with her."

Battling a grin, he murmured, "She *is* appealing."

Brodie chuckled. "But will she demand the sword of Chapling from her father and bestow the Highland crown on you?"

"If I'm remembered of it correctly," Revas admitted, "she said the sword would crumble with rust before she touched it."

Brodie angled the blunt cheese knife toward the

window until the light caught the blade and reflected a splash of sunshine on the ceiling. "Perhaps she's peevish because she's been away from us for so long?"

Revas wished it were so. "She claims Scotland is a land of monsters."

"You exaggerate. Surely she favors you a wee bit."

Sinking low in his chair, Revas recalled her words. "Were I her only choice of mates, she pledged to go to her grave a virgin."

Brodie shrugged. "I suppose you told her you were saving yourself for the marriage bed?"

Revas saw through Brodie's ploy; he was now trying to make Revas smile. He did, and with ease. "She is bonny, isn't she?"

"Bonny enough for a butcher's son who'll one day wear the crown of the Highlands."

Feeling rash, Revas wiggled his eyebrows. "She has a temper, too."

Brodie grew serious. "She's no longer a frightened and maligned child."

On this point, Revas was well versed. "There you are wrong. She's scared to her soul, and make no mistake."

"She has the ill humors of the Macgillivrays," Brodie grumbled.

"She took nothing from Cutberth, but 'tis wrong to ignore the man who sired her."

"As if anyone could ignore that war-loving bastard." Brodie put down the knife and crossed his arms over his chest. He'd removed his battered war bracelets, but still wore his chain of office. "What angers her most?"

Regretting every word of the tale, Revas explained his abduction of Meridene.

"Sweet Saint Columba, Revas! What made you act so boldly?"

Revas felt like a green lad having his first go at the quintain. Deservedly so, for he had erred. But after wanting her for so many years, he'd lost his good judgment. Never had it crossed his mind that Meridene would reject him.

"Well?" Brodie prompted.

Revas resigned himself. "To my dismay, Ana did not color up her stories of Meridene's hatred for all things Scottish. I had no choice but to take her by force."

In exasperation, Brodie rolled his eyes. "Very Scottish of you."

"I could not linger in merry old England." Recklessly he added, "The food would've killed me."

Although his mouth puckered with humor, Brodie did not smile. "What will you do now?"

"I'll teach her to love us, one day at a time, and I have made progress," Revas couldn't help boasting. "She favors her new lodgings."

Brodie waved him off. "A blind Cornishman would favor that palace you built for her."

Revas felt a burst of pride at what he'd accomplished. The Maiden deserved luxury. As her husband, he was duty-bound to provide it. "I always knew she would come home to me, Brodie."

Fondness glowed in his weathered face. "So you've said since the day old King Edward gave her to you."

Through a flood of sentimental visions, Revas thought about how she'd looked when he left her hours ago. "You should have seen her with her new handmaidens. I tell you, Brodie, she gives orders like a marcher lord on campaign. She was born to rule."

"Came from her grandmother, most likely. 'Tis for certain the Macgillivrays bequeathed her little, save a penchant for war."

A familiar weight pressed in on Revas, but he was becoming accustomed to the up-and-down changes in his moods. Now his fosterlings were in jeopardy. "If I do not stop Cutberth now, he'll spread his poison to every clan in the Western Highlands, not just the Munros."

"Aye. You've worked too hard to gain the trust of those chieftains. Should you sit idle while Cutberth tries to regain the power, others will follow Munro's lead. Fraser may send for his lad next. Then Macpherson could call his son home. Your dream of unity will die."

Years of negotiations would go for naught. The clans would disperse, and little wars would again plague the Highlands. But the damage wouldn't stop there. Flanders and the Nordic states would cancel the trade agreements Revas had worked so hard to gain.

Unless he took action. But he must move cautiously. "'Twill go worse when Cutberth learns that I've brought his daughter home."

With a callused hand, Brodie worried his chin. "He's not heartless enough to send another assassin after her, is he?"

That possibility angered Revas to his soul. Harm would not befall Meridene; he'd watch her like a hawk, accompany her on the smallest of errands. "Pray he does not; if so, the Bishop of Inverness will pass along Cutberth's plans to our Father Thomas."

"Can the bishop be trusted?"

"He'll take the side of the Scottish church, as he did last year when the pope excommunicated King Robert. The Vatican will not like it, but 'tis a risk he'll gladly take in the name of self-rule. All of our clergy will."

"As will Elginshire." Brodie rose and walked to the pedestal table where the Covenant of the Maiden had rested for thirteen years. "What words of wisdom does the first Meridene offer on the subject?"

Brodie, too, was fond of the tales put down in the book by Meridene's namesake. "She was not so fortunate as we are. In her time, the clergy were untrustworthy and lecherous. When she wanted information, she sent a whore to loosen the priest's tongue."

"Surely your Meridene cannot find fault with her namesake. There's one Scot she'll remember fondly."

"She wants nothing to do with the Covenant."

Brodie whistled. "What will you do?"

"Change her mind."

Smiling crookedly, Brodie returned to his seat. "Pity her, then, for I've yet to see you target a lassie's heart and come away wanting."

The compliment emboldened Revas. "She thinks I keep twenty women."

As serious as sin on Sunday, Brodie said, "Do you?"

Revas leveled him a look reserved for the randy Summerlad Macqueen. Then he couldn't help laughing.

Brodie cleared his throat. "Who told her such a tale?"

"'Twas Ana, and I doubt her stories stopped there. She was angry at my taking Meridene in the dead of night."

"Worry not, Revas. John Sutherland will control his daughter. But when will you tell Meridene about yours?"

Revas had sired an illegitimate daughter, and the lass Gibby lived in comfort with her maternal grandparents in the nearby village of Aberhorn. Her mother, Mary, died of a fever shortly after weaning Gibby, and the girl was the very joy of her grandparents' life.

Would Meridene grow angry when she learned of his by-blow? Lord, he hoped not, for Gibby was a fine lass. "I haven't decided when to tell her. 'Tis early yet, and she'll not find fault with dear Gibby."

Brodie waved his hand in agreement. "Everyone loves the lass."

Revas noticed new blisters on the sheriff's hand.

Normally that palm was smooth. "Have you been wielding a sword with your left hand?"

"Aye, that young lad from Tain fights offhanded. Now tell me. What news of the parliament at Saint Andrews?"

The occasion had been a milestone in Scottish history, for it marked the first true Scottish parliament. "Nothing more surprising than the event itself. To Bruce's relief, the members voted to decline the French king's invitation to join him on Crusade."

"Did Macgillivray take his seat there?"

"Aye. Cutberth strutted about like a ripe bull put to a pasture of seasoned cows."

"Did he wear the sword of Chapling?"

Revas knotted his fists. "Aye. He took pleasure in taunting me with it."

"You crossed words?"

The subject of Meridene's father troubled Revas to his soul. "Let's speak of cheery occasions."

Brodie nodded in sad commiseration. "What has the king planned?"

"Our sovereign is so pleased to have a sitting parliament, he's decided to make a pilgrimage through Scotland this summer. A sweep of his kingdom, he proclaimed it. I've invited him for Midsummer's Eve."

"He warned you about compelling Lady Meridene. Does he think she came willingly to Scotland?"

The lie troubled Revas, but he'd stretched the truth before, and he would do it again, if the fate of Highland unity hung in the balance. "Aye."

Brodie chuckled, but his laughter was wrought with pain. "I'll take over the training of those ruffians you enjoy fostering. You'll be busy with matters of the heart."

Revas eagerly awaited the challenge. "My thanks."

"'Twill be entertaining, Revas, to see you try to woo an unwilling lass."

"She'll come around."

Someone pounded on the door. "Revas Macduff!"

Meridene's voice. Excitement buoyed his spirits again. "Did I not say 'twas so, Brodie? She seeks me out already."

"Aye, you did. But she sounds angry."

The door flew open. An outraged Meridene stood on the threshold. Her hair was still wet from the bath and trailed to her waist. She'd donned Serena's smock and bliaud.

An hour ago she had melted in Revas's arms and kissed him with the immature passion of a woman on the brink of falling in love.

Now she glared at the sheriff. "I must speak privately with Revas. Immediately."

Revas stood. "Brodie, see what's keeping Munro and the luggage cart."

She breezed into the room, ignoring the sheriff's exit.

"Why are you wearing Serena's clothing?" Revas asked.

If wrath were a mantle, she was cloaked in it from head to toe. "She took mine to the laundry. Did you order her to take my clothes away?"

"Nay. It never crossed my mind."

She slammed her hands on her hips and began pacing the carpeted floor. "You must have been too busy reading my property and spreading tales from here to there. How dare you tell Ellen that my grandmother bathed with my grandfather."

She referred to one of Revas's favorite entries in the Covenant. He had shared the story with all who would listen. "You didn't tell me not to read the book. You said I was to keep it from enemy hands."

Halting, she whirled and pointed a finger at his chest. "You *are* the enemy! You told these people that you would find me."

Her feet were bare, and her toes were beautiful. "I did find you."

"You've been telling them that for over ten years!"

Hoping to quell her irritation, he gave her a lop-sided grin. "I'm a stalwart lambkin."

She clenched her teeth and marched up to him. The fragrant smell of heather filled his nose. "Hear this, Revas Macduff. I would stab you with my dirk had Ellen not taken it to the cutler."

The tension in the air between them grew as thick as Montfichet's porridge. "'Tis my good fortune, then, that you've been disarmed."

Through gritted teeth, she said, "Do not mock me."

He held out his hands, palms up, in surrender. "My apologies, Meridene, for whatever wrongs I've done you."

"Now he begs my pardon," she said to the ceiling. "You've had these people saying prayers for me every Sabbath. They don't even know me."

He thought it best to tell her all of it. "They also honor you twice on Hogmanay in observance of your birthday. They abide by the Covenant."

Bracing her hands on the table, she leaned toward him. Her eyes glowed with contempt, and her sweet breath fanned his face. "You have a twisted mind."

Serena's yellow smock fitted Meridene too tightly, and the fabric strained across her breasts, which were heaving with the force of her anger. He wanted to kiss her fury away.

As if burned, she moved back. "You're leering at me. Stop it!"

A lame denial came to mind. Too late he saw her spy the tray of food and the knife. In a flash, she snatched up the dull blade.

She wasn't like other women; she was self-reliant, and she'd been wronged. Flattery was a mistake.

Cajolery proved a worse error. Revas wisely backed away. "You have a knife in your hand, Meridene. Please, put it down."

Ignoring his polite request, she began pacing again. "How could you give these people false hopes year after year?"

The garments were too short and her ankles too distracting. Was she naked beneath the borrowed clothes?

"I could have been dead."

Revas tried to shelve his unseemly thoughts, but he couldn't, for the simple fact that she was here, in his life at last. And he wanted her with a yearning that burned in his gut and lower.

"How could you?" Her knuckles gleamed white from clutching the knife.

He took a deep, calming breath. "They needed hope, Meridene."

Her shoulders slumped. She walked to the hearth and stared into the flames. "How considerate of you."

He hadn't intended to say it that way, but he had always believed he'd find her. Wretched as Edward I had been, he did not hang the daughters of his enemies. He gave them into the keeping of the church.

As he observed Meridene now, garbed in a too small smock, her hair a concealing black blanket, she looked small and childlike. A deception, his manly heart argued, for she was a woman to her soul.

"I will not stay." She shook the knife at him. "I'll take the veil first."

No, she wouldn't, but she was too angry for him to broach that argument just now. "'Tis a drastic move."

She threw her arms in the air and sent the knife sailing across the room. Droplets of water rained from her hair and landed, hissing, upon the hearth. The knife fell harmlessly on the floor. "Drastic? Kidnapping me was not? By God, Revas, I'll go to King Edward."

If Edward II knew that Revas had taken her against her will, he could use her abduction as an excuse to continue his father's war on Scotland. Alone, Revas could not hope to prevail. The combined armies of Revas and Robert Bruce were too great for the English, but Bruce would not commit his forces until Revas possessed the sword of Chapling. Cutberth Macgillivray would not yield it; only Meridene could take the sword from him.

"I cannot allow you to bring King Edward into our marriage."

"You have a queer notion of marriage. I'm your prisoner."

"Only if you force me to play the tyrant. Come, Meridene, let us not fight all of our battles today. Montfichet has prepared pheasant and barley cakes. You cannot deny 'tis your favorite."

"Ana told you that. What else did the gossiping fool tell you?"

She had given him an opening to lighten the mood. Revas grasped it. "She also told me about the time you donned that chastity belt."

Color blossomed on her cheeks. "She was not there at the time."

"Nay, but I fear the tale has grown with the telling. I cannot imagine you marching to the smithy and having good Kentish iron forged into a spoon."

She smiled. "A trivet was commissioned of it."

"Montfichet once said he couldn't acquire a chastity belt for Sibeal because they'd have to mine half of England to get enough iron."

"I doubt she likes being so large."

Revas rejoiced, for she had exhausted her anger.

Distracted, she said, "Where is the Covenant?"

He glanced beyond her to the pedestal table in the corner. A lamp illuminated the ancient book. "I thought you wanted nothing to do with the legend."

She followed his line of vision. "That's still true."

Making a lie of the declaration, she padded across the room and touched the book. "But it's my property."

"It belongs to the Maiden. Are you she?"

She looked up, her eyes a lush green in the lamplight. "The Maiden is no more."

"Then reacquainting yourself with the contents of the book shouldn't interest you." He suspected it did, and very much. He took heart, for he'd found an even spot of ground in the rutted road their lives had taken. Casually he said, "'Tis only rules and tenets for the survival of Highland unity."

All righteous and wronged woman, she lifted her chin. "It was written by my mother and her ancestors. By right, their words are mine."

In truth, her mother hadn't added a word to the legacy of the Maiden. Not all of the women had taken up a quill. Had they, no one volume could have contained the words.

Revas had laughed and cried while reading the chronicles of a few of those brave and entertaining women. Not even if he lived five lifetimes, with a dozen wives in each, could he learn more about the workings of the female mind and the craving of their hearts than he had in that tome. He would not give up their precious legacy, not to one who impugned their honor.

He strove for a reasonable tone. "Their words belong to all of the people of the Highlands."

She tried to hide her feelings, but her hand shook as she traced the symbols on the bindings. With the tapered nail of her index finger, she lifted the front binding. Her eyes were alight with interest, and she sighed with what he knew was relieved longing. How could he use the book to his advantage? He did not know.

Noise from the castle yard drifted through the open window. The luggage cart had returned. While

Meridene was preoccupied, Revas walked to the door. "Excuse me while I speak with young Munro."

She drew the book to her breast. "I must go."

He hadn't expected to broach the subject of the matter so quickly. But he had no choice. "The Covenant must stay here, unless you'd like to discuss a trade."

Her gaze sharpened. "What trade?"

He girded himself for another battle. Thank goodness she'd tossed the knife away. "The sword of Chapling for that book."

Interest turned to disbelief. Then she threw back her head and laughed. "You wretched Scot."

He hadn't expected her to agree, but the insult stirred his ire. "I cannot allow you to take the book."

"Pray tell why not? It's mine."

"Yours to cherish or to destroy?"

In her typical queenly fashion, she stiffened her graceful neck. "To do with as I please."

She'd lose this battle, for Revas treasured the chronicle. Munro would wait. Revas would prevail.

He held out his arm to indicate the chairs by the hearth. "Then sit. We shall enjoy the Covenant together."

"I hate you."

"Ah, well, you've said that before." She was also cradling the book as if it were precious to her. "Do you wish to peruse the Covenant or not?"

She glowered at him. "What I wish is to see your head on a pike at London Bridge."

Revas couldn't stop a shiver.

She smiled wickedly. "And your heart and liver pitched to hungry eels."

Enough was enough. Determined to subjugate her, he took a powerful stance. "If you harm that book, I will beat you." He wouldn't, of course, but she needn't know that. "I will lock you in the dungeon and visit my lust on you until you give me a daughter who will honor the women in that book."

"I'll see you dead first."

"You'll need help to bring me low."

She took a moment to assess him, from his head to the toes of his boots. "You've made a success of low behavior on your own."

Their argument was growing too heated. "Yield, Meridene, for I'm a fighting man, and you have no weapons against me."

A calculating look glimmered in her eyes. "Since you have a penchant for superstition, I'll call up the ghosts of my kinswomen and watch them nibble away at your precious manhood."

The image of that lusty love play made Revas smile. "Summon them now."

"You're pleased?"

"I'm delighted. 'Tis a truly inventive punishment." He held out his hand for the book.

She clutched it in a death grip. "You're demented."

"Nay, I'm inspired." He strolled toward her. "And someday, my virgin wife, I'll show you why the notion of having my manhood nibbled holds great appeal."

Her heart pounding in fear of his intent, Meridene backed away.

"Well?" he challenged, anticipation dancing in his devil-dark eyes.

She would escape him. In the meantime, she had to read the Covenant. The servants knew more about her heritage than she did. At every turn she faced some ritual prescribed in that book—even the particulars of her bath were dictated by custom. Not that she was overly curious; she simply hated feeling outside of events, especially when they concerned her toilet. She would leave the book here, as he had insisted. It wouldn't do to have him suspect she was interested in the legacy.

"Have you no more cutting words for me, Meridene?"

He looked so determined and powerful, she couldn't resist saying, "I do have one wish, Revas. I hope that you die without issue and your bones rest in unconsecrated ground."

With a rueful shake of his head, he sighed. "You're a passionate woman."

At his all too obvious ploy, her anger melted. She marched to a chair, plopped down, and opened the book. At the edge of her vision, she saw him leave. Fare thee well.

The lock slid into place.

She read the first sentence.

Her mind was suddenly fixed on the words of a woman who had lived centuries ago.

I stand naked before my husband. I do not quake in fear of the marriage bed, for I am Meridene, the first Maiden of Inverness.

CHAPTER
5

After a meal eaten in silence, save a compliment for the cook, Meridene excused herself to the privacy of her apartments. Serena had spoken truthfully of her knowledge of looms, for the frame had been assembled properly and placed before the now-darkened windows. The girl had even hung a lamp overhead.

Meridene took refuge on the stool and stared at the half-completed tapestry. From the Covenant she had learned that her namesake had also been skilled in the weaver's art, and the first cloth of Clan Chapling had been a gift to her husband.

Husband.

The word and the man terrified Meridene. Unlike that first Meridene, she had no desire to rule. Too much was expected of her. She had no love in her heart for Scotland; her father's cruelty and her mother's indifference had purged that affection long ago. She felt used, alone, adrift in a sea of strangers with only a few pots of ink and a loom to call her own.

As she tied off a thread of precious lavender silk,

Meridene couldn't stop thinking about the words of the other Meridene, a brave woman who had changed the course of Scottish history.

> *To cleanse a man of his warring ways, join him naked in his bath. But not often, unless you wish to beget a son for the effort. If ever a lad is born to you with green eyes and black hair, he shall be named the Prince of Inverness.*

Meridene thought of her own mother and the healthy sons she'd borne. Both William and Robert were fair and resembled their father. Try as she would, she could not imagine her aloof parents languishing naked in a pool of warm, scented water. A glance at the tub in the adjacent room made her wonder if Revas expected her to join him in a bath. She remembered the kiss they'd shared earlier in the day, and now, as then, an unwanted yearning stirred deep in her breast.

He had asked for a kiss of thanks for the luxurious lodgings he had provided. Fool that she was, Meridene had relented. He had taken the spark of her gratitude and fanned it into a fire of wanting.

He kept twenty women.

She wasn't surprised. He wanted them for pleasure and companionship. He wanted her for ceremony.

Her spirits sank, for she had no weapons against his sensual expertise, except anger.

"Meridene?"

She jumped at the sound of his voice. It was as if she could summon him with a thought. Quickly she glanced at the door to be certain it was locked.

As if reading her mind, he said, "Open, Meridene, else I'll use my key."

Resigned, she went to the door and opened it.

Still dressed in the dark blue velvet he'd worn at table, Revas stood smiling down at her. Pinned at his shoulder was an ornate silver brooch bearing the lion of Macduff. Not a strand of his hair was out of place, and he looked at ease.

Her gaze flew to his hands. Empty. He hadn't brought the Covenant. She hated herself for wanting to read more of the book.

"May I come in?"

He might have a key to the door, but she had the means to refuse his intentions. "The servants have left. It wouldn't be proper."

"Perhaps not in English propriety." As if he owned all of the British Isles, he strolled into the room. "In Scotland we honor our women with our presence before marriage."

He sounded so righteous, she couldn't help nicking his pride. "Do some of you marry?" she chirped. "How modern you've become."

The sloth laughed. "Oh, Meridene. You are a delight. Such vinegar after your favorite meal. I shudder to imagine your ill humor when the food is not to your liking."

He shouldn't act so friendly, not when he'd kidnapped and threatened to beat her. "I could fill my belly with pomegranates and still despise the sight of you."

"Then I expect you'll live your life much as poor Isobel did."

"Isobel?"

"Aye. Meridene's granddaughter and the third Maiden. She brought her tragedies upon herself, poor lass."

Meridene had read only a few pages in the book. Her belongings had arrived shortly after Revas left her in his chamber. She had no knowledge of this Isobel. Would that woman's chronicle prove as disturbing as her grandmother's?

Bother the book and the ancient stories; Revas

could take them with him to the grave. Meridene would see the priest on Friday. Revas was being agreeable tonight. Their angry exchanges exhausted her. She would persevere.

"What do you want?" she asked.

He walked around the room, touching first her clothes trunk, then the quills and ink on her writing desk. He paused at her loom, which was large by any weaver's standard, but he dwarfed the wooden frame.

The casual pose belied the determination in his gaze. "What do I want? My needs are simple. I want the Maiden at my side, a friendly ruler at my back, and a long purse."

So much for an evening passed in friendly camaraderie. "Rejoice, then," she said. "For you have two of three: friends and money. A good showing in the best of times."

"I'll have them all." As if he were strumming a harp, he raked his fingers across the still unwoven threads of the tapestry. "'Tis a beautiful scene."

His wrists were bare of the war bracelets, and his hands moved with unexpected grace. The observation surprised her, and she chastised herself. Admiring even one aspect of her kidnapper was cause for alarm.

"The heather is especially well done," he said.

"It was for Johanna—" At the verbal blunder, Meridene gasped and quickly said, "I meant to say, of course, that the tapestry is for *Clare* Macqueen."

"Drummond's wife." Leaning close, Revas examined the details of the scene, which depicted a moorland in summer. Hares and squirrels frolicked in the field. Butterflies and a blazing sun would crown the work. "You must not hold either of them to blame."

Meridene had been raised at the abbey with the twins, Clare and Johanna. With absolute surety, she said, "In this, I cannot accuse Clare Macqueen." Clare was dead. Johanna had taken her place.

"Good. I expect them to visit after her babe is born."

Sister Margaret had gone to assist in the birth, leaving the abbey defenseless. "Ana told you Sister Margaret was taking the guard."

He sat on her padded stool, his long legs extended and crossed at the ankles. "The cushion still bears your warmth."

His intimate words embarrassed her, but a cozy place to rest himself was all the warmth he'd get from her. "You were only able to kidnap me when you did because the guard was elsewhere."

"Guard?"

"Aye, the duke of Cumberland's soldiers, not that we needed defending before you blackened Scarborough with your evil presence. Had you come when the knights were there, they would have prevailed."

He gave her a bland, handsome stare. "The absence or presence of a few Englishmen-at-arms had little to do with my plans. Although the sport might have proved entertaining."

She was certain of one thing about Revas Macduff: He did not lack confidence. "When did Drummond tell you where I was?"

"Before fetching you, I attended our first parliament. 'Twas held in Saint Andrews."

She read between the vague words. He hadn't made a special journey on her behalf. That bothered Meridene as much as his affable mood. "So you just extended your travels to include a jaunt to England to retrieve me."

He shrugged. "I go there from time to time. They always have Spanish oranges. I have a liking for fresh fruit."

Oranges. He dodged questions like a warrior avoiding an opponent's blow. With every parry, she grew more frustrated. "Why have you come to my room tonight?"

He fished a rosary from his pouch. "To take you to chapel."

Relief lightened her mood. "Church. I will pray that your teeth blacken and fall out."

That winning gleam in his eyes portended trouble. Before he could make any more mischief in her life, she snatched up her purse and cloak and preceded him out the door.

Flaming torches of bog fir illuminated the castle yard. The pungent smell stirred an old memory in Meridene, but she was too conscious of the man beside her to explore the past.

He took her arm and guided her down the front steps. Breathing deeply through his nose, he exclaimed, "It smells of a Hogmanay fire."

She didn't want to talk to him, especially when he was so attuned to her thoughts. If she ignored him, she could forget the alarming fact that he was her husband. She wanted no part of belonging to Revas Macduff. No shared baths, no sons. No glorious wedding night as her namesake had enjoyed. Her destiny lay in the peaceful confines of Scarborough Abbey.

"You must have had special celebrations," he said cordially, "since Hogmanay was also your birthday."

He must have garnered that information from the book, then spread it like cheap gossip. Meridene had not told him when she was born. No stinging retort came to mind, and she hoped her silence maddened him.

He waved at Summerlad Macqueen, who stood just outside the glow of a lighted torch near the well, the handmaiden Serena at his side.

"Will you join us at the chapel?" Revas called out to them.

"We've just prayed."

"We'll pray later."

Said in unison, the contradictory answers drew a gasp from Serena and a groan from Summerlad.

"'Tis true," Summerlad rushed to say. "I've been to chapel. Serena came to tell me about Lady Meridene's fine loom."

Revas grew still. "I see."

The embarrassed girl shrank inside her cloak, but Summerlad stepped fully into the light. He wore the sedate red and black tartan of Clan Macqueen. Tossing an end of the plaid cloth over his shoulder, he bowed to Meridene. "My lady."

Meridene again looked up at Revas, whose stern expression had darkened. According to custom, his responsibility toward Summerlad went beyond battle prowess and horsemanship. Honor and loyalty stood at the forefront of a guardian's duty.

"Bid Serena good night," he said. "Then relieve Forbes on the wall."

The youth wanted to object, for his eyes darted here and there in indecision.

"Unless you'd care to join us?" Revas added.

"No, sir."

"Then my lady and I will leave you with your *honorable* intentions."

With the slightest pressure on her arm, Revas steered Meridene toward the side yard.

"I favored the sweet cakes at Hogmanay." He spoke in a friendly fashion, as if they were boon companions.

Hogmanay was a Scottish ritual. Meridene wondered if he had truly put the exchange with Summerlad aside or if he was hesitant to discuss it. Having a choice of subjects, she gladly took up the holiday. "I don't remember the sweet cakes," she replied.

"Sibeal Montfichet makes a fine batch. Look there!" He pointed overhead. In a trail of twinkling light, a star fell from the sky.

"Do you make a wish on a tumbling star . . ."

Without thinking, Meridene finished the rhyme. "The angels will favor you from afar."

After a moment's contemplation, he said, "I wished for a gesture of peace from your father."

He spoke casually of a man Meridene despised. "You cannot voice your wish, else it will not come true."

"Then our wishes are well met." He looked her in the eye. "For I suspect you asked for a means to break your wedding vows."

He was too close to the truth to suit Meridene. With an effort, she sought a reprieve in the surroundings.

Unlike the courtyard at Scarborough Abbey, the castle yard came alive with sounds. A prowling cat screeched, a dog bayed at the half-moon. From the outer bailey, cattle lowed. Closer, a babe wailed.

Ignoring her lack of participation in the conversation, Revas said, "I hated sweeping the stoop at Hogmanay."

He spoke of superstition, of the age-old Scottish custom of sweeping the stoop at the turn of the New Year. The old luck and bad spirits were swept away from the dwelling. But women usually wielded the broom. "Where was your mother?"

"She left us for a fisherman out of Tain."

He had told her that years ago, but like so much of their one day together, she had forgotten. She felt bound to say, "How old were you?"

"Two or three. I do not remember her, but I recall clearly the other lads teasing me for wielding that broom on Hogmanay."

He had been different as a youth, and as much as she hated to admit it, she had liked that butcher's barefoot son. But he had changed. He was now a warrior bent on using her to lead his unruly brethren. "You can seek retribution now. You are the chieftain of Clan Macduff." She intentionally omitted the title he coveted most: king of the Highlands. Without her assistance, he would never sit on that throne.

"Seek revenge against lads playing pranks? Nay, I've better things to do."

"Such as kidnapping."

"You wound me, Meridene."

He sounded so sincere. Looking up, she studied his face. Bathed in moonlight, his manly features appeared comely beyond the telling. Twenty women wanted him. Did he walk them to chapel? Did any of them now stand in darkened windows watching him escort his wife to prayers? Did the women pine for him?

"I never wanted to take you by force, Meridene. But Ana said you had turned against me."

She hadn't truly forsaken the lad Revas had been. To the contrary, his sweet concern had helped her through the hardest day of her life. But that was then.

To change the subject, she said, "What do you do when not engaged in kidnapping?"

His eyes shone with glee at her inquiry. Eager to set him straight, she said, "Take no softhearted meaning, Revas. It was merely an attempt to make conversation."

"None taken, Meridene." He mocked her serious tone. "I trade wool, timber, and hides to Flanders in exchange for foodstuffs, iron, and salt."

She pointed to the noisy barracks. "You also command an army."

"When I must. At present I foster a number of Highland sons. By sponsoring them, I make alliances and avoid war," he said civilly, ignoring her gibe.

Dodging a blow, she thought, was the better description of his methods. But she was forced to admit that he had managed the Macqueen lad with the skill of a diplomat. Her brothers would have fought to exhaustion or injury—all in defense of bruised pride.

"My father died before I united the clans."

Thirteen years ago, during their short time together, he had spoken often and fondly of his father. She shouldn't feel sorry for him. In a sense, she'd lost both of her parents, all of her family and friends, yet she had survived. "What of the Macgillivrays? You have not brought them into your fold."

He wagged a finger at her and chuckled. "Careful, Meridene. One might think you harbor an interest in Scottish politics."

She bristled and pulled the cloak tighter around her. "I loathe Scottish politics."

"So do I," he said meaningfully.

"Ha!"

"Truly. I'd rather watch armor rust."

"You a peaceful Scot? That's a contrary notion."

He dropped an arm around her shoulder. When she tried to draw away, he pulled her to his side and whispered, "Spoken by one who is well versed on contrariness."

He'd all but named her a shrew, which was particularly odd, since he was holding her in an unbreakable embrace. "You're to blame, Revas."

He gave her a gentle squeeze and let her go. "I know. Just do not teach Serena your ill humor. Summerlad likes her as she is."

That brought to mind a question, and for the first time Meridene could quote the Covenant, Maiden and verse. "According to the book, Serena is old to serve as a handmaiden."

"True," he said. "But I could not follow every tenet, else I would have come for you years ago."

"How?" she challenged. "Without the loose tongue of Drummond Macqueen, you never would have found me."

"I paid men to look for you, but the old king hid you too well. Still, I would have found you."

To her profound surprise, the admission that he had looked for her warmed Meridene. Frightened by the feeling, she struck out with words. "So Ana wasn't your only spy. She was simply the most treacherous."

"Did you know that in Elginshire lots are drawn for the honor of serving as handmaiden? I know, 'tis not in the book, but since you weren't here to select them, we had to make do."

He could keep improvising until angels perched in the mews. She wanted no part of it. "What an inventive solution," she said, meaning nothing of the sort.

"On the occasion that Serena's name was drawn, Ana Sutherland had been among the unfortunate."

"I sense that you think I should sympathize with her."

He paused at the corner of the barracks and scanned the castle wall. "The sum of it is, Serena will be leaving service. Since you are newly arrived and unfamiliar with the people, you will have to draw another girl's name. Will you do so in good humor?"

According to Serena, the first handmaidens in Elginshire had been chosen twelve years ago. Since then, some girls had married and been replaced. That baffled Meridene, for without hope that she would be found, Revas had carried on the tradition of the Maiden.

Tradition be damned. "I have a better solution," she said. "The next time you draw names, pick yourself another wife."

Evidently satisfied that marauders would not scale the castle wall, he started walking again. "Serena is to become a wife. She and Summerlad wish to marry. Her father and his brother have come to accord, and the betrothal is set."

That bit of information piqued Meridene's curiosity, for Serena had said nothing on the subject. "Drummond Macqueen's brother is marrying a weaver's daughter? I'm surprised he would choose a girl of common birth."

His mouth twitched at the words "common birth." He probably thought she referred to him. Hooray for her.

"Serena Cameron is not of common birth. Her father is the earl of Clyde. Her family weaves the finest cloth in Perwickshire. She's an heiress."

Meridene's own servants possessed more wealth than she. *I am Meridene, the first Maiden of Inverness.* Her own legacy was not one of coin, but of mettle and intelligence, leadership and honor.

"What troubles you?"

The devil with leading Scots and honoring clan wars.

"Has Serena been unkind or rude?"

If Serena Cameron had willingly become a hand-maiden, then the legend of the Maiden was celebrated by the Camerons. But they were midland Scots and traditionally content to leave the Highlanders to their petty wars. Had Revas truly expanded his dream of peace to a shire so far to the south?

"Has she behaved poorly?" Revas asked again. "Tell me and I will discipline her and write to her mother."

"Nay, Serena is overeager. Does her father swear fealty to you?"

"Only to unify Scotland against England and any other nation that threatens our sovereignty. 'Tis a different sort of alliance. The chieftains now regularly exchange correspondence. Soon we hope to establish a system for delivering messages between all peoples of all cities."

"But your alliance is based on defense."

With a promise in his voice, he said, "We will unite against a common foe."

He did indeed rule the Highlands and more. The extent of his power grew with every conversation.

They arrived at the chapel, and Meridene repeated

her wish that the priest return early. Disappointment awaited her when Revas escorted her inside, for the church was empty.

"Do you remember this place?" he whispered.

Twin rows of wooden pews flanked the carpeted aisle. The altar and its ancient trappings gleamed in the torchlight. She and Revas had exchanged wedding vows before that very altar. The priest had been hesitant to marry them so young, especially when Meridene had been too ill to stand alone. But the will of King Edward I had prevailed. With a hand at her waist, Revas had helped her kneel, assisted her to her feet, and offered encouraging smiles throughout the ceremony.

Would the priest take her side again? Riddled with uncertainty, she retrieved her rosary from her purse.

"Wait," Revas said. From a niche in the wall near the poor box, he withdrew a small pouch. "Here."

The pouch had been stitched by Ailis, Meridene's grandmother, and it housed an ancient and mismatched rosary. Meridene remembered it well, for she had begged her mother to let her pray with it. She could not bring herself to touch it now, not in the house of God and not with deception in her heart.

"You keep it, Revas," she said. "For I tell you truly, I am smothered by so much ceremony."

Sadness filled his eyes. "'Twill be here when you change your mind." He returned the purse to the niche.

She anointed herself with holy water and genuflected. After Revas did the same, they started down the aisle.

"Have you the same priest?" she asked.

"Nay. Father Clarence was called to Rome."

He helped her kneel, then went about his prayers. She couldn't help peeking up at him. Head bowed, his hands clasped, he looked like an archangel. His fair hair, damp from the evening air, gave the impression of a halo. He must have felt her gaze, for he smiled and turned slightly toward her.

When he opened his eyes, she felt bathed in admiration, and her heart tripped in response. Her rosary slipped from her hands and landed, in an explosion of sound, on the stone floor. They both reached down at the same moment, and their shoulders touched. He retrieved her rosary, and taking one of her hands, he let the beads fall into her palm. He leaned closer, until his forehead rested against hers. His eyes drifted shut, and he tilted his head to the side and kissed her.

His lips were soft and supple, as before, but this kiss contained a wealth of sensations that went beyond racing hearts and rushing breaths. It was as if he were trying to draw out her soul and commune with her very spirit, and like a bird too long in captivity, she stood on the threshold of her cage, but could not seek the freedom he offered.

He pulled back, his eyes clouded with confusion. "I cannot keep my mind on prayer." Then he gathered his composure. "I'll await you outside."

So profound was her sense of loss that she almost called him back. But what could she say? That she had forgiven him for ripping her life apart? That she was happy to be in a land of monsters?

He could have sent her a message, rather than stealing her away in the dark of night. They could have exchanged letters. He might have asked her to return. But she wouldn't have come, and he knew that. He hadn't bothered with sweet words and the ritual of courting. He had not cared that she was frightened. He wanted a sword and a kingdom, and only she could provide him with both.

Sadness overwhelmed her, and she bowed her head and prayed for an end to her misery. When the pain eased, she dried her tears and walked out of the church.

Revas sat on the steps. He rose quickly, and from the smile on his face, she decided his mood had also lightened.

Pretending that the deeply emotional experience had not occurred, she said, "Who is your priest?"

"Father Thomas, the younger son of the duke of Ross."

That man's holdings were vast by anyone's standards. At the time Meridene left Scotland, His Grace had ruled even the Western Isles. "Is the duke of Ross an ally?"

"A most staunch ally. Your handmaiden, Ellen, is his favorite granddaughter."

Meridene groaned inside, for if what he said was true, the extent of her husband's influence knew no boundaries. "I suppose Lisabeth is also an heiress."

"Oh, nay. Lisabeth's father is the miller, but she will be valued as a princess when her service is done. Same as the others before her, she will receive a dowry for her service."

Meridene had heard enough for one night. To her relief, Revas was also content to walk in silence. Until they passed the barracks.

He stopped abruptly, listening, his eyes scanning the wall. When his gaze fell on the battlement near the main gate, he said a quiet curse. "Wait here."

Making little sound, he climbed the steps leading to the wall. Moving swiftly on the high walkway, he passed beneath the intermittent torches, ignoring the sentries as he went. When he reached the main gate, he disappeared into a darkened barbican.

A feminine shriek rent the air.

In the next instant, a cloaked figure burst from the enclosure and into the torchlight. It was Serena, her red hair gleaming like copper. Summerlad followed, his muted tartan unmistakable. Then came Revas. A very angry Revas.

In single file, the three marched along the wall and

down the steps. At the base, Revas stopped and addressed the couple. He spoke too softly for Meridene to understand the words, but the reprimand in his voice was clear.

Serena looked so forlorn, Meridene approached them.

"What's amiss?" she said.

Revas glowered at Summerlad. "I fear Serena needs a protector."

The young man's features were frozen in indignation. "We are betrothed, Revas," he said.

"That does not give you the right to anticipate your vows."

Shocked, Meridene said, "You mean he would dishonor her?"

"He's too young and randy to see it as that," Revas replied. "I'm certain he thinks to *honor* her with his lusty attentions."

He sounded so wise and so outraged—an oddity, considering he had reclaimed by force his own unwilling wife.

"'Tis not all his fault, Revas," Serena pleaded. "He did not carry me up those stairs. I went to him willingly, and I'm still a virgin. I swear on my wicked soul."

Revas rounded on Summerlad. "No thanks to you."

"I only kissed her," came the grumbling reply.

Serena began to cry. At the sight of her tears, Meridene drew the girl aside and clutched her hands. "Worry not. You're to be married."

Between sobs, she said, "You must be completely disappointed in me. But Summerlad and I have waited forever."

"How long have you been betrothed?"

"Five years. We've only held hands. But then you came back, and . . ."

"And now you can be wed."

"Aye. Unless Revas tells Randolph."

She sounded fearful, and Meridene's heart went out to her. "Who is Randolph?"

Her breath shaking, Serena said, "He's Summerlad's older brother and chieftain of the Macqueens. He was against the betrothal because I'm a lowland Scot. But I love Summerlad, and my father likes the match. Revas did also."

"Shush," Meridene said. "One kiss will not change his mind."

"Truly? Will you talk to him?"

Under the circumstances, she had to agree. But when she turned to him, words died on her lips.

Once a butcher's barefoot son, Revas Macduff now stood, hands on his hips, his considerable wrath directed at an unrepentant lad of noble birth.

"If I see you within sword's length of Serena before your vows are said, I will come after you. Do you understand?"

Summerlad's blue eyes widened in alarm. "I'm no match for you. You'll force me to yield."

Revas flung an arm toward Serena. "What did you ask of her?" he spat. "I will not let her fall to your winsome ways. She is a fair flower of Scotland. You will tend her, for she has given you leave to rule her life."

"I will husband her well."

"By God, Summerlad, you have stooped low. 'Tis a blessing Randolph is not here to witness your fall from grace."

Completely shamed, the young Macqueen stared at his boots.

Revas sighed and in a lighter tone said, "'Tis for certain you love her well, lad. Everyone knows 'tis true. What will you do now?"

So quietly his words sounded like a prayer, Summerlad said, "I beg your pardon, and henceforth, I will honor her. On that you have my word as a Macqueen."

Revas slapped the lad on the back. "Well said, and we'll seal that bargain with a tankard of the brewer's best. Go along. I'll join you there shortly."

Summerlad headed for the tavern. Revas approached Meridene and Serena. Smiling fondly at the girl, he brushed her hair from her face. "How fare you, lassie mine?"

"Oh, Revas." She flew into his arms, and he held her, rocking from side to side, his big hand cradling her head on his shoulder.

"Fret not, sweeting," he murmured. "What has occurred here will stay with us."

Meridene was reminded of another heartsick girl he had comforted long ago. He'd been rail-thin and his voice had warbled with youth. His honest concern had seasoned with age.

"I'm so ashamed," Serena cried. "And I do so want to be a goodwife."

His gaze fell on Meridene. She saw tenderness there and something else. As if speaking to her, he said, "There's more to being a *good*wife than meaningful kisses in the dark of night."

CHAPTER
6

❧

Two evenings later, Meridene sat at her desk and pressed her seal on a letter to Sister Margaret. After telling the nun of Revas's abduction, Meridene assured her she was well. In closing she had asked for assistance in fleeing both her husband and the dangers of Scottish intrigue.

She hadn't seen Revas since Wednesday night. According to Sheriff Brodie, her husband had gone a-hunting.

She hoped he fell off his horse and landed in a bush of nettles. The wretch had secured his chamber door, and none of the castle keys would spring the lock.

I cannot allow you to take the book.

Splendid. Deciphering the Covenant of the Maiden would wait. Understanding Revas Macduff would challenge the brightest Oxford mind. One moment he acted the caring gallant by rescuing Serena from Summerlad. The next, he left without a word to his wife.

His absence thrilled her beyond measure. Her anger stemmed not from a wayward husband, but from a cowardly priest. Even now, her hands clenched and her eyes narrowed at the memory of her meeting earlier today with Father Thomas.

Overly tall and thin, with brown hair perfectly tonsured and a beard so neatly trimmed, a servant had surely done it, Father Thomas had towered over her. If his place in the clergy weren't influential enough, he had the powerful duke of Ross behind him. Revas had chosen well and wisely in picking this man for his priest.

After denying her request to petition the pope for an annulment, the goodly Father Thomas had ordered her to confess her wifely lapse to Revas Macduff.

She had flatly refused to obey him. "No kind priest would make such a demand of a woman concerning her husband."

"Tell him, Lady Meridene, else I will."

"In your capacity as a messenger of God? I think not. You base your decisions on the needs of Scotland."

His gaze slid to a statue of the Madonna. "God has chosen Scotsmen to serve. He meant for us to honor our kinsmen, else he would have summoned only Romans to tend his Christian flocks."

Meridene had chuckled at his attempt to use religious justification for pure deviltry.

"My lady!" The girl Ellen skipped into the room and twirled in a circle. Meridene gladly put aside the disheartening memory of the pious Father Thomas.

"They've returned, Lady Meridene," Ellen chirped. "And you'll never guess who's standing in our very own stables at this very exact moment."

Although she knew the answer, Meridene couldn't help teasing the excited girl. "Has my husband perchance returned?"

"Oh, aye." Hands clasped, Ellen stared in dreamy fixation at the ceiling. "But someone else—someone truly enchanting—has come."

Budding with womanhood, the girl discovered at least one new passion every day. Meridene couldn't help enjoying her company or teasing her. "Has the pope graced us with his presence?"

Like a bird eager to build her first nest, Ellen darted about the room, her wavy blond hair bouncing as she went. "Oh, my lady, you are the very cleverest of women, and I am hopelessly speechless at *his* arrival. Should he cast eyes on me, I shall surely wither like a sickly English rose."

According to Serena, Ellen's interest in the opposite sex had begun at May Day last. "Yesterday you swore the Leslie lad was all a woman could hope for in a devoted husband."

"My devotion was misplaced with Lord Leslie." As if it were a matter of her salvation, Ellen said, "He doesn't play a harp or sing ballads—or captain his own ship."

Meridene ducked her head to hide a smile. "Who is this newly arrived model of chivalry?"

Sighing as if to swoon, Ellen hugged herself. "Randolph Macqueen."

Revas had spoken of him. "He's Summerlad's brother."

"Aye, and chieftain of all the Macqueens. When the elder brother, Drummond, fell prisoner to old King Edward, Randolph braved unspeakable perils to assume leadership of his clan." Having emptied her lungs, she took a deep breath and kept going. "The woman he chooses will know much happiness and wifely bliss. Serena says that Macqueen men cherish their women as kings unto queens."

For the sake of her best and oldest friend, Meridene hoped that was true. "You'd like to wear his crown?"

"Oh, my lady. He is the very noblest of minstrels,

and handsome beyond words, and better with a sword than even the Holy Roman Emperor." She sucked in a breath. "They say the countess of Buchan was so completely besotted with him, she took a short sword to his mistress and forced the woman naked into the street." Her complexion blossomed red.

"Then you had best conceal your interest, Ellen. You have only a dirk for weapon."

Youthful adoration turned to pure alarm. As quickly, the girl relaxed. "Revas will protect me from her evil clutches."

If his concern for Serena was any indication of his devotion, Revas would indeed take up his sword in defense of the handmaidens of Elginshire. He would win, too, if the priest's assessment of his skill was to be believed.

But what would he do when Meridene told him of her request for an annulment? She didn't know, but postponing the inevitable seemed cowardly. Her cause was just, her reasons true.

Eager to have it over and done, she capped the ink. "Ellen, please seek out Revas, and tell him I wish to see him alone and at his earliest convenience. And should he attempt to bring along Randolph Macqueen, I expect you to engage that man in conversation—without withering."

"Aye, my lady." She skipped to the door, murmuring, "Good evening, Lord Randolph. Are you enjoying your stay? Shall I show you the mews?"

The moment Ellen stepped into the hall, her girlish demeanor vanished. Her back went pike-straight and her strides were as smooth as those of a princess.

Her own courage fleeting, Meridene couldn't sit still. She must tell Revas about her visit to the priest, else Father Thomas had promised to do so himself. The Judas.

She went livid at the thought of those men discussing her behind her back. Men exercised too much control over women, and asking her to sacrifice her life for Scotland was unfair. As a child she'd been isolated from the people because of her birthright. At eight years of age her estrangement had been complete.

Father Thomas's blunt rejection of her request had shocked her into challenging him. "What of the church's obligation to keep confessions secret?" she had demanded.

"You did not ask me to hear your confession. You insisted, without good cause, that I petition the pope to dissolve your marriage."

"Good cause?" she had argued. "I was eight years old and suffering the effects of my father's poison. The priest even suggested a betrothal rather than marriage. King Edward compelled him."

"Greater concerns were at stake."

"Concerns greater than the life of a defenseless child?"

"Aye, if she is the Maiden of Inverness."

Scorn ripped through her. "I will never, never wear the crown of rowans. You people have no right to ask it of me."

"All the better, then, that you surrender yourself to the care of Revas Macduff. He will protect and cherish you."

His loyalty should not have shocked her. Priests yielded to the will of kings and to men who aspired to rule. "In exchange for the sword of Chapling."

"It is your destiny, Lady Meridene."

A truly regrettable phrase, she thought. "And if my father again tries to rid himself of an unwanted daughter? Who will protect me then?"

"Revas will, and if a better swordsman resides in Christendom, you'll find him ruling the Holy Roman Empire. The sons of Macqueen, Leslie, Macpherson —all of the other skilled soldiers who follow him will take up your cause." He spoke confidently, but the cool expression in his eyes told her he did not believe her father would be so bold.

Clan pride. She knew it well.

Too angry to speak, she had clutched the back of the pew until her fingers cramped. When she gathered her composure, she moved into the aisle. "You shame the robes you wear. How dare you put the concerns of the clans above the souls of those you are beholden to serve."

Unmoved, he had reasonably said, "They are often one and the same. Had you not been away so long, you would remember that. Much work awaits you here, and the people will reward your sacrifice with devout friendship."

Now, in the privacy of her solar, the memory of that meeting fired Meridene's temper anew. She would tell Revas, but not for the reasons Father Thomas had insisted. She was unashamed to seek a destiny that opposed Scottish interests.

She looked at the hour candle. Rings were carved into the wax at intervals, each to mark an hour's burning time. It was after six. As she waited for Revas, she took comfort in the knowledge that Father Thomas was still occupied with Vespers.

What would Revas say?

When the knock came, Meridene put her letters in a trunk with Sim's precious ransom. Then she went to the door.

Leaning casually against the frame, he appeared at ease, and his eyes glowed with merriment. His hair was smoothed back and tied at the nape with a strip of leather. The style accentuated his high forehead and strong cheekbones. A stubble darkened his cheeks and circled his mouth, drawing attention to his lips.

The memory of their soul-searing kiss jolted her.

"You summoned me?"

Was he, too, thinking of that moment in the chapel?

"'Tis a bonny dress, Meridene. The yellow favors you well."

He *was* remembering, and she had the impression that he wanted to kiss her again. Annulment, she told herself, and the devil with romantic notions. She had business with him. "Come in."

She offered him wine. He held up a tankard. Why hadn't she noticed it in his hand? Because she'd been too consumed with worry. As if to prove the point, her palms grew damp.

"Ellen said you wished to see me alone."

Lord, she'd kept the girl's company too often of late, for Meridene couldn't carry an idea from one heartbeat to the next without a thought of Revas Macduff getting in the way.

"Yes. I did want to speak with you."

"Good, for I have news as well."

A reprieve. "What is it?"

He took a long drink from the tankard. "You first. I insist."

She went to the table and poured herself a cup of wine. Then she walked to the loom and examined the newest work. Her effort had been poor; she'd woven acorns on a rowan tree. The mistake was Revas's fault.

And she was flitting about like Ellen.

"You're limping, Meridene. Have you hurt yourself?"

Her toe smarted every time she thought about his locked door. But she wasn't about to explain the injury to him. "No."

"'Twould be best if I heard it from you."

At his stern tone, she started. "Heard what?" The words came out as a squeak.

He chuckled. "Whatever it is you're trying to hide. Secrets are poorly kept in Elginshire."

Except his twenty women. Even the handmaidens

knew nothing of those tarnished souls. "What makes you think I keep a secret?"

He joined her at the loom. "You're being cordial to me. That's an odd rowan tree."

She blocked his view of the tapestry. "The light was poor last night. Everyone here is always nice to you."

"They know me."

His self-importance knew no bounds, and he looked taller, broader, in his rugged hunting garb.

"Have you blackened Sim's name?"

She took a swallow of the honeyed wine. "No."

"You've run off the Montfichets?"

That made Meridene smile, and the guessing game relaxed her. "If Sibeal cannot force her husband to leave your service, how could I?"

"Have you turned the handmaidens against each other?"

On the ship she had threatened to wreck his household. He shouldn't be so clever as to throw her words in her face. She shouldn't like him for it, either. But she did. "No. Ellen, Lisabeth, and Serena are the most loyal of companions."

"Out with it then, Meridene."

Catching his gaze, she lifted her chin. "I went to see Father Thomas."

He raised his brows as if waiting for a revelation.

"I asked for an annulment."

His gaze sharpened, but he did not move. "Our humble holy man refused."

"Humble? Have you spoken with him?"

"Nay."

"Then how did you know he refused?"

He gave her a smile she was coming to loathe and waved his mug toward the dressing room. "You haven't packed your belongings."

She seethed with rage. "How dare you take me lightly."

Stopping at the bed, he leaned against one of the posts. "What did Father Thomas say?"

His carefree reaction baffled her. "He told me that no one in the Highlands would aid me."

"'Tis better said that everyone in the Highlands seeks your happiness."

"So long as I find it here and with you."

He sighed and shook his head. "How do you know 'tis not here with me?"

Her heart's desire lay in the safety of England. "Because I could never be happy within a king's mile of my father."

A muscle twitched in his jaw. Through gritted teeth, he said, "Your father wants no one in the Highlands to be happy."

"How delightful that you've found someone to despise. In that we are evenly met."

"He has sworn to destroy the Community of the Realm, rather than see me wear the Highland crown."

Bruised feelings made her say, "I do not care a blunted needle for clans, crowns, and garlands of rowans."

At her angry words, he dropped onto a chair and threw back his head. Arms dangling, eyes closed, he looked as if he'd expired from his own fury.

Wondering why he acted so odd, she circled him. "If your bad humor has killed you, I am not aggrieved."

He smiled and his chest rocked with suppressed laughter.

"Will you attend me?" she demanded.

"Have I a last wish?"

Baffled by his quick change in moods, she spat, "Only if it doesn't involve me."

"Not at all," he said much too expansively. "I should like you to call up those nibbling Maidens to welcome me into heaven. A man of eternal patience deserves a reward."

Realization dawned. "You're drunk."

"Drunk. Hum." He savored the word. "'Tis true I've had a full measure of Macqueen's best ale. At first, I feared that your biting wit had wasted the effects." Toasting her with the tankard, he said, "Thank the saints, the spirits have prevailed. I am impervious to your scorn."

Drunk. For days she'd thought him away providing meat for the table and contemplating their last embrace. He'd been making merry with one of those wretched Macqueens. "Get out."

He breathed deeply through his nose, his jaw again taut.

"Shall I call the porter?"

He began to drum his fingers.

The wrath that had been simmering since her unsuccessful meeting with Father Thomas now came to a full boil. "Pity your purchased priest is occupied. I should think he'd make the perfect nursemaid. He tends your business well."

His hand curled into a fist.

Relishing his loss of control, she pushed onward. "Perhaps one of your twenty women will carry you back to your cave."

In the blink of an eye, his smile returned.

Her better judgment fled. "You admit to keeping those women?"

"Would you believe me if I said I did not?"

"Would you give them up if I asked?"

"Ah." He studied her over the rim of the tankard. "Once again, we have the pleasure of facing a quandary."

"Your favorite pastime."

"My second favorite." He gave her the full power of his smile. "You are my first."

Ignoring the voice of reason, she said, "I'm certain those women want you. That kiss in the chapel meant nothing to me."

Like the lion that was his symbol, he sprang from

the chair and pinned her against the wall. "Then why mention *that* kiss? You were interested, Meridene, and your passion came not from obligation. You like me, and it frightens you."

"I loathe you, and it delights me."

He leaned into her, pressing his chest against hers. "What are you doing?"

"Guess."

"Past crushing me against the wall, I haven't a notion."

His chest jerked with laughter. "You've a fire in you, Meridene, and I like it well. But know you this, my jealous wife, I am resolved to our marriage."

"Jealous?" She fought the force of his will. "You want me only for the sword."

His expression softened, and his gaze grew hungry, exploring her face and neck. "I am also resolved to having you lie naked beside me. I will discover if your breasts are as lovely as I imagine. Then I will suckle them, and when I've had my fill, I will taste and nibble your other sweet places. You will rejoice in our marriage bed."

Vivid pictures rose in her mind. "I doubt you'll find the time, and I will not yield."

His grin turned wicked and he held the tankard to her mouth. "Everyone yields to Macqueen's brew. Would you care for a taste?"

He wore good humor like a cloak. She had concessions to gain. "Thank you, no. Since you are so *resolved* to keeping me, am I to have any money of my own?"

"Am I to know what it's for?"

"Messengers to deliver my letters. I've written to Sister Margaret and others."

"Sister Margaret knows where you are."

"Drummond told her."

Suddenly exhausted, he rested his forehead against

the wall, his cheek almost touching hers. He smelled of the forest, of woodsmoke, of a long ride in the sunshine.

"Randolph will take your letter to Sister Margaret. He leaves tomorrow for his brother Drummond's estate."

"I've also written to the pope."

"'Twill gain you naught. Moray has twice challenged the church to reinstate your betrothal to him. Twice was he denied. Our vows stand."

At her father's command, Meridene had been promised at birth to the man who was now the earl of Moray. Their betrothal had been formalized on her fifth birthday. "The pope has not heard *my* plea."

"Very well. If you will do something for me, I will send your message to the pope."

Now that he had conceded, she stood firm. "I will agree to nothing that involves Clan Chapling or the sword."

"So you've said. But will you try to enjoy yourself for as long as you are here?"

His ploy was as clear as rainwater. He thought to seduce her into staying. *'Twill be enjoyable, seeing you yield to the lure of the Highlands.* He'd said that shortly after kidnapping her.

"Have I your word?"

She'd mastered the art of feigning happiness at an early age, and she rather liked the idea of making friends of her handmaidens. After she returned to England, she hoped they would speak well of their mentor. "I swear."

"'Tis a bargain we've struck. Do you go back on it, I will punish you."

"You've already promised to beat me and toss me in your dungeon. I am suitably frightened of your wrath."

"And fearful of all else," he murmured.

He thought her a coward. Her first instinct was to prove him wrong, but he was too close, and a confrontation favored him. She hadn't the small advantage of flight, not with his shoulders blocking her view and his warmth seeping through her clothes.

"Unless," he went on, "you can find the courage to seal our bargain with a kiss."

Would the kiss be as stirring as before? Surely not. "It's your custom."

"The Macgillivrays avoid bargains."

Her family were strangers. She knew more about Ellen and Serena than she remembered of her own kin. "I am not like them."

"I've always said 'twas so."

Calmness spread through her, and she had the strangest desire to thank him. She had given her word to put aside her reservations.

"Too late," he murmured, and put his mouth on hers.

Her back instinctively bowed, and his hand curled effortlessly to support her waist. As easily as needle slips into thread, they settled into the intimacy. A sense of belonging engulfed her, and her mind flew back to a girl and a boy who had faced an enemy king.

The vision alarmed her. She broke the kiss. "I'm certain you'll want to return to your drunken friends now."

He studied her for so long, she thought he would refuse to leave. Still watching her, he pushed away from the wall. "Give me your letters."

Before he could change his mind, she fetched the messages and handed them to him. "You swear you'll have them delivered?"

"I swear on my honor as chieftain of Clan Macduff." He walked to the door.

She remembered that he'd also wanted to talk to her. "What did you wish to tell me?"

Over his shoulder, he said, "Ana and John Sutherland have gone missing."

Revas closed the door behind him. Like a plunge in the ocean, that kiss had cleared his head of the effects of Macqueen's brew. Regrettably sober, he made his way to his chamber, his body tense with desire, his mind spinning with her confession and his own lie. He'd send a messenger to the pope, but he'd give young Leslie instructions to go by way of a tour of his family's French estates. By the time the emissary delivered Meridene's letter, she'd be too busy suckling their third or fourth child to think of dissolving her marriage.

Revas couldn't forget the feel of her lips and the gift of her surrender. Although short-lived now, her yielding moments were on the rise. For the hundredth time he remembered kneeling beside her in the church and feeling her watching him, answering his immediate prayer. The kiss had stunned him, for in that brief moment of intimacy she had lowered the barrier to her heart and given him a glimpse of the enchanting woman within.

She wanted to love him; he could feel her need, but the cruelties of the past were too fresh in her mind. His plan to woo her was simple enough. Now she'd given her word to put aside her intolerance. It was a place to start, and if that last kiss was a sign, his vanguard was on the move. He'd succeeded in uniting the Highland clans, save one. The very jewel in the Macgillivray treasure belonged to him. And she kissed like a woman eager to solve a puzzle.

Fired by determination, he called for a hot bath, then took the steps in a run. He found Sheriff Brodie waiting for him outside the locked door to his chamber.

"The lass tried to open it at least a dozen times while you were away," Brodie said.

Revas couldn't help grinning. "She did?"

Brodie couldn't hide his concern. "Oh, Revas. What sins have you committed to reap her for penance?"

"Not my sins. Probably the sins of Hacon, her namesake's husband."

"God also gave him a spirited woman."

Taking the key from his sporran, Revas opened the door and motioned Brodie in before him. "Yet he lavished stubbornness on my wife." And gave her a mouth to adore.

"Aye." The sheriff knelt before the hearth and kindled a fire. "When she discovered she could not open your door, she kicked it so hard, she limps still."

Revas had noticed her discomfort. He also understood why she had not shared the details of the injury. Stubbornness. On the edge of a dilemma. He knew the exercise well.

"I heard gossip that ill has befallen the Sutherlands."

Revas grew weary, for his life moved from one obstacle to the next. But he took heart, for great reward awaited him on every front. "Pray Cutberth isn't behind their disappearance."

"Let the Sutherlands fight that battle. You have a greater challenge here."

"Peace in the Highlands is my challenge. If the unified clans cannot defend their Sutherland brethren, then we have defeated our purpose in uniting."

"But everyone knows Cutberth's quarrel is with you."

"Then let's hope the Sutherlands boarded the wrong ship."

"What happened to them?"

"After leaving Elgin, they made port in Cromarty. John and Ana went ashore."

"And did not return."

"Aye. The tale came from a sailor out of Nairn, who swore that Macgillivrays were seen in Cromarty."

"King Robert will get wind of it."

"Aye, and if Bruce wants to rule all of Scotland fairly, he'd better learn to dirty his hands in Highland affairs."

"He expects you to manage Cutberth."

Revas yanked off his pouch and threw it on the desk. "Then our king must think again. He once rode with Cutberth against me." Revas held up his hand to put a halt to the discussion. "Enough of Cutberth. The sound of his name fair sours my stomach. Yet a thought of his daughter warms my wicked heart."

Brodie howled with laughter.

Feeling jovial again, Revas pointed to Meridene's letters. "My wife has written to the pope asking him to dissolve our marriage."

"Others have tried and failed."

"True. Does young Leslie still crave a visit to his French relations?"

"Aye, his cousin is to be betrothed soon to one of Burgundy's lads."

Ignoring a stab of guilt, Revas said, "He has leave to stay until his cousin births her first child. At which time, he's to deliver Meridene's letter to the pope."

"Leslie's cousin is but five or six years old."

"Then Leslie's stay will be an extended one, and the message tardy."

Brodie whistled. "I'd not care to be in your boots when she learns the truth."

"My boots will rest beneath her bed by the time she receives a denial of her request from the church."

A knock on the door brought Sim and a trail of servants carrying buckets of steaming water. Handing Revas a small chest, the steward said, "The Maiden's flower pennies."

According to the Covenant, the original flower pennies, as they had been called, were golden coins. But misfortune had turned them to wood, and they were henceforth given as tokens of affection and rewards to children. During the lean years, the pennies had been used as currency.

Revas raised the lid of the box. Larger than the silver coins minted by Edward I, these wooden pennies would mark the return of the Maiden of Inverness.

Would Meridene accept and distribute them with good grace? Lord, he hoped so.

When the servants left, Revas stripped off his clothes and settled into the tub. Brodie lounged in a chair and examined the wooden coins.

The water leeched Revas of his woes. "What comings and goings while I was away?" he asked.

"The stonemason took his leave. A wheelwright from Aberdeen arrived last night. Says he's looking to settle here."

"Has he a wife and children?"

"Nay, but he has fine tools, and the blacksmith thought him skilled."

Revas welcomed families into Elginshire. Unattached tradesmen and landless adventurers always brought trouble. "See he doesn't spend too much of his time in the alehouse."

"I'll put the Grant lad to watching for him there."

Scooping up a handful of the pine-scented soap he favored, Revas lathered his hair and torso. "What of commerce?"

Brodie returned the flower pennies to the box and closed the lid. "Gordon's factor came to purchase salt. Maclean declares that the lambing is nigh. Father Thomas returned this afternoon. Lady Meridene went to see him. I fear their meeting went poorly for our cleric. He twice misspoke at Vespers and shouted at the almoner."

Revas could imagine the loyal and blue-blooded Thomas chiding Meridene for her request. He could better envision her wrath. He'd tell Thomas that the matter was closed. More amiable subjects awaited. "The old hunting lodge is yours."

"My thanks. I've always wanted such a place."

"You've earned it, my friend. I'm building a new one in the last bend of Serpent Creek."

"'Tis a bonny spot. I wondered why you returned with so little game. I thought 'twas the company of Lord Randolph."

The idea of building a new lodge had come after a hotfoot ride through the forest. When exhaustion had eluded Revas, he spent the day felling trees in frustration. He wielded the axe in hopes of obliterating thoughts of Meridene, that kiss, and the passionate consummation his body craved. Once begun, the construction of the lodge provided a needed diversion. The arrival of Randolph Macqueen had cut short the work.

"I'm naming it Macduff's Halt."

"Why?"

Revas rinsed the soap from his hair, then began scrubbing the rest of his body. "'Tis where my patience ends."

"Your patience for the charms of a raven-haired maiden?"

Her promise to look favorably on her new life bolstered Revas's good humor. "Aye."

"Pray she never goes there."

"If she does, she'll forfeit her innocence, for I vow, Brodie, I have only so many weapons against her."

"But the rewards will be great. Think of the sons she will give you."

"And the lassies."

"Have you told Gibby of the Maiden's arrival?"

Thoughts of his ten-year-old daughter made Revas smile. "Aye. When I mentioned that the wood-carver was making flower pennies, she pledged to earn the very first one."

Staring into the now-blazing fire, Brodie smiled fondly. "When will you tell Lady Meridene about Gibby?"

Revas reached for a drying cloth and stepped from the tub. "Soon. My lady will be drawing the name of another handmaiden. I'll invite Gibby to the ceremony."

"Pray she doesn't put her name in the pot."

"Worry not. Gibby loves her grandparents well. She'll not leave their tender care." He sat before the fire and drew on his trunk hose. "Now. I've a perverse desire to see Randolph's face when he sets eyes on my bride."

"If he wants to greet her properly, he'll have to pry young Ellen off his arm."

"Tomorrow will find her smitten with some other lad."

"Will the morrow find Lady Meridene smitten with you?"

Feeling lighthearted, Revas stretched. "I predict there will be smiles at table tonight."

The boast proved true. Almost. But the smiles were not of the kind he'd hoped for.

CHAPTER 7

From the moment Meridene opened her door, she knew trouble was afoot. Scrubbed and groomed and garbed in black trunk hose and a short black tunic trimmed in gold braid, Revas Macduff looked like a man living his destiny. His head appeared naked for lack of a crown.

In his hands he held a small chest. "For you. Something you never thought to see."

Was he giving her his mother's jewels? No. His father had been a butcher and his mother left them for a fisherman. Meridene relaxed, for she could with good grace refuse any gift, save his family heirlooms.

She took the chest. "Come in."

As was his habit, he went to the loom. "You look bonny in that dress."

Her surcoat was a perfect match to his tunic. The garments were cut of the same cloth; even the golden trimmings and belts were exactly alike. "Ellen told you that I had chosen this gown tonight."

"Aye."

131

Honesty did not excuse his maneuvering. "Then you sent her on an errand."

"'Twas you who told her to attend Randolph."

"Have you matched our entire wardrobes?"

"Nay. I'd look foolish in pink silk."

The remark did not shock her; she was growing accustomed to his irreverent humor. "Then allow me to exchange this gown for the pink."

"Certainly." He sat down in the chair, as if to watch.

"You're despicable."

"Nay. I'm hungry, and you haven't opened your gift."

Had she hurt his feelings? Yes, if his disappointment was as earnest as his admission. Just hours ago he had allowed her to petition the church for an annulment. Now he connived to present them as man and wife. That or watch her disrobe.

She'd look at his gift and decide if she could, in good faith, keep it. Then she'd send him ahead to table and don a different overdress.

Expecting a scarf or a set of knives, she lifted the lid. Her animosity fled, for the chest was filled with wooden coins. They were called flower pennies and were the subject of a fairy tale. Her grandmother had had one of the trinkets, and it was so old, the edges were worn smooth and the wood darkened with age.

A fond image danced on the edge of her memory. She'd been five years old and fretful after the long journey to Sweetheart Abbey and the endless ceremony betrothing her to Moray's heir. John Balliol, the king of Scotland at the time, had been in attendance. Her maternal grandmother, who lived in that faraway place, had also been there. After giving Meridene the ancient penny, Grandmama told her a story of a beloved wife who had been captured by the enemy. As ransom, the husband forfeited all of the gold in his kingdom. But the moment the evil villain touched the coins, they turned to wood.

The story had cheered Meridene then. It confused her now. How had Revas known of the tale? The Covenant? Yes. Her instincts told her that the ransomed wife had been one of the Maidens of Inverness, another fact her mother had omitted.

"You read about the flower pennies in the Covenant," she said.

"Aye, and your handmaidens argued over what you would do when you opened the chest. Serena said you would cry." He peered at her dry eyes. "Good. I worried that the pennies would distress you. Most Scottish things do."

"With good cause."

"I cannot dispute that."

"Yet you seek to change it."

"So I've said. Lisabeth, however, predicted that you would count them twice. Why would she say that?"

Meridene was trying to teach the girl to cipher. "Because she cannot correctly sum three and four, and she refuses to learn."

He folded his arms over his chest, revealing the war bracelets. Against his elegant black clothing, the manly symbols appeared harmless ornaments. But, as Meridene was coming to realize, Revas Macduff was anything but harmless.

"Care you to guess what Ellen said?" he asked.

She had agreed to enjoy herself while here in Scotland. He had made promises, too, but he wasn't bound to keep them. Bother it. His honor or lack of it was his own affair. Happiness was hers. "Did Ellen dance around the room?"

"Nay. 'Twas much more dramatic. In the words of our most fervent romantic, you will fall swooning at my feet, and to revive you, I must anoint your wrists and a spot just here—" he touched his neck below his ear "—with lavender water. Then I'm to take up the harp and sing your melancholy away to the depths of gloom."

He made it sound both preposterous and possible at once. Yet beneath the contradiction, his affection for the girl shone clear. Meridene replied in the only way she could. "It befits her nature to think up such a thing."

"She also predicted that a touch of your hand would turn the flower pennies back to gold."

He knew the details of the story. Or had he embellished the legend? To learn the answer, she must ask him, thereby admitting she had not been allowed to read the Covenant, or she could bide her time, gain access to the book, and glean the truth.

Be cheerful, she told herself. "A valuable skill in a wife, turning wood to gold."

"Aye. Especially if we lived in a forest."

His good humor reached out to her. "How would we keep warm?"

He opened his mouth, but decided against saying whatever was on his tongue. A moment later, he said, "A point well made. Dear Ellen will need your patience and guidance more than Lisabeth and Serena."

He allowed Meridene to think he'd let her return to England, but he acted as if she had no intention of leaving. The assumption shouldn't have surprised her, for she was coming to learn that stalwart perfectly suited her husband's methods.

Resolve described hers. "Passing out a few keepsakes to deserving children and advising Ellen does not mean that I wish to be your wife."

"Nay." His gaze was steady, his mood suddenly serious. "And refusing both the gift and the custom renders you petty beyond salvation."

He excelled at drawing her into intimate discussions. Theirs was a pretend marriage made by an

English king whose purpose had died with him. Revas had discovered a different use for those vows, and for the second time, Meridene Macgillivray found herself a pawn in Scottish politics. But giving flower pennies to Serena, Lisabeth, and Ellen was a small concession.

Meridene closed the lid on the chest. "To which one shall I give the first penny?"

"To me, of course. 'Twas my idea."

He shouldn't make her laugh. She shouldn't enjoy their verbal jousts or his company.

He pointed to his boots. "Unless you'd like to try Ellen's method of gratitude."

The challenge in his eyes begged for a clever reply, for he suggested she fall at his feet. Applauding herself, she said, "Do you sing?"

"Do you swoon?"

Lord, he was clever. "Not with any grace."

"Then we are, as you often say, well met."

The room grew warm and close, and Meridene had the oddest feeling of comfort, of familiarity. At that moment, she felt as if she'd known Revas Macduff all of her life. In some ways, she was forced to admit, she had, for when she recalled the most important events, Revas had been there.

His appreciative gaze settled on her unbound hair. "You do that gown justice and more."

She held out the skirt of her surcoat. "Allow me to change in private."

"You cannot unlace that garment and don another without assistance. At this moment, I am your only choice of handmaiden. Since you refused my offer of aid, you are done up for the night, Meridene."

"But I look like I belong to you."

Rather than crow with self-importance, he frowned and shook his head. "I doubt anyone will notice me. They'll all be admiring you."

He'd been conniving, a trait at which he excelled. "All? Who have you invited?"

Standing, he offered her his hand. "Just the lads and a few pretty lassies. And if Randolph Macqueen plays the gallant, I'll rescue you."

As it happened, Randolph Macqueen played both friend and fiend. Darkly handsome, with a smile that would enchant a city of women, Summerlad's brother sat at the far end of the high table. Lisabeth and Ellen hung on his every word.

When Revas and Meridene took their places, Randolph left the company of his adoring females and approached her.

"My lady." He bowed over her hand. "I am both happy and sad to make your acquaintance."

"Happy and sad? How can that be?"

"I am happy that you have come home to us. Yet I am saddened if the change in residence displeases you."

Gallant words from another Highlander. Her perception of Scotsmen as war-hungry and despotic was proving faulty. For among the three of them, Randolph, Summerlad, and Revas possessed charm enough to spare.

But Meridene saw through his twisting of words. "I shall remember your honesty."

He glanced at Revas. "Did I not face certain defeat at the sword arm of your husband, I would claim you for myself."

"Is that loyalty?" she countered.

"Nay, 'twas flattery."

After the meal of suckling pig, barley pudding, and winter greens, which Father Thomas blessed with great ceremony, Revas invited Meridene to join him in a game of chess. Randolph and his admirers occupied the corner table. With the sheriff, the priest, and a dozen young noblemen looking on, Revas captured Meridene's king in ten moves.

Having nothing else to forfeit, she promised a

second flower penny to him and surrendered her place at the table to Summerlad Macqueen. Serena took the spot beside her betrothed.

"Sit with me." Revas patted the empty space next to him on the bench. "You'll be warmer here."

Had he said, "Sit here," she could have declined gracefully. But by including himself in the accommodating request, she must either reject him in the presence of his friends or comply. Giving him high marks for strategy and silent praise for daring, she walked around the table. As she stepped over the bench, he offered his hand and helped her sit.

Quietly he said, "Is Ellen sleepy, or on the verge of a swoon?"

Meridene glanced at the corner where Randolph Macqueen was holding forth. Elbows on the table, their chins propped in their palms, both Ellen and Lisabeth looked exhausted. "They've had a busy day."

"Aye. Especially Ellen."

Serena murmured, "Adoring Summerlad's brother is exhausting work."

"What about adoring me?" Summerlad said.

Revas pointed a finger. "We'll have no lovers' talk here."

Meridene had found the perfect excuse to retire. "I'll send the girls to bed."

Serena stood up. "Please, my lady, allow me to do it. If Ellen doesn't turn down your bed and Lisabeth doesn't set out your nightrail, they'll fret for days, thinking they've disappointed you."

More ceremony, thought Meridene, and everyone at the table awaited her concession.

Revas leaned very close and said, "I'd be willing to turn down your bed and undress you."

More seduction. "That's lovers' talk."

"Will you fall in love with me, Meridene?"

Words failed her.

With a parting smile to Summerlad, Serena roused the girls. Blinking off sleep, they trudged from the room.

Glancing at the young men Revas fostered, Meridene saw understanding and approval in their expressions. Whatever their expectations of an evening with Revas and his bride, they were obviously satisfied.

Their acceptance of her position was to be expected, but their comradeship surprised her. When first she'd spied this room, with its wall of Highland regalia, she had diminished its significance as ambitious decor. But as she scanned the room, she saw a Forbes man dicing amiably with a Highland Mackenzie. Near the hearth, a Grant lad strummed a harp while a Macgregor sang the words to a song about a shepherd's daughter and a wolfish suitor. Was she witnessing honest Scottish camaraderie? Was Auldcairn Castle truly a Community of the Realm?

The term still puzzled her. Everyone knew that Scotland would never enjoy peace, not unless the island cracked and England fell off the edge of the earth. That, or all of the clans united permanently.

Again she looked up at the wall. Matching face to symbol, she paired the Mackenzie lad with the shield bearing the stag. The singing Macgregor belonged to the emblem with the lion's head. Through marriage, Serena would bind the upland Macqueens to the midland Camerons.

The fortunate girl had found love in her betrothal. But if the past was a harbinger of the future, tragedy awaited. Highland women always lost their men, if not through war, then through duty, for they first answered the call of clansmen. Serena appeared untainted by Scottish politics now; Meridene had been ill used by the clans and estranged for too long to care.

The serving maid approached the table, a small keg under her arm. With a wave of his hand, Revas declined.

"Have you lost your taste for Macqueen's best?" Summerlad asked.

Earlier today, Revas had overindulged of the ale. He must have lost his fondness for it; he'd taken water with the meal.

Sagelike, he spoke to Summerlad. "Heed me well, lad. If you ever down a pint of that brew and then have the poor judgment to engage in an argument with a woman, you deserve the tongue-lashing you'll get."

The men laughed. The serving girl giggled. When Revas slid Meridene a smile, she fought a blush of embarrassment.

Like Revas with his young charges, Sister Margaret had often sat at the table and given advice to Meridene, Johanna, and Clare. But her lessons involved stewardship of the land and governance of the people.

"You bested Revas at words?" Summerlad asked of her.

Not in years had Meridene sat amid a room of men who discussed her. But her father, Moray, and old King Edward had looked upon her as property. These people treated her as an equal participant.

She felt beholden to respond in kind. "It was no real feat, Summerlad," she said. "The brew encumbered his wits."

From his spot in the corner, Randolph slapped the table and declared, "Be it with ale or good mother's milk, women *always* best men at words."

"Truly?" Summerlad asked, his face blank with uncertainty.

Revas looked down at Meridene. "Always," he said, but she knew he didn't mean it. Too often he tricked her with words.

"Then if you gentlemen will excuse me, I shall withdraw while I'm still victorious." Standing, she held out her hand. "I should like to write the names of my handmaidens in the Covenant."

He must yield the key or make their conflict public. A quandary; his second favorite pastime, or so he had said. "Your namesake began that tradition with her handmaidens."

To her relief, he yielded the key. Meridene went to his chamber, and by the light of a brace of candles, she read the book until she found the reference to the flower pennies.

I am Eleanor, the tenth Maiden of Inverness, and I stand chained to the wall in the dungeon of my husband's enemy.

Blinking back tears, Meridene read the true account of what had become a fairy tale. Poor Eleanor. She'd been with child at the time of her abduction. During her captivity, she made a promise to God. If she was freed and her babe delivered safely, she would relinquish the title of Maiden. True to her word, Eleanor had complied, and to Meridene's dismay, one hundred years passed before another woman took up a quill and revived the legend of the Maiden.

"My lady?" Serena stood in the doorway.

Still caught up in the past and eager to get back to it, Meridene dashed away a tear. "Yes?"

"You must be reading about poor Eleanor," Serena said.

Meridene closed the book. "I was indeed."

As if to hold in her own sorrow, Serena hugged herself. "How could she give up so much?"

Because she'd been taken away from her home, same as Meridene. She'd been alone and frightened. "She had few choices."

"Women fare better today."

Some did, Meridene was forced to admit. Serena was content with her lot. One of a thousand questions niggled at Meridene. Learning the answers meant delving into the lives of these people. She risked forming affections that an annulment would break.

She wanted no more memories of this place to haunt her; enough demons plagued her life.

Yet tonight she couldn't summon the will to resist. "How did you come to be a handmaiden?"

Grasping the invitation, Serena took the chair opposite Meridene. "My father allowed me to put forth my name. Many other girls wanted to be chosen. But I was the lucky one."

"How old were you?"

"Eleven."

The answer posed more questions. Serena was one and twenty. A decade ago, Revas had set in motion the events that had changed the future of the Macqueens and the Camerons. He'd been but ten and six at the time. Baffled by his youthful ambition and fearful of the consequences, Meridene felt the first real doubt in her convictions. What if he refused to let her go? What would her father do?

Troubled anew, she retreated to the safe company of Serena, who more each day reminded her of Johanna Benison. The loss of that precious friendship sparked a need in Meridene that begged to be filled. "How many girls have expressed an interest in your position?"

"Let's see." Rising, Serena walked out of the circle of candlelight and returned with a small whitewashed keg. She placed it on the floor before Meridene and pulled off the top.

Inside were swatches of cloth in every fabric and color: green silks and heavy damasks, soft wools and even a square of butter-soft leather. Some had purposefully frayed edges; others were painstakingly hemmed with blindman stitches; still others were finished with elaborate borders.

Serena rummaged through the barrel and came up with a square of plaid fabric. "Here. This is Summerlad's sister's piece. See? Her name is embroidered in the center."

In looping script, the word "Lili" stood out sharply against the boxlike plaid.

Stunned, Meridene stared at the overflowing barrel.

"Revas picks from one of these. Well," Serena demurred, "he used to do the picking. He said you would choose the one to take my place."

"You'd like me to pick Lili Macqueen?"

Serena took the small cloth and held it closer to the light. "Her needlework is passable, but she's five and ten. A younger lass will stay with you longer."

Stay. The word gave Meridene a chill, and though her heart had ceased pounding like thunder, she could not suppress her anticipation.

"When will you draw the name?" Serena asked.

Revas had not mentioned an exact date, and making the decision herself gave Meridene's independent nature a much-needed boost. "On Saturday after Vespers. You may spread the word."

Serena held the cloth of the Macqueens to her breast. "Summerlad wants us to wed on Whitsunday."

May was just weeks away. "So soon?"

"'Tis an eternity. Randolph says we must wait until the Macqueens harvest their fields."

"What will you do?"

Her eyes twinkled. "I'll offer him a tankard of his own ale and broach the argument. He says men always lose to women. And Revas got a tongue-lashing from you."

"Good luck."

Her course set, Serena dropped the cloth into the barrel and returned it to the corner. On her way to the door, she paused.

"Was there something else?" Meridene asked.

"Nay. Revas asked me to look in on you."

Probably to see if she'd made kindling of the Covenant. "You may tell him that I am fine."

Now tentative, Serena stared at her feet. "Did you truly write my name in the book?"

Meridene hadn't yet; she'd been too engrossed in the tragedy of poor Eleanor. "I will on the morrow."

"Oh, thank you." She curtsied and dashed from the room.

Meridene opened the book and turned the page.

I am the Maiden Catherine and newly acquainted with the office. The year is 1174, and our beloved king, William the Lion, has been captured by Henry II of England and forced to acknowledge him as overlord of Scotland.

While renovating her husband's castle, the bride Catherine had found the Covenant sealed in a space behind a niche in the solar wall. With the ancient book, she discovered a fine golden belt. To preserve them for future generations, she copied the chronicles to heavy vellum and polished the chain of office.

For almost two decades, the Maiden Catherine acquitted herself with honor, and in 1189, the year she passed the Covenant to her daughter, Scotland had recovered her independence.

Meridene sighed. The lives of her ancestors were fraught with war, kidnappings, and hard-won ransom.

"You look unhappy."

She gasped in alarm. Revas stood in the doorway.

"How long have you been watching me?"

Moving into the room, he stopped before her. "Not long enough."

Her hands curled around the book. "I thought you would be with one of your women."

His brows rose, and with sheer determination, he said, "I am with my woman."

Flustered, she sprang to her feet and returned the Covenant to the pedestal. Her feelings for Revas were twisted with her hatred for a family who had yanked her from the nursery, given her to an enemy king, poisoned her, then abandoned her.

War, kidnapping, and ransom.

"I'll just say good night." She tried to move around him.

He caught her arm. "I've often wondered how I could make a place for you here—where we live the simple, country life. Now I—"

"Wait." Freeing herself, she held up a hand. "Our marriage will be annulled. Thank you for the flower pennies. Good night."

To cut off a reply, she left the room and hurried to her own. After locking her door, she took a drink of water and sat on the bed.

Just when her heart stopped racing, the lock clicked. Revas threw open the door and marched inside. Covering the distance between them in three long strides, he towered over her.

"You are mistaken and rude to interrupt a man to accuse him of a blunder he has yet to commit."

"I knew what you would say."

"Enlighten me."

He wanted another intimate discussion. She didn't want to know him well enough to share her opinions. "No."

"Accuse me or acquit me."

He looked tired and overwrought and eager for a confrontation. Knowing he'd win, she again capitulated. "I knew you would try to cajole me into liking this ghastly land of warriors and petty kings."

"Wrong. I had intended to say that I have stopped wondering how I could make a place for you here, because I decided 'twas best if you did that for yourself."

How could he hand her her independence, then take it back? "You are generous to a fault."

"I also came to tell you that Leslie has departed with your letter to the pope." He handed her a leather purse. "And I wanted to give you money of your own."

Coins chinked in the bag. "Thank you."

"Rest well, Meridene." He strolled from the room, but did not lock the door.

Too discomfited to sleep, she went to her loom, but the tapestry was almost finished and the repetitious work bored her. She needed the challenge of starting a new piece. But on what theme, and would she be here long enough to finish it?

After breaking the thread twice and stabbing her finger, she gave up the effort and went to her desk. With quill and ink she began to sketch.

The effort relaxed her, and before she'd finished the design, she yawned. Satisfied that she'd committed enough of her idea to paper, Meridene went to bed. As she closed her eyes, she thought of the Maiden Eleanor, chained to a dungeon wall in the castle of her enemy.

"Revas!"

Dragging himself from sleep, Revas opened his eyes. Serena stood over him, a lighted candle in her hand, her long red hair in disarray.

Alarmed, he sat up. "What's amiss, lass? Has Summerlad—"

"'Tis Lady Meridene. She's screaming in her sleep. I tried to rouse her, but she would not awaken."

Revas almost sprang from the bed, but remembered he was naked beneath the covers. "Fetch a cup of Macqueen's ale and bring it to her room. I'll meet you there."

"Aye. In a trice."

"Tell no one about this, Serena. We cannot have everyone whispering about her troubled sleep. She's been cloistered in England, you know."

"Wretched monsters. I hate them all." Cupping her hand around the candle flame, Serena hurried from the room.

Revas bounded from the bed and drew on his

breeches and slippers. As he snatched a cloak from the wall peg, he thought of Meridene's fitful dreams on the ship. He hadn't been able to comfort her then. Now he could.

Making little sound, he hurried down the hall, past Brodie's room and down the steps. He eased open the squat door leading to her apartment. The drapings were open and the glow of the brazier shed faint light on the bed and its occupant.

She thrashed and moaned and cried, "Nay, nay. I want to stay with you. Do not let them take me, Mother." She thrust out her arm, her fingers grasping for the hand that was not there. "Mother!" she wailed.

The sound of her cries went straight to Revas's heart. He raked back the covers and climbed into bed. Dodging her flailing arms, he wrapped her in his own. "Shush, Meridene," he whispered, struggling to hold her still. "Shush, sweet lass. All will be well."

"Please don't make me go with the king." She clung to him, her fingers clutching in a death grip. "I'll be good. I promise I'll be good. I swear I'll never touch your sword again, Papa."

She jerked as if struck. Her pleas turned to sobs and her hands relaxed as if she were defeated. "Oh, Papa," she moaned.

Damn Cutberth Macgillivray. What decent parents could ignore the entreaty of their own child? They'd left her with a legacy of fear. Ripping apart an innocent girl's life had not been villainy enough; they had also spoiled a woman's dreams.

Her skin felt damp and her braid had begun to unravel. Holding her tighter, he scooted to the head of the bed and rocked her. "Meridene?"

She did not hear; the nightmare had her in its grip. "Mother, please! William, where are you!" She grew frantic again. "Robert, help me! William!"

She called out for her brothers, men Revas knew, men he had wenched with and later faced in battle.

Although older than Meridene, they had been youths at the time she'd been taken away and unable to help her. Did they mourn the loss of the sister as much as they despaired the loss of the Maiden of Inverness? He suspected they had put the event behind them, while Meridene was forced to live it again and again.

She'd been only eight and still in the nursery. Would that those men could see her now and witness the cruelty their father's lust for power had wrought.

"Oh, please, someone help me!"

A tear trickled down Revas's cheek, and his soul ached for her. No wonder she hated Scotland and everyone in it; they had banished her to England with only demons for companions. "I'm here, Meridene. No one will hurt you. No one will take you away."

Praise God, she grew still. But in the next moment she drew up her knees and curled into a ball. She felt small in his arms, too small to carry so great a burden of fear.

He heard another voice crying quietly. Serena stood beside the bed, a candle wavering unsteadily in one hand, a tankard in the other. "Oh, Revas. How awful for her."

His own throat was thick with sorrow, and he managed a quiet "Aye."

"What will you do?"

"I'll protect her with my life."

She put the tankard on the table by the bed. "What else can I do?"

"Stand at the door and let no one enter."

He saw her leave, but his attention was focused on the woman in his arms. He thought of his daughter and the times he had comforted her—when she'd lost her front teeth, when her puppy had broken a leg. But Gibby's life, aside from a few slights regarding her bastardy, had been a May Fair compared to Meridene's.

The weight of his responsibility pressed in on

Revas. The law gave him the right and the duty to claim his wife, even against her will. Morally, he questioned his decision. She had good cause to despise Scotland and its people, yet he had good reason to change her mind.

But how much of his determination stemmed from ambition? The better portion, he was forced to admit, and at times like this, he wished he had taken up his father's occupation. As a butcher, he wouldn't worry about alliances between clans, about Scottish unity, about the safety of those in his keeping.

What if dear Meridene had refused to drink from that poisoned cup so long ago? Left here with Revas, she surely would have grown to love the people and cherish the legend that was her destiny.

Don't fret over a dull blade. Sharpen it, his father had often said.

How much more Scottish blood would be spilled before Cutberth Macgillivray yielded the sword of Chapling and joined the Community of the Realm? Revas hadn't a guess; only the woman in his arms could make it so.

But how could she when ambitious men ruled her days, and demons ravaged her nights? How could he help her when she thought him the blackest villain of all?

Sometime later she slipped into restful sleep. Revas unfolded her arms and legs, and holding her against his chest, pulled up the covers.

She'd feel ashamed when she awakened and found him here. What would she say, and how could he reply?

CHAPTER
8

❦

A pounding head awakened Meridene. Her joints ached, as if she'd been beaten, and her sleeping gown felt damp.

The nightmare.

Limp with exhaustion, she stared up at the scenic canopy. Faint light seeped through the closed bed hangings. The tapestry overhead depicted a family of roe deer in a moonlit clearing. Angels hovered in the starry sky.

No guardian angel watched over Meridene Macgillivray.

The maudlin thought disgusted her. She had survived the dream again, and with less damage than on some occasions. No scratches irritated her skin, and her jaw did not cramp. She hadn't even kicked off the covers. Yet her head throbbed and her eyes burned with dryness.

Rolling onto her side, she parted the drape, but closed it immediately when a shaft of sunlight blinded her. What time was it? She felt as if she'd slept for days. Where was Ellen? Lisabeth? Serena?

Had Revas again sent them on errands?

Revas. He governed her actions, but more and more, he occupied her thoughts. She couldn't pass one hour to the next without thinking of him. His distinctive smell seemed to linger with her even now.

On that ridiculous notion, she threw back the covers and sat on the side of the bed. A tankard rested on the lamp table. Ellen's thoughtfulness, no doubt.

She needed more guidance than the others, Revas had said.

Will you swoon at my feet? he had asked.

Will you sing? she had replied.

Will you fall in love with me?

Like lifelong companions, they traded quips and discussed servants, but beneath the friendly banter lay unspoken demands and silent refusals.

Dismayed, Meridene took a drink and almost choked. It was ale, of the kind Revas had drunk yesterday. She had smelled the pleasant honey aroma on his breath. The taste was deceptively refreshing, and she now understood why he had cautioned Summerlad about partaking too much of the spirit.

But how had the tankard come to be here—beside her bed? He must have left it yesterday afternoon, and in the excitement of Randolph Macqueen's arrival, Ellen had overlooked it.

As she dressed, Meridene counted off the day's tasks. She must meet with Sim to approve his tally of the household account. Using some of the money Revas had given her, she would buy another loom and thread for the new tapestry. She would also order a bridal chest for Serena.

Meridene would be gone by the time the girl spoke her vows. Willingly, for Serena wanted Summerlad. No political agenda dictated their love and guided their future.

Meridene had attended only one wedding: her own, and it had been a lonely, sad day. But later, when the pain of exile had eased, she found freedom in England. She would have it again.

The Leslie lad had left for the Vatican. Randolph Macqueen would take her message to Sister Margaret. Help was on the way.

On the desk she found a note from Serena.

Lisabeth and I are spreading the word of the handmaiden's drawing on Saturday. Ellen plays shadow to Randolph M.

In the dining hall, Meridene heard Ellen's voice. Looking through the hearth and into the common room, she saw the girl perched atop the table. Randolph Macqueen sat on a bench nearby. He wore spurs, chain mail, and his battle sword. His traveling bag and tartan cape rested on the floor at his feet.

Ellen turned pleading eyes to him. "Is it true that you were chained in an enemy's dungeon, beaten, and starving for the sight of your beloved? And Elizabeth Gordon braved great peril to rescue you. Does her love for you know no earthly bounds?"

"Aye, lass. Only her service to the king delays our vows."

Ellen wilted in a fake swoon. "I knew 'twas true. Lost love found is so very romantic."

Meridene walked through the hearth. "As I'm sure you will discover in five or six years, Ellen. Now bid Lord Randolph farewell and fetch the tankard Revas left by my bed."

Ellen's eyes bulged. "Revas came to your bed last night!"

"Of course not. He left it there yesterday afternoon."

"In the light of day!" Ellen squeaked.

Randolph choked back laughter and twisted his war bracelets.

He had played the gallant last night. Today he'd lost

his charm. Meridene glowered at him. "You know precisely what I meant."

"Aye," he said. "Revas will keep to the letter of the Covenant."

The tenets of the Maiden dictated that she must be a virgin to demand the sword of Chapling from her father. Everyone knew Revas wanted her only for the power she could gain him. They certainly weren't timid in voicing their opinions, either.

Better that, she thought, than rumors about him visiting her bed. "Ellen, you are to tell no one where you found the tankard."

"I swear. I will tell everyone he worships you from afar."

"Should you tell anyone my business, I will order you to count the peas in the pantry."

Her country-fresh face contorted into a fearful frown. "I will speak only of trivialities."

"Then you may work on the tapestry if you like."

"Thank you." She dashed through the hearth and down the hall.

Meridene turned to Randolph. "My thanks to you for offering to deliver my message to Sister Margaret."

"I did not offer. Revas asked me to do it. I shall tell the good sister that you are hale and happy. Although I doubt 'tis true."

Meridene stepped back. "Have you been gossiping about me?"

"Nay. I watched you with Revas last night." He scratched his thick black beard. "Women are usually more attentive to the man who united the Highlands and will one day wear the crown."

Of course they were. Twenty women. Twenty-one, were anyone counting. "Let him boast where he may, but he cannot claim the title, for he hasn't the sword of Chapling."

"Get it for him. 'Tis your duty to the people of the Highlands."

"Duty. Have you a duty to me?"

"Aye. To protect the Maiden of Inverness with my life."

"The Maiden is no more, but you may take my message to Drummond Macqueen." Bother the clans and the Macqueens. None of them knew her well enough to judge her reasons for avoiding Scottish affairs. "Tell your brother that if ill comes of my sojourn in Scotland, the sin rests with him."

"With Drummond?"

"Yes. He told Revas where to find me."

He pointed to the shields on the wall. "As would any of those Highlanders did they come by the knowledge. Old Edward had no right to take the Maiden from us."

She recognized his loyalty; a woman's desires were subject to the concerns of men. "I will not be a pawn in your wars."

His expression stiff with consternation, he moved closer. "Then your namesake should have wed a Dane instead of a Scotsman. That would have saved us centuries' worth of meddling Maidens of Inverness!"

"How dare you!"

"Because this is my homeland. You are the Maiden of *our* time, Meridene Macgillivray. Although we should have expected as little from the loins of your sire."

A chill passed through Meridene at the mention of her father.

"Ask her pardon, Randolph." Garbed in chain mail and war boots, his sword belt slung over his shoulder, Revas stepped through the hearth. He carried a heavy sack. "She's not to blame for her father's ill deeds."

Randolph stared at the wall, his face tight with anger. "Ill deeds? Putting Nairn to the torch again is foul beyond that. 'Tis the blackest of sins."

"Aye, but your anger stems not from my beloved,

153

but from your own, estranged as you are from the Lady Elizabeth."

As quickly, Randolph's anger fled. "You speak the truth, my friend." He smiled at Meridene. "I meant no offense to you, Maiden. Too much of my own brew and a Gordon woman are to blame."

"Those things," Revas said, "and ignoring your own advice. I told you Meridene was too clever for you—especially since you are straining at the bit to say your wedding vows."

Her father had attacked a village with families; yet these men chatted about personal matters. She looked from one to the other. "When was Nairn set afire?"

"'Twas at the close of Vespers last," Revas said. "The city was well armed and manned, so all was not lost."

"What will you do?" she asked.

His calm expression told her no more than his silence. "You will not retaliate?" she said.

He handed Randolph the sack. "Montfichet has prepared a feast for your journey to Fairhope Tower. Give my best to Lord Drummond, and tell Lady Clare we wish her a swift and successful delivery. Now, if you both will excuse me."

She didn't know this distracted, stern Revas Macduff. "Where are you going?"

"To take provisions to Nairn."

"You're leaving her here?" Randolph said.

Revas paused at the hearth. "Much as I'd like to take my wife with me, the accommodations will be lacking."

Randolph put down the sack. "I'll stay until you return."

Revas looked pointedly at his friend. "Thank you, but 'tis not necessary. Brodie and Summerlad will be here, as well as a company of Forbes."

They discussed her protection, but spoke as if she

were a child to be tended. And kept uninformed. "Does my father come? Does he know that I am here?"

"The gates of Auldcairn Castle are open to one and all. People come and go at will. 'Tis possible that someone has told him you have come home," said Revas. "But I assure you he visits his evil closer to his own."

Pray God he stayed there until she could flee Scotland. "When will you return?"

Irony tinged his smile. "So soon that I doubt you will even miss me. But if I do not return tonight, Summerlad will escort you to table."

Each of her childhood excursions had included an armed guard. Soldiers had even followed her and her mother to church. But her father always had enemies at the gate. "Why must I have Summerlad for a guard?"

"I had hoped you would keep an eye on him. Not the other way 'round."

The lighthearted comment sounded forced. He was leaving, and suddenly she wanted him to stay. Impossible. His absence would afford her freedom. He was privy to the state of affairs in Scotland, and if he thought her safe, why should she worry? She would not. "Have a care on your journey, Revas."

He smiled. "I shall, Meridene."

He spoke her name with ease, as if they were boon companions or something more. Too aware of herself, she stared at the kettle simmering on the hearth fire.

"I'll ride with you to Elgin's End." Randolph moved to Revas's side. "Farewell, Lady Meridene."

"To you," she murmured, struggling to get her mind off Revas's departure.

She walked to the window and watched them mount. Revas rode a dappled gray warhorse, his shield and helmet fastened to the saddle. Macpherson, the

Grant lad, and several others flanked him. At least a score of mounted soldiers followed. Behind them, three overburdened wagons rumbled down the lane.

At the gate, he drew rein and hailed Summerlad Macqueen, who patrolled the wall. The youth raced down the steps and halted beside Revas. Leaning in the saddle, he spoke briefly.

Summerlad straightened, and Meridene could almost hear him say, "Aye, sir."

Bracing his hand on the horse's rump, Revas turned back to the castle. His gaze moved to the window where Meridene stood. He nodded, smiling, then kicked the horse into motion.

How had he known she watched him? Did he now trust her? Curiosity drove her to his chamber, which she found unlocked. The Covenant rested on the pedestal, and like a siren, the book called to her. She found her place and turned the page.

I am Margaret, the first Maiden of that name, and the last, I fear, to wear the crown of rowans.

Spellbound, Meridene read the account of a woman who had borne six healthy sons and three daughters, all with hair as pale as sunbeams. At eight and twenty, Margaret despaired of conceiving a dark-haired girl to carry on the legend.

Superstition dictated Margaret's every move. The priest counseled her to wear only black. The chambermaid anointed her mattress with salt water. The midwife advised against conceiving again at her advanced age. When she did blossom with child, King William's surgeon ordered her hair shorn and the black tresses placed in the awaiting cradle. The cook dusted her food with soot from the hearth.

At the hour her labor began, Margaret was moved to the dungeon so that no light would taint the coloring of her child.

She died in that dark place, a smile on her face, a raven-haired daughter in her arms.

Her husband had been so aggrieved that he had ordered the felling of every rowan tree in sight.

I am Angus, he had written in the book, *and I loved well the Maiden Margaret. Would it bring her back, I would gladly cast the sword of Chapling into the sea.*

Heartbroken and confused, Meridene closed the book. She'd read no more stories of women who gave their lives for a legend. Not when her father waged war a few hours' ride away.

She thought of her own older siblings. Like her father, they were fair. Had her mother prayed for a dark-haired girl during those births? By turning to the last page, Meridene could read her mother's account. But she preferred to read the entries in the order they were written. In light of the great sacrifices revealed thus far in the book, anticipation was a small concession.

And she had to admit that she rather liked seeing the story unfold in stages. She knew she would open the book again, but not today.

Other concerns intruded, and as she went in search of Sim, Meridene questioned whether Revas told the truth when he said he was going to Nairn. What if he was now planning a siege of her father's castle? He rode north toward the port city of Elgin's End, not west to Kilbarton Castle, her father's home. Once out of sight, Revas could easily change directions.

What if her father slew him in battle? The answer made her tremble, for she would be returned to Kilbarton Castle and married to the man of her father's choosing.

As she made her way down the lane to the carpenter's shop, she couldn't stop wondering if Revas had ridden into danger. What would become of these people should ill befall him?

She surveyed the castle wall and counted only ten guards on patrol. The gates stood open. In the tiltyard,

Brodie observed the swordplay of Summerlad and one of the lanky Macphersons.

If her father posed a threat, no one here took it seriously.

Neither would she. She had business in the village, and she'd dallied too long in her unsuccessful search for the steward, Sim.

With squealing pigs and honking geese for accompaniment, the people of Elginshire conducted their affairs. Smoke hung in the air over the thatched roofs of the houses that lined the hay-strewn lane. A broom boy hawked his hardiest sweepers. A woodsman peddled peat from a cart. A red-haired lad and his younger sister tugged on the leading rein of a braying ass.

As she walked through the village, the purse of marks and flower pennies slapping against her thigh, Meridene tried to remember similar excursions in Daviot, the city that stood hard by her father's castle. But she'd been small at the time and unable to see past the armed escort that always surrounded the members of her family.

In Elginshire, every day brought some new happening, some challenge to meet. Men did not cast furtive glances her way. Women did not gaze in sympathy at the lonely girl who longed to play with the others her age.

The people of the village called out greetings and asked after her health. She spoke to old women and young, to children both bold and shy.

The stubborn ass nudged the red-haired girl into the mud. Her brother gallantly helped her up and dried her tears. For his kindness, Meridene awarded him a flower penny.

A burst of boyish pride squared his shoulders. "I'll be the best man o' the Highlands when I grow up."

As if she were looking at a jeweled crown rather than a wooden coin, his sister peered into his hand. So endearing was the girl's awe, Meridene handed over another penny.

Passing the laundry, she heard Serena informing the maids of the drawing on Saturday next to choose a new handmaiden.

Meridene grappled with her conscience over the upcoming event, for she dreaded giving the impression that she intended to stay. But Revas knew of her determination to end the legend, and after reading the Covenant, he must agree that only misery visited the Maidens of Inverness.

Resolved that the Highlands would carry on without her, Meridene continued her search for Sim. It ended at the carpenter's shop, where the steward stood over a table and, with the craftsman, examined a drawing.

She paused in the doorway.

"Remember who the bed is for," the steward said. "Revas cannot have his feet dangling off the end."

The carpenter nodded. A hail of wood shavings drifted from his hair and shoulders. "I'll fashion it after the Maiden's bed. He said 'twas fair perfect for him."

She grew uneasy at the thought of Revas in her bed, and that he had commissioned it to accommodate his larger frame. An ambitious move that was doomed to failure, for he'd never join her in it. Still it offended her to hear these men discussing her bed. In thirteen years at Scarborough Abbey, Sister Margaret had seldom mentioned Meridene's personal effects, and only then to remind her to tidy her room.

"No fanciness," Sim was saying. "Remember, 'tis for a hunting lodge."

"Aye. Revas said he needed no canopy or carvings."

Meridene stepped into the shop.

The carpenter straightened. "My lady. May I help you?"

"I wish to discuss a loom."

He pulled a face and glanced at the drawing. "But there's to be tables and benches and shutters for the Halt."

Same as all the people of Elginshire, he spoke English, but his words confused her. "The what?"

Sim grew nervous. "The uh . . ."

"Revas's new hunting lodge," said the carpenter. "He calls it Macduff's Halt."

The job was obviously of such great import to him, she felt bound to say, "Macduff's Halt. What an inventive name." She hoped the property shared a border with the Holy Land.

Sim rolled up the drawing and tucked it under his arm.

The carpenter put away his tools. "'Tis where his patience ends."

Past her own limit of patience, Meridene admitted defeat. "Good sir, I merely wanted to discuss a loom for me and a bridal chest for Serena. Trouble yourself no more about my loom, but build the chest at your first opportunity and deliver it to Serena."

"You're certain, my lady?" asked the carpenter.

Meridene edged toward the open door. "Truly. Sim will tell you that I as yet have a tapestry in my loom. Oh, Sim, we'll meet tomorrow morning to discuss the accounts. Will you ask Cook to serve the ham tonight —and the barley soup, if it has not spoiled?"

Not waiting for a reply, she eased out the door and into the sunshine. Her discomfiture puzzled her, for she did not consider herself shy or retiring. The men were discussing work. They did not know she sought an annulment. The fault lay with her. She simply wasn't accustomed to so many strangers and lay-people.

From the pie house someone yelled, "My lady."

Turning, she saw a squatty fellow with a pale beard as thick as lamb's wool. Only slightly taller than she, he wore a long woollen tunic belted with a wide strip of leather that held a short axe and wedge.

He doffed his cap. "I walked past the carpenter's shop and heard you asking after a loom."

Compared to the carpenter's halting speech, this man's good diction was a welcome relief. "Yes. I am in need of one."

"I'm a wheelwright by trade, but I've built many fine looms for my kinswomen."

She should have known that a village as large as Elginshire would support more than one carpenter, but she'd lived in isolation for too long. "Where is your shop?"

"Aberdeen's my home. I work from my wagon." He motioned her to the path beside the chandler's shop. "I thought to leave Elginshire today, but for you, my lady, I'll linger."

His accommodating manner didn't surprise her; everyone in the village was eager to please. Well, almost everyone.

From her basket, she withdrew the measuring strings she'd prepared earlier. "It's to be as long as the white thread and as wide as the brown. How soon can you build it?"

He took the coarsely spun cords in his callused right hand. His left palm was oddly smooth—a condition peculiar to wheelwrights, she decided.

"Two days, do I find the proper wood."

At the current wage of a penny for a day's labor, the price was more than fair. "It must be crafted of aged oak," she warned, "with the edges smooth and the surface free of oil. Should you deliver as we have agreed, I will give you an extra coin."

"Thank you, my lady. Trust me to make you a loom you'll be proud to pass on to the next Maiden."

Not likely, she thought, and bade him good-bye. She had yet to visit the mercer and select the thread. On her way there, she passed the church, but did not look inside the open doors. A corrupted priest interested her not at all.

In the noisy weaver's shop, an older woman greeted her. Meridene's list of supplies was well received, until she mentioned the need for red thread.

The weaver's wife tapped her chin. "Gibby'll have the red dye. She's the best at leeching the color from rowan berries."

Meridene couldn't remember hearing the name Gibby before, but she'd met so many new people, she doubted she'd ever remember them all. "Where can I find this Gibby?"

The portly weaver stepped between them. "I'll be after finding the lass. We'll have your thread tomorrow."

His manner was anxious, but Meridene did not question it. Her most pressing errands done, she made her way back to the castle proper.

The small round structure that housed her apartment was dwarfed by the twin towers of Auldcairn. Through the open windows of her solar, she saw Ellen bent over the loom and working vigorously on the tapestry for Drummond Macqueen's wife. Serena sat on a pallet near the ring of budding rowans, but the girl did not tend the trees; her attention was fixed on the tiltyard and Summerlad Macqueen. A crowd had gathered to watch.

Steel slammed against steel as the distinctive young warrior battled a formidable opponent. Who was the slender, taller man? Not Brodie, for the sheriff stood nearby in the company of a group of men who wore the colors of Clan Forbes.

Curious and hesitant to leave the warm sunshine, Meridene changed direction and approached the tiltyard and joined the crowd.

Young Summerlad acquitted himself admirably, but his more experienced opponent proved relentless.

As the latter came on strong, Summerlad stumbled. A feminine scream sounded behind Meridene, and in the next instant, Serena raced into the yard.

As the girl knelt and fussed over her betrothed, Meridene waited for the victor to remove his helmet. When he did, she sucked in a breath.

It was the cleric, Father Thomas. Extending a hand, he said, "Well done, Summerlad. Another year and you'll have Revas on his back."

So the good priest was also a fighting man. She shouldn't have been surprised; he was the least spiritual of any holy man she'd met.

Spying her, he left the uninjured Summerlad to Serena's tender mercies and approached. "Lady Meridene. You did not accompany Revas to confession this morning."

His friendly tone didn't fool her. "Oh," she said lightly. "I have the gist of it now. When you dress as a warrior you take up the office of priest. When you wear your robes, you do your duty to clan politics. Were you a Knight Templar by chance?"

The insult struck a blow, for sweat trickled over his cheek and clenched jaw. With his battle helmet, he waved toward the western sky. "In yonder cemetery rest the bones of good Elginshire men who gave their lives so that you could achieve your destiny."

"A destiny I scorn."

"Then you scorn God, Meridene Macgillivray, for He hath made you who and what you are. And He guides the sword of your husband."

Men hadn't died for her. They'd perished by their own ambition and warring ways. "No. Revas led them to it."

His apologetic smile laid bare her indifference. "Revas Macduff is the finest man o' the Highlands. He has done naught but keep the vows he spoke before God."

First Randolph Macqueen, and now an ordained

priest. How many more men would disparage her for events beyond her control? "I was already legally pledged to another. I was forced to wed Revas Macduff."

"In the matter of husbands, few of *your kind* have been so blessed. I will pray for you." He turned on a heel and walked away.

Her kind. The words opened an old wound. *Our kind,* she recalled her mother saying, *do not choose our mates. We are as prized bitches held out for the mightiest dog in the pack.*

As if the years had spun backward, Meridene saw clearly her mother's toilworn face. The image so disturbed her that she blocked it out.

Not until that evening when she retired did she try to bring back the memory of her mother. She failed, and with sad acceptance, for the truth of it was, she could not remember being anyone's daughter. Not like Ellen, who had a satchel full of fond letters and keepsakes from her mother. Not like Lisabeth, whose parents lived nearby and cherished her well.

Meridene had simply been the future Maiden of Inverness.

When the nightmare awakened her hours later, she knew what she must do.

CHAPTER
9

Two evenings later, Revas found her in her apartments, seated at a new and smaller loom. Facing away from him, she wore a pale linen surcoat over a bliaud of darker blue. Her long hair was gathered loosely at her nape and hastily bound with a length of red yarn that matched the thread attached to the shuttle.

As always, he anticipated her reaction. As never before, he hoped for swift acceptance. Unless she soon demanded her father's sword, five small clans, under pressure from the Macgillivrays, had threatened to withdraw from the Community of the Realm. Munro would as yet stand fast with Revas, but if Cutberth did not soon step down, dissension would spread. Signed treaties would become kindling.

If he was honest with himself, Revas had to admit that he understood her reluctance. To prevail in the Highlands today, the victor must be stouthearted in his love for the land. She had few emotional ties to Scotland, and those were dark and ugly. Therein lay his task, and if she would but give him a chance, tonight he would build for her a fond memory.

"You have a new loom."

She started and turned, then put away her shuttle. Her smile lifted his spirits. Her inspection of his person gave rise to more earthy feelings.

"You are unharmed," she said.

"And very glad to be home. 'Twas an arduous two days."

"What of Nairn?"

Revas rejoiced; she did care about her people. "Restored. Ana and John Sutherland have been safely ransomed according to custom. All is well in God's good land of the Scots."

"Who kidnapped them?"

A prevarication perched on the tip of his tongue, but he could not voice it. Kidnapping was a long-accepted practice in Scotland and often used to avert bloodshed. At an early age children learned the meaning of words such as *ransom* and *forfeit*. Coloring up the truth would not do. "Your father."

She blanched. "Is Ana hurt?"

On the day Meridene had wed Revas, she had borne her father's mark. Rumor said he visited cruelty on his wife and his kept women. Meridene probably thought Cutberth had beaten Ana.

To quell her apprehension, Revas recalled the lighter moments in the negotiations. "Quite the opposite. Ana claims that during her capture your brother Robert developed an affection for her."

She looked beautifully baffled. "My brother? How did Ana reply?"

"I believe she told him she would marry a poxed Cornishman before she'd give herself to him."

"But she hates the English."

His fingers itched to smooth away the frown that marred her forehead. "'Twas a point well made, don't you think? The bishops of Nairn and Inverness, who conducted the negotiations, agreed that poor Robert was stricken low by her rejection of his admiration. William laughed until tears came to his eyes."

"You sound as if you like William."

Now, Revas thought, was the time to change her mind, for according to Ana, William was ready to break with his father. "Your brother is a goodly man. Did you know that years ago they tried to make him join the church? He refused, saying 'twas unfair to deprive the women of Scotland of so able a man as himself. The cattlemen and shepherds within his authority prosper."

She grew pensive, and Revas hoped she was thinking favorably about the one member of her family who still had a care for her.

After a lengthy silence, she said, "How did you come to know William?"

Those had been learning years, years when Revas had perfected his sword arm and celebrated his manhood. "'Twas on my first visit to Inverness. I was but five and ten."

"You and he are of an age," she said, as if it were a revelation.

More discoveries awaited her. "Aye, though at the time I was much greener than he. I'd never been farther from home than Elgin's End."

"How did you—" She turned away and yawned. "Have you eaten?"

She hadn't meant to inquire after his appetite; of that, he was certain. Seldom was she solicitous of his needs. A change had come over her, but what had caused it? Whatever the source of her friendliness, he was too happy to question his good fortune.

He preferred to think he'd made progress. "Nay, I've not supped. Summerlad said the hare at table tonight was particularly fine. Will you join me?"

"I've eaten."

A bit of cajolery seemed appropriate. "Then sit

with me, and tell me what has occurred while I was away."

She shrugged. "Nothing of any real import. The days have been frightfully boring."

"And your nights, were they filled with dreams of me?"

"Of course. I dreamt that you discovered a fondness for ships and took to the sea."

If she didn't care for him, she would not jest. "Truly?"

She sighed. "In truth, nothing eventful occurred."

"With Ellen about? Come." He held out his hand. "Partake of a tankard and tell me what lucky fellow currently holds her affections."

She extinguished the lamp and pulled the yarn from her hair. Their eyes met. "I have not changed my mind about annulling our marriage."

Not yet, but she had changed her mind about something, and he could hardly wait to discover what it was. "I am ever willing to hear your opinion, Meridene."

Draping a veil of pink silk over her hair, she fumbled with the coronet that held it in place. "I simply think that if we . . . if you try to respect my position, the matter will be settled with the least disruption in the lives of all concerned."

It was just as he thought: She was beginning to like the people of Elginshire; they were not monsters, but concerns.

Revas righted her lopsided veil. "Have you visited the village?"

"Why do you ask?"

She became excited at the casual question. Moments before she had shown only slight trepidation at the mention of her family, a subject proven to stir her ire.

Intrigued, Revas said, "'Tis my duty to keep abreast

of comings and goings, and I did ask you to chaperon young Summerlad."

"Father Thomas bested him at swords."

Revas guided her out the door and slowed his steps to accommodate her shorter strides. "The priest won with ease?"

"Misfortune. Summerlad tripped."

As she walked, the veil fluttered around her, and the clean smell of heather teased his senses. "I'd not like to be a penitent on the morning after Thomas loses to the lad. Sinners and better swordsmen are the bane of his life."

"Which are you?"

"Both."

Rather than chide him for vanity, as he expected, she looked determined and comfortable with her purpose. "We had words."

"Who prevailed?"

"Neither of us. I refused to confess my sins to a priest who lacks compassion. He refused to grant me a voice of my own."

Alarmed, Revas said, "What of the danger to your immortal soul?"

"Father Thomas has a predictable way of defining sins, especially when they disagree with his vision for Scotland. He forgets that I spent many years in the shelter of the church and enjoyed the counsel of a goodly nun and the absolution of a kindly priest. I face danger at the hands of your cleric, but only if I take up a sword against him. My soul is in God's keeping. I have not sinned by seeking to undo the wrongs visited on an eight-year-old girl."

Revas had to admit that her honesty was admirable, her logic undeniable.

They entered the common room, and he exchanged greetings with the guardsmen who gamed there. Eager for privacy, he motioned her through the hearth and to the empty table. "I'll speak with Thomas."

"You needn't bother. I shan't be here long enough for it to matter."

And he was a Toledo blacksmith, laboring in the Spanish heat. She'd grow old here, sheltered in his arms and blessed by the devotion of their children. Addressing her dissatisfaction would sour her mood, and tonight he longed for sweet company.

When they were both served, he sprinkled a pinch of salt on his food. "Did the carpenter fashion your new loom?"

"Nay." Over the rim of her cup, her eyes twinkled with devilish intent. "He's too busy furnishing the end of your patience. Macduff's Halt, indeed."

Revas almost choked on a swallow of ale. He'd discouraged his people from discussing but two things with Meridene: Gibby and the hunting lodge. Both could prove sore subjects to his reluctant bride. Eventually he planned to show her the lodge himself. Introducing her to Gibby was another matter.

He'd wanted to be present when she heard his daughter's name for the first time. When the moment came for them to meet, he'd planned to rest his hand on his Gibby's shoulder and proudly present her to Meridene.

"I am encouraged to know," she went on, shaking her head in rueful humor, "that you can summon tolerance when you choose."

Lord, he loved bantering words with her. "Why?"

"For it gives me hope."

Blithely said, the reply inspired him. "Hope, patience, and a loving wife," he quoted. "Was it not our own Saint Columba who said that a fortunate man was possessed of all three?"

"Ha! I suspect it was said by Revas Macduff when cajolery failed him."

"I yield the point, Meridene, and beg you, return to the safe topic of who crafted your new loom."

With a fingertip she rubbed at the ring her tankard

left on the oaken table. "I do not know his name, but he said he was a wheelwright by trade."

"Ah, yes. The fellow from Aberdeen who has the speech of an Invernessman."

She shrugged. "One Scot speaks the same as another to me."

In this instance, he liked her indifference, for it wouldn't do for her to take up with a stranger, not until Revas had questioned the man himself. "When did he deliver the loom?"

"Earlier today, during evening prayers."

That explained why Sim hadn't mentioned it when he met Revas at the door. He disapproved of strangers entering the castle, but the staff had been occupied with devotion when the man had brought the loom.

Other more pleasant subjects beckoned. "What gallant has captured young Ellen's heart?" Revas asked.

"Glennie Forbes."

"What chivalry did he perform?"

"She dropped her flower penny and he picked it up."

"When did you give it to her?"

"Yesterday. She misplaced it twice before noon. As chance would have it, one of her gallants found the coin each time."

For thirteen years, Revas had imagined conversing with Meridene on just such ordinary topics. He added another blessing to his already bountiful life. "You like her."

Turning to the side, she laughed. "How could I not? She hasn't an ill word to say against anyone, least of all you." Her eyes caught his. "And do not say you are a lambkin."

His heart pounded like a signal drum. With his forearm, he slid the trencher aside and leaned close to her. "Shall I prove it?"

"Only if your men stand as witness."

"Do you truly wish an audience to our lovemaking?"

She shied; he'd been too bold. "You haven't touched your food. Aren't you hungry?"

"Aye." *For food, too,* he thought, and turned his efforts to the hare, mince pie, and oat cakes.

She sipped honeyed milk, and her attention moved to the shields on the wall. "Did you see my father?"

Revas's respect for her grew; she showed bravery in broaching the painful subject. "Only his mark of destruction."

"Was anyone killed?"

Courage be damned; he wanted to talk about more pleasant things. "Nay. Only a few burned fingers and scorched beards. Nairn was fortunate. What did Ellen say when you gave her the flower penny?"

Again she locked her gaze with his. "Where is my father now?"

"He returned to Kilbarton Castle. Would you like to go riding tomorrow?"

"Tomorrow?" she said, as if her days were filled with urgent obligations.

"Have you other plans?"

"Of course not. I'm your captive."

"Meridene." Again he pushed his food away.

"My apologies, Revas. I would not have us quarrel tonight."

His first impulse was to question her; his second was to enjoy the accord. "My thoughts exactly. Would you care to come to my chamber? William has sent you a gift by way of Ana. I thought you would prefer to receive it in privacy."

"What gift?"

"I did not open it. 'Tis yours."

Meridene believed him. She was doubtful, however, about her brother's sincerity. None of the Macgillivrays lamented the loss of an exiled kinswoman, else years ago they would have rescued her. She had long since made peace with her feelings toward the family that had abandoned her.

Now she must put a finish to her time with Revas Macduff, retrieve the Covenant, and flee. The wheelwright had agreed to take her to Aberdeen. They would leave before dawn. From Aberdeen, she'd find a ship to London and the safety of the court of Edward II.

With her father ravaging the land, it was only a matter of time until he turned his wrath on Elginshire. Meridene would not be the reason for a siege of Auldcairn Castle. The people here were innocent, and they had treated her kindly. She would not repay their generosity by putting them in danger.

Her decision made, she accompanied Revas to his chamber. Once in the room, he took her into his arms.

"You are different tonight, Meridene."

Alarmed, she looked at the pedestal. A package rested atop the Covenant. "Is that from William?"

"Aye. What has happened?"

Tomorrow at this hour, she'd be well away from his compelling charms. Denying him a greeting could rouse his suspicion. "You surprised me. Welcome home, Revas."

"Kiss me," he said with gentle persuasion.

She wrapped her arms around his neck.

As if he needed no more encouragement, he lifted her and joined their lips in a kiss very much like the one they'd shared in the chapel. She felt a yearning in him, a manly call that found an answer in her woman's heart, and with bittersweet understanding, she knew that he wanted and cared for her. Had circumstances been different, she would have returned his affection.

On that contrary thought, a greater intimacy beckoned, leeching her will to withhold her heart from the man who had pledged to honor her. But he was too skilled to resist, and she was kissing him farewell. As her senses spun and her own need grew, she thought of his kind gestures: the flower pennies, the lovely wardrobe, the handmaidens.

Gratitude spurred her to meet his passion and savor the last embrace they would share.

He noticed the change and grew adventurous, nibbling at her lips and whispering, "Open your mouth, love, and let me taste your sweetness."

Love. Like a treasured gift at last bestowed, the word and the emotion it spawned went straight to her heart. Held securely in his arms, an escape on the horizon, Meridene grew brave. He'd have twenty women to console him. She would have her peacefully quiet and comfortable life. But feminine pride compelled her to leave him with a kiss he'd remember.

Pulling him closer, she threaded her hands through his hair and slipped her tongue into his mouth.

He turned eager, and his hands roamed her sides, pausing at her waist, then sliding higher to cup her breasts. So pleasant was his touch that she sighed into his mouth and moved in harmony with him. She felt his fingers dallying with her nipples, caressing her, awakening a craving for the touch of him in other, more intimate places.

Then she was lifted, and the familiar furnishings wheeled in and out of view as he carried her to the bed. Bracing a knee on the mattress, he lowered her, following and settling his body over hers.

She felt his maleness against her thigh, hot and heavy with physical need. The urge to surrender thrummed inside her, melting her loins and deafening the voice of resistance.

He undulated against her in a slow, circular motion that matched perfectly the thrust and retreat of his tongue. She felt light, and her head whirled with glorious images of lovers entwined and hearts united in bliss.

Lifting his mouth from hers, he looked into her

eyes. "Put a halt to our loving, Meridene, for I swear I haven't the will to end it."

The plea set her pulse to racing, and her heart cried out for more of his love words.

His expression softened and regret served an odd counterpoint to the desire that burned in his eyes. "Stop me, sweet lass. 'Tis too soon for us."

Too soon. Not yet, Meridene. At the moment, we cannot fit you into our plans. Wait until we want you. All of her life she'd heard similar promises. In the case of Revas Macduff, he asked for a sword.

He wanted her, but only when the time was right. She felt hollow inside, ashamed, and unimportant to the depths of her soul. Yet the cause was none of her doing. Same as the affection of every Scot she had ever known, Revas Macduff's feelings for her were based on reason, not love. His passions were not for Meridene Macgillivray, a woman who loved the smell of clover and the scent of the air at dawn. They were for the Maiden of Inverness, a person she could never be.

"I believe you are ravishing me."

Groaning, he collapsed beside her, his fists knotted in the bed linens, his shoulders, arms, and back bulging with ropes of muscles. Her ache felt deep and exhausting; his was hard and angry.

When he'd mastered his emotions, he sat up and raked his hands through his hair. As he righted his clothing, she knew what he was thinking. *Pardon, Meridene. I cannot love you until*—She blocked out the hurtful thought.

Scottish people had always made her want, but never did they give. This was a people of pain and cruelty. In this land, something else would always be more important than her. Like one more fork of hay on an already backbreaking rick, another condition would weight her happiness.

But only if she allowed it.

Faking a yawn, she mustered a casual air and walked to the pedestal. "You must be exhausted."

"Meridene . . ."

"I'd almost forgotten William's gift." She turned her back to him, and with shaking hands, unwrapped the package. Tied with a string from her brother's bow and adorned with a faded green ribbon was a bird nest. Rather than speckled eggs, the nest held a tiny rolled parchment. A message from William. William, who had played a flute and sketched ships in the dirt. William, the brother who put thistles in her bed and filched sweet cakes from the kitchen.

She unrolled the parchment.

Welcome home, little Maiden, and heed my words. You are in danger.

How could William know? Did Revas? She must learn the answers, but her senses were raw from Revas's halted seduction. Delving into Scottish politics would create an emotional storm too great for her to weather just now.

The bed linens rustled. She put the package back into its wrapping. Turning, she blinked in surprise at the misery on Revas's face.

"'Tis good you did not kiss me downstairs," he said. "I'd have much to answer for to Summerlad and the others."

In any event, she would have kept her maidenhead, for Revas would not risk losing his chance to wear the crown of the Highlands. Not even to prove he loved her. As always in Scotland, sentiments of the heart fell prey to political ambitions. Harder to accept was the fact that she'd fallen in love with him.

The weight of the admission saddened her. She looked down and took refuge in the package that contained the bird nest, a keepsake of one special afternoon in the lives of a brother and sister. She'd had so few fond remembrances of her childhood.

This, then, was one.

"I should reacquaint myself with the handmaiden ceremony." She picked up the Covenant. "The drawing is tomorrow."

"We should talk, Meridene. Greater concerns dictate the intimacies of our lives."

The truth came easy. "I'm embarrassed, Revas, not ashamed of what we almost did."

"Good. Until the morrow, Meridene."

Indeed.

After a fitful night Revas sought out the wheelwright, but found him gone. He gave the man little thought until an hour later, when a distraught Ellen burst into the armory.

"Revas! Lady Meridene's bed has not been slept in. And she's nowhere to be found!"

Concealed beneath a mountain of stifling, smelly blankets, Meridene tried to brace herself against the wagon's bumpy ride. Her benefactor, the wheelwright who bore the common name of Robert Dunbar, had not slowed the team since helping her inside hours before.

The postern gate behind the chapel had offered the only unobserved escape from Auldcairn Castle. Wearing a dark cloak and carrying a sack of personal items and her bag of coins, Meridene had exited the castle proper through the buttery. Like a thief in the night, she had kept to the shadows and slipped through the back gate.

Crossing the inner bailey had proven uneventful, but a pair of lovers strolling in the moonlight forced her to crouch near the newly mortared outer wall. Their tryst went on and on, and not until later, when Meridene pulled the rough blankets over her head and felt the wagon move, did her heart cease its pounding.

Now, desperate for a glimpse of the outside world, she lifted her head and peered over the back of the wagon. The rising sun almost blinded her.

They should be traveling east, not west.

She felt the first shiver of alarm.

Carefully she craned her neck and spied the driver. Hunched over the reins, he was engrossed in guiding the team through the boulder-strewn field. He had been insistent that they avoid roads and travel quickly. That made sense, for she expected Revas to give chase.

Revas. Her heart flip-flopped at the thought of him. Rather than ignore the pain, she faced the longing, and just when the agony made her stomach float, she shoved it away. She'd dealt with loneliness before. But saints guard her soul, a woman's pain made trivial the hurts dealt to an exiled and lonely child.

Pray Revas did not find her, and surely he would not, considering the direction the wagon traveled.

Perhaps the driver was merely circumventing a town or an impassable stream. A forest lay just ahead, and if he did not change direction soon, she would question him.

Hoping to find a more comfortable position, she scooted to the front of the wagon, but stopped when her hip struck something hard and sharp. Lifting the blanket higher, she spied amid the cushioning hay a veritable arsenal of broadsword, dirk, mace, and a deadly short sword.

A second shiver stole her breath.

Why would a wheelwright have need of so much Spanish steel?

She found the answer beneath the board on which the driver sat. Reaching blindly into a bulky sack, she discovered a battle shield. Without benefit of light, she relied solely on feel. Even as she traced the shape of the heraldic device emblazoned on the shield, she could not picture the design.

Why did he conceal his family crest, unless his mission was sinister? She couldn't be sure, but instinct told her she had erred in trusting this man who traveled west to reach east.

Like a lackwit, she had fallen prey to yet another Scotsman. Out of a skirmish and into a battle, she lamented.

Then an image of Revas popped into her mind, and she willed him to rescue her.

Terrified to her toes, she ducked under the blankets again and tried to think what to do. She must flee and soon, but how?

"My lady?"

She froze.

When he called her again, she moaned, as if he'd awakened her. They would enter the forest soon. Once there, she'd make good an escape.

"Are you hurt, my lady?"

Yawning, she lifted her head and gave him what she hoped was a sleepy smile. "Have we reached Aberdeen?"

She saw through his confident grin.

"Never as yet," he said. "'Twill take the better part of the day to flee Macduff's land."

The speech of an Invernessman. Was it true? She did not know, could not remember the manner in which her kinsmen spoke. But something about the way he said "Macduff" gave her pause.

"Is aught amiss, lady?"

Not unless lackwitted counted for anything, she morosely thought.

Desperate for courage, she tried to sound aloof. "Wake me an hour before we arrive, so that I may tidy myself."

When he turned back to the team, she felt for the hilt of one of the swords. Unfortunately, she found a blade first. Wincing, she curled her fingers against her palm. They came away sticky with blood.

A perversely humorous notion crossed her mind: She would not soon pick up a shuttle or thread a needle.

As the wagon rumbled on, she made her plans. She would toss the short sword out first, then carry her sack of belongings. The search to retrieve the weapon would waste valuable escape time, but she knew better than to take a blind leap with a deadly blade in her hands. Especially since the sword was already stained with her blood. More, she must have a weapon.

When all was ready, she lifted the blankets and breathed the blessedly sweet smell of the forest. Slowly, cautiously, she tunneled beneath the blankets to the rear of the wagon. Wedged into the corner, she braved a peek at her escort. His back to her, he flipped the reins and urged the draft horses to greater speed.

The forest moved past in a blur of naked hardwoods and an occasional splash of verdant pine. Before her courage fled, Meridene grasped the handle of the sword and pitched it out. Quick as a frightened hare, she again ducked beneath the blanket.

She counted to twenty. Taking a deep breath, she swung a leg over the back.

Revas held up his hand and called for silence. Macpherson and five of the Forbes clansmen grew quiet.

As a precaution, Brodie, Thomas, and the bulk of the soldiers had stayed behind to guard the keep. If eight trained and dedicated men couldn't find one woman, Revas might as well surrender to the Macgillivrays.

Summerlad cursed. "How could a wheelwright snatch the Maiden from beneath our noses?"

"He's clever," spat Glennie Forbes.

Fortunate better fitted the wheelwright's circumstances. Unlike the guardsmen, Revas knew that

Meridene had left willingly. Escaped, as she probably put it. Gone. Again.

The burden of thirteen empty years returned. Even the relief he'd felt at finding her in England could not quell the new loss in his heart.

Revas wanted to place the blame for her flight on the gift from William, but he could not. Unless the note tucked inside the bird nest had contained some other meaning than danger. Revas had inspected the package. He felt no guilt at lying to her. With her safety at stake, he trusted none of the Macgillivrays, least of all his scheming wife.

Her decision to leave him had been made long before she opened her brother's gift. At table last evening she'd been agreeable and intimately earnest because she knew she wouldn't be there to face the consequences.

Had she been thinking about the departure when she kissed him? No. She had wanted Revas. Hers had been the passions of a woman in need of her man.

Last night her desires had been uncluttered by schemes and destiny. Meridene Macgillivray held an intimate affection for her husband. Although he would have chosen a different path for the quest for her affection, he must now bind her to him with the pleasure of physical love. Her heart would come later.

First he had to find her.

As they followed the westward tracks of the fast-moving wagon, Revas let go of his anger. Manly pride forgotten, he raged at the folly of what she'd done. Her recklessness could land her in the hands of the very evil she avoided.

She knew better; she'd been Highland born and raised.

Kilbarton Castle teemed with soldiers eager to throw down a gauntlet. Her father's demesne attracted landless adventurers who lacked the tools to prosper on an estate, even did they win it.

He hoped she had been lured by a stranger with false promises. The openness of Auldcairn Castle afforded ample opportunity for a villain to come and go. If Revas closed the gates and subjected the people to searches and interrogation, he ran the risk of spreading fear and encouraging isolation. Grim alternatives when his success had been built on free travel and the commerce it spawned.

But if strangers were free to prey upon his people, he had a duty to identify the culprits and vanquish the worst of the lot. Discretion must be his tool, and diligence his method.

Henceforth, soldiers would mingle in the village, and the gatemen would take notice of those entering and leaving Auldcairn. Pray the first arrival to be noted was Meridene Macgillivray.

If she wanted to be free of Revas, why did she travel toward the family she despised? He did not know, but was certain the answer lay ahead.

In the field near Alpin's Moor, they lost the wagon tracks in stony soil. The men fanned out and searched. At the edge of the forest, they again found the trail.

An exhausted and bruised Meridene sat on a boulder amid a stand of concealing bracken. Relief at escaping her captor gave way to confusion over what to do next. When no plan came to mind, she opened the Covenant.

> *I am the Maiden Mary, and I stand over the cairn of my last son. Now I must bargain with the villain who slew all of the lads of my womb, for he has demanded my little princess in exchange for the life of my beloved husband.*

The story brought an ache to Meridene's heart and tears to her eyes, for it confirmed her worst fears about the warring practices of Scots. But as she continued to read Mary's dramatic chronicle and several more, she felt her apprehension ease.

Although Mary had not known it at the time, she had made a decision that benefited all Scots for generations to come. Her daughter and the next five Maidens had thrived. A result, according to the chronicles, not of a softening in Scottish temperament, but of the ongoing Crusades in the Holy Land. Side by side with Romans and Englishmen, Highland kings had defended the faith. Yet in their zeal and their absence, they had almost ended the legend. Were it not for the courage of Sorcha, a Maiden of one and twenty years, who traveled to the Holy Land to find her husband, Meridene's great-grandmother would not have been conceived. The following spring, the sword of Chapling had fallen to a heathen's scimitar. The widowed Sorcha had done her duty.

What would Meridene Macgillivray do? She closed her eyes and held her breath, hoping a sense of loyalty would guide her. She felt a deep affection for Revas Macduff, but no great devotion to a land and a people who asked for more than she could give.

With sad acceptance, she opened her eyes.

The sun offered little warmth, and the sight of Revas riding through the forest chilled her even more. He had not noticed her; her plain woollen cloak blended with the dried brush.

What would he say?

When her hands began to tremble, she put away the Covenant, laid the sword across her lap, and followed the progress of the approaching men.

They rode two abreast, with Revas and Summerlad in the lead and Macpherson and five of the Forbesmen behind. The gray warhorse thundered across the forrest floor, clumps of sod flying beneath his hooves. Taller and broader of shoulder than the others, Revas stood out like an oak in a field of saplings. He rode with the ease of a man well suited to command. The shield of Clan Macduff rested against his knee, and his powerful legs hugged the withers of the mighty horse. Sunlight glinted on silver spurs and golden bracelets, and the wind ruffled Revas's overlong hair.

She had blundered in her attempt to escape him and the political pitfalls of the Highlands. Another option remained: seduction. By yielding her innocence, she forfeited the Maiden's right to claim the sword of Chapling. But more, she avoided facing the father who cared more for his falcon mews than his daughter.

How could she make it appear that Revas had compromised her and yet keep her innocence? She'd need a witness, but who?

Ah, she knew just the one.

She also knew the exact moment Revas spotted her. Although slight, his reaction was marked.

What would he do?

"Meridene," he called out, as if they were old friends being reunited. Yet, like a hunter, his eyes scanned the perimeter.

Without words, he conveyed orders to his men. With a look, Summerlad lifted the visor on his helmet and guided his horse around the bracken behind Meridene. Each man in his turn did the same until she was surrounded. Only then did Revas approach her.

A wall of bracken separated them from the others.

"How did you find me?" she asked.

He gave her a look rife with waning indulgence. "What happened to your hand?"

"A minor cut."

She didn't like the knowing gleam in his eye, but even if he had threatened to beat her, she would have welcomed the sight of him just now. As much as she wanted to deny it, he looked like a prince in a land of monsters.

"When did you depart the company of the wheelwright?"

Even now she could not quell her relief. "An hour ago. He's no tradesman."

"Nor is he a Dunbar, I'll wager."

"How did you find me?"

He held up a scrap of linen. "'Twas snagged on a thistle near the path of the wagon."

The hem of her gown had been shredded by the winter-dry underbrush. "Thank you for finding me."

"My men believe the wheelwright kidnapped you."

Although plainly put, the statement held a complex meaning. Revas knew she'd run away, but he would not say it, for he was more concerned with the opinions of his men. A wayward bride would be an embarrassment.

"If that is so," he went on, "why did you flee him?"

"Why ask me if you know the answer?"

Quietly he said, "You thought he would take you to Aberdeen."

"Yes."

"Whereas he thought to take you to villains unknown."

Unknown. To her, but not to Revas Macduff. She asked, "Which villain?"

"You will not like my answer."

"If you tell me who sent that man, I will know better next time."

He stared at the sun. "You know, no one else will bother to help you, Meridene. You're too much trouble."

The burr in his voice rolled over her, reminding her of a childhood spent under the control of ambitious Scotsmen. "Then give me a horse, and I'll be on my way."

"Give me the sword of Chapling, and I'll empty the stables on your behalf."

"You *are* angry."

"Summerlad!" he yelled out. "Take three of the Forbes and introduce yourself to the wheelwright. He cannot be far ahead. Find out who sent him. Meridene will not choose the new handmaiden until you return to Auldcairn."

"Aye, Revas." Summerlad lowered his visor and in turn pointed to three other men. Sawing reins, he wheeled his warhorse around and galloped into the forest.

Leather creaked as Revas dismounted. "Where did you get the sword, Meridene?"

She gave him the weapon. "The wheelwright has an arsenal in his wagon."

"Macpherson! Take Glennie and Douglas and follow Summerlad."

"But—"

"Go. Lady Meridene has cut her hand. I believe I can escort one frail woman as far as my own holdings."

"Aye, Revas." Macpherson and the remaining men hurried into the forest.

"Come, Meridene."

Revas could have held out his hand. Obviously even that small gesture was beyond him. Graceful acceptance was her most rational choice, so she picked up her belongings and stepped off the boulder.

Withdrawal shielded his emotions as surely as chain mail armored his body. Splendid. She didn't care a knotted thread how he felt. Call her frail, would he?

Lifting her chin, she moved closer. As if it were kindling, he snapped the sword over his knee and flung the pieces aside.

"A warning to your enemies?" she asked.

"Nay." He lifted her into the saddle, then mounted himself.

"Then why the show of animal strength?"

"I was merely marking my territory."

Odd as it was, she wanted to laugh. "I'm not afraid of you."

He kicked the horse into motion. "But you are

afraid of yourself and what you feel for me. 'Tis why you ran away."

"You know so much."

"I know that you want me."

"You want a sword."

"I did not seek the sword of the Highlands, but I must have it. I'm baffled by why I want you."

"Then enjoy your quandary alone, for you'll get no help from me."

"How can you ignore the harmony you see? Do you not wish it to prevail? Think of Sim, of Brodie, of Lisabeth. With peace in the land, the lass will have a husband to give her children. Her father will cherish her babes. Her brothers will not seek their destiny on a field of battle."

His eloquent speech touched her deeply. "Yes, I wish them that happiness and more."

"'Tis enough for now." He hugged her.

"Enough what?"

"Enough trouble from you," he grumbled.

She looked up at the sky. "But the day is young."

CHAPTER

10

A spyglass pressed to his eye, Revas stood in the guard tower and scanned the horizon for a glimpse of Summerlad and the others. They should have returned by now; he'd been watching and waiting for hours.

Just when he'd decided to mount yet another rescue, the riders popped into view. Pennons fluttering above their heads, they were a powerful gathering of Scottish youth and valor. Expert horsemen all, they rode their steeds in perfect vanguard formation. As they approached the break in the curtain wall, Summerlad raised his arm. The others fell back into columns.

Revas raced down the steps and arrived at the gate as the first of the horses thundered into the yard.

Stable lads converged on the lathered animals; squires attended the toilworn riders.

Revas searched each man for signs of injury. He found none, but Summerlad's trunk hose and leather battle jerkin were stained with blood.

"Are you injured?" he asked.

His mouth tightened, but his countenance spoke of victory. "Nay, Revas."

"What delayed you?"

"The wheelwright admitted to having accomplices awaiting him at Elder's Bow."

Macpherson said, "We ventured ahead to spy them."

"We found a nest of Cutberth's mercenaries," Summerlad hissed.

Meridene's father so close to Elginshire? Revas didn't believe the action signaled war; Cutberth enjoyed leading an army himself. He'd sent the wheelwright to abduct Meridene, and the mercenaries for escort. In her desire to escape, she had aided her father's cause. "How many mercenaries?"

Summerlad removed his helmet and shook his head. "A score and some."

Revas looked pointedly at the bloodstains. "You led your men against a force three times as great?"

Again Macpherson stepped forward. "Nay. We wanted to engage them, but Summerlad bade us return before they saw us. He earned his bands on the wheelwright."

Summerlad had slain the man in a fair fight; of that, Revas was certain. He'd also prevented his men from waging a battle they were sure to lose. His leadership ability had been tried, and he had prevailed. "Dunbar died well?"

"You spoke the truth. He's no Dunbar," Summerlad said. "His shield bears the bull of the Macleods, barred."

The black bar of illegitimacy. Such men were often more ruthless than foreign-born mercenaries. "A hired-out bastard."

"He would not yield his sword to me," Summerlad said. "When I made the offer the second time, he swore to slice off my manhood and present it to Serena."

"Thereupon," proclaimed Macpherson, "Summerlad did the slicing."

Revas looked for a change in his fosterling, a hardness and acceptance of the need to slay another man. To his relief, he saw a shadow haunting those blue Macqueen eyes. He motioned to Summerlad. "Come with me."

Oblivious to the people in the lane, Revas hurried to the church and ushered Summerlad inside. Father Thomas stood near the altar, and when he took a step toward them, Revas held up a hand to stop him. The cleric would take Summerlad's sin to God; Revas had other counsel to offer.

"Even a black soul deserves a prayer," he said. "Never forget that, my friend."

Summerlad jammed the helmet under his arm. "Tell me, Revas. Would I feel differently had he kidnapped my own Serena?"

He was hoping for a respite; good men always did. Revas offered the wisdom taught him years ago by Kenneth Brodie. "No matter the crime, a soul is lost. Is one soul of more importance than another? That is for God to decide. You must give it up to Him, Summerlad."

With stern insistence, he said, "I will never forget the man or the moment."

"Nay. Nor will you forget the sight of that first carrot-haired son your beloved Serena gives you."

The crease in his brow smoothed. "Or her smile when I declared my love." He grew pensive. "Is that a woman's place, then? To ease the ache that killing brings us?"

"Aye. For that blessing and infinitely more are we gifted with God's loveliest miracle."

"'Tis good then, for on my oath, I feel little joy at ending that man's life, villain though he was."

The bond that had begun years ago between them grew stronger. At two and twenty, his friend had indeed become a man. "You are wise beyond your years, Summerlad Macqueen."

"I thank you, Revas, for this and the many other wisdoms you've bestowed upon me."

Revas squeezed his arm. "With Father Thomas's help, we'll now make our peace with God. Then we shall see your Serena put away her handmaiden's smock and don that costly gown you gave her."

Meridene thought Serena looked like the goddess of all harvests. Beneath a surcoat of golden velvet, she wore a bliaud of orange that turned the color of her hair to fire. Anticipation glittered in her eyes.

Nearby, Lisabeth and Ellen, dressed in their yellow smocks and wearing garlands in their hair, accepted greetings and shared gossip with the crowd. Near the well, the elderly villagers sat on stone benches and chatted among themselves.

Serena sighed.

"Your gown is beautiful," Meridene said.

The girl flushed. "'Tis Summerlad's doing. When he saw the clothing Revas commissioned for you, he bought this." She caressed the fabric of her sleeve.

Meridene's own gown was sinfully beautiful. Of soft white wool, adorned with butterfly shells from the sea and seeds from the orchard, the garment and its matching veil were fit for a queen. Or for the Maiden of Inverness.

If only Revas would relent on the matter of her demanding the sword of Chapling, she'd gladly wear sackcloth and bare her feet. But ambition ruled her husband. He'd doubled the holdings given to him by the English king and cast his fortunes in Scottish politics.

The people wanted him, believed in him, and that was their choice. They'd rallied for other men. The last Alexander to rule Scotland had captured their hearts. With Revas's help, Robert Bruce might well do the same. If Meridene delivered the sword and the Macgillivrays, accord for all of the Highlands could follow. Her father must yield, else his kinsmen would abandon him. His land would fall to the crown, and he'd be left with only foreign soldiers and legal sons to lead. Even if Daviot and Kilbarton Castle flew the flag of Chapling, Revas would become the king of the Highlands.

For how long? Peace reigned now in Elginshire; the people had turned out in droves to witness the choosing of the handmaiden. A subject, she realized, that held greater appeal to her than Scottish politics. By ending her time as handmaiden, Serena would embark on a new life, a mate to Summerlad Macqueen. Serena had failed in her attempt to convince Randolph to hold the wedding on Whitsunday. The couple would wed at harvest's end.

Now Meridene must put into motion her plan to seduce Revas Macduff.

"Serena," she said, and waited for the girl to turn. "Will you come to my room later and accompany me to table?"

Completely flattered, Serena smiled. "Oh, aye."

Setting a trap pricked Meridene's conscience, but she had no other choice. If Serena stumbled upon Revas and Meridene in a compromising position, it would appear that Meridene had lost her innocence. Then no one would expect her to face her father and demand the sword.

"How is your hand?" said Ellen, who had come to stand beside them.

Meridene's hand was sore, but her spirits were high. "It's only a scratch."

When Revas, Father Thomas, and Summerlad joined the throng, Serena almost quivered with excitement. Revas approached her. Around her neck he placed a string of amber stones shaped like arrow-heads.

He said, "You have done good service, Serena the Handmaiden, and we thank you."

Tears pooled in Serena's eyes when she touched the necklace. "Oh, Revas, you truly are the best man o' the Highlands."

Oh, the sweetness of ceremony, Meridene lamented, watching Revas kiss Serena's cheek, then move to stand beside his wife.

But Scotsmen weren't supposed to value their women. They surrounded them with armed guards, traded them for land, and to save their own hides, abandoned their daughters to the enemy.

But not the Scots of Elginshire.

These people admired Serena, just as they admired Summerlad for his prowess with a sword and his willingness to govern. The young girls gazed at Serena Cameron with loving envy, as if to say they would be as she when they left their youth behind. Husbands smiled fondly at wives, who did not demur as she expected, but nodded as if accepting a deserved word of praise.

Summerlad stepped to the front of the crowd and held out his hand to Serena, palm down. In a gesture as old as the honor of the fighting man, she matched her palm to his, then raised her arm, signifying that she willingly bore the weight of his sword arm and accepted him for the soldier he was.

That's when Meridene noticed the golden bracelet on his wrist. Summerlad's arms had been bare before. What life had he taken to achieve the symbols of manhood?

The wheelwright.

She waited for the old pain to steal her breath and sour her stomach. To her amazement, it did not come. Because of her, a man was dead. Not a man, but a villain bent on treachery. When, she wondered, had she learned to judge and condemn a man, then easily accept his death?

The crowd exchanged murmurs of approval. Revas had yet to say a word to her.

She looked up at him. "The wheelwright is dead."

"Aye, but 'twas his own doing. Summerlad twice gave him the chance to yield his sword. His name was Macleod."

What if Summerlad had lost? Revas would shoulder the blame and the loss of a kinsman. But the responsibility was not solely his. "Are you angry with me still?" she asked.

He scanned the crowd, probably searching for a distraction. "'Tis possible."

He was a Highlander and accustomed to shedding the blood of his fellow Scots. If he hadn't brought her here, the man named Macleod wouldn't have fallen to Summerlad. Still, her actions had played a part. "I did thank you for coming after me. On our return I spoke at length of my gratitude."

"Welcome words from a wayward bride—" he glanced at her "—who looks very well cared for."

She had not asked for fine clothes and adoration; he'd given the garments freely and schooled these people to revere her. She wanted no such devotion. "You're a man of pride and ornament, Revas Macduff."

"I'm a lam—" She put her hand to his lips. She knew what he would say.

His eyes danced with challenge, and she sensed a power in him, an unbending determination. He had a right to his anger. She had no quarrel with that. What troubled her was her own need to seek his understanding and receive fair judgment.

She dropped her hand.

He gave her a look that said she'd made a wise choice in yielding. How could he speak so plainly to her with only an expression? How had she come to know and love him so well?

He picked up the white keg and held it before her. "Meridene?"

Gathering a thought proved impossible. She stared at the parti-colored swatches of cloth. The ceremony. Choose a handmaiden.

Composing herself, she reached into the mass and pulled out the square of butter-soft leather. Scripted finely in red dye was the name of her next handmaiden.

To the crowd she said, "I have chosen the girl named Gibby."

The crowd stood in shocked silence. Revas took the marker from her hand and examined it closely. Then he gave it to Macpherson. "Fetch the lass."

Brodie said, "I'll accompany him."

Baffled, Meridene said, "Who is Gibby? And why do you look so bothered at the notion of her being selected as a handmaiden?"

Revas felt as if he'd taken the butt end of a Yule log in his gut. Gibby, his daughter, had put forth her name. Not once had she mentioned an interest in the position. He had not discouraged her; the subject had simply never come up.

Bless the saints, what would Meridene say?

"Come." Taking her arm, he pulled her through the throng and into the castle. In her apartment, he released her and moved to the new loom. Searching for words, he stared at the tapestry she'd only begun.

Moments passed. The weaving drew his gaze, but Meridene was certain that his mind was fixed on something of great import. She recalled a similar instance when he had interrogated her.

She could pry information just as well as he. "'Twould be best if I heard it from you, Revas."

He tensed. "Heard what?"

Had he not been so somber, she would have chuckled. "Whatever it is you are trying to hide. As you are fond of saying, secrets are poorly kept in Elginshire."

He lifted his head and pinned her with his gaze. "Gibby is my daughter."

Had he proclaimed himself the king of France, Meridene could not have been more surprised. His daughter. A bastard. Twenty women. The sloth.

Questions tumbled in her mind, and she broached the subject that had too often troubled her. "Have you a large family?"

He gave her a remarkable look.

She replied, "You think I am shocked?"

"You weren't as sheltered as *that*, Meridene. I pray you will understand."

Righteous anger stiffened her spine. "Make no mistake, Revas Macduff. I understand you well."

"Look." He shifted his weight and held out his hands. "Gibby is not to blame for my . . ."

She lifted a brow. "For your . . . ?"

He set his jaw. "For my life before you came here."

He spoke as if she'd come of her own free will. The word "kidnapping" had conveniently fled his vocabulary. If keeping vows were the subject of the conversation, the word "wife" had deserted him long ago. "Had you planned to tell me about her?"

"Of course. She's not hidden away in a crofter's hut or living under another's name."

No. She lived with her mother—the woman he loved. "My father kept women, and it caused trouble in our household. I ask you not to bring her mother here until Leslie has returned with word of our annulment."

He hadn't expected the request, and he searched for a reply. At length he said, "Mary died shortly after Gibby was born. The lassie is the joy of her grandparents' lives." Ruefully he added, "And mine, more oft than not. I love her well, Meridene, as I will love all of our children."

Before she could disabuse her husband of the notion of legitimate progeny, Sim appeared in the door.

"Gibby has arrived," the steward said.

"Then bring her," Revas said.

When Sim departed, Revas asked, "Will you treat her kindly, Meridene?"

This vulnerability was new in Revas Macduff. What manner of woman did he think she'd become? Surely not one who'd punish a child for the father's sins? She of all people understood the unfairness in that.

"She's a good lass, bright and thoughtful," he went on.

"Bright and thoughtful," Meridene mused. "She must favor her mother."

He nodded, obviously relieved. "That she does. Wait here."

He stepped into the hall and stared toward the common room. Meridene knew the moment he spied his daughter, for his face glowed with pride and love.

Meridene's throat burned with envy; her father had never looked at her in that manner. Much as she wanted to deny it, she found another reason to love Revas Macduff.

A moment later a delicate girl came into view. The top of her head barely reached his elbow. She had short-cropped, fair hair and a storm of freckles on her cheeks and her upturned nose. Meridene looked for resemblances between father and daughter and discovered several. Gibby's fair brows arched with the same elegance as his; her tentative expression was reminiscent of the smile of a barefoot boy who once faced the king of England.

Revas knelt beside his daughter.

"Are you angry with me?" she asked in a voice as soft as thistledown.

"Nay. I'm very proud of you, Gibby my own."

"Good, for I'll try my best."

Thickly he said, "You always do."

A fortunate girl, Meridene thought, and pledged to show her the kindness she'd been denied.

Standing, he put his hand on Gibby's shoulder and drew her into the room. "Meridene, this is my daughter and your new handmaiden, Gwendolyn Mary Margaret."

The girl's face puckered in disgust.

Meridene smiled. "You prefer to be called Gibby."

"Aye, my lady."

"How did you come by your name?"

As if she'd told the story countless times, she took a deep breath. "When I was a wee bairn, I was sickly. My nose was a runny mess, and I was forever sneezing. When I spoke, I talked like this." She pinched her nose. "Gibby a drink of milk. Gibby a sweet cake. Gibby this, gibby that." She clasped her hands. "That's why they call me Gibby. Isn't it true, Papa?"

"As true as the sweetness of your soul."

She rolled her eyes. "He's a lambkin, you know."

Meridene fought to keep her gaze on Gibby. She lost, and when she caught his eye, he gave her a knowing smile.

She couldn't resist saying, "All men are lambkins when they choose to be. But now I'm interested in you, Gibby. How old are you?"

"Ten."

Meridene's gaze flew back to his. He'd been only five and ten or thereabout when he sired this girl.

His hand tightened protectively on Gibby's shoulder. She looked up, confused. When he winked, she became flustered and turned her attention to the loom.

Watching the loving exchange was like a caress to Meridene. Legitimate or no, this daughter was loved by Revas Macduff. Meridene said the first thing that came to mind. "The mercer spoke of you, Gibby. You made the red dye for my thread."

"Aye."

"'Tis well known," Revas declared, "that she also makes the truest greens and blues in all of the Highlands."

Gibby ruffled with pride. "My grandmama showed me where to find the plants and how to mix the colors."

"Do you know the duties of a handmaiden?" Meridene asked.

"Aye." She swallowed hard. "I'm to make fast the windows against the night air, bank the fire, and tend the rowans."

Revas said, "Gibby can make even a stump grow. 'Tis said she can walk on rocky soil and a trail of posies will sprout up in her path."

"Papa!" She cringed in embarrassment, her arms stiff at her sides.

Seriously he said, "You'll have the chamber next to mine, Gibby."

She beamed. "What of Jaken? May I keep him with me?"

"A dog? In here?" He sent Meridene a questioning look.

Gibby rushed to say, "He has the king's own manners, my Jaken does."

"Which king would that be?" Meridene asked.

Gibby cocked her head. "A goodly one, I am certain."

Bright, he'd said of her, and Meridene agreed. "Yes, you may keep your dog. Where is it now?"

"It's a him, and I'll fetch him." She dashed out and returned with a black and white terrier no taller than Meriden's calf. The dog's back leg was crippled, withered, and curled up tight against his wiry body, but he trotted as well on three.

"He's the veriest gentleman. I swear." Bending from the waist, she addressed the dog. "Swear fealty to the lady, Jaken."

The dog trotted to Meridene, sat before her, and held up a paw. She took it. His stubby tail thumped the stone floor, and his short ears stood at attention.

Inspired, she patted the dog's head. "I dub you the official keeper of the bones and chaser of the cats."

Father and daughter shared laughing glances. Meridene watched in envy.

"To me," Gibby called.

The dog trotted back to his place at her heel.

"Wash your hands and face and wait for us in the common room," Revas said to the girl.

"I know all that, Papa. I'm not a bairn."

"Wait." Meridene went to the trunk and took out a yellow smock. "You should have this now."

Her eyes wide with excitement, Gibby hugged the garment to her chest. On its good back leg, the dog hopped in place.

"When you've unpacked your belongings and donned your new dress," Revas said, "we'll all go to table together."

Eager for a moment alone, Meridene said, "I'll join you both there."

When Gibby and the dog left, Revas closed the door. "And leave you to ruminate on my past frolics? Nay, Meridene. We'll have this out now."

"Have what out?"

"Whatever is on your mind—as pertains to my past."

"Your past? A mild word since you've spent the last thirteen years plowing women like a farmer with a new hoe."

He propped his hands on his hips. "Where did you hear such a vulgar thing?"

Ana Sutherland had been the source, but girls

always spoke boldly among themselves, and a blessing it was, for if men had their way, women would stay ignorant of intimacy until the marriage bed. "I'm not *that* sheltered, remember? You said as much yourself."

He had steady eyes, eyes that said, *I'm at ease with the way you see me, and with what I see in you.*

"Gibby is my only child."

Meridene fumed. "How moderate of you."

"You left moderation behind with your swaddling clothes."

"But I stayed chaste."

"Shall I praise you for keeping *one* of your vows to me?"

"Only when I praise you for keeping a flock of women."

"A flock? Who told you that?"

"Ana. She said you had twenty women."

He looked so incredulous, she lost her train of thought.

"Meridene. No man can have twenty women. 'Tis impossible foolishness."

"What was to stop you? Your *wife* was not here."

Plaintively he said, "My bed would break beneath the weight of twenty women."

Like butter left in the sun, her anger melted. "Why do you try so hard to make me like you and this ghastly land?"

"I believe," he said, staring at the tapestry, "that if Scotland cannot keep her finest sons and her fairest daughters, she will fall the way of Wales, her culture crushed beneath an English hammer."

"I am not one of Scotland's fairest people."

He glanced up, his eyes glittering with raw emotion. "Oh, aye, Meridene. *You,* of all her people, are."

More to convince herself than him, she said, "I am not your wife."

He feigned bewilderment. "Have I a wife?" he growled, and flung out an arm. "Pray send her in to wash my back and pour my ale."

"You want a servant."

His pride rightfully nicked, he stepped back. "True. But I'll admit my mistake if you will explain what you know about being a wife."

"After you tell me who sent my kidnapper. He did not wear Macgillivray colors."

"'Tis what troubles you—the thought that he may have been one of your kinsmen. Worry not who sent him. He thought to sell a bonny lass to a sea captain in Tain."

She felt an odd sense of relief and vindication; Scotland teemed with kidnappers. Her father had no allegiance with Clan Macleod; by marriage they were aligned with Robert Bruce. Unless that Macleod had broken with his family.

"Now," Revas said with finality. "Define a good-wife."

"As it applies to me?"

"Aye, and to the letter."

He wanted a battle with words. Obliging him came easy. For effect, she poured him a glass of ale and shoved it into his hand. "First, a goodwife must choose a good husband. Since I was spared that luxury, our discussion on the subject ends there. And here. And now."

"You learned such verbal trickery in the English church?" Shaking his head in wonder, he plopped down on the weaving stool. "That explains why their country's on the verge of civil war."

"Scotland coined the word."

"With your help, the Highlands will know peace, Meridene."

She should defend herself. She couldn't find the words. Serena would appear soon. Meridene must entice Revas into a compromising position. "What know you of good husbandry?"

"Listen well. The happiness of a wife is the husband's responsibility." He put down the ale and walked toward her. "Does the wife prefer tender lamb? Then 'tis the husband's quest to seek out the shepherd every spring."

He came closer, his eyes compelling, his voice rich with meaning. "If fat partridge be her desire, then he must string a bow and walk the fields at harvest's end. If memorable conversation rouses her mind, then he must sharpen his wits to match her keen thoughts." His voice dropped, and he was almost close enough to whisper. "If sweet words and tender touches nourish her soul, then he must tell her that her mouth is like a delicious flower and that her skin is the softest of God's textures." He clutched her shoulders. "Should she crave nearness as much as this, then her husband is bound to take her in his arms."

Her mind became a still lake yearning for the touch of the wind. His breath fanned her face, and she drew him down for a kiss that emptied her soul. Then he was giving back, filling her with a desire so real that even her fingertips tingled with it. She clutched his tunic until her hands were knotted and cramped in the velvet.

Seeming to know, he pulled her hands free and threaded his fingers in hers, taking care with the bandaged hand she had forgotten. Both of his palms were rough from labor, but his skin felt oddly tender next to hers. The tension flowed from her, leaving a lassitude and a need to cling.

As if warming up to a dance, he moved his hips from side to side, brushing against her, urging her to join him. She did, and as passion worked its way up her spine and down her legs, she began to sway.

He understood and moved their clasped hands

behind her, supporting her, enabling her to sway as she would. But she couldn't quite find the ideal movement or gain her balance. For better footing, she parted her legs, and he stepped into the void. Her breath caught at the sheer perfection of the fit. Then he bent her back, over their clasped hands, and kissed away her senses, save those that yearned for him.

"Forget vows and allegiances. You are all that I desire."

After breathing the words into her mouth, he took her lips in a kiss that set her on fire for him. She pulled her fingers free of his and cradled his cheeks, feeling the kiss with her hands, sealing the union with her touch.

He felt it, too, for his hips bumped gently against hers. She cried out in surprise and pleasure at the movement, and his tongue plunged into her mouth even as he nudged her again.

Begging proved to be her next option, for she wanted him with a need beyond pride and past reason. This, too, did he know, for he worked at the lacings on her gown, but never broke the kiss or the rhythm.

She heard the patter of shells striking the wall, felt the rending of precious woollen cloth. "Yes," she said, willing him to take off the dress.

He did. And swept her up and carried her to the bed. Tearing his lips from hers, he drew off her bliaud. She stood before him, naked but for her stockings. His hungry gaze fell on her breasts, and his arms floated upward, until his fingers grazed her nipples.

She understood that he wanted to indulge himself in touching her, so she covered his hands with her own and pressed him closer. His head tipped back and his throat worked, as if he were savoring the taste of a fine wine. Her own thirst for him grew, and she tunneled her hands beneath his tunic to the laces of his hose.

He jerked away, then moved so close that she felt his desire straining at the fabric that bound him. Knowing what he wanted, she curled both hands around him and languished in the extent of his need for her—for Meridene Macgillivray, a woman who treasured a good loom and hated Scotland.

On a soft groan, he ripped his mouth from hers and drew her down onto the bed. Then he fastened his lips onto one of her nipples and suckled a soft moan out of her. That done, he moved to the other breast and teased and laved until she reached for his manhood again.

He knew, and stripped off his tunic and hose. Chest heaving, his eyes wild with desire, he stood beside the bed. With gentle insistence, he parted her legs and walked his fingers up her inner thighs. Her pulse hammered in a rapid thud, and anticipation robbed her of speech.

As if peering at a gift, he admired her most intimate place. A flush warmed her skin, but she did not feel shame. She felt adored, cherished, and eager for what he would do next.

His arms grew lax, and he lowered himself until she felt his breath on her private desire.

"So bonny," he whispered, and kissed her there.

Her head went blank, and her back arched like a bow. Sweet Saint Mary, she should tell him to cease, but a drum had begun to beat beneath his lips and the pounding was sweet with the promise of glory.

"Bonny mine, bonny mine," he said, again and again, until she sensed that he wanted her to give to him, which was odd, since she was near to exploding with pleasure. When it did come, she felt like a bird flung to freedom and caught up on the currents of a hot summer wind.

"For me," he said between devilish licks that prolonged her pleasure. "For me."

Through a haze of blissful oblivion, his meaning became clear: A wife's happiness was a husband's responsibility, and Revas Macduff took up his office with zeal. But what of his joy? What of the empty ache that throbbed deep inside her?

"Let me give you pleasure, too, Revas." She grasped his shoulders and pulled him up, her gaze fastened on the magnificence of his desire. Of their own accord, her legs parted and her hips rose to meet him.

The powerful muscles of his shoulders and arms strained with the weight of his need, and he stared as if entranced at the sight of his flesh poised so near her own.

She said his name in a yearning whisper.

His head came up, and his eyes were dazed, his chest heaving. She gave him a smile that trembled with uncertainty.

Awareness flashed in his eyes, and she knew what he was thinking. *If he took her innocence, he would forfeit the sword of Chapling.*

To thwart him, she lifted her hips. He grimaced and sucked in a breath. *Take my innocence,* she silently willed him, *and prove you love me, not a legend.*

He hesitated, obligation pulling him from the clutches of passion.

"It is not me you want, Revas. I'm not the passion in your life."

He blinked, and his eyes went out of focus again. Seizing the moment, she grasped his hips. Beneath her fingers, muscle turned to steel. She cursed his power for the punishment it dealt her. Doubting his motives was an elusive thing; the proof was like a knife in her chest.

She should have known better than to yield to a Scotsman. Her hands fell to her sides. The candle sputtered. Shadows danced on the walls. It was odd, but nothing in the room had changed, and yet everything was different. "Let me up."

"I cannot." His gaze fell on her. "Your sorrow has undone me, Meridene."

We are well met, this butcher's son and I, she thought. "Then make me yours."

He did, and time stopped for Meridene. It was as if a bell had sounded, marking the end of what had been and, at the same moment, heralding what was to come.

The completeness of their union struck her first. They fitted together like hand to favorite glove, and the absolute peacefulness of their souls filled the very air.

She sighed in contentment. "I feel wonderful."

"Hum. For this pleasure," he said, "I would lie comfortless and hungry in the heather."

A flutter of pride made her smile. "I would bring you sustenance."

He moved inside her.

A twitch of pleasure almost ended it for Revas. Passion squeezed his loins, but he'd waited over a decade to bind this woman to him. He'd not have it end in a quick quenching of lust. He'd make a banquet of their desire, a feast of their loving.

Her innocence surrounded him, new and yielding. The joy or lack of it that she received tonight would set the pace for their intimacy. He'd succumbed and taken her innocence. They would go on from here as man and wife. Politics be damned.

Now he intended to love her until the memory of this night never left either of them, and when next she expressed displeasure, he'd spirit her away to a quiet place and remind her of the bliss they could enjoy.

On that glorious thought, he pulled back, then thrust deeper, a little at a time, until he could go no farther. She moaned in delight and ground her loins against his. Her eagerness drove him to finesse, for he was very close to spending his seed.

A gentle challenge in his eyes, he said, "You are the passion of my life, *Meridene Macgillivray."*

She blossomed like the finest flower in Scotland. "I know not what comes next."

"Then allow me to show you."

Revas grasped her hips to hold her still while he dragged himself from her warmth, then plunged in again. Her eyes fluttered shut, and with the ease of a woman who'd lain in his arms a thousand times, she lifted herself to him and followed his lead.

When he asked her to wrap her legs around him, she did, and her slender thighs were surprisingly strong, gripping and urging him at once. Sweat dampened his skin, and lust pooled, hot and heavy, in his loins. She smelled of heather and contented woman—dangerous scents to a man as close to climax as he.

To master his passion, he thought of trivial things: his new chain mail, the dwindling supply of flint stone. He even pondered the latest nick in his favorite broadsword.

"Have you lost interest in me, Revas?"

At the sound of her voice, he blinked. Her eyes gleamed with sated desire, and her luxurious hair fanned the linens. He'd pictured her just so, but the reality made dull work of his musings.

She pinched his waist. "Have you?"

The Maiden was his, his to hold, his to love, his to cherish, until God called them home. He swelled within her.

"Oh! I can tell you have not."

He gave her a grin he suspected was crooked. "'Tis safe to say, though, that my interest is peaking and quickly."

She raked a fingernail over his ribs. "Are you riding hotfoot to passion's gate?"

He shivered and latched on to the diversion. "Have you been reading that randy Frenchman, de Lorris? Those words sound like his."

She flushed prettily. "I've been listening to Ellen."

He felt like a crossbow, cocked and ready to fire. "Henceforth, you should listen to me."

Laughter vibrated in her breasts and mock defiance glittered in her eyes. "Are you commanding me— here in my own bed?"

Her casual acceptance called up the best in him, for he wanted a lifetime of just such moments with Meridene Macgillivray. "I offer only the truth. Stay very still, or we'll both be sorry for it."

Enlightenment gave her serenity, and she fairly glowed with feminine power. Knowing she was eager to wield it, he felt bound to say, "I warned you, Meridene."

"Even so . . ." Her hips snuggled his loins, and a shaft of anticipation seared him. He gave up the fight.

Now dedicated to his lustful objective, he thrust quick and hard, and when his passion burst, she squeezed him sharply, over and over, until he thought she'd drained the very soul from him.

At the edge of his euphoria lurked a shadow of danger. Trouble would come, for he'd broken his word to the people of the Highlands. Curse him for a faithless Christian, but he did not care. Of all the rewards he had received, this one woman was to be his foremost prize, and the time just spent, his greatest boon. But he'd put his cart before his horse, and if the worst prevailed, he'd jeopardized Highland unity.

"Now who's sorry, Revas?"

How did she manage to know him so well? How could he tell her the truth without spoiling the moment? *Oh, Scotland,* he thought, *you ask too much of an ordinary man.*

He scooted to the head of the bed and pulled her with him. When he'd tucked her to his side, he said, "My only regret is that I did not prevent you from drinking from that poisoned cup so many years ago. Had I stayed your hand, we could have been together all this time."

With the flat of her bandaged hand, she drew lazy circles on his chest. "What of the sword of Chapling?"

According to tradition, she could not seek it now; her father would keep the symbols of power. But Revas possessed the grand princess of the Highland folk. If he was fortunate, the Macgillivrays would follow the old ways and abandon Cutberth in favor of the Maiden, even if she did not demand the sword.

It had happened before, but the circumstances and clans had been different. Centuries ago, the father of the unwed Maiden had stayed too long on Crusade. In defiance of her greedy uncles, she had chosen her husband and together they had ruled the Highlands in relative peace. Precedents aside, Meridene Macgillivray did not think of herself as the Maiden, did not possess the devotion of her predecessors.

Would she ever? Perhaps seeing William again would rouse her loyalty. Revas would send a message to him, asking him to visit. Would her brother come? Yes, and by that time, Revas prayed she would accept her circumstances and claim her birthright.

In contradiction to his thoughts, he said, "You mustn't think of the sword now. If I'm to reign, the sword of Chapling and the crown will find their way to me. And if you keep fondling me, you'll find yourself calling up Saint Mary again."

Her hand stilled, and she slid him a curious glance. "There's no blood on the linens . . . or on you."

Her candor charmed him. He also felt pride at the care he'd taken with her. "You looked closely at me?"

"I—You're just there—and I couldn't help— seeing—you."

She flustered beautifully, which brought him quickly to life again. "You were innocent. The lack of virgin's blood means nothing. By my oath, I swear you were pure of body."

Vindicated, she grew brave. "You've had many virgins, I suppose."

In the absence of an acceptable reply, he kept silent and prayed for a miracle.

"Have you nothing to say?"

"I was praying for divine intervention." He took her hand and moved it to his desire. "'Twould appear I've been blessed."

Engagingly curious, she caressed him. "That wasn't what you were thinking, but for the moment, I'm too bewitched to quarrel with you."

It was a far cry from *I love you,* but she was his now. "You'll be sore if I make love to you again."

Pinning him with a direct gaze, she said, "Will your regret double?"

Only a fearless woman would pose such a direct question; only a fool would answer it, but risks came easy to Revas, especially where she was concerned. "You are my wife, Meridene. I have a duty to you."

"Did you learn that verbal trickery in the Scottish Church?"

She had an odd way of mastering bewitchment. "Tossing a man's words of devotion in his face must surely be a sin."

On a particularly sensitive stroke of her hand, she said, "What of lusting after worldly pleasure?"

"Enough teasing." He drew her beneath him and settled himself between her legs. "I'd rather lust after you."

She was a woman apart from the one he'd imagined. He hadn't expected spontaneity and daring, and as he touched his lips to hers and pressed against her yielding form, he thought himself the most fortunate of men. When she wiggled her hips until their bodies were perfectly joined again, he couldn't think at all.

A knock sounded on the door. "Lady Meridene?"

She gasped. "Oh, goodness. I've let you— Oh, my. It's Serena. I told her—I didn't tell her— Gibby's waiting for us. Oh, wretched misfortune."

Gibby would live in his home. Meridene would guide her. No misfortune there. Over his shoulder, he said. "Not now, Serena. I'm having a word with my wife."

Giggling, Meridene undulated beneath him. "A word?" she whispered. "If she opens that door, she'll get a very mortifying view of your fall from grace."

"Serena," he called out. "Ask Sim to tap a fresh keg. Meridene and I are not to be disturbed. We'll be along when we've had our discussion."

"Aye, Revas," the girl answered.

Cursing himself for not locking the door, he moved to draw the curtains into place around the bed. Meridene looked mysterious in the shadowy light. His wife. The future spread out before him, prosperous and satisfying.

"What if someone else comes?"

He kissed her nose, her cheeks, and her brow. Meridene Macgillivray, the wife he had waited over half of his life for, was now in his arms. "You forget that I'm laird here."

"You're very good at giving orders."

Tunneling his arms beneath her shoulders, he braced himself on his elbows and wedged his loins into the nest of her womanhood. "'Tis my second best quality."

She languished, smiling. "And your first?"

"Lightsome questions are disallowed."

"You're a devil, Revas Macduff," she scoffed, and turned her head away.

He chuckled and took her to the edge of release.

When next she said his name, a pillow muffled the joyous sound.

An hour later, after they'd both dressed, Meridene brushed her hair and watched Revas gather seashells from the floor. She couldn't stop picturing him naked or cease feeling him inside her still, pleasuring her out of her mind. Beneath his dark green trunk hose and leather tunic was a body she knew intimately. Her limbs relaxed at the thought.

"What shall I do with these trinkets from your gown?"

"Give them to me." The woollen surcoat could be mended and the ornaments reattached. She folded the garment and held out her hand for the shells he'd gathered. "I'll put it all in the clothes chest until I can mend the gown."

He lifted the lid of the trunk. The Covenant of the Maiden rested atop her heavy cloak, and he picked up the book.

He was so close, she could see shards of golden light in his brown eyes. She hadn't noticed the color before.

"I never meant to tear your clothing." He rubbed his nose against hers. "But I was beset with a craving for you."

He'd paid a high price, too, and his honesty tugged at her conscience. But she refused to feel guilty for what had just happened. She'd freed herself of the duty of demanding the sword of Chapling. In the scheme of things, he'd been the true loser; yet no sense of accomplishment swept over her. Rather a deep abiding peace thrummed in her breast. "I understand, Revas."

"Much has changed now."

"Yes, and I'll wager the treasury of flower pennies that you never even meant to kiss me."

"Then you'll lose, Meridene."

As if to prove it, he kissed her, and her fingers curled until the edges of the shells bit into her palm. Knowing she'd yield again, she said, "I should hide these."

"You don't want your handmaidens to know?"

The need for privacy came naturally to one raised in a convent. She shouldn't feel sad for wanting to keep secret their intimacy, but she did. "Do you?"

He shrugged. "When you conceive, they will know."

When, not if. Too stunned to answer, she ducked her head and busied her hands with putting away the gown. He had beguiled her, for she'd forgotten the one tie that would irrevocably bind her to him: a child.

Logic urged her not to worry, but a greater danger dawned. Their marriage was sealed. No annulment would be forthcoming. Her plan to have them caught in a compromising position had gone awry; she'd lost more than he. "We consummated our vows."

He grinned. "Aye, and quite satisfactorily. Your namesake would have been pleased."

Blaming him was unfair, but she couldn't help doing it. "You took advantage of me."

He gave her a dubious frown. "'Tis dishonorable of you to cry foul now, Meridene. You fairly begged me to love you."

Anger ripped through her at his notion of honor and love. That her scheme of seduction had gone awry only added to her ire.

She slammed the lid of the trunk. "I never begged." But she had, shamelessly, wantonly.

"I suppose 'tis better said that you made a convincing request, and I hadn't the will to resist."

Both of them had paid a high price: he a sword, she a safe future devoid of Scottish intrigues. Why did he have to be so understanding and engaging? "You have an obliging conscience."

He tucked the Covenant under his arm. "And a ravenous appetite. Shall we fill our bellies, then later indulge ourselves again? What say you to breaching passion's gate a third time?"

And run the risk of conceiving a child? No. She'd achieved her goal, though she hadn't fully counted the consequences. Now she must sort through her options. Denying the desire that lingered even now promised a new dilemma. "I'm rather tired."

He lifted her chin and looked into her eyes. "Did I hurt you?"

Only if rapture could be considered an injury, she wanted to say. Instead, she spoke a heartfelt truth. "No. You made a lie of the fearful tales of the marriage bed. For that I thank you."

He took great pleasure in her answer, for his eyes shone with joy, and as he led her from the room, Meridene made a remarkable discovery. For the second time in her life, she felt completely at ease in the company of a Highlander. On the first occasion he'd been a boy anticipating his own demise at the hand of a foreign king. On the second, the Highlander was a man who'd given up achieving through ceremony the unity of Scotland to claim the hand of a desired wife. She'd spent years honing her hatred for Scotland and her people. In less than a fortnight, Revas Macduff had dulled the edge of her enmity.

She paused in the torchlit hallway. "Do I look different?"

With the same hand that had touched her so intimately, he caressed her cheek. "Only to me, Meridene."

"How so?"

He kept his voice low. "You bear the glow of a woman well loved, but you are frightened of what you feel, and you hesitate to trust me."

Honesty compelled her to say, "Scottish people have seldom concerned themselves with what is best for me."

"Not the Scots you know today. Certainly not I. You are my foremost concern, and I swear on the soul of my father that we will thrive in peace here."

All of that changed the next morning when he returned from confession. Standing in the common room with the steward, Meridene watched Revas barge into the castle and scale the stairs three at a time. No sooner had the doors closed than Sheriff Brodie burst inside and raced after him.

A quarrel ensued, but she could not make out Revas's angry words or Brodie's equally forceful replies. Amid a clamoring of shield, sword, and spurs, a mail-clad Revas barreled down the stairs. Ignoring her and Sim, he gave the doors a mighty kick, then stormed into the yard.

Meridene closed the ledger. "I would say he is vexed, Sim."

The steward whistled. "Pity the man who gained his wrath."

Brodie started down the stairs. "Then say a prayer for our cleric."

Sim gasped. "Oh, no. They've never crossed swords in anger."

Brodie made a fist. "'Twill be a fight for certain this time."

"How Scottish of them," Meridene mused. "Why do they quarrel?"

"I suspect the cleric took offense at Revas's confession."

She studied their worried faces, but found no end to

her puzzlement. "What black sin could Revas have committed, and when? The day is young, and he's just broken his fast."

The sheriff stared at his boots. "I do not know the particulars."

He lied; his withdrawal told her so. But she was more concerned with the danger to her husband. She snatched up her veil and headed for the door.

"You shouldn't watch, my lady. When bad humors are upon them, they are bloody wicked fighters."

Meridene ignored Brodie; curiosity had her in its throes.

A crowd had begun to gather in the tiltyard. Flanked by Summerlad and Glennie Forbes, Revas stood near the quintain, his sword and shield at his feet. Rage hardened his features, and his arms were stiff with restrained fury. Small wonder he led so many Highland clans; battle-ready and determined, he looked as if he could conquer all of Christendom.

With renewed vigor, the agony of her dilemma returned. She couldn't live among these people, a crown of rowans on her head. They deserved a Maiden who believed in the Covenant, not some English-raised stranger whose dreams were plagued with Scottish monsters. Yet where else had she to go? How would she get there? Whom could she trust?

Having no answers, she pushed away the quandary and picked up her step. As she approached Revas, she called his name. He watched her, but his attention was inwardly focused.

"Excuse us," she said to his young escorts.

When Summerlad and Glennie moved out of hearing distance, she put her hand on Revas's arm. The chain mail felt warm and imposing beneath her fingers. "Why have you and the cleric come to odds?"

His smile was forced. "No reason that you should concern yourself with."

"Why not? Because it involves swords and words between men?"

"Meridene." He rested his arm on the quintain post. "I know what you are thinking."

In the span of a night, he'd changed from a devoted lover to a dangerous soldier bent on salving his bruised pride. He looked so imposing, so set in his ways, she dropped her hand and said, "Tell me what I am thinking."

"You think us animals for settling our differences in the tiltyard."

He'd gotten it all wrong. She knew well the warring practices of Scots, but Revas Macduff was no animal; none of God's other creatures cherished the females of their breed. Revas had made her shiver with longing and weaken with the promise of a happy future. She simply wanted to be a part of his life. A need, she decided, that had been born of their intimacy. Foolishness, for he excluded her at will. She did not fit in here. Never would.

Bother his ill manners; she could not give up without a fight. "What did Father Thomas do to earn your wrath?"

"He overstepped himself."

"That shouldn't surprise you."

Grudgingly he said, "He's a good priest."

"For his fellow man perhaps. It's only women he ill serves."

That notion distracted him. He tilted his head to the side and stared into her eyes.

"What has Father Thomas done?" she asked.

"He admonished me when he should have counseled me."

"That's no answer. What did you do?"

His anger vanished. "I made love to you."

As always in personal matters, she felt inclined to reticence. But if the cleric knew, others would find out. She scanned the crowd to see if his soldiers were listening. They were not. "You told him about us? About last night?"

He stared at something behind her. "He is my confessor."

"But you committed no sin." She, on the other hand, had erred by giving him leverage to keep her in Scotland. But, Lord, the experience had enlightened and satisfied her and made her think for a little while that her dreams could come true.

"Nay, I have not sinned, except to a cleric who cares more for politics than souls."

Aha! "I told you he was such a man. He condemned me for ignoring my vows."

"He condemned me for consummating them."

"Because I cannot now claim the sword of Chapling."

"Exactly. He said you tempted me. Can you imagine such a thing?"

Hedging might be best, for she had planned a seduction of sorts. She hadn't considered that she'd fall prey to her own wanton desire. "He's a poor priest, and yes, the memory of what passed between you and me is quite vivid."

As if trying to hold on to his anger, he folded his arms over his chest and grumbled, "He was always better with a sword than a Psalter."

At least he realized the priest's faults. "You can best him, can you not?"

"'Tis probable."

She took note of the equivocation. The sheriff had said that, too. "Explain yourself."

"Never have we battled in anger, and I committed a folly."

On the field of errors, Revas Macduff was a rank amateur compared to her. She had fallen in love with a man who would force her to live among her demons. He asked the impossible of her. "Go on."

"I boasted that I could defeat him with one arm tied at my back. He'll hold me to it."

In her heart she knew Revas Macduff would prevail. Still, she felt bound to aid him. He had rescued her. She could not claim the sword. Her purpose in Scotland had not been served. "If you allow him to make a widow of me, I will kill you myself."

At the absurdity of her words, he laughed. "We haven't had a moment alone. You retired early last night. Are you truly well?"

She understood what he meant, and his concern pleased her. "Aye."

"You have no discomfort?"

"Only a guilty conscience." She hadn't counted on loving him so much.

"Now you cannot seek an annulment."

She wasn't sure she wanted one. A pity they weren't ordinary people—wheat farmers with weather and pestilence as their most serious concern. A curse on swords and crowns and kingdoms. "No one else has to know, and it needn't happen again."

"I know what occurred." His voice dropped and his gaze sharpened. "And I intend for us to be fruitful and multiply."

Try as she would, she could not separate the man from his heritage. Neither could she do the same with her heart and her hatred for Highland ways. "If I give you sons, you will teach them to be soldiers."

"I'll teach them to cherish and govern and defend this land."

"With a mace and siege engines and no care for their souls?"

"With fairness and strength and a care for their mother's heart."

Mother. She'd have children to nurse and love. Lads to send into battle. Innocent daughters to barter like sheep. "No."

"You're afraid."

A son to be carried home in a litter, his body broken, his soul unshriven. "I hate this warring land."

He clutched her upper arms. "Then help me bring peace to it," he said through clenched teeth. "'Tis within our grasp."

So strong was his conviction, she felt her hatred waver. But other men were ambitious too. "My father enjoys wearing the sword of Chapling and the crown."

"I know. He strutted about the parliament like a cock in a hen yard. 'Tis an empty kingdom he rules."

"While your kingdom is full of righteous-thinking Scots."

He waved an arm. "See you any discord?"

Resolution blanketed her. "Only a man ready to slay a priest."

Rebuffed, he snatched up his gauntlets. "I will not slay him." Again he glanced past her. "Gibby is coming. Will you keep her beside you?"

"She cannot watch. What if you're injured?"

"She's a Highland lassie and accustomed to displays of Scottish valor."

"If taking up a sword to decide a matter of faith is heroism, I'm the queen o' the May."

"Nay. You're the grand princess of the Highland folk, and I am your champion."

"Mine? You said the cleric found fault with you. Has he also belittled me?"

"Aye."

"I'll not be the excuse for bloodshed."

"I must defend your honor."

Realization dawned, and with it came welcome relief from the guilt she felt for loving him. She threw up her hands. "Your valor is misplaced. I suspect he defamed not me, but the Maiden of Inverness. What precisely did he say?"

"He said you sinned as Eve, that you seduced me."

"Your reply?"

"I told him you were innocent."

"You discussed me as if I were a fractious horse that pitched you into the bracken? I'm mortified, Revas. How could you?"

His mouth broadened in a fake smile. "Gibby," he said, drawing his daughter between them. "You're to stay with Meridene."

"Gibby," Meridene said, nudging the girl toward him. "You're to stay with your father." Then she headed for the church.

Male pride be damned. She wasn't some serf's daughter trapped in the justice of the ruling class. She was the Maiden of Inverness.

She almost stumbled at that hated thought. No ceremony. She was a daughter of nobility—nothing more. She would be heard.

She found Father Thomas dressed in battle gear and kneeling at the altar. So sacrilegious was the air in the chapel, she did not genuflect, but waited.

The door opened behind her. Revas stepped inside. The priest rose and came toward them. Flanked by a well-intentioned husband and an angry priest, Meridene lost her patience. "I condemn both of you for poor Christians. Kill yourselves if you will, but not because of me."

Father Thomas radiated condescension. "We do not fight to the death."

"I see. Only until one of you is maimed."

"First blood," said Revas, obviously eager to shed it.

"Why not settle your squabble with bows and arrows and a stout oak for target?" she asked.

Father Thomas slapped his gauntlets against his open palm. "Why not settle it yourself and praise God in the doing by demanding the sword of Chapling? Cutberth cannot know you've lost your innocence."

Like a spent candlewick sputtering in a pool of wax,

her patience waned. "You speak of me as if I were some vessel, necessary to quench your thirst, but bothersome otherwise. How many other women have you served in so shoddy a fashion?"

All imperial and goodly servant of God, he glared down at her. "You have a duty."

She turned to Revas. "You ask why I hate this land of monsters? Look at yourselves and you will see my demons come to life. You're no different than my father or any other Scotsman who covets power. Bend a knee to each other if you will, but leave me out of your rituals!"

Too distraught to continue, she left them there and locked herself in her room. Darkness found her bent over her loom, her heart aching with regrets and her soul heavy with sadness. As she readied herself for bed, she thought of her room at Scarborough Abbey. She thought of the fishwife who made creamy mullet stew. She thought of Sister Margaret and longed for the nun's good counsel. Looking ahead to tomorrow and the next day and the life that yawned before her, she shivered with foreboding. She saw Macgillivrays pouring over the wall and slaying the people of Elginshire; Sim, lying in a pool of blood; Sibeal screaming in terror as they hacked Conal to pieces; Serena and Summerlad ripped apart. Lisabeth and Gibby . . .

She awakened screaming, and she found herself held securely in Revas's arms.

"Shush, Meridene." He rocked her gently. "'Tis over. No one will hurt you now."

She felt chilled, damp, and hollow. "How did you come to be here?"

"You cried out."

A deep shame settled over her. "Did the others hear?"

"Only Serena, and she is unfailingly loyal to you."

"I'm sorry I disturbed you."

"Had you come to table tonight, I would have said that very thing to you."

"Why?"

"'Twas true, what you said in the chapel about Thomas and me. We value our pride more than those we have sworn to protect. For that I am deeply sorry."

"It's all those oaths you swear. You rob yourself of volition."

He gave her a gentle squeeze. "You put it nicely, Meridene. We are selfish creatures who remember warring and forget the things we truly love."

He couldn't love her, not when she feared unto death making a home here. "Are you hurt? Who prevailed?"

"Nay, I haven't a scratch. I bested him at arrows."

They'd taken her advice. The knowledge lightened her weary spirits. "Pity the penitents on the morrow."

A concerned frown creased his brow. "Father Thomas has gone. He felt the need for a pilgrimage to renew his vows. He gave me a message for you."

"I'm not certain I wish to hear it, Revas."

"'Twill cheer you."

"Tell me then."

"He said you were correct about the role of the church. He also said there is no greater concern for a priest than the well-being of God's children, especially eight-year-old girls with no one to protect them."

As Meridene had been. But she'd left that lonely child behind. "It does cheer me, but who will say mass?"

"I've sent to Inverness for a priest. Are you thirsty?" He offered her a tankard. "'Tisn't your favorite, but you might like it."

The honey ale quenched more than her thirst; it answered a question. "You were here once before when I had the dream. You left a tankard of Randolph's ale by the bed."

"Aye. On the night before I relieved Nairn."

She hadn't conjured his smell or imagined his comfort; both had lingered. "How long have you been here tonight?"

"Since high moonrise."

Hours. Yet the fire still blazed. "Have you slept?"

"I've been thinking and occasionally reading the Covenant."

"You respect it more than I."

He shrugged and took a sip from the mug. "I've had years to enjoy it. It must seem odd to you, reading those accounts now that you are an adult and a wife."

More than he knew. "Yes."

"They were very important women, and their writings were helpful to a lad who knew more about skinning animals than leading men."

A butcher's son. "How so?"

"By studying their legacy, I found the courage to break with Edward the First."

She realized how little she knew about his rise to power. "It must have looked insurmountable to you at the time."

"Aye."

"You swore fealty to King Edward in the church before we spoke our vows."

"I had no choice. At three and ten I was too scared to do aught else. He also left an armed guard."

"Did you slay them?"

"Nay." He kicked off his slippers and wiggled his toes. "I took their wealth in tournaments."

"When did you learn to wield a sword?"

"Soon after Edward took you away, Brodie began training me. He would have nothing less than excellence."

"When did the English soldiers leave Elginshire?"

"The last was ransomed by his family five years after you left."

"You were eight and ten, and you bested the Plantagenet guard?"

"I had Brodie and the assurances of the Forbes. Enough about me. Tell me every moment of your sojourn in England."

"Sojourn? I made my home there, and friends, too. And don't change the subject. How did you make so many alliances?"

"I hosted the Highland games and came to know the chieftains. The Macqueens were my first allies. Drummond had been taken by old Edward, and Randolph had just risen to chieftain of his clan. I bested him, and for a reward, I asked to foster Summerlad. We were boon companions from the start."

"What of the Macgillivrays?"

"They attended the games twice. Thereafter only William came. To my disappointment, he also eventually stayed away."

"He sent me a message."

Revas's reaction was slight, a quick movement of his shoulders, but she knew he was surprised. "When? How?"

He must have spoken truthfully when he said he had not looked inside the package containing the bird nest. He had respected her privacy. How *un*Scottish of him, she thought. "He put a note in the gift you brought."

"What was his message?"

"That I was in danger."

CHAPTER

12

"You are in no danger, Meridene," Revas said.

For a week they had argued the point. "You must think me a simpleton."

They stood near the circle of rowans. Traffic had slowed in the yard. Sunlight glinted on the silken coronet that held her veil in place. Revas couldn't stop picturing her beside him in bed, her mouth turned up in a smile of satisfaction, her voice husky with words of devotion.

Buoyed by hope, he said, "I seek only your happiness."

"With armed guards flanking me everywhere I go?" She glared at Summerlad and Brodie, who had accompanied her and Serena on their errands. "Would you enjoy your life were you surrounded by soldiers?"

Pointing out that he was a soldier would only anger her, and Revas was desperate to ease her mind.

Across the yard, the stable doors swung open. A courier in Chapling livery guided his horse into the sunshine. Thank the saints she faced Revas and could not see the rider depart. The message Revas had just received from her father promised trouble, and if Meridene did not acquiesce on the matter of her guard, danger could result. But he knew better than to tell her that.

"Well?" she demanded, her features rigid with determination. "Have you nothing to say?"

"Only that the bachelor's life had its merits."

She tried to look indignant and failed.

He rushed to say, "Summerlad is here to carry your basket and pay court to Serena. Brodie is here to watch them."

"Ha!" She stepped so close, he could feel her resolve. "You will not cajole me into accepting my own personal army. Surely Brodie is enough."

Brodie had offered to escort her now, but her brother William had sent word that he was coming to visit. As soon as he arrived, he could squire her when other matters called Revas away. "Brodie will not carry your basket as Summerlad does. 'Tis beneath him."

Bless Brodie; he folded his arms and planted his feet.

She glared at the war bracelets on the sheriff's wrists. "Naming them porters will not change what they are and what you set them to do. I can carry my own basket."

Be reasonable, Revas told himself. She must agree to protection; events of the last hour confirmed it. Even now, the messenger plodded toward the main gates. "Of course, you can carry your own basket, but then Summerlad must forgo the pleasure of Serena's company."

"He can court her in the common room or at the well." She flung her arm in that direction.

Knowing she would look there, Revas took her hand and held her attention. "His courting is better done with you looking on."

Serena joined the effort. "You cannot go out alone, Lady Meridene. 'Twouldn't be proper."

"Not in the Highlands," Meridene scoffed, her heated gaze fixed on Revas. "It's the fashion of the ladies of Scotland to travel with an army."

He couldn't help saying, "If this is an army, I'm a milkmaid."

She leveled him a look that made Serena cringe. "I will not allow you to make quibbling of my legitimate complaint. I am a prisoner, and I like it not."

Respect for her tempered his reply. "'Tis only for a while, Meridene. Will you abide it to please your husband?"

She closed her eyes and breathed deeply, as if summoning patience. She would not engage in a personal discussion, not with an audience; of that, he was certain. He hoped she would relent and speak privately with him, but since comforting her through the last nightmare a week ago, he had been unable to get her alone. His key to her apartments had disappeared, and watching her elude him in public had become both entertaining and frustrating.

Today he'd had enough, and he sensed she felt the same about their separation. She was just too proud to admit that she missed him.

"Will you?"

She opened her eyes. "Yes, if you will take me riding. Alone."

The contradiction in her request gave him pause. The challenge in her eyes inspired him to deviltry. "Only if we ride hotfoot to pass—"

She slapped her hand over his mouth, cutting off his lover's sally. He kissed her palm.

She jerked her hand away and demanded, "Do you agree?"

He should decline, considering the message in her father's dispatch. But Revas Macduff hadn't gained the respect and allegiance of the Highland chieftains by yielding to Cutberth Macgillivray. Outsmarting him had become a way of life.

"Will you?" she insisted.

The gates swung open. The messenger took his leave of Auldcairn Castle.

Revas relaxed. "Aye. The lilies are blooming in Lord's Meadow. Have Conal pack a basket, and we'll stay the afternoon." He hoped to languish in the field with her and speak of ordinary things. "If you would care to go there?"

That got her attention, but she was still wary; he could see it in her eyes. "The day will be gone before you can ready an army to escort us," she said.

Victory awaited. "'Twill be you and me, Summerlad and Serena."

"No one else?"

"As you say, 'twould take too long to outfit a guard." When her features smoothed out in disdain, he added, "And we do not need an escort."

Insistently she said, "We're going outside the walls, just the four of us?"

"And our mounts."

"Not the plodding mare that brought me here."

She had either forgotten that Revas had taken her up in the saddle with him or chose to ignore it. The latter was logical, for she was ever tentative, especially with others looking on.

Teasing her came naturally. "A stallion?"

Her gaze sharpened. Rising on tiptoes, she leaned close to him and whispered, "Only if he is fleet of foot and soft of mouth."

He was momentarily stunned by her bold innuendo. But he rallied, murmuring, "Your stallion has been known to ride throughout the night and never lose his wind or break his stride. If you have forgotten that his mouth is soft, he is ever willing to refresh your memory."

She drew back, her cheeks pink with embarrassment. Then she shoved her basket toward Brodie. "Will you hold this please?"

Caught off guard, he forgot his role and took the basket. "With pleasure, my lady."

Looking like the queen of the May, she smiled. "How pliant of you, Sheriff." To Revas she said, "I'll speak with Montfichet, then change my gown and meet you in the stables."

"I'll await you there."

She marched off, Serena on her heels.

When they were out of earshot, Brodie sighed. "Forgive my slip of the tongue, Revas. She's too clever for me."

"I know the feeling well, but now we have other business. Both of you, come with me to the stables." When Brodie and Summerlad fell into step, Revas lowered his voice. "Brodie, you're to send Glennie and a dozen men into the forest near Lord's Meadow. They're to stay out of sight while we're there. I want no surprises with Meridene and Serena along. We'll return before nightfall."

Brodie said, "But what of your flank?"

"Send a few men after us, but at a safe distance. If even one of them shows himself, they'll all spend the next fortnight cleaning chain mail."

Brodie called out for Glennie Forbes and relayed the instructions.

Summerlad looked confused. "Why does she refuse a guard?"

A dozen reasons came to mind, and they all involved her hatred of Scotland. What had her childhood been like? With Cutberth Macgillivray for a father, Revas could only guess. When the time was right, he'd ask her. Now he had to keep her safe and make her happy, ofttimes contradictory quests.

"According to the messenger, Clan Davidson has returned to Cutberth's fold."

Not breaking stride, Brodie passed the basket to Summerlad. "How could they be so impatient? They know the Maiden has returned. The Bishop of Nairn swore that word of her arrival has spread over all of the Highlands. Her father even sent one of those hired dogs he calls mercenaries to kidnap her."

He'd forfeit the Halt to have been a spider beneath his throne on the day Cutberth learned that his princess had come home. But a better experience awaited Revas: the moment she donned the crown of rowans and demanded her birthright. "She has yet to call for the sword. Cutberth claims she's an imposter or unwilling. In either case, the Davidsons have always been loyal to the old ways."

"Backward-thinking Highlanders," said young Summerlad. "If a badger held the sword of Chapling 'tween his teeth, the Davidsons would fall to their knees before the beast's lair."

The bittersweet humor of it made Revas smile. He could not send assurances that Meridene would seek the sword, and he could not sway her if he couldn't get her alone. She was coming to like Elginshire. She knew the staff and most of the villagers by name, a result of her determination to avoid Revas.

He'd been of two minds about her strategy. By mingling with the people, she witnessed their contentment and reaped the benefits of their friendship and loyalty.

He'd grown up in Elginshire. With the support and encouragement of the people, he had taken up the cause of unity. Now that hard-won harmony was in jeopardy. But the people had done their part. This afternoon Revas would do his, once he got her alone, and he must, for time was running out.

He waited until they'd passed a crowd at the pie house. "There's more ill news," he said. "Cutberth has sent messengers to every chieftain in the Highlands. If Meridene does not demand the sword, he claims the right of guardianship over her."

Brodie stopped and grasped Revas's arm. "He would take his daughter back, even though your marriage is legal?"

And consummated. Revas suppressed a surge of desire at the memory of the joy they'd shared in the marriage bed. He wanted more from Meridene, and he knew with certainty that passion and physical need would not earn him her trust and friendship. "Aye, and with an army at his back. Cutberth's given her until Whitsunday to appear before him."

Brodie cursed out loud. The noise scattered a gaggle of geese.

It was an impossibly short time, even to a determined man. "She's not to know of her father's ultimatum." He looked from one man to the other. "Have I your word?"

They both nodded.

Summerlad said, "What if she saw the messenger?"

Revas looked at the main entrance. In accordance with his new and unpopular policy of recording comings and goings, the gate was now closed. Could she have seen the rider? He hoped not, for if she had, he would be forced to tell her part of the truth. But her back had been to the gate, and the man had exited before she walked to the castle moments ago.

To satisfy Summerlad, he said, "I doubt she saw the fellow. She was too concerned with bedeviling me."

Brodie said, "What will Bruce do?"

The king of Scotland wanted an alliance with the king of the Highlands. He preferred to parlay with Revas, but Bruce would wait only so long. By showing indecision on the matter of Highland leadership, he looked weak. His patience had its limit. "That depends on how many clans Cutberth can rally before Meridene demands the sword."

Summerlad's face had darkened with anger. "Counting the Davidsons, he's already won back six. The Macqueens and our liege men stand with you."

Drummond and Randolph had been Revas's first allies, Summerlad his first fosterling. "We all stand for the Highlands," Revas said. "If Cutberth comes for Meridene, we will prevail." Rather than receive the crown in the traditional way, Revas would take the sword in battle, reducing the king of the Highlands to a warrior's title.

He despaired, for he wanted to rule according to custom. He wanted Meridene to present him with her father's sword. With good reason, she hadn't the will or the confidence to face her sire. "Summerlad, I'd like private time with Meridene today."

"I understand, Revas."

Revas wanted to woo his wife. He almost chuckled at the innocent thought, for he must keep a tight rein on his desire. Should his passions run amok, he pledged to seek a diversion in the safe topic of Gibby and her new duties as handmaiden. "Meridene has been away a very long time."

The lad sneered. "With the heathen English. They've ruined her for us."

"They only influenced her. She fears her father." As soon as the words were out, Revas regretted speaking them, for he knew how dearly she regarded her privacy. Henceforth, he would respect it.

"Are we to arm ourselves?" Summerlad asked.

"Only with dirk and short sword. We're porters, remember?"

Summerlad laughed. "You're the salt to her spice, Revas."

Lord make it so, he prayed, for he longed for harmony between them. "You're to leave your war bands and your husbandly ambitions here."

Now cocky, Summerlad replied, "What of yours?"

His instinct was to expound, but loyalty stopped him. Meridene would consider their discussion an intrusion of her privacy. Revas had another reason for avoiding the subject; only Brodie and Father Thomas knew of the consummation. "My vows were said years ago."

"And you're too noble to seduce her before she fulfills her duty as the Maiden and claims the sword."

Revas should have felt guilty, but he did not, for he was beholden to a greater cause. "True."

Summerlad shook his head in youthful awe. "She must have been a bonny wee lassie."

"Oh, aye," said Brodie. "All green eyes and hair as dark as moonset. Never was a prettier Maiden born to the legend."

Revas remembered a gentle and clever lass with skin smoother than anything a common lad had ever touched. At the time she knew more about Scottish politics than he. Now he'd taken her part, and she his. Pray that changed, too.

"You were smitten with her from the start," Brodie taunted. "You should have seen him, Summerlad." Brodie elbowed Revas in the ribs. "Soon after King Edward took her away, our butcher's son became a swordsman, and a devil with mace and spear. And the lance—all of his targets were the bloody Englishmen who held his bride."

Too guilty to protest, Revas said, "Let's hope they taught her to ride. Now go and hurry the Forbes."

Meridene guided the spirited stallion toward Revas, who stood with his own mount near an ancient stone structure just inside a stand of towering larches. Dressed in well-worn trunk hose and a quilted leather tunic, he looked like a gentle man, rather than a warrior eager to command all of the Highlands.

He had kept his word. On the far side of the broad

meadow, Summerlad and Serena watched a storm of yellow butterflies frolic in the lilies.

Birdsong filled the air, and squirrels foraged noisily in the trees.

Meridene was alone with her husband.

Grasping her waist, he set her on the ground. "You enjoyed the ride?"

His friendly tone demanded a like reply. "Yes, and thank you."

He leaned against a tree, his shoulders so broad, they blocked out the trunk. "I must confess that I doubted your riding skills. I was wrong. You handle a horse very well."

No wonder the people of Elginshire sought his counsel; his easy manner and friendly smile could melt the coldest heart. But not hers, not when she was a prisoner. Not when her jailer received her father's messenger and kept it to himself.

She'd lost her innocence to him, but she would keep her pride. And if he attempted to seduce her again, she'd fall back on her duties as chaperon for Summerlad and Serena. "There is much about me that you do not know."

Banked passion smoldered in his eyes. With hands equally suited to wielding a broadsword or rousing her passion, he cupped her face. When his lips were only a breath away, he whispered, "I treasure knowing even your most trivial thought."

The urge to fall into his arms nudged at her determination to get to the truth, but she'd come too far to retreat. "What message did my father send?"

Alarm sharpened his features. "Your father's messenger?"

Did he think her a lackwit? She'd spied the rider through the closing gates. "I've seen the livery before."

His jaw grew taut. "You said you wanted nothing to

do with Scottish politics. Have you changed your mind?"

"He's my father."

He moved his hands to her shoulders. "The message does not concern Meridene Macgillivray. 'Tis the business of the Maiden of Inverness."

"How convenient for you. When it suits your purposes you claim I cannot be one without the other. Now that you wish to exclude me, the matter is none of my affair."

"'Twill become your affair when you face the truth that is in your heart."

The canopy of fragrant pine boughs closed in on her. "What truth?"

He picked up a cone and plucked at the seeds. "You scorn tradition, yet you perform the Maiden's duties with a skill to rival Catherine."

The Maiden who revived the legacy of Chapling and Inverness after a century of obscurity. Her mate had been the best swordsman of his day, same as Revas. "I perform ceremonies and school handmaidens."

"'Tis the duty of nobility, Meridene. I did not ask for so much responsibility. I was happy to be a butcher's son." He crushed the pinecone. "You and the tradition that bred you have made my destiny. When other lads were stealing kisses, I was learning to read."

"Was Gibby's mother your teacher?" Meridene flinched at her own cruelty. "I'm sorry."

"Mary was older than me." His expression softened. "And yes, she was a teacher of sorts."

She felt ashamed, but couldn't contain her curiosity. "Did you love her?"

He looked past her. "I cared for her, but you needn't feel jealousy."

Curse him for reading her thoughts. To bedevil him, she thought up a lie and created an imaginary suitor.

"Then you needn't envy the marshal of Scarborough his affection for me."

"Oh, but I do envy the Englishman. Pray he never crosses my path, for you belong to me, Meridene." He tossed aside the remains of the pinecone and pulled her against his chest. "God has ordained it so. 'Tis true we were both young for the ceremony, but time has eased our way. That and the glorious consummation of our vows."

The air smelled crisp with the flush of spring, and the cadence of his voice lulled her into baring her soul. "If my father comes, I will not be the cause of a siege of Auldcairn Castle."

"Will you be the cause of a siege of Scarborough Abbey by your English marshal?"

He referred to her thought-up beau. "You know the answer to that."

He turned her around so that her back pressed against his chest. With a sweep of his hand he indicated the field of white lilies. "Behold this land. You've a kingdom at your feet, love. Many men covet you, but you belong to me." Turning her again, he wrapped her in his arms. "I would sooner pledge my sword to the Saracens as let you go."

Even as he bathed her neck in kisses, she found fault with his declaration. "You think of me as your property."

"Mine to hold." His lips moved to hers. "Mine to admire, and I am yours to enjoy."

The first kiss made a mockery of the word, and the loneliness of the last few days vanished like bees at sunset. A sliver of resistance remained. "What message did my father send?"

His lips were damp from the kiss, his gaze clouded with reticence. "He sent word to the Maiden of Inverness." His eyes met hers. "Are you that woman?"

A denial popped into her mind, but it was a scant echo of her usual reply. "I am his daughter. Did you respond in my stead?"

He sighed and stared into the distance. "Do you not envy the trust Summerlad and Serena share? I fair covet their happiness."

Knowing she would return to the subject of her father's message, she allowed Revas the diversion and turned to spy the young couple. Summerlad paced the field. Serena laughed.

"What are they doing?" Meridene asked.

"He's marking off the dimensions of the castle he intends to build for her. 'Tis his second favorite activity when in her company."

When Serena gestured a protest, Meridene said, "She disagrees with his design?"

"When last I heard them discuss their home, she vowed to live with him in the meanest croft, were that the extent of his holdings. She calls his plans ambitious."

At the sweetness of the sentiment, Meridene felt tears sting her eyes. "She's smitten with him."

Revas kneaded her shoulders. "'Twas not always so."

"What changed her mind?"

"She came to know the gentle soul that lies beneath the warrior."

Weakness spread through Meridene. "Do not expect me to think he learned it from you. You're no lambkin, Revas Macduff, and you do not heed the advice of women."

Close to her ear, he said, "Did I not take up bow and arrow to settle my dispute with Father Thomas?"

"Aye, you did."

"Because I swear on my soul, yours was the better way."

"You flatter me only to seek your own end."

"The line is narrow 'tween flattery and gratitude. I was very angry, and you spoke the truth about Thomas. Do you blame me for heeding your good counsel?"

"And if I counsel you on the merits of returning me to England?"

"I would call you clever, then speak of other things."

"What things?"

He watched the young lovers for so long, Meridene thought he would not answer. At length he said, "I would turn the conversation to Gibby. Does she please you?"

His honesty disarmed her. "Yes. She's eager, but I think she misses gathering plants and making dyes."

"Would you care to don an old dress and go a-foraging with us?"

She tried to summon the old enmity, but failed. "You accompany her?"

"Since the day she first uttered the word 'berry.' She used to stand atop my shoulders to strip the rowans bare. For dowry, I've given her the forest at Elder's Bow."

At the patriarchal duty his admission implied, she thought of her own sire. "What message did my father send?"

"Though it distresses me mightily, I cannot say."

He *wouldn't* say, was more the cause. "And if I proclaim myself Maiden of Inverness?"

"You would have to demand the sword."

"Sorcha did not claim it. She commissioned a new blade. I could do the same."

"Her sire fell in battle and that weapon was lost. Sorcha acquired the very one your father wears."

"What if I duplicate the thing? Why cannot you both be king of the Highlands?"

"For the same reason there can be only one king of Scotland."

"You're trying to trick me," she said.

"Nay, Meridene." Taking her hand, he guided her to a crumbling stone wall. "I'm trying to love and befriend you."

She shivered, but whether from the cool of the shade from or desire, she did not know.

He adored her mouth, nibbling at first, then tasting. Knowing their intimacy had limits, Meridene indulged herself.

At length, he drew back, deep in thought, his breathing labored. "Do you like this place?"

He hadn't intended to discuss the landscape; of that, she had no doubt. Studying him closely, she said, "What was this structure?"

With the flat of his hand, he grazed the ancient stones. "'Twas a settlement, a dwelling of those who came before us. 'Tis primitive, but an improvement over a cave. We've come far since these people laid claim to the land. Someday I hope to pave the road to Elgin's End and line it with merchants—perhaps even an inn."

The pride in his voice drew her, and she understood that his ambitions did not end with the sword of Chapling and the crown of the Highlands.

"What makes you smile?" he asked.

"You're ambitious. You would make a Londontown of this place."

"Aye. Commerce begets prosperity."

His confidence revealed an interesting truth: He aspired to greatness. "You will not seduce me again, will you?"

To her surprise, he laughed. "You cannot hope to lay all the blame on me for the loss of your innocence. You wanted me, yet you questioned my motives. You encouraged me, and in the next breath, you accused me of wanting you merely for political gain."

"I stand by my accusation, Revas."

He picked at the dead vines that covered the old wall. She knew what he was thinking. He had erred in succumbing to desire. He would not do so again. She should have been happy at the knowledge. Instead she felt bound to challenge him.

"Will you deny that you covet the Highland crown?"

He turned and their gazes met. She drew in a sharp breath at the anguish he did not or could not conceal. Like comfort to suffering, she was drawn to him. "Revas—"

"Nay." Looking away, he pretended great interest in the ruins. "You said there was much about you that I did not know. I would have you remedy that. Tell me where you rode and about your English mount."

He spoke of her life in England as if it were as much a thing of the past as the civilization that once inhabited these ruins. Somehow she couldn't summon the will to argue. "The mare's name is Argent."

"A gift from the marshal?"

"No."

"You thought him up because of Gibby's mother."

He'd seen through her ploy. If he expected an admission from her, he'd go wanting until a Scot sat on the throne of England. "What of your twenty kept women?"

Humor flashed in his eyes. "Shall I teach you swordplay to fend off my score of lemans?"

"They are welcome to you, and with my blessings."

"Once, you wanted to cut out my heart and feed it to the eels. Today you would cast me off like a worn glove."

It seemed an age ago that she'd cursed him with so much emotion. Her feelings for him now were softer —loving, and dangerous. "Becoming fish bait is not your destiny."

On a half laugh, he said, "Thanks to you."

"What do you mean?"

"Only that being the chandler's son suddenly has its appeal."

"Because then you wouldn't have been forced to wed me."

In neither expression nor movement did he reveal what was in his heart, but she suspected he was sorry he'd married her.

She pressed on. "You said you favored the bachelor's life."

"I was sorely vexed at you." He sighed and added, "Every man wants an heir."

She hadn't thought of that. "You have Gibby."

"She should have siblings."

Brothers to fight clan wars. Sisters to barter like cattle or banish to a foreign land. Never. "We should see what Serena and Summerlad are about."

He hesitated, then took her elbow. At the edge of the ruin he stopped and held her back. "Shush."

A fat badger waddled across the forest floor, one of her young in her mouth.

Quietly Revas said, "She moves her nest. Be very still or she may forsake the others."

As Meridene watched the animal disappear into the brush, she thought of her own mother and the pain of separation. But the ache didn't come. Somewhere along the way, Meridene had made peace with the mother who bore her, then abandoned her. A new criticism surfaced, and with it came scorn for a woman who, as the Maiden of Inverness, shunned her duties and refused to pass on the legacy to her daughter.

It wasn't that Meridene wanted to wear the crown of rowans. She had disdained the office for too long. But for the first time, she wondered if her rejection was of her own doing. Never had her mother spoken proudly of the legacy; such had been Meridene's schooling and preparation of her destiny.

Revas's hand tightened on her arm. Meridene cast off the disturbing doubts and saw the badger retrace her path. The animal moved toward the spot where their mounts were hobbled.

Leaning up, Meridene whispered behind her hand, "Will the horses frighten her?"

Revas drew her back into the shelter of the ruin. "'Tis only man who threatens her."

"We could rescue the little ones."

"If necessary, but 'tis best to leave mothering to mothers."

Hurt clogged Meridene's throat. She looked away.

"Except where you are concerned," he said softly, and drew her against him. "Do you remember the last words I spoke to you before the old king took you away?"

She felt like a charitable cause, a waif in need of comfort. She'd have none of it. "Repeating a lad's vow changes nothing."

"I swore I would come for you. Upon the souls of all my kinsmen, I pledged to help you fulfill your destiny."

In a matter of weeks he'd changed her opinion of the day that had altered her life. With gentle words and unflagging determination, he'd turned a time of bitterness into a fond memory.

Then he kissed her in the fashion she favored, unrestrained, intense, yet heartachingly tender. She was drawn to his warmth and to the contentment that awaited her.

A soft breeze wafted across her skin, cooling the heat that blazed between them. The forest grew quiet, and if yearning were a sound, it thrived in the beating of her heart and the singing of hot blood through her veins.

Unleashed, his need spoke to her in the language of intimacy, urging her to take the last step and put her soul into his keeping. Caught up in the lure of his persuasion, she ignored the voice of her conscience and yielded her heart.

On an agonized sound, he said, "We should not."

Rather than dash her ambitions, his denial spurred her to change his mind. With hands now familiar with his form, she caressed his trim waist, then moved to the hard ridge of his desire.

A manly groan set off an answering sigh of surrender. Splaying his fingers, he kneaded her buttocks, and his mouth took hers in a devilishly deep kiss. Cool air touched her ankles, her knees, her thighs, and although she did not understand how, she knew he would love her here, where they stood.

As eager as he, she reached inside his hose, and when her hands closed over him, she felt her knees tremble with weakness. Then he was lifting her, setting her legs astride his hips, and she knew what he would do.

Her senses spinning with anticipation, she pushed his tunic up and his hose down, and in the next breath, he made them one.

Relief, as pure as heavenly light, spread through her, but it was only the beginning. His back against an ancient wall, his legs planted firmly in the soft ground, he thrust deeper, setting a rhythm that both primed her need and made kindling of her desire. He took her too close to the edge of rapture, and fearing a quick end, she broke the kiss. "Slowly, Revas."

His eyes drifted open, revealing so joyous an expression, she lost control. And as she yielded to the first tremor of satisfaction, he smiled and joined her. Throbbing in unison, in perfect harmony, they held on tight, until the rapturous moment ebbed, then flowed into absolute serenity.

A blessedly sweet kiss followed, which led to a near bone-crushing hug. "By my oath," he said, "I had not intended to do more than hold your hand."

On the heels of their mind-jarring loving, the anguished confession made her smile. "Shall I shoulder the blame for corrupting you?"

Wincing, he lowered her to the ground and righted his clothing. She did the same, never taking her eyes from his worried frown. "What troubles you, Revas?"

"What if you conceive the next Maiden?"

Euphoria lingered, keeping her misgivings at bay. "If I conceive, it will surely be a lad."

"How do you know?"

It was common for women to speak among themselves of their birthing experience. Conversing with a man on the subject of creation unsettled her. A silly notion, she was forced to admit, considering the intimacy they had shared.

"Don't be shy. Share your thoughts with me."

Oddly comfortable, she said, "Because my mother had three sons before me. As did her mother and grandmother. The Maidens always bear their sons first."

He brushed leaves off his shoulders. "Always?"

"Always."

"How did you know that? I saw no mention of it in the Covenant."

Feeling smug and contented, she trailed her index finger down the front of his tunic. "Not all of the legend is written."

An idea had him in its grasp, yet he slapped his hand over hers. "Ah, womanly secrets inspire me."

She welcomed the leverage of knowing more than Revas on at least one subject, for he was quickly becoming an expert on her. "Inspire you to what?"

Drawing her hand to his lips, he kissed her palm. "To strip you of that bonny blue dress and love you again, unless we attend Summerlad and Serena."

A shiver stole her composure.

"Come, love, the day wanes."

Riding four abreast and laughing all the way, they returned to the castle. In the yard, the sheriff approached them, his face drawn into stern lines.

"A word, Revas," Brodie called out.

Pulling her along, Revas said, "'Twill wait, my friend."

"I fear not."

Revas stopped. She withdrew her hand and left them on the steps. Just as she opened the door, she heard Revas call her back. On the threshold, she stopped, stunned, for there—at a table near the hearth—sat an aging priest. Beside him stood a man who looked so much like her father, she cringed.

"Welcome home, little Maiden."

CHAPTER

13

Revas raced up the steps and into the common room.

Back rigid, hands clasped tightly, Meridene faced her brother, who gazed at her with unabashed affection. The priest stared from one sibling to the other.

A cauldron simmered over the hearth fire. Empty benches and stools had been pushed beneath the tables in preparation for the evening meal. All appeared normal, save the tension that hung like a storm in the close air.

Revas moved quickly to her side, but she was unaware of his presence.

"I thought never to see you again." Her voice was devoid of warmth or scorn.

William's bulky shoulders sagged and his lips thinned. Even in disappointment, he bore a striking resemblance to their father. Did that likeness hold Meridene back, or had she spoken truly when she said she had no love in her heart for her kinsmen?

"And I you, dear sister. Though I prayed for a word

from you. You are well?" His inquiring gaze slid to Revas.

"Well enough, William," she said.

No cutting remark about Scotland. No praise for England. Looking down at her, Revas was reminded of the lass he'd met and wed that day so long ago. Yet time and circumstances had changed her; the brave girl had become a poised woman.

Into the tense silence, Revas said, "Welcome, William and Father John. We've been a-fielding." With a look, he implored William to have patience. "If you will excuse us, we must tidy ourselves."

He felt her awareness a moment before she glanced up at him, and Revas was unprepared to see her green eyes barren of emotion. An hour ago, they had shimmered with excitement and passion.

He swallowed hard. "Shall we rid ourselves of the smell of horse and forest?"

Please, her expression said.

Compassion flooded him, and he cursed himself for thinking her brother's presence would make her happy. Did the demons of her nightmares brave the light of day?

He took her hand. It quivered like the wings of a frightened bird, and her palm was damp to the touch.

As a lad, he'd been unable to protect her. As a man, he'd fared no better. He hadn't thought beyond the physical harm she might suffer. To his dismay, he now knew that Meridene's hurt lay deeper. It was a bitter admission to a man who prided himself on his ability to understand and lead the people of this land.

He turned to escort her from the room.

"Meridene," William called out, as if hesitant to see her go. "I've brought you something." He picked up a large sack that was tied with a rope and held it out to her. "'Tis a letter from my beloved and gifts from my children."

Her breathing grew shallow, and her hand began to shake in earnest. Revas took the package.

A puzzled and waiting William tilted his head. "The other is yours, by right and title."

As silent as a stone, she allowed Revas to draw her from the room. Once in her chamber, she pulled her hand free and poured herself a drink of water. The goblet shook, even though she held it with both hands, and she breathed so deeply, her shoulders rose and fell.

Thinking she needed a moment to order her thoughts, Revas walked to his favorite spot. Half-completed, the new tapestry depicted a massive tree, but what began as the trunk became the torso of a man wearing an empty sword belt. Rather than branches, two arms stretched out toward the tapestry's edge and spread great shadows on the forest floor, where the sword of Chapling lay. Whose face would crown the work?

Brilliantly imaginative in scope and exquisite to each pass of the shuttle, the piece, when finished, would inspire conversation. Unfinished, it engaged his curiosity.

As did its creator.

"Why has William come?"

Tapestry forgotten, Revas approached her. "His arrival does not cheer you?"

"Cheer me?" Color flooded her neck and face. "You expect me to rejoice at the sight of a Macgillivray?"

He felt alone, as if he stood before the gates of his enemy's stronghold with only riderless horses at his back. "Your happiness is my foremost concern."

She put down the goblet, and with much effort, smoothed the wrinkles from her gown. "I thought my safety was."

William had written that she was in danger. "Do you fear him?"

A glimmer of challenge shone in her eyes but was quickly gone. "I do not know him."

But she knew herself and governed her emotions too well. Her feelings were there, in her heart, locked up tight. There he would go. "He favors Cutberth in appearance."

Turning her head to the side, she folded her arms at her waist. "As I recall, yes. Our kinsmen are all fair of face and hair."

William was Revas's age, only a few years younger than Cutberth had been when Meridene last saw her father. No wonder she trembled. The passage of years had not altered her image of the man who spoke to his daughter with his fist and thrust her into the hands of a foreign king.

Her scars were old, long festering, and he must help to heal them. "Tell me how you feel, Meridene."

She sat on the arm of the chair and examined her fingernails. "Honestly, I do not know."

"Are you saddened? Angry?"

"Rather I feel scattered."

Revas knelt beside her. "Should I have asked if you wanted to see him?"

She tried to smile. "As if you would obey me."

Self-pity wouldn't do, not if she was to meet and conquer the ghosts of her past. Reassuring her came easily. "Command me, then," he said. "For I am your champion until the withering of the last thistle."

She sighed and touched his shoulder.

"What," he implored, "is in your heart?"

Her eyes were full of sorrow, and her voice distant. "Past hurts and confusion. The urge to run." She gazed out the window. "An absence of destination."

Like a petal floating on a slow-moving stream, she drifted away from him. Desperate to keep her, he clutched her wrist. "If you will run to me, I will listen. By my oath, I will stand beside you and offer up my life to please you."

Her chin quivered; she pressed her fingers there. "You will expect too much of me."

Of every man, woman, and child he knew, only his daughter spoke so frankly to him. Gibby trusted him. Was Meridene coming to believe in him as well? "Tell me what you wish to do."

Meridene almost scoffed at the question. What could she do? He had made no offer to send William away. He'd given no assurance that her father did not follow. Revas was destined to make her face a past that loomed like a great black void. A tragedy, for in the span of a day she'd soared to the heavens, only to plunge into the depths of despair. Uncertainty and the unknown awaited her.

In his note, William had said she was in danger. From where? Whom?

Fear squeezed her chest, and she longed to retreat to a quiet place where only harmless thoughts and happy days awaited.

Revas held out the sack to her. "Will you accept William's gifts?"

Unaccustomed to hearing her brother's name spoken casually, Meridene didn't know what to feel about the only one of her siblings who'd bothered to befriend her. But William wasn't an adventurous boy. In Meridene's absence, he had acquired a beloved wife and children. No legacy had prevented him from following his heart. No traditions dictated his future.

Bitterness cast a pall over the joy she'd felt earlier in the day. But she must move on, else she'd dwell, helpless, in a bog of sorrow.

Revas was doing his part to aid her, and she did trust him. His reasons for wanting her were plain; he hadn't colored up his ambitions with love words or deceits. From the moment he'd faced her in the ship's cabin, he had been forthright in his mission.

That she'd come to love him felt natural of late. Even so, the future looked bleak. "Yes," she said with all the confidence she could manage. "Let's see what William has brought."

"I love surprises." Revas's agile fingers worked at the knot. So dear, he was, and so willing to run before her troubles.

Anticipation gleamed in his eyes as he peered into the sack. "A letter for you." He plucked it out and put it on her lap.

William had mentioned a message from his beloved. Read it later, her heart pleaded. Learn what other tokens he'd brought, her courage said.

"A gift of—" Revas held a small sack to his nose and sniffed. "The original and very rare scent of heather. From your niece." The bundle joined the letter. "The wee lassie is named for you, the best of all the Macgillivrays." He jiggled his fair eyebrows. "Since Hacon dragged your namesake into his cave."

At the comical image and the artless compliment it implied, Meridene felt her indifference waver and her composure falter. He was playing a part to please her, and in the doing, he revealed yet another delightful aspect to an altogether enchanting man.

Not waiting for a comment, he again delved into the sack. "A string of pinfeathers," he announced. "From William's son to his favorite aunt. The plumage of the black cock brings the bearer good fortune, you know."

Impatience forced her to say, "Leave off, Revas. The boy doesn't know me. I cannot be his favorite."

An expression of mock injury gave him a jolly air, and with great ceremony, he again thrust his arm into the sack. He twisted his wrist, feeling for the items within. Metal chinked. He ignored it and went on with his search.

"Revas?"

His hand stilled. He grew serious.

"What have you found?"

Slowly and with much hesitance, he produced a velvet pouch. Threadbare in places and repaired in many more, the cloth had once been very fine. He worked open the frayed drawstring, but his gaze stayed fixed on her. When he tipped the bag, a golden chain tumbled into her lap.

The other is yours by right and title.

Her first thought was to reject the symbol, but she must overcome the cowardice that made her quake. Willing her hands to still, she picked up the chain.

Catherine's written description had not over-flattered the chain of office. Using the crude tools of his age, the goldsmith had done credit to his craft. Cloverleaf-sized links in the shape of cinquefoils were connected with small discs, each bearing a thistle, the ancient symbol of Clan Chapling. The belt symbolized the marriage of the Maiden to the king of the Highlands.

"The Maiden's belt?" Revas asked.

Without doubt, it was, but Meridene had never before seen it. "Why didn't my mother wear it? She styled herself the Maiden."

"Perhaps she was like Isobel and took up only some of the duties. Not every Maiden served with the dedication and authority of Meridene."

She spread her hands over the items in her lap. "I do not seek the legacy, Revas. And I am unprepared for so much responsibility."

He watched her closely. "'Tis your choice to make, and I must confess the pocked keys to Auldcairn Castle will surely corrupt your golden chain."

Charm came effortlessly to him; another of his admirable qualities. He also seemed vulnerable—odd, considering she was the one facing the demons. But not alone, not if she wished his help.

Decisively he returned the items to the sack, taking great care with the feathers. "'Twill wait," he said, as if her decision were none of his affair. "I'm certain you'd like to bathe."

She thought of their heated coupling amid the

moss-covered stones. The last safe moment she might ever know, for her life was irrevocably changing. "Because of what we did at the ruins?"

"Nay." He kissed her nose. "Because you smell of the *other* stallion."

Before she could protest at his vulgarity, he rose. "I'll send in your handmaidens and have Sim show Father John to Thomas's quarters. Then I'll settle William in the south tower."

"How long will he stay?"

Plaintively he said, "Till Whitsunday, I would suppose, unless you wish it otherwise."

Whitsunday was a fortnight away. "Did you send for him, or does he come at my father's bidding?"

"He will break from Cutberth. He even wears the Macgillivray tartan, not the cloth of Chapling."

She hadn't noticed William's garments; she'd been unable to take her eyes from the face she remembered all too well. "He called me little Maiden."

"'Twas the first time?"

"No, but why would he address me so, unless he thought I had returned to Scotland willingly?"

He cleared his throat and glanced at the door. "I cannot speak for William Macgillivray."

He avoided the subject. Why? "You led the people of Elginshire to believe I'd returned cheerfully."

Looking like a man who didn't know what to do with his free hand, he rubbed his thigh. "I am guilty of that."

"But not without remorse of late."

"Aye. I am, as you say, ambitious and overeager to grow old in peace among these people. I should like to see all of my children and all of their children christened in the chapel."

Simply said, the noble thought spoke loudly of his sense of duty. So seldom had she been a party to such unselfish stewardship, she felt honor-bound to endorse it. "The people of Elginshire are fortunate to have you."

He acknowledged the compliment with a poignant smile. "What will you do?"

After a bath and a little more time to reassure herself, she would face her brother. "Ask William to join us at table. Shall you and I go together?"

The sack hit the floor. A broad smile perfectly transformed him into the lad she'd known long ago, a butcher's son who'd promised to come for the Maiden of Inverness.

He swept her into his arms and hugged her fiercely. "Always, my love."

His devotion disarmed her, and if she didn't watch herself, she'd grovel at his feet and find herself nose-deep in Scottish intrigues, a crown of rowans on her head.

"Wait!" he said, and held her at arm's length. "What if Montfichet serves your English fare?"

He looked so engrossed in the dilemma, she grasped the opportunity to lighten the mood. "Stuffed eggs and spring greens?"

"Not," he said with great effect, "the typical Scotsman's fare."

An odd choice of words, for he was anything but typical. "Then I shall eat more than my share," she said. "And William will have an adventurous meal. But what will you do if Montfichet serves haggis?" Revas hated haggis.

He looked deeply into her eyes. "I shall persevere." Softer he said, "The new tapestry is exceedingly fine."

Pride glowed inside her, and she almost flung her arms around his neck. But she'd been alone with her feelings for too many years, and decorum reigned. "Thank you."

"Do not forget," he said sternly. "You were a clever lass when last you saw William. Shall I tell him of the siren you've become?"

The ruins. The lovemaking beneath a canopy of larches. If Revas spoke of their—

"'Twasn't *that,* Meridene." Hands on his hips, arms akimbo, he looked affronted to his soul.

A smile brightened her spirits and embarrassment heated her cheeks. He'd done his best to banish her fear; she must return the favor, and with friendship. "You're a devil and more, Revas Macduff."

"So Brodie often says, but I swear the sound of it is sweeter upon your lips." He cupped her cheek. "Name me the grandest fool o' the Highlands, but I think I should summon your handmaidens."

The courteous remark and loving gesture smacked of evasion, for Revas Macduff was ever the rogue. He was prepared to leave, but why? Unless—The truth dawned, and she didn't know whether to accuse him of intrigue or compliment him for a gallant. "You wish to speak alone with William."

He licked his lips and stared at her lap. "I wish to ease your troubled mind and await your pleasure."

When he did not move, she knew he'd trapped himself with contradictions. To learn the truth, she must make him squirm in the lair. Boldness was her tool.

She lifted her brows. "You would depart, rather than pour my bath?"

Immediately alert, he looked deeply into her eyes. Bless his roguish heart; he was weighing his options. She lifted her brows.

"'Tis unfair, Meridene, to pose a quandary now."

"You haven't always been fair to me."

"Fairness often fails in matters of the heart."

A devil snatched her tongue. "'Twasn't your heart I hoped to engage in the bath."

His mouth dropped open, and he blinked in surprise.

A smile tickled her cheeks, but she held her composure.

"Siren doesn't suit you." He pointed an index finger at her. "Vixen does."

She did smile then, and when his eyes narrowed, she thought the exchange singularly fine.

His jaw worked, and his thoughts showed clearly in his keen gaze. Then his expression turned doleful. "Heed me well. Should I stay and visit upon you the lust that gnaws at my loins, 'twill make us inexcusably tardy. 'Tis poor manners, you must agree, in any man's house."

She flamed with mortification, but pressed on. "Especially when the object of your lust is a wife who is known to be chaste?"

"If you are chaste," he said pointedly, "then I am a Cornishman."

She laughed and truthfully said, "And I've exhausted my lovers' sallies."

He grasped her chin and lifted her face. Moving close, he murmured, "'Tis enough spice from you."

"Be gone, Revas."

"And should you wear that pink silk concoction to table tonight, I shall revive Hacon's part."

She flustered. "You never would!"

In a trice, he thought, and let the desire flow over him. Praise Saint Columba, he'd been given a prize for wife. He forced himself to kiss her cheek, when he wanted to suckle her breasts.

"Curse you, Revas Macduff, for leaving me with one of your dreadful quandaries. I adore the pink gown."

He left her there, her lovely features pert with challenge, his loins afire with lust, and went in search of William Macgillivray.

"I had hoped for so much more at my first meeting with her. What has happened to Meridene?"

William stood near the mullioned windows in the south tower, his arm propped on the casement. Revas sat on a wooden bench near the brazier, his mind whirling with indecision.

He chose the truthful path. "She has suffered mightily at the hands of her kinsmen." Guilt forced him to add, "And mine, too, for she did not embrace her return to Scotland."

"You forced her?"

"She's my wife."

"But abduction—"

"'Twould not have been necessary had the Macgillivrays not forsaken her thirteen years ago."

Squinting, William stared into the yard. "'Tis a wretched lot, having Cutberth Macgillivray for father."

"Especially for the only daughter."

Lips pursed, William shook his head. "She was a bright lass, sooner to walk and quicker to learn than any of us. Our little Maiden."

"She noted that you addressed her just so."

"And felt the butt of my father's knuckles, did he hear of it."

The first Vesper bell sounded. Soon the din in the village would cease. Stalls would close as the faithful of Elginshire thronged to evening prayers. Civility made him say, "Will you attend church?"

"Not this eve. I accompanied Father John from Inverness. He has heard my confession."

William's misery was heart-deep, and Revas felt bound to ease it. "I believe you can revive her affection, if you go slowly."

"She said as much?"

"Not in so many words, but I'm certain 'tis true."

"What else did she say of the past?"

"She wondered why your mother never wore the Maiden's belt."

"'Twas always in our father's keeping. I took it on my last visit to Kilbarton."

Revas grew fearful. "What will he do when he finds it missing?"

William scoffed. "'Twas hidden in his sanctuary and buried 'neath a layer of dust."

"Your mother never pined for want of the chain of office?"

"Not that I ever heard of. Our mother is—" He stopped and sighed. When he spoke again, it was with an apology. "My father never honored the traditions of the Maiden. He's fond of saying that had our mother not been a good breeder, he would have cast her off. Thank God she delivered all of her children safely."

Revas stared in confusion. "What of the miscarriage?"

"Oh, nay," he said with much emotion. "Not our mother."

A lie. Their mother had miscarried her first child; of that, Revas was certain. She had put it down in the Covenant.

Pity they had not broached the subject years ago, when William attended the Highland games at Elginshire. Still, Revas intended to learn what he could about the workings of the Macgillivray family. "Your mother set down no words in the Covenant." Not words. Only dates.

"True. My father bragged of it. But how do you know that?"

As always, Revas felt a part of the traditions. Years of studying the chronicles had made it so. "On the day we were wed, Meridene left the book with me for safekeeping."

William crossed the room and plopped down in the chair that faced Revas. "Ah. Father wondered how you knew so much about the customs. He calls you a cur pup who favors the ceremonies of women and says you are too cowardly to try to take the sword from him in battle."

By way of gossip, Revas had heard that insult and a dozen more. "'Tis a mistake for Cutberth to recall my greener days."

"He tries to goad you into war again."

In the fall of 1307, with Bruce's army at his back, Cutberth had commanded Revas to surrender, else he'd put Nairn to the torch. Outnumbered and outsmarted, Revas had no choice but to retreat to Elgin. Two days later, word had come of Nairn's fall. Upon hearing of Cutberth's treachery, Bruce had distanced himself from Highland politics. Cutberth returned to his Highland throne, but the taunts continued.

If he engaged Revas again, he would see a different soldier. "Your father wears a bloody crown."

William laughed, but the sound held no humor. "Who better than I knows the cruelty of which he is capable?"

Revas's throat grew thick. "Meridene knows. His treatment of her is beyond redemption. Never has he cared about her."

"How could he care for her when only God and she could alter his destiny? From the moment she understood the importance of her birthright, her fate with Father was sealed. He knew he must one day yield his power to her."

Revas reached for his dirk. "Do you defend him?"

"Sweet Saint Ninian, nay, and sheathe your blade." When Revas did, William continued. "Our father scarcely looked upon Meridene, and always with scorn. Poor mite."

Affection for that forlorn girl filled Revas with rage. "He's a fool."

William shot to his feet. "Never take him for that, Revas. He is clever beyond pride, and if you value your life and hers, you will hurry my sister to Kilbarton to claim the sword."

"Easier said than done, William."

Sadness wreathed his features. "How fares her heart?"

With great pride and satisfaction, Revas smiled. "'Tis mine, and her affections, too."

"Then why the delay in claiming her birthright? She spoke of little else as a lass." He chuckled at the memory. "Bedeviled Mother so often for the Covenant, 'twas finally put away and forgotten."

Ah, so she had cherished the legacy at one time. "'Tis facing Cutberth that she fears. What is he about?"

William rubbed his face, then shook his head, as if to clear it. "The king of the Highlands has petitioned the king of Scotland. If Meridene does not claim the sword by Whitsunday, father demands that Bruce bring his army northward and put an end for all time to your claim to Clan Chapling."

Unity would crumble. The Highlands would revert to a land of warring clans. "Robert tours the land in goodwill. He swore as much to me at parliament. But we shall see. Meridene does not know of your father's ultimatum."

"Is that fair to her?"

"She needs time, William. She's been away from us more years than not."

"I ken your meaning."

"Good, and I'm to invite you to join us at table tonight."

Hope sprang to William's eyes. "Her words or yours?"

"Both, and a word of warning, my friend. Recall only the happy moments when you speak of her childhood."

He grinned. "Many of those times did she and I share."

Satisfied, Revas got to his feet. "I wonder what delicacy has Montfichet prepared."

"For the gift of my sister's company, I will gladly dine on swill and leavings."

Meridene pushed aside the leeks and toyed with the braised hare on her plate. Conversation at the crowded table settled to a dull din. Revas occupied the lord's place at the head. Brodie sat at the far end with the best of the soldiers. Summerlad sat between Serena and Lisabeth. Ellen chatted with Glennie Forbes. With the new priest on her right, Gibby sat beside Revas and across from Meridene.

Her attention strayed to the man on her left. William, the brother who'd cherished a bird's nest and taught his sister to whistle.

At the sentimental thought, her stomach floated.

Revas took her arm. "I've made a dreadful error."

Seated at the head of the table, he looked so serious, her discomfiture grew. "What have you done?"

A roguish twinkle appeared in his eye. "I warned you against wearing the pink gown, but I misspoke. The green is more pleasing to my eye and other parts."

The tension left her, replaced by a flush of impatience. Behind her hand, she said, "Bother you and your other parts. You speak boldly to distract me."

As charming as a prince on coronation day, he grinned expansively. "How am I faring?"

She shook her head. "Well enough, and you know it. I should slap you."

"Much better options await those bonny hands."

"Oh, yes," she teased in a breathless whisper. "After we sup, I shall capture your king in twelve moves."

"Meridene," said William. "Do you remember the berry tarts Cook used to make?"

She latched on to the reprieve from Revas's seductive conversation. A fond memory popped into her mind. "Aye, I remember the tarts."

"And the nutcake with trinkets inside on your birthday?"

The cook hadn't gone to any trouble. The cake, baked with an assortment of toys, was actually a Hogmanay tradition, and her birthday happened to fall on the holiday of New Year's. She shuddered to think of the fare had she been born on Hay Stack Night. "You broke a tooth on the little drum."

"You almost swallowed the tiny sword."

To the table at large, William said, "Once, our brother, Robert, filched a keg of October ale from the stores. We hid in the dungeon and drank ourselves sick." He rolled his eyes in embarrassment. "'Twas Hogmanay, and our parents were in Inverness. Had Meridene not found us first, we'd still call that dungeon home."

Remembering, Meridene smiled. "The smell of their retching drew me down there."

"How old were you?" Revas asked.

"Five, I think."

"Wrong," said William. "You were four and still small enough to hide under our beds and spy on us."

"Yet she braved a dungeon to save you," said Revas.

William nodded, affection glowing in his eyes. "Aye, she was ever the stalwart lass."

Revas stared at a point over Meridene's shoulder. She turned, but saw no one behind her. "What is it?"

Then Revas was grinning.

"What?" she insisted.

He shook his head, but some jest had him in its throes.

"A game of chess, Revas?" asked William.

Expansively he said, "Only if my lady watches me win."

Revas's good humor grew as he captured William's king for the second time.

William slapped the table, then pushed to his feet. "Losing twice is enough."

Revas touched Meridene's arm. "Will you play? I've a mind to win a flower penny."

"Revas gave you flower pennies?" William looked from one to the other.

He'd brought to life a favorite tale of true chivalry, but not without a price she must pay. "He is ever generous in matters concerning the Maiden."

Admiration softened William features. "Do you remember the old penny Grandmama Ailis had?"

"Yes."

"Now our children will have their own." In a gesture of goodwill, he clasped Revas's shoulder. "They'll pass them on to our grandchildren."

When it came to legacies, Meridene had experienced the dregs. Even in her own family, she had fared the poorest, except her mother. *"If* the children are not killed in battle or bartered."

He sent her a look he'd learned from their father. "I value my children."

Years of loneliness came rushing back. "A lesson you learned after the family gave me away."

Revas cleared his throat. "Sleep well, William."

Meridene glowered at him, then at her brother. "You're being sent off to bed."

"Meridene . . ."

The admonition in Revas's voice sounded so paternal, she thought of her own sire. "I should like to have seen father's face when he learned of my return."

William studied the shields on the wall. Everyone in the room, from Brodie to Serena, stared expectantly at Revas. Only Gibby and the other handmaidens were unaware of the anticipation.

"Well?" Meridene insisted. "What did he say?"

The stillness was broken by Revas, who raised his arms and stretched. "I'll wager Cutberth feared you would turn the flower pennies back to gold and make me the richest man in Christendom."

Relieved laughter settled like a blanket over the

others in the room. With quiet insistence, Meridene addressed William. "You have not answered me."

His eyes found hers. "I was not there when the news reached him."

But he knew, and he'd keep the information to himself. He was welcome to it, for she didn't care a soiled slipper what her father thought of her return. She simply wanted to anticipate what he would do. How frightened should she be?

"In any case," Revas went on, "'tis late to broach the subject of Highland politics. I intended to ask William if he remembers how to thatch a roof. Macduff's Halt awaits."

Meridene wasn't fooled. She stood. "If you'll excuse me, I'll practice turning wood to gold."

"While you fill my treasury," Revas said, "tell your handmaidens the tale of Hacon. A lass should be prepared for the likes of him."

CHAPTER

14

At his cleverly worded threat, Meridene retired. Standing near the loom, she watched as Gibby banked the fire and made sure the windows were closed tight. Ellen laid out Meridene's sleeping gown and turned down the bed. Lisabeth helped her undress, then brushed and plaited her hair.

Too confused to sleep, she sent Gibby to fetch the Covenant from Revas's room. When the girl returned, she excused all three. Lighting the lamp, she climbed into bed and broke the seal on the letter from William's wife.

To Meridene, the Maiden of Inverness:

Praise God you have come home, my lady. I entreat you, in the name of your ancestors who lie buried here among us, to take our cause close to your heart, that you may make haste and assume the duties to which you were born. Forsake us no more.

Forsake *them?* Bitter laughter welled up inside Meridene, and she tossed the letter aside. Where were their concerns when a Scottish child cried herself to sleep on a narrow cot with only cold abbey walls to hear? She knew her English friends missed her even now, and the people of Elginshire had prepared for her return.

Take the Macgillivrays' cause close to her heart? What of her causes? Bother her family. She owed them nothing. Their needs were none of her affair.

She opened the Covenant to the page written by her grandmother.

I am the Maiden Ailis, daughter of Sorcha, and I fear I have given my own daughter to a monster. Cutberth Macgillivray came honorably to ask for my Eleanor's hand. With my eternal soul as ransom, I swear I did not know of his cruelty and his obsession to end the legend of the Maiden. Should I tell my husband, he will storm Kilbarton Castle and demand the return of our lass. But Cutberth enjoys his prime, and his skill with a sword is legend. I will not trade the life of my beloved. I am the most wretched of mothers and the poorest of Maidens.

Sorrow choked Meridene, for she remembered her grandmother as a contented and kind woman who told tales of villains turning golden coins into flower pennies, and she had exhorted Meridene to honor the traditions of the Maiden.

Her last words to Meridene took on new meaning. It was years ago, on the occasion of Meridene's journey south to celebrate her betrothal to Moray's heir. She'd been a child in awe of an ancient wooden coin.

"Your time will come, Meridene," Ailis had said. "My Eleanor has named you for the first and the best of us. I pray you have been given to a man who will honor us all and save the Highlands from the wrath of Edward Plantagenet."

Meridene thought of Revas. Were Ailis alive today, she would have rejoiced at Meridene's husband. Their marriage was particularly ironic, for it had come at the command of the very English king Ailis feared.

Grandmama had been correct in her judgment when she named Cutberth Macgillivray a monster.

Now Meridene had but to turn the page and read her mother's words. Did Eleanor bemoan her life and curse her husband? Did she lament the loss of her daughter?

For a dozen reasons, Meridene stilled her hand. She felt pity for her mother. Eleanor deserved better than Cutberth; every woman ought to have a husband to cherish and honor her, to protect and nurture all of the children of her womb, not just the boys.

A flick of her wrist would reveal her mother's reflections on her reign. Would her words to Meridene be kind and at last loving? Would she express regret at her indifference to the tenets?

The door opened. She looked up to see Revas step into her room. Like a youth fearing detection, he eased the door shut. But when he turned, he bore the look of a man determined to claim his woman.

Still miffed at his despotic behavior, she gave him a bland stare and closed the book. "What do you want, Revas? Or should I name you Hacon?"

That look of tried patience was too familiar to mistake. For effect, he slid the bolt into the jamb. "If you would but try," he murmured, "I'm certain you can reason out why I am here."

"I reason better on English soil."

He blew out his breath and approached her. "Shall we make a quarrel of it, Meridene?"

His boldness should not have surprised her, but it did. "I'd sooner argue with a braying ass."

The mattress crackled beneath his weight. "Shall I scour the village and find you one?"

She scooted to the head of the bed. "Only if Leeds is the village you scour."

The beast laughed and snatched the Covenant from her hands. "You cannot wound *me* with your ready tongue—not when William has sharpened it. You are not truly angry with me."

"You aided him when he would not answer me."

In exasperation, he stared at the tapestry over the bed. "I thought to keep peace in my own castle. You could have taken your argument elsewhere. Why should Brodie and the others witness you and William squabbling like children?"

She hadn't considered that, hadn't imagined their discussion would be perceived as a disagreement between siblings. Most times she thought of herself in a singular fashion. "It would not have come to a squabble."

He held up his thumb and forefinger in measure. "You were this close."

Drawing her legs beneath her, she sat up straight. "Ha! I do not know him well enough to engage in an argument."

He fell back across the mattress, his arms behind his head. "You do not speak openly of yourself when others are listening. You are a private person, although not so much as when you first came home. Still, I feared you would regret revealing so much of yourself in public."

True, she had changed. That he had anticipated her feelings filled her with joy. "You thought to spare me embarrassment later."

"Aye. I know the both of you. I spent years with William, drinking and wenching—" He stopped and gave her a pained expression.

Her mind latched on to the word. "Wenching?"

Suddenly affable, he touched her knee. "Look,

Meridene, 'twas nothing. Just lads reveling . . . and . . . foolish talk."

Had she not been so jealous, she would have enjoyed seeing him squirm. "Foolish? I doubt that. I'm certain you take your wenching seriously."

"I don't suppose you would be willing to look upon those times as preparation for my marriage to you?"

It was the last thing she expected him to say. She said the first thing that popped into her mind. "Had I been cloistered, I would know better than to believe that worthless chaff."

He lifted his brows in entreaty. "Then could you perhaps view it as the misspent youth of a poor butcher's son?"

For a man of his size and strength, he squirmed handsomely, with grace and charm. She seethed with satisfaction. "Not even if your wenches were toothless crones."

"You would have preferred a chaste husband?" He drew lazy circles on the bedcovers. "Here in your bed?"

"I would have preferred no husband at all."

With the tips of his fingers, he touched her forearm. "You cannot deny that you enjoy our intimacies."

He wanted to drop the subject of his transgressions. Relishing his discomfort, she resisted. "You wish to practice your wenching here? Now?"

Far too reasonably, he said, "A man cannot wench with his wife."

"For that base logic, I should be grateful?"

His hand stilled. "Gratitude is not what I seek."

Oh, no. Not Revas Macduff. He lounged in her bed as if it were his own. And according to the law, it was, along with all of her possessions. "You hope to make me forget your sordid past?"

"I hope to hear you again say my name and God's in the same breath."

Warmth pooled in her belly. He moved up and over

her, his face a hand's length away, his eyes filled with longing. "But were I given only one wish, 'twould be to hold you in my arms tonight and have harmony between us."

Conversing with him was the easiest endeavor she had ever known. He exuded warmth and honesty.

She smiled in appreciation of yet another of his attributes. "Do you know what my father said when he learned that I had come home?" Why had she named Elginshire home?

He jerked away and put the Covenant on the table by the lamp. Sitting on the edge of the bed and staring at the wall, he said, "Nay, and I'd trade my place in paradise to have been there."

He meant it, and she felt their closeness grow. "You know him far better than I. What do you think he did?"

"What any frightened coward does. He found a weaker man and spent his wrath."

"A frightened coward? My father?"

Turning, he glanced at her over his shoulder. "'Tis for certain he fears *you*—even above the king of Scotland."

"That's preposterous. Why should he fear me?"

"Because, my cloistered lass, he must yield his power to you, the Maiden of Inverness."

"You cannot be so certain of that. Even if I did— and I have not said I would—declare myself the Maiden of Inverness."

With his index finger, he tapped her nose. "*You've* been away too long. You belittle your importance in the matter of who wears the crown of the Highlands."

Ten lifetimes wouldn't be long enough to evade Cutberth Macgillivray. "My father will not hand over the sword to me."

Yes, he will, Revas's expression said. "He has no choice, not with his people as witness and his sons flanking him."

"A public spectacle." She cringed.

"May we please speak of happier things?" He flipped onto his back and settled his broad shoulders into the mattress. "I am weary of Scottish politics, and the mention of your father fair sours my stomach."

"On that," she declared, "you have my complete agreement." But her mind held an image of her father on bended knee, yielding up the sword of Chapling to the daughter he'd wronged.

"Would you care to tell me what message William's wife sent?"

What if Cutberth could tell she was no longer a virgin and publicly shamed her for it? She fled from the horror of that possibility and harkened back to the subject of her sister-in-law. "You would hear her words, even if they are political in nature?"

He kicked off his slippers. "I take back the question. Share a pleasantry with me. Tell me the plans Serena and Summerlad have made for their finest hour."

Lamplight flickered on the moonlit scene on the tapestry overhead. The goings-on below appeared just as peaceful to Meridene. "Their wedding is also political."

"Then I forbid you to—How can speaking their vows . . . ?" His expression turned sly. "'Twas a jest you were making."

She faced him boldly. "Yes."

"At my expense."

"Completely."

He winked. "Good housewifery, that."

Flattered to her naked toes, she smiled down at him and thought herself as fortunate as her namesake. "Hacon, indeed," she scoffed.

He sighed contentedly and closed his eyes. "Leave off, and tell me again about your fine English mount."

"Why?"

"I'm tempted to go a-raiding for new horseflesh and delicacies."

Delicacies. She understood. Rather than admit he'd come to England solely for her, he had praised the English ports for their fresh fruit. So well tended was the memory of that conversation, Meridene felt she had always known his tastes.

"Unless the beast has a rough mouth and plodding gait. Then I would hear you retell the tale of donning that chastity belt." Laughter rippled his chest and danced in his eyes. "I'll wager you played the tart that day."

Pleasant moments from her past clamored to be shared. When he took her hand, Meridene told him about the day her mare had outdistanced Johanna Benison's exalted hunter.

He spoke of the Highland games at Elginshire and the year the duke of Ross traded five-score sheep for a yearling from Revas's stallion.

He kissed her good night and left. Meridene fell into a restful sleep. A popping sound awakened her. She opened her eyes and screamed in terror.

Flames climbed the bed hangings.

Hours later, Meridene stared, shocked, at the destruction the fire had wrought. Serena mopped up dirty water from the stone floor. Summerlad pulled the scorched mattress from the bed frame. Sim yanked the charred remains of the bed hangings from the canopy. Gibby huddled in the corner, her shoulders shaking, her face buried in her hands. At her feet, the terrier whined in confusion.

Revas paced the floor, his hair singed, his face dusted with soot. The acrid smell of smoke hung in the air, a constant reminder to Meridene that her beautiful sanctuary had been invaded. Thank goodness no rushes covered the floor. Her looms were spared, and her clothing untouched. The fire had been contained to the bed and several of the small floor tapestries.

Who could have wreaked this havoc?

The answer did more than lay blame for the near tragedy; it told her just how desperate her father was and how frightened she should be of him. Without doubt, this was his work, for she had no other enemies in Scotland.

Her own father had tried again to kill her.

The knowledge bewildered her, and she turned to flee the room.

William made an untimely entrance.

"Sweet Lord, what happened here?"

Looking at her brother, Meridene was reminded of countless and long-suppressed confrontations with Cutberth Macgillivray. She did not try to hide her scorn. "I should think it's obvious."

"Are you hurt?"

"No." Not where anyone could see.

"I'm sorry we quarreled, but I thought you wanted no part of your heritage."

Her first thought was to keep her own counsel, but the urge to express herself won out. "I did not ask you what my father thought about the return of the Maiden."

He opened his mouth, then closed it. "I do not understand. You *are* the Maiden of Inverness."

Even William could not separate the woman from the legacy. She considered reminding him that she was also a child of Cutberth and Eleanor Macgillivray, same as he, but he wouldn't understand that, either.

A hand touched her shoulder. "*I* ken your meaning," Revas said, then addressed William. "Have you come to help?"

"Aye. What can I do?"

Revas jerked his head toward Summerlad. "Help

him haul out what's left of the bed. We'll discuss what happened here later."

To Meridene's relief, William nodded, picked up one end of the blackened leather mattress, and dragged it out the door. Sim followed, his arms filled with the ruined velvet drapings.

Serena leaned on the mop handle. "What could have happened?"

A father tried to kill his daughter, Meridene thought morosely. But did Revas speak the truth when he said her father plotted against her out of fear, rather than hatred? Did her mother know and condone Cutberth's treachery? Did the answer lie in the Covenant? Meridene glanced at the book and knew that she must find the strength to read her mother's words. But heaven help her, she'd had enough shock for today.

"'Twas my fault."

Gibby's tearful admission broke the silence.

Revas knelt at his daughter's side. "Nay, lass."

"I banked the fire poorly." She gazed up at Meridene. "I'm sorry."

Her misery pushed Meridene into action. She, too, moved to comfort the girl. "The brazier was perfectly tended."

"I've ruined it all. I'm unfit to be a handmaiden."

Revas pulled her into his arms, dwarfing her tiny form. "Never say that, sweeting."

"Misfortune was the cause," Meridene insisted, her heart aching for the girl.

"'Twas a villain's work," he said.

Gibby cried harder. "I'm wretched to my soul."

He squeezed his eyes shut. "Oh, nay. You're my special gift from God."

The girl leaned back and looked her father in the eye. Chin quivering, she said, "I should not have come here to live. You're only being nice because you love me."

His chest swelled, and he clutched her to him in a death grip.

"'Twasn't your fault, Gibby." He carried her to the window. "The glass was broken from the outside. See the shards on the floor? Had the damage been done from here, the glass would have fallen outside, into the flower garden."

He was speaking of an intruder. Gibby was thinking of the fire itself. To aid his failing logic, Meridene said, "Gibby, did you clip the candle wicks when Lisabeth forgot?"

Gibby twisted in his arms. Her yellow smock was smeared with soot from his soiled hands and clothing. "Aye."

"Didn't Ellen thank you twice yesterday for sweeping the floor after she spent too long in the common room?"

She sniffed and rubbed her nose. "Aye, but she fetched the stool so I could reach the windows."

"You complete every task in great good cheer, and you have made friends with the other girls. You do not even laugh at Ellen's carrying on."

Revas shot Meridene a look of sheer gratitude. To Gibby he said, "You're a thoughtful girl who never gathers wool."

"Nay, Papa. I gather berries and lichens for the dyes."

He made a funny face and pointed to his head. "Woolgathering."

She tucked her chin to her shoulder. "Oh."

"The brazier did not start the fire," he insisted.

Gibby searched the room. "What did?"

"A devil came through the window."

Serena dropped the mop. The wooden handle clattered loudly on the stone floor.

Gibby's red-rimmed eyes widened in surprise. "Someone tried to hurt Lady Meridene?"

That explanation wouldn't do. Meridene had to

help them. "You both are wrong," she said, keeping her voice calm and reasonable. "The brazier door was latched tight, as were the windows. The glass was shattered from the heat of the fire. I was reading in bed and forgot to put out the candle. I was the careless one, not you." She glared at Revas. "And certainly no intruder."

As serious as Meridene had ever seen him, he said, "I do not color up the truth for Gibby."

"Is that the Highland way?" she challenged. "Spare the children nothing?"

He stared at his daughter, but didn't actually see her. "We'll discuss it later, Meridene."

Eager to see Gibby put the matter behind her and get back to being a bright and contented child, Meridene stood her ground. "We'll make an argument of it now, Revas Macduff."

She smiled at Gibby. "Serena will walk with you to the tanner. You're both to wait there with Ellen until he has sewn my new mattress."

Uncertain of what to do, Gibby looked up at her father. "Are you going to quarrel with Lady Meridene?"

"Most certainly, he is," Meridene rushed to say, then smiled. "He fancies himself clever with words."

Eyes agog, Gibby drawled, "He is."

Serena choked with laughter and moved into the hallway.

Meridene propped her hand on her hip. "Then I shall see how well acquainted he is with the word 'humility.'"

"Papa, what's humility?"

"A hard-won trait, sweeting. Especially when a vixen demands it of a softhearted fellow who is justified in his opinions."

Concern creased Gibby's brow. "Because you're a lambkin?"

"To the bottom of my Scottish heart."

She giggled. He put her down. "Go with Serena, and tell Ellen she's not to pester the tanner with her romantic musings."

A purpose in mind and the terrier on her heels, the girl skipped out the door. Revas slammed it, then rounded on Meridene.

Fatherly concern fell prey to ruffled male pride. "Well?"

In the face of his anger, her courage wavered. "Well what?"

"Why do you make light of this destruction?" He pointed to the charred bed frame and soot-stained ceiling.

"Should I hurry to Kilbarton Castle and accuse my father? Lot of good that would do."

A steely calm settled over him. "You can take his power."

There it was. The sum of their differences. "And give it to you?"

He hadn't expected the blunt challenge; his blank stare was proof. But he recovered quickly. "I am your husband. I have earned the crown!"

"While I worked night after night to earn forty pence at that loom."

He marched to the windows and braced his arms on the casement. Staring into the yard, he said, "Did you believe your life would unfold without misery or hardship? None of us can expect so much good fortune."

"Pardon me for sparing your daughter *one* misfortune."

"We live in troubled times. But 'tis not about Gibby that we argue."

"It is! I will not visit my troubles on an innocent child. And if you tell me the Maiden's business is everyone's concern, I'll . . ."

He turned to face her, his arms crossed over his chest. "You will what?"

No worthy retribution came to mind. "I shall make certain you regret it."

"I'm too angry to cross words with you now." He started for the door. "I must speak with Brodie about trebling your protection."

More armed guards. "Why not manacle me to the well? Then everyone can watch me. You can make a sport of it. The tale will spread to every village and farm. The curious will flock to Elginshire."

Twisting his neck, he stared at her. "'Tis unwise to taunt me, Meridene."

"Next you'll say it's my own doing."

He slapped the doorframe. "I'm not so prideful as that!"

No. He was gloriously determined to right a wrong and wear a crown. "I thought you were a lambkin."

That stopped him. "I thought the blood of your namesake thrived in you. And cease calling me that."

"I will forget you are a lambkin, if you will return me to England."

Oh, that look. Even with soot on his face and ashes in his hair, he seethed with restrained civility. "England is lost to you."

"I hate Scotland."

"Do you dislike Lord's Meadow? Does Montfichet's porridge thicken on your tongue? Do your handmaidens ill serve you?"

His questions were unfair; he knew she could voice no complaint on those subjects. "I dislike the treachery of the Macgillivrays."

He grew serious. "Do you think William set the fire?"

"Nay," she said without thinking. More calmly she said, "He has put his trust in you."

His eyes glittered with mock relief, and he wiped his hands on his hose. "I shall rejoice, then, for I've found *one* Macgillivray who knows the meaning of loyalty."

"Meaning I do not?"

His jaw grew taut, and the muscles in his neck stiffened. "Meaning that some of your clan are overeager. Others are not."

The cryptic observation begged for a defense. "I did not deceive you. From the beginning, you knew that I wanted no part of—" She almost said "this life," but that was not entirely true, not anymore. "I made clear that the office of Maiden of Inverness holds no interest to me."

Through clenched teeth he said, "Then you are overeager in *that!*"

She stepped back. "I thought you were too angry to cross words with me."

He threw up his arms and shouted, "By the saints, I am. But know this, Meridene Macgillivray, our marriage is not a banquet. You cannot pick and chose only the things that please you and leave the dregs to some other soul."

He spoke the truth, and she lacked the courage even to defend herself. "There's no talking to you now, Revas."

"Nor will there be until your appetite changes."

Revas stormed from the room, so enraged he did not see the pile of wet tapestries in the hall. After picking himself up off the floor, he continued. As he made his way to the barracks, he berated himself for breaking his vow to never argue with a woman, least of all a stubborn wife who took freely of the rewards her marriage offered, but shouldered none of the responsibility.

The Maiden of Inverness.

He paused near the quintain. He was being unfair to her. She was more than a title. William didn't understand that, but Revas did. Cutberth's villainy was not aimed at his daughter, for never had the king of the Highlands looked at Meridene as a product of his loins, his child to protect.

Yet in spite of her father's selfishness, Meridene had a kind heart, was generous to one and all—except those who never looked beyond the celebrated green eyes and distinctive raven hair. Beneath the traditions that bred her lay a hurt and frightened woman who had suffered greatly at the hands of those who were bound by the laws of God and humanity to cherish her.

Even tormented by her father's treachery, Meridene had thought first of Gibby.

How could he have overlooked Meridene's pain? Last night she had called Elginshire home. He felt hollow to his soul, for he must make Auldcairn Castle her prison, until she called for the sword.

Would her need for revenge against Cutberth prevail where her love for Revas had not? Or did she truly love him? Beneath her indifference to Scottish politics lay an independent woman who had, since the age of eight, fended for herself in a foreign land. If Revas could convince her to seek the sword for personal reasons, rather than tradition, the outcome would be the same. He would wear the Highland crown. She would rule beside him, tempering might with the goodness of the Maiden of Inverness.

His quest was fraught with pitfalls, for she was ever on the lookout for coercion from him. It was a painful revelation, for he loved Meridene Macgillivray more than duty, cherished her beyond all obligation to the Highland people. Were he afforded the luxury of following his heart, he would relinquish his claim to the throne and honor her wish to refuse the office of Maiden of Inverness. As simply the chieftain of Clan Macduff and his lady wife, they would govern Elginshire. They would prosper, until one of Cutberth's assassins succeeded.

At the thought of losing her, Revas felt his chest grow tight and his senses quicken. He became aware of noise in the yard. The goose girl drove her flock through the open gate to complete their morning trip to the pond in the outer bailey. The sun had fully risen; the village teemed with movement.

He felt an indifference to the ordinary events, and it saddened him, for normally he took great pride in seeing the day unfold. But rather than watch the sun rise on his kingdom, he'd spent the early hours of dawn fighting a fire that could have destroyed his future. The quarrel was another unsettling matter. She must call for the sword. The alternative spelled doom, and quickly, for Highland unity.

Angered anew, he hurried to the barracks and found Brodie addressing Glennie Forbes and a dozen of his clansmen.

"You're to detain and question every stranger. Find out who set fire to Lady Meridene's room and bring the culprit to me."

One look at Revas and the sheriff ordered the men out. When they were alone, Brodie waited.

Disgusted with the turn of events, Revas gazed at the row of cots but didn't really see the furnishings. "We are victims of our free commerce. Assassins and kidnappers may come and go, same as tradesmen and travelers. We'll never find the culprit."

"Nay, we will not. He's surely halfway home to Kilbarton Castle by now."

"Damn Cutberth Macgillivray!"

Brodie twisted his war bracelets. "Is she no closer to claiming the sword?"

"I had thought so, but Cutberth has turned her against us. I had hoped she'd ask for the sword out of revenge—if for no other reason."

"'Tis wifely devotion you seek, my young friend."

"Young friend," Revas mused. "You haven't addressed me so in years."

He grasped Revas's sword arm, and his cheerful tone belied his serious expression. "Not since you bested me with this demon."

That day seemed a lifetime ago. Back then, Revas had naively thought he'd find Meridene, bring her home, and begin their joyous reign over the Highlands. Now he must petition the king of Scotland for aid and advice, for he could not risk her life again. If he studied his motives closely, he had to admit that seeking help nicked his pride, but better he suffer a bruise to his dignity than lose Meridene.

He shook off the ghastly thought and turned his attention to Brodie. "Bruce should have arrived at Moravia Keep for his tour of John Sutherland's holdings. Send Macpherson with word of Cutberth's attempts on Meridene's life and have him await Bruce's reply."

Brodie nodded. "The lad should take ship at Elgin's End. With fair winds, he'll be back in a week. We have a little time yet—before Whitsunday."

"Make it so, and put a sentry atop the south tower. Bid him watch hawklike over the windows in Meridene's chamber. I want no other intruder finding his way into her rooms."

"Summerlad and I will share the duty, unless you will give up your nightly visits?"

If his anger at her lingered, Revas would not seek entrance to her chamber. She cared for him, he was certain of that, but not enough to face her father. That truth wounded Revas deeply.

"She needs comfort and protection," he said, as much to himself as to his mentor. But when next they spoke of the troubles between them, she would broach the subject. Not Revas; he'd found that well dry too many times.

"Ask the women of the village to seek her out more often. Have them anticipate the pilgrimage."

Brodie sighed. "'Twill surely help the poor lass. 'Tisn't fair to twice suffer her father's wrath. Pity his soul should he succeed, for his life will be forfeit to you."

"God forgive me," Revas swore, "but I cherish the mere thought of hacking that bastard to pieces." Distracted again, he headed for the door.

Brodie followed. "Where are you going?"

"To the cooper's shed. A beast rages within me."

With the same hand that had taught Revas to wield a sword and helped him stack the stones on his father's cairn, Brodie slapped him on the back. "'Tis your way, Revas, and an honorable one. Better you spend your anger chopping wood than splitting heads."

But even as the day waned, Revas could not forget her last bitter condemnation of Scotland and her continued insistence that he return her to England.

Did she know the pain her cruel words dealt him? Did she care? When she did not come to table that night, Revas went to the south tower. His vantage point offered an unobstructed view of the windows in her chamber. Looking as forlorn as he felt, she sat at the loom amid a pool of golden lamplight, her hands working the shuttle back and forth.

She stopped and, from a nearby table, picked up a book. He suspected it was the Covenant of the Maiden; a peek at her through the spyglass confirmed it. With the aid of the instrument, she appeared close enough to touch, but the image, much like the woman herself, was deceptive.

She started to open the book, but paused. Taking a deep breath, she stared out the window. Then she again moved to examine the chronicles of her forebears.

Still she hesitated.

"Do it," he whispered, urging her to delve into her legacy and find the strength to bring greatness back to the women of her line.

The need to go to her, to persuade, to compel, rose like a tide within him. But he could not. He had done his best, and she had rebuked him.

In dismay, he watched her put the book aside and blow out the candle, extinguishing the light of hope he'd held for so long in his heart.

On Monday he sent Gibby to ask Meridene to go a-fielding with them. Citing her duties to Sim, she declined.

On Tuesday he sent Sim to her with an offer to spend the day in Lord's Meadow. With Gibby's lessons as excuse, she refused.

On Wednesday he directed Serena to invite Meridene to view a horse race in the outer bailey. Explaining a meeting with William, she sent Revas an apology.

In church they knelt side by side. To outward appearances, nothing was amiss. But when they exited the chapel, Meridene went her separate way.

On Thursday he penned a note, wherein he threatened to commission a chastity belt. She replied with a threat of her own: *Do it, Revas, and I shall tell the entire village that we have lain together.*

They would lie together again, he pledged to himself. She wasn't truly angry with her husband. The politics of Scotland had spoiled her disposition.

Revas could wait her out. She had nowhere to go, not unless an armed guard or a flock of women followed her.

When she did seek him out a week hence, her first words shocked him.

CHAPTER

15

"I'm here to barber your hair. You look like a shaggy hound." Even as the words were out, Meridene wished them back, for she hadn't intended to sound commanding and aloof.

She set the Covenant atop the pedestal table, but did not move farther into his chamber.

Sitting near the hearth, he carved a comb from a piece of smooth, dark wood. His bloodred jerkin contrasted handsomely with his fair hair and dark eyes. But he looked as tired and as lonely as she felt.

Sparing her a glance, he said, "Do not expect me to lift a paw and beg as Jaken does for favors."

She gripped the shears tighter and moved to stand before him. She had come to make amends. She must begin again. "The coldness between us cannot continue. I should not have spoken so sharply, but do not expect me to grovel."

"You, grovel?" Holding the comb to the light, he examined it, then blew off a shaving and continued carving. "I'd sooner pray for riches and a face as handsome as young Summerlad's."

"Modesty is unnecessary. You are handsome enough—especially so in that color." When he lifted a brow, she added, "It's pride you possess in overabundance."

In a tip of his head and a half smile, he honed aloofness. "And you do not?"

"More, I would venture, but you are stubborn, and I am not. Our quarrel is adversely affecting everyone. Ellen hasn't fallen in love once since we argued. The priest goes on and on about the sanctity of wifely devotion. Gibby is confused and blames herself."

"You did not come here to discuss my daughter, or my hair, or my pride, or your stubbornness."

The trickster. He'd twisted her words. "I have no intention of—"

"Being stubborn? You? Nay." He laughed mockingly.

"We must settle this."

He looked pointedly at her hand. "Then why come to me with another purpose? Sibeal will shear me without motive."

The troll intended to make her mission as difficult as possible. She had been wrong to ignore his gestures of reconciliation, but she'd been plagued by confusion and fear. She wanted peace between them. Especially now. A jest might work. "What you said about Sibeal grooming you may be true, but she cannot call up her ancestors to nibble at your manhood."

That got his attention. His hands stilled, and his measuring gaze surveyed her from head to toe. "You would use your charms to make peace between us?"

"Charms? It was meant as humorous conversation."

He tapped the comb on his thigh.

"Oh, very well," she said. "I meant it as an insult to your manliness."

"Then you erred in the attempt, for you do not grasp the meaning of the jest."

Everyone, even the mercer, swore Revas couldn't hold a temper for long. Sadly, they were wrong, for he gave no hint that he would come easily to terms with her.

She moved closer. "Please enlighten me."

"An ardent man suckles his woman's breasts. If she is so inclined, she returns the favor by nibbling his manhood."

A vivid picture shamed her, and she blurted, "I did not conceive, and why must you use such rough talk?" Why had she revealed something as personal as the coming of her cycle?

He put down the knife and comb. "Rough? Hardly. You broached the subject, and suckling your breasts is my second favorite pastime."

How dare he name her stubborn. The toad. "Then your first love is Scottish politics."

He gave her a roguish grin and a villainous laugh. "Again you err."

Her patience fled. "I am trying to make pleasant conversation."

"If this is pleasant conversation, you must be speaking French." Softer he added, "Do you suffer with your menses?"

Civilly put, the question dashed her embarrassment. "No. I am average in that respect." She worked the shears. "Shall I trim your hair?"

"Aye, but do not nibble my ears." He handed her the half-finished comb. "And try this."

Into the wood, he'd carved a cinquefoil. She realized the comb was to be a gift for her—a peace offering. He'd always been thoughtful and generous where her personal needs were concerned.

Inspired, she walked around behind him and drew the comb through his hair. Thick and wavy near his scalp, the uneven strands turned frayed and singed. In a hail of cinders, he'd beat out the fire and saved her life.

She wanted to throw her arms around him and tell him that no one had ever put her welfare before his own. Few women enjoyed so much husbandly devotion.

"Is something amiss with the comb?"

"No." Her voice was thick with emotion, and she cleared her throat. "It's a very fine comb."

He shrugged, and she wished she could see his face. As she clipped the singed ends of his hair, she prayed he would soon speak to her in the friendly banter she missed.

To encourage him, she said, "Shall I close-crop it, like the Normandy men prefer?"

"Do and I shall toss you into the pond with the geese and the toads."

She leaned close and whispered, "Ellen said I should leave braids at your temples." He trembled, and she continued. "They are the mark of a man of great import."

He swallowed loudly. "What do you think?"

"That I cannot nibble your ear with your hair covering it."

He cocked his head to the side and raked his hair out of the way, effectively presenting his ear. "I'm here to please."

Words she should have spoken earlier came rushing out. "I should have said that I am grateful to you for putting out the fire, and I'm sorry you burned your hair."

Dropping his hand, he turned, and his look was steady, as if he knew she had more to say.

"I was stubborn and afraid."

"Others may not have been offended and worse, but to me, you were unreasonably stubborn."

He meant that she should have considered his feelings. He was correct. "Yes."

"And I was blinded by anger because I failed to protect you."

A man as powerful and honorable as he would suffer. To give him ease, she said, "Worry not, for I am so safe, only Elginshire midges brave my presence."

When he gave her a slight nod, she broached an important matter. "William said you sent word to King Robert of what my father has done."

Staring at her lips, he licked his own. "You have resolved your differences with your brother?"

With William looking on, she had finished the new tapestry. Together they had explored the years of estrangement. He was no longer the cheerful young lad, but neither was he cold and deliberate like her father and her other kinsmen. "I confess I do like him."

His gaze slid to hers. "You gave him a flower penny?"

Were they hers to give, she'd bestow the stars upon Revas Macduff. But so guarded were his feelings, she read no emotion, no need, in his eyes.

"I gave William two flower pennies. They are for his children. What do you think the king will do?"

Blinking, he glanced away. "I think he will do nothing. You are sleeping well? No unpleasant dreams?"

"Would you have come to me, had I awakened in fear?"

Like a compass needle swinging true, his attention came back to her. "In a trice. 'Tis a husband's duty to comfort his wife."

They could have been discussing the ceiling beams, so amiable was their exchange, so uncommitted their words. He showed no feelings, except for that tiny glimmer in his eye, which she intended to explore. A moderate topic would be best. "Gibby is learning to weave."

"So she said."

A tent of apprehension dropped over them. Meridene's heart began to pound. "You went a-fielding with her on Monday."

Silence was his reply.

He had invited her, but she'd been too stubborn and prideful to accept. "I should have gone with you," she admitted. "I regret that I did not."

His gaze sharpened. "I should like you to give me the sword of Chapling. I regret that you have not."

Bluntly said, the statement went to the heart of his purpose. Disappointment awaited him, and for that she was truly sorry. To fortify herself, she took a deep breath. "There is no claim to make against my father's throne. I am a virgin no more."

He grew eager. "You have considered demanding the sword? It has crossed your mind?"

She had done little else since their quarrel, save think of her future and the man she loved and had alienated. By facing her father, she could seek the reward of revenge. After so much suffering at his hands, she wanted retribution. "Yes, but it matters not, for I have lain with you."

His brief smile dented the solemn mood. "Your mother had lain with Cutberth before she gave the sword to him."

Disbelief turned to puzzlement. "How do you know that?"

"How could you *not* know it?" He pointed to the book. "'Tis in the Covenant for all to see. Eleanor miscarried a fortnight after speaking her wedding vows."

Now was the time for truth. Meridene put down the shears and walked to the pedestal table where the Covenant rested. Where Revas had kept it for so many years. Once he cared more for her heritage than she, but no longer. "I have not read my mother's chronicle."

"Perhaps not of late, but surely you remember her poor legacy."

Poor legacy. An apt description of Eleanor's motherly devotion. This latest transgression didn't surprise Meridene, for her mother had withdrawn from her children early in their lives. "As a child, I was not allowed to touch the book. My mother locked it away with the Maiden's belt." And just because she could, Meridene laid her hands on the book and caressed the ancient bindings.

"But on the day we were wed, you gave it into my keeping. You were ill from the poison, but surely you remember."

She did, but the pain of that day had diminished, along with so many heartaches from her youth. "I gave it to you one day after my mother placed it in my hand. I could not let the English king see it. I was not alone on that journey here, save at night, and they did not provide me with a lamp."

If eyes could speak, his verily trilled a welcome. "You were so lovely, Meridene. I still remember the clean smell of your clothing and the softness of your skin. You were quite the bonniest sight I'd ever seen."

As she basked in his flattery, she remembered him saying those very words to her and more. The butcher's son who feared for his own life, yet found the strength to reassure a frightened and abandoned girl. "You were the most gallant lad I'd ever met."

"You do not know what your mother put down in the book?"

Meridene had picked up the book countless times, but couldn't find the courage to read it. "No."

"Shall I tell you? Will you take the word of a butcher's son?"

Coming from him, the words might not be so hurtful. She relaxed and leaned on the high table. "Please. What did she write?"

His expression turned sad. "No words. She only listed the dates of her children's births and the miscarriages."

The knowledge should have saddened Meridene, but she was growing accustomed to her parents' selfish ways. A mother who cursed her child wouldn't bother with words of encouragement, even if she was the Maiden of Inverness and bound to ensure continuation of the legacy. Her own troubles must have caused her indifference, for Ailis, in her own hand, had taken the blame for giving Eleanor to Cutberth.

"My mother suffered the loss of two babes."

"Aye, and the first was a fortnight after she gave the sword to Cutberth. The second child was lost 'twixt William's birth and yours."

Indifference toward her mother turned to scorn. "She cheated! She was impure when she demanded the sword from her father."

"She was not the first. I have reasoned that other of your ancestors anticipated, for good reasons and true, their vows."

Bewildered and disappointed, Meridene wilted into a chair. "You have proof that they also deceived the Covenant?"

"Only suspicions and birthing dates that occur too soon after wedding vows."

All of her forebears listed the dates they birthed the new Maiden, but only some listed when their sons were born. Although she knew Revas had ferreted out the details for ambitious reasons, she couldn't help praising him for his interest in her birthright. "I don't know what to say."

"You must not think less of them. Mary faced an invasion from the Norsemen. With her father in the

Holy land, Sorcha anticipated her vows because she risked ending the tradition altogether. Your straits are not so dire by comparison. You face the loss of Highland unity. I cannot say you cheated, for I seduced you."

A familiar and comforting warmth infused her. "Cutberth seduced my mother."

"Do you know, 'tis the first time you've said his name without fear in your voice?" He leaned forward and extended his hand, palm up. "Forget your father. Think of today and of our future. I'm no monster, Meridene. I'm the husband who loves you."

Happiness flooded her, and she flung herself onto his lap. "I do love you, too."

She kissed him with promise, commitment, heart and soul. But would she fulfill her destiny?

Before he lost control of his passions, Revas drew back. Her dreamy gaze almost got the better of his conscience.

"Do you think you will find contentment in England," he began, "after living among people who have made a place in their hearts for you?"

"I have friends in England. The fisherman's wife."

"Then I shall give her husband leave to plow my waters."

"You govern the sea?"

"Not exactly. Jamie Forbes's father does."

"And he swears fealty to you."

"Aye, and provides Montfichet with fish aplenty. If the English fisherman and his wife choose to remain where they are, you may write to them as often as you please. I do think 'tis not too ambitious to say that one day soon we will have messengers traveling throughout Scotland."

Now he spoke of aiding progress. Was there no end to his honorable intentions? "These men will cross the land with no other purpose than carrying letters?"

"Even the common man's words. The king likes the idea." His voice dropped. "Will you demand the sword?"

Meridene's life stretched before her, joyous and complete, and in the distance she saw a daughter with raven hair and green eyes and a father who would meet death to protect all of his children.

Clare was dead. Johanna had found happiness with Drummond Macqueen. What truly awaited Meridene at Scarborough Abbey? Nothing, she had to admit. Her life was here.

"Will you redeem the honor of the women of your line?"

She thought of the first Eleanor, pregnant and chained to a dungeon wall. And the aging Margaret, who sacrificed herself to bear the next Maiden. She remembered her mother's cold words. *Our kind do not choose our mates. We are as prized bitches held out for the mightiest dog in the pack.*

Meridene looked at Revas. Beneath his pleasing form beat a heart that was true and constant. A better man, she would not find.

"Yes, I will demand my father's sword."

In relief, he closed his eyes, and a smile as big as Scotland spread across his face. "Praise God."

Giddy with relief herself, Meridene laughed. "You must also credit the women of the village. They have *sung* your praises morning, noon, and night."

"'Tis kind of them."

"Kind? It's better said that they followed your orders."

As jovial as she'd ever seen him, he threw back his head and laughed. "They need no command from me to befriend you. They love you well, and you cannot dispute that. I see them dancing in the lane when you wear the crown of rowans."

The rowans. The vows. Her letter to the pope.

"What will we do when Leslie returns with our annulment?"

"We'll . . . ah." He squirmed, his eyes darting from the hearth, to the lamp, to the table. "'Tis a bridge better crossed when the time comes."

"You're stammering. What's wrong?"

He looked like he'd swallowed a fish bone—that or the truth was stuck in his throat.

"Tell me."

"I have it." He snapped his fingers. "We'll marry again. We'll say our vows willingly—with the entire village looking on. Oh, what a celebration 'twill be."

"Revas?"

"There'll be dancing and merrymakers. And you can throw flower pennies to the bairns. Have you enough?"

"Enough of your evasions. Has the annulment come?" The thought and the consequences propelled her off his lap.

He drew her back down. "Nay. No annulment comes."

It was an odd way to phrase it—too final, too confident. "How can you be so certain?"

"I am certain the annulment will be a long time coming."

If she had to drag the truth from him, so be it. "You did not send my letter, did you?"

"I did," he insisted. "With young Leslie."

His discomfort was so obvious, she wanted to laugh. But the situation wasn't funny. "You sent the letter with Leslie—but what else?"

"But I told him to first visit his French relations and await the birth of his cousin's first child."

Reality and relief swept over Meridene. "And this birth will be a long time coming."

He shrugged, his expression as sheepish as a caught thief. "A decade or so, I should think. Although betrothed, his cousin is still a child and resides in the nursery."

Bold didn't begin to describe this butcher's son who'd captured both her heart and the loyalty of the Highlands. "I should hate you for tricking me."

"But you love me instead. Say it."

"Much as I'm certain it will forever plague me, yes, I do."

"You will make the finest of mothers."

Children. "I owe the Macgillivrays no progeny."

"The Macgillivrays, you say? What of the Douglases? Sorcha was of their kin. Ailis was a Macdonald. Mary, a Leslie. The Maiden has ties to many clans. Will you abandon all of those people, whose blood mixes with yours, just to spite one wretched Macgillivray?"

He made a convincing argument, but she still had reservations. "If I bear you a child, it will be a Macgillivray."

"When you bear my *children,* they will be Macduffs. And handsome ones, too."

He was so confident, she couldn't help but tease him. "Given names such as Hacon?"

Sharply alert, he rubbed his chin. "I had not thought of that. Hacon." He tested the sound. "Hacon, 'tis a—"

"Dreadful choice of names."

"Oh, aye." But the notion had him in its grasp, and he was favorably considering it.

"Revas . . ." she warned.

"Utterly unthinkable and unromantic, as Ellen will surely attest. What name would you choose?"

With Hacon behind them, she grew generous. "Duncan or Kenneth."

He fairly oozed affection. "And for our wee Maiden?"

Johanna was her favorite name, but wait. A child

would change her life. "I do not think I would like a child immediately."

"On that point, your body and God's will shall prevail."

"But I am not sure that I wish to have a child."

"Why not? We've much to recommend us. Your hot temper aside. But with a lambkin for a sire, good will prevail."

"How did you divert me from the subject of the annulment?"

He kissed her cheek. "I believe 'tis because our conversations usually run to the pleasant."

It was true, but while they were speaking honestly, she had a few objections to make. "I will not abide your raiding."

"You fear for my safety?"

His smug expression inspired her to deviltry. "No. I haven't the coin to waste ransoming you."

He nodded, engrossed in the dilemma. "'Twould beggar us, most likely."

"You think highly of yourself."

"And value my future with you."

She remembered his threat to raid the abbey's stables. "Enough to honestly acquire the mount I left in Scarborough?"

"A Highlander *buy* a horse from an Englishman?" As if it were absurd, he laughed.

"Englishmen say the same. They are much like you. They love their wives and their children. They say their prayers and mount their horses from the left side, same as you."

"They covet Scotland."

With a certainty she had never hoped to feel, Meridene said, "'Tis a place worthy of it."

A second later Revas grasped the importance of her words. She no longer hated Scotland, and of all the matters they'd settled tonight, this one resolution most warmed his heart. She loved him; she would seek her destiny, and at last she favored the land of her birth.

His eyes misted with tears, and he hugged her tight. She worked her arms free and, cradling his face, drew him down for a kiss. The embrace ignited the embers of passion banked days ago, and as their desire burst into flame, Revas knew he must end it.

"Revas!"

Through a fog of physical longing he recognized the sound of Brodie's voice.

"The herald, Lady Elizabeth Gordon, seeks an audience."

"Who?" Meridene asked.

His high spirits plummeted. "Our king's herald."

"Oh, my." She tried to rise.

He held her. "Be still. You're my wife, and she is only a messenger of the king." Revas had assured King Robert that Meridene had returned of her own free will. The messenger would look closely for any sign of discord between Revas and his wife. A loving embrace fitted the occasion perfectly.

"You know her well?"

"As well as any man, save one."

"I don't think I like the sound of that."

Revas liked very much the sound of her jealousy, but he didn't reply; the second most celebrated woman in Scotland, and the most gossiped about at court, glided into the room.

Wearing an ankle-length tunic of gold velvet, emblazoned with the scarlet lilies of the king of Scotland, she moved with purpose and grace. Overly tall and now thinner than he remembered, her gray eyes glowed with cold obligation.

She doffed her feathered cap, and moisture dripped from the plumage. Her red hair was coiled tight at the crown of her head, drawing the eye to her slender neck and heart-shaped face. While she executed a formal bow, her gaze stayed fixed on Meridene.

"Are you truly the Maiden of Inverness?" she asked.

Her face reddened with embarrassment at being caught on Revas's lap, Meridene jumped to her feet. "Aye. I am Meridene, wife to Revas Macduff. King Edward the First brought me to Scarborough Abbey, where I lived for a very long time."

If his chest swelled any more, Revas knew he'd burst the seams on his jerkin. His wife. A promise given, a prayer answered.

As solemn as her office dictated, Elizabeth Gordon said, "Welcome home, my lady. You are glad to be among us again?"

Revas held his breath until he heard Meridene say, "I am content."

Elizabeth nodded. Her expression turned grim. "A moment of your time, Lord Revas."

"I prefer the simpler address. I am a butcher's son."

A smile pinched her lips. "As you wish, *Revas.*"

She was a born Scot from a noble family older than most, yet she served as a herald. But Elizabeth Gordon was Randolph Macqueen's puzzle. Revas had other business with her. "What word from King Robert?"

She threaded her long fingers together. Her gloves were soft leather dyed the same golden color as her clothing. Her voice was pure music. "While our sovereign lord understands your plight, he reminds you that Cutberth Macgillivray wears the Highland crown."

"Cutberth hires foreign mercenaries to raid any clan that resists him. That is no way to rule his fellow Highlanders."

"The king of Scotland does not bestow the crown of the Highlands."

Revas looked at Meridene.

She must declare herself now, and to the king's herald. There'd be no going back. She must look her father in the eye and force him to yield all that he held dear. She must accept the sovereignty of the Highlands with dignity and purity of heart. Then she must pass it to Revas Macduff.

"I will ask my father for the sword."

The weight of uncertainty left Revas. Thirteen years of struggling and hoping were over. He wanted to touch Meridene, but Elizabeth Gordon would notice his relief. The king must believe that all was well in Revas's marriage to the Maiden of Inverness.

Catching the herald's gaze, he lifted his brows in challenge.

Her nod was subtle, almost missed. "Then allow me, in the name of King Robert, to pay homage to you." Lady Elizabeth went down on one knee and bowed her head. "May your reign be long and prosperous, Maiden Meridene, and your daughter a gift to those who come after us."

Too overcome to say more, Meridene murmured, "God make it so."

With fluid grace, Elizabeth rose. "When will you demand the sword?"

"She has not yet set the date."

"In June at Summer's Eve," Meridene said.

The herald stiffened. "But she must go before Whit—"

"Nay," he interrupted, determined to keep the herald from revealing Cutberth's Whitsunday ultimatum. "Meridene will accept her destiny when she decides. Not before."

Catching his meaning, the herald nodded and donned her cap. "Now I regret that I must journey in all haste to—I must go."

"To where?" Revas asked.

As if grasping a name from air, she said, "To Calais."

She lied; Revas knew it. "I'm to name France as your destination, even should the king inquire?"

Turning away, she stared at the floor. "Our sovereign lord will find me."

"But Randolph Macqueen will not. You are so sure?"

"Lady Meridene," she said by way of dismissing Revas and changing the uncomfortable subject. "Lest I forget, I also bring you a message from Lady Clare. She says Englishmen are lambkins compared to Scots, and she implores you to be wary of the devious ways of Highlanders."

Revas's eyes grew large.

Meridene fairly cooed with pleasure. "A wise observation on her part. Do you agree?"

Her gray eyes were wells of sorrow. "In my experience, nay." As quickly, she recovered her composure. "Lady Clare also says Scotsmen are boors and bids you ignore them."

Revas laughed, but much too gaily. "She did not include Drummond Macqueen in her condemnation."

"Most definitely and colorfully did she include her husband. Drummond will not let her lift so much as a quill to sum the accounts. Sister Margaret goes between them."

"They fare well?" Meridene asked. "The abbess and Clare?"

"The kind sister enjoys good health, and for one so stubborn, Lady Clare thrives."

Grumbling, Revas said, "'Tis a trait of the English —teaching stubbornness to innocent lassies."

"Let us not dwell on the cruelties of men toward the fairer and more intelligent sex. With your permission, I shall take my leave of you."

In a swirl of dignity and royal livery, she marched out.

"A most curious and beautiful woman," Meridene said.

"And a love story to rival any in the Covenant."

"Tell me."

"Only if you sit with me."

When she returned to her place on his lap, he held her in a loose embrace. "Elizabeth Gordon gave her heart to Randolph Macqueen, but the king holds her to a bargain she made to serve him."

"That is why Randolph is rude."

"Aye, he suffers bad humors."

"How long will our king make them wait?"

Our king. With every word, she knitted herself closer to the people of her homeland. "Bruce needs her now. She is the only messenger he trusts."

A sigh bowed Meridene's shoulders. "I'm glad we face no such obstacle."

She didn't know it, but the risk taken by Elizabeth Gordon and Randolph Macqueen paled when compared to the responsibilities Meridene had promised to undertake. She was just too naive of Scottish politics to see it.

"What were we discussing before these weighty matters commanded our attention?" he asked.

Looking like a woman with knowledge she should not have, she smiled. "You were about to explain the particulars of how an inexperienced woman nibbles her husband's manhood."

His ability to think drifted south and settled in his loins.

"Have you nothing to say?"

"'Tis unfair to bedevil your husband at this time."

"Oh, very well. Let's discuss my new bed. Did you know that the tanner put goose down among the straw? It's very soft and quiet."

"After your menses have passed, I will repay you for teasing me."

"Then I have another day's grace to bedevil and tease you."

Not so long, for a patient man. But when Revas went to her room two nights hence, he found her sick unto death, the odor of poison on her lips.

Crowns and thrones forgotten, Revas knelt beside Meridene's bed and prayed twice to every saint he knew to save the life of his beloved.

The barley water she'd drunk last night had been poisoned. A frantic Montfichet had awakened Revas at dawn, wailing as he told of tossing the boiled grains to the chickens, as he always did. The carcasses of two score of them lay stacked in a pile awaiting the torch. Revas had ordered every grain of barley in Auldcairn Castle tossed onto the pyre.

No intruder had stolen into the kitchen or the granary and tainted the stores. Entry was unnecessary. The eager-to-please Montfichet had unknowingly bought the poisoned barley from a stranger who approached him outside the brewer's shop. The cook suspected nothing sinister; he often purchased foodstuffs from peddlers in the lane. He could not have known that the man had been sent by Cutberth Macgillivray.

Would she live?

ARNETTE LAMB

Revas's stomach roiled at the alternative, and he cursed himself for thinking he could protect her from the ruthless man who sired her.

Against her black hair, her skin was snowy white. So still did she lie, he wet a finger and held it beneath her nose. The breath of air was faint, like the brush of a feather, but enough to tell him she clung to life.

"Cling harder, beloved," he whispered.

Tears tightened his throat and burned his eyes, but Revas could not let them fall. Should she awaken and see him so distraught, she could lose hope.

And hope was all they had, according to the healer. The poison had done its work and gone to her heart, which even now thrummed softer than the beat before.

Old King Edward's physician had saved her once, but on that occasion she'd had only a sip of Cutberth's poison. According to Gibby and Lisabeth, Meridene had drunk a tankard full last night.

"She is in God's hands," the healer had said.

Would the last entry in the Covenant be the words of a bereft husband who had underestimated his enemy and watched his Maiden die? Would the tradition end with a woman named for the one who'd begun it all? Was this the closure of a great circle of time?

"Pray God, nay," he whispered, and clutched her hand.

Her skin was warm and her fingers supple, but lifeless.

Silently he begged the Lord to save her. He offered up his service in every waking moment for the rest of his life in exchange for hers.

Behind him, the door opened. William stepped inside.

"Oh, why, Revas? Why did you bring her back to Scotland?"

Rising, Revas went to him, and the pain and

accusation in William's eyes was almost his undoing. "I know not, and I'll go to my grave seeking an answer that eases my mind. But if she lives, I swear on my soul, I'll send her to safety. Edward was right, you know. And she, too. We are a land of monsters. Look what tragedies we make."

Softly, as if to convince himself, William said, "She has a strong will. Even as a child, she did not yield easily."

As a child she'd been a bride—his bride—and even as he watched her hang on to life, he knew her father was just as determined to destroy her.

The years fell away, and Revas was once again a frightened lad facing the king of England. Edward's rage at seeing her brought low and his conviction to save her from Scottish monsters had seemed heroic to Revas. Because he hadn't loved her then—not with a man's passion and a husband's duty. He hadn't come to this place in his life when he anticipated the simple pleasures of seeing her work at her loom, or watching her teach Gibby how to inventory the pantry stores. As a lad, he hadn't felt the soul-deep sorrow and heart-wrenching pain of losing her.

Life was a gift of God, or so the priest had counseled Revas. With a stronger conviction than he had ever known, Revas was certain that God had played no part in this treachery. Men had determined the course Meridene's life would take. Now it was time for Revas to shoulder the blame and do his part.

He caught William's gaze. "She belongs in a sweet place with people who have a care for her, not with a self-important butcher's son who has overreached himself, and a father whose soul is crusted with sin."

William dashed tears from his eyes. "You cannot blame yourself for Father's treachery. She loved you well, Revas. If she lives, she will not leave you."

"She can love me as much from England." He grasped handfuls of William's tunic, and when they were nose to nose, he said, "You must help me convince her. Compel her, if that is the only way. She will go with you—back to Scarborough Abbey, if we do our work well."

"What work?"

Revas told him of his plan.

In resignation, William sighed. "I will do as you ask, if she lives."

Meridene ached all over. Her stomach growled, and she felt like she'd eaten spiny rocks. A dry bitterness coated her mouth. What had happened? She felt leeched out, exhausted. This was no rancid food she suffered, and her hands and arms bore no marks or blotches from a plague. Yet she felt bludgeoned from the inside out—as if she'd been poisoned again.

Her shoulders tightened. Yes, the sickness, the soreness, the aching exhaustion. The same leavings as that poisoned cup she'd drunk from so long ago.

Her father had sent a generous wheelwright. When that failed, he sent a faceless intruder to set fire to her room. Now poison. Even the rank taste on her tongue was the same as before.

Hatred coiled inside her. She reached for the tankard on the bedside table. Weariness and fear clouded her head, but after several swallows of the cold, sweet water, her thoughts cleared. She became aware of a strong presence beside her.

Revas. In her bed. She thought it heavenly odd that she could sense his presence. Her sworn protector was nearby. He'd rail at her father and worry with guilt. But they would be more careful in the future, and once Revas wore the crown, Cutberth wouldn't dare come after her again.

Her fear ran like hounds after the hunt, and her exhaustion followed. "Curse you, Cutberth Macgillivray," she swore out loud.

Sitting up and holding the mug in both hands, she

turned to watch Revas sleep. But he was awake and watching her.

"'Twas the haggis," he said. "Your handmaidens have been brought to bed, and half the Forbesmen are struck low."

"It was poison in the barley water."

"Nay. No one else drinks it, and many of us are sick. 'Tis not the first time, though. Two years ago, a brace of tainted moorhens sent us running to the privy and then to our cots."

He had it all wrong. "My father tried to poison me. He sent that Macleod after me, then he had someone set fire to my bed. Now he's had someone poison the haggis."

"Impossible. No one save Montfichet touches the haggis. He always cleans the umbles himself. Even Sibeal takes no hand in the making of haggis." Wry laughter made him groan. "Smart lass, that Sibeal. 'Twas your fault, though."

How could he be so sure? "It is not my fault, and put away your charm. It's wasted now."

Wincing, he rubbed his stomach. "Last night you coaxed me into eating the haggis, Meridene. Not since I left my father's house has the vile stuff passed my lips. Until you forced me."

Even in the aftermath of poison, he played the gallant. But she was not fooled. "If you will not color up the truth for Gibby, why do it for me? I tell you it was poison—in whatever food."

"'Twas the corrupted liver from an old hart." Scooting to the head of the bed, he smoothed the covers over his lap. "Montfichet swears to it. You are cruel to make quibbling of my legitimate complaint."

She'd said those very words to him, and he did look ill—his eyes were red and his youthful features were lined with fatigue. If Montfichet was certain about the meat and others were ill, then bad haggis must be to blame.

"I'm glad you understand," he said. "And do not think for a moment that Sibeal has not exacted a price for her husband's poor work." Pausing, he ruffled his now shorter hair. "She has a bloody wicked tongue, that Sibeal."

"What did she say?"

"I know not, but in reply, Conal said he no longer lamented not giving her a chastity belt, for he would sooner spend his coin on a muzzle to keep her quiet."

Meridene pictured the sapling-thin cook berating his rotund wife, and the image made her smile. "She'll not wear a chastity belt."

Revas rolled his eyes. "Of course not. The weight of the thing would stagger her."

Their conversations always ran to the pleasant. It was true, and Meridene laughed, then groaned, for her ribs were sore from vomiting.

Revas threw off the bedcovers. "I should summon Sibeal to help you. I'm certain you'll want to bathe."

He seemed nervous, and he was fully dressed, while she wore a thin sleeping gown. He'd complimented the garment at length. Why didn't he notice it now? Did his illness consume his thoughts?

Hoping to make him feel better, she said, "Were you striving for a gentle way to tell me that I smell?"

His eyes grew glassy, and he looked at her with sad longing. "Nay," he said thickly, and crawled off the bed.

"We could share a bath and see if my namesake was correct about begetting a male child."

Instead of a roguish grin and a naughty remark, he swallowed hard and looked at the hour candle. It was nine in the morning.

"Brodie and the others await."

He hurried out the door, and she had the oddest thought that he wasn't sick at all.

* * *

At midday she went to the kitchen. Montfichet was dutifully conscience-stricken, and Sibeal looked disgusted with her husband.

"Damned Macgraw!" the cook spat. "He slew that hart a sennight ago, not two days as he swore when I bought it. Turks'll plow this land before I spend good coin on another of his kills. There's fresh barley from Aberhorn—acquired just this morn. Shall I make you a broth, my lady?"

Standing at the worktable, Sibeal huffed and ground her knuckles into a mountain of bread dough.

Conal wagged his finger at her. "And if you challenge me, woman, I'll be visiting the blacksmith for that special head ornament I promised you."

His wife hefted the dough and threw it at him. By the time he'd peeled the sticky mass off his face and yelled in outrage, Sibeal had fled out the back way.

Choking with suppressed laughter, Meridene fled to the steward's pantry.

Sim, too, had eaten the accursed haggis, but his tale of woe was overdone, for he tended to be a quiet fellow, or at least efficient with words.

He sat at his desk, the ledgers piled high around him.

"A wretched night I spent, my lady," he went on, twisting the quill. "Too weak I was to do more than blink once for water and twice for help getting to the privy."

He almost recited the words, and his choice of them was odd, for she couldn't imagine him mentioning the private workings of his body—not to her or to any other female—of that, Meridene was certain.

"A wretched sickness, my lady, to all of us that caught it."

All? "Has everyone recovered?"

"Aye. Revas fared the best. Off he's gone, taking the new furniture to the Halt."

Surely not. Moving furniture was the last thing he'd do, knowing she'd just risen from the sickbed. She peered out the window. Glennie and Summerlad practiced with short swords, but Revas was not among the bystanders. "You must be mistaken, Sim."

"Nay." His gaze flitted to her, then dashed back to the quill. "He was driving the carpenter's wagon when he said he was on his way to the Halt. He'll be home before Vespers, he said. But you're not to wait."

Meridene didn't wait. She wanted the old rosary. Henceforth, she would pray with the Maiden's beads and give her own to Gibby. She found the rosary in the niche where Revas had kept it all these years.

Her husband. Revas Macduff. At Vespers she thanked God for blessing her with so fine a man. The best man o' the Highlands, the villagers said of him.

Happiness propelled her from the church. Revas had gone to his lodge because he was planning a surprise for her there, some gallant gesture to melt her heart.

She would pretend surprise just to please him.

Then she would present him with a gift: the new tapestry. Tonight, in the company of their friends and the entire household, she would give it to him.

Hoping to fetch it before he returned, she hurried into the castle. Only Summerlad sat in the common room.

"Where's Serena?" she asked.

"She went with the soldiers to see Gibby home to Aberhorn."

But Sim had said the others were on the mend. "Why? Is Gibby still ill?"

"Nay, the lass is fit, as is my Serena. Revas sent his lass home."

To be with her grandparents. Most likely they were worried about her. "Then Revas is back?"

"Aye, we returned before Vespers." As he spoke, he twirled one of his war bracelets. The casual gesture

was out of place, for he valued the bands second only
to Serena. They were not toys; he took his duties to
heart.

Now Meridene understood. He simply missed his
sweetheart and awaited her return.

At the cheerful prospect of seeing her own sweetheart, Meridene forgot the tapestry and almost ran up
the steps. Revas must have wanted to bathe before
seeing her, and that was why he had not sought her out
upon his return.

She found him in his chamber studying a map, not
lounging in the bath. William sat beside him. Neither
looked up when she approached.

"Are you planning to build a road?" she asked,
remembering what he'd said about traveling messengers.

Her brother started, but Revas barely spared her a
glance. "'Tis Kilbarton Castle and the grounds. Surely
you recognize it."

He sounded disinterested, cold. This morning he'd
been evasive.

Thinking he'd fallen ill again, she took a stand.
"You should have stayed in bed another day."

"Oh, nay. I'm eager to see your father's face when I
demand the crown."

When he demanded it? Of all the odd com-
ments and strange behavior she'd witnessed today,
his was the most peculiar. "Do you think he'll be surprised to see me?" She knew the answer, but had to
ask.

He took a long drink from a tankard. "I'll not give
him that satisfaction. Your declaration is enough.
There's paper, quill, and ink. Just put down your
words, and I'll take them to Cutberth."

She balked. The Revas she knew would not refuse
her a moment of revenge. "What's wrong with you?"

His gaze caught hers. He swallowed hard. "Important matters."

"Yes, important matters that concern me. You said as much."

"I did, and sooner or later you must put down the words." His attention dropped to her waist and the Maiden's belt she'd donned for the first time. "'Tis prescribed in the Covenant."

Knowing he spoke the truth and certain she could change his mind, she went to the desk and penned the traditional demands. The scratching of the nib on the vellum was the only sound in the room, yet her heart thudded with pride. She was bothered, though, because Revas hadn't commented on the fact that she wore the golden belt. He'd said the choice was hers, but in matters pertaining to the Maiden, he was ever the champion of tradition.

After signing her name and sketching the cinquefoil of the Maiden, she sprinkled sand on the ink. When it dried, she handed it to Revas.

He scanned the page, then rolled it up and put it in his chieftain's pouch.

"When will we go to Kilbarton?" she asked.

"Not we." He sat down again, all cold stranger. "You will stay here."

"When fish sprout feathers!"

"You will stay."

It wasn't like him to be unreasonable. He must still think her too afraid of her father to face him. "Seeing me take the sword from my father is all you've talked about since you brought me home."

"Not all," he murmured meaningfully. "You know well my favorite subject."

She almost relished the roguish comment, even if it was spoken in her brother's presence. But Revas could not cajole her into giving up the opportunity to face her father, not when he knew it was her destiny. "What farce do you play?"

"No farce, Meridene." Honesty glimmered in his

eyes. "Unless you wish to see me slay your father and stuff his head on a pike?"

Her knees went weak at the horror. "Give me back my letter."

"Do not be angry. You've been away too long." Leaning back, he enlisted William with a touch on his arm. "Faced with an army of women, Cutberth will laugh. Isn't that so?"

"Very true, Meridene. Much has changed, and for the better."

How could they scheme to shut her out? Side by side, they formed a convincing front, but she was not done. "Curse you, William, for agreeing with my noble husband." She sent Revas her most withering stare. "I'm important to the Highlands. The people will support my claim. It's the tradition."

Revas rudely waved her off. "'Twas colored up. From you they want flower pennies and sweetness, which you admirably provide. We're not so ceremonious in our time about the passing of the sword."

"I'll be the judge of which of the Maiden's ceremonies I perform and when."

He snatched up the tankard and drank again, as if to fortify himself. Slamming it down, he said, "I expected stubbornness from you, but it will not work this time. You will do as your husband bids."

She planted her feet. "I'm going to Kilbarton Castle."

"Very well, Meridene. Since you leave me no choice, I'll tell you all of it." He wiped his mouth on the sleeve of his tunic. "Your father swore that if you came for the sword according to tradition, he would slay every woman with you. Is that what you want?"

She did not fear her father now. "His kinsmen will not support him, and William will be with us."

"William matters not to Cutberth."

For confirmation, she looked to her brother.

"Revas speaks the truth, and I do not wish to die for a ceremony. Father's hired mercenaries receive a boon for every man, woman, and child they slay. The price on your head and mine is a hefty purse in itself. Revas is the only one they are not to touch. Father has saved that pleasure for himself."

"There you have it," Revas said with finality. "None of us wants to perish to see you don a crown of rowans and speak a few words from that book."

She could take no more of their cowardice. "Then drive the mercenaries from Scotland!"

William stepped closer. "How can we when they wear Macgillivray colors? Who's to tell them from my brother Scots?"

"Worry not, Meridene." Revas smiled but without warmth. "I'll bring you the crown—but not with your father's head attached."

He was different—cold and ruthless—and she longed to know why. "You swore there would be no bloodshed. You said you wanted peace through treaties and progress."

A broadsword through his heart would hurt less than the words Revas must say next. He must drive her away, and quickly.

He spoke the words he'd practiced. "I lied, Meridene. There will be bloodshed aplenty. The Macphersons have left the Community of the Realm, which you would have noticed had you looked at the hearth wall and the shields that dwindle as we speak. Even Munro has thrown in with Cutberth. 'Twill be war. Should I fall in battle, you will be provided for."

She swayed, as if the words had been a blow. Then she rallied. "It's my right to help you get those alliances back. Together we will unify the clans of Scotland."

"And we shall," he said much too amiably. "You will help by giving me a castle full of wee Macduffs to marry among the better families."

Not if he lived three score years would Revas forget the agony she didn't try to conceal. But he could not relent; she must leave Scotland. On reliable information from the priest, Revas knew that even now, her father marshaled an army to march on Auldcairn Castle.

"You will not barter my children like sheep."

"Come, Meridene," said her brother, crossing the room. "Revas is not the hero we thought."

"Why, Revas?" she implored. "This isn't like you."

"I'm afraid it is," William said solemnly. "Ever has he been thus, until you came."

Revas felt his heart sink, but he must play his part a moment longer. If she did not leave now, his alternative plan would crush her spirit.

"It was all a ruse, wasn't it, Revas?"

Another moment, a few more coarse remarks, and she'd be on her way to safety. "'Tis Scottish politics, plain and simple. You were raised with it. Do not pretend otherwise."

"But you aren't like Father. You want peace."

"And I'll have it at the hands of this peacemaker." He grasped the hilt of his broadsword. "And you'll stay behind these walls."

William grasped her arm. "He's always like this before a battle."

"A battle? I thought he was jesting. I thought—"

"That I'd give Cutberth your message, and he'd trip over his war boots in his haste to yield the sword to me?"

William shouted, "You promised you wouldn't tell her—"

"You know the way of things, brother-in-law." Revas lunged to his feet and turned his back on them. "She'll get used to it."

Meridene decided Revas was again suffering too much strong drink. Why else would he sway and his hands shake? He wore the same clothing as this morning, and he did not look ill from the haggis.

She would wait him out, hear his apology, and forgive him. They had disagreed before. They would argue again. But when he did not come to escort her to prayers the next morning, she went after him.

"He's at the Halt," said a preoccupied Brodie.

They stood inside the stable door, where the sheriff was inspecting a harness.

Revas's favorite mount wasn't in any of the stalls. He must not be suffering the effects of drink, and since she felt much better, she would take her search a little farther. "Then I'll ride there. How do I find it?"

"You cannot go to the Halt, my lady. 'Tis his private place. He's just put in the bed and—He wouldn't want you there."

Confused, Meridene searched Brodie's face for some sign that he jested. But his weathered features were stoic as always. She must get to know him better; other than at meals, she'd shared few conversations with Revas's mentor.

In the face of his obstinacy, a direct approach would be best. She called out to the stableman to saddle her horse, then turned back to Brodie. "If you will not tell me where the lodge is, someone else will."

The harness snapped, and he tossed it aside. "Nay, they'll all abide by his wishes."

"Revas told you to keep the location a secret—even from me?"

"The few who know, aye. Even the carpenter was kept out of it."

Sim had said Revas drove the wagonload of furniture himself. Why the secrecy? Ah, she remembered. "Sheriff Brodie," she said patiently, "I promise to act surprised."

He blew out his breath. "'Twill be a surprise sure enough, if you go there."

* * *

Only William was willing to accompany her, but as they rode abreast across Lord's Meadow, she saw regret and hesitance in her brother's eyes.

Tucked into a bend in a river they aptly called the serpent, the lodge was smaller than her apartments. Rough-cut logs sealed with mortar formed the walls of the structure, and the roof was of thatch.

A frowning William helped her dismount.

She took the tapestry from her pouch, having decided to give it to Revas now. "What's wrong, William?" she asked. "You look like we're going to a funeral mass."

Distracted, he guided her up the steps and opened the door. "'Tis most likely the remains of that rancid haggis."

A feminine giggle gave Meridene the first impression that something in the lodge was wrong. Naked to his waist and barefoot, Revas sat in one of the new chairs, the hated map spread before him on the low table.

The smell of newly cut wood permeated the air. A vase of freshly cut spring lilies caught her eye.

He looked up, surprised, then glared at William. "You knew better than to bring her here."

Meridene couldn't make her feet work. "I insisted."

Revas glanced at the bed. "You did not knock."

She expected stubbornness from her husband; his belligerence was something new.

"Revas," trilled a voice from behind the bed curtains. "Send them away, and come back to bed. I promise to nibble your manhood again."

Meridene jerked and stared, transfixed, at his bed. He had a woman in there, and she used lovers' phrases that Meridene had spoken to him in confidence. He'd delivered the furniture himself so that no one else would know about this place and the sins that went on here.

Gathering courage, she moved closer. "How long has she been your leman?"

Suddenly sullen, he stared at the beamed ceiling. Beside her, William shuffled nervously.

Wringing the tapestry in her hands, she counted to ten, then to twenty, but he did not answer. Like a hot wind, anger blasted through her. "Bid farewell to your legitimate heirs, Revas Macduff. I'm going back to England."

Still staring overhead, he clucked his tongue. "You'll come back to me."

"When badgers fly!"

He looked at her then, and his eyes were cold with purpose. "Who will pay for your keep at the abbey? Surely not the husband of a runaway wife."

Rage, hurt, and confusion battled within her. Rage won out. "Do not trouble yourself about me, Revas Macduff. I managed well enough for many years without you."

"I'll take you there," William said. "We can be packed and gone in an hour's time. Leave him to his wenching."

A cajoling Revas started to rise. "Now, Meridene."

She held up her arm to keep him in place. "Stay where you are, you wretched snake."

"Look," he wheedled. "'Tis a rocky patch we've arrived at, but now that you understand, 'twill be better."

"Better? I'd rather face a pack of hungry wolves on the Great North Road than live here with you. You adulterer!"

"You cannot begrudge me one woman."

Fearing she would cry, she implored William with a glance. He took her arm, and she wanted to wilt into his. "Come, sister."

"Leave the Covenant," Revas said. "But you may take the belt."

Her control fled. Shaking William's hold, she

marched up to Revas and threw the tapestry in his face. In a blur of unshed tears, she stormed out the door.

Revas's knees wouldn't hold him. He collapsed into the chair and unfolded the cloth. Even after he heard them mount and knew she was gone, he couldn't take his eyes from the cloth. The face that crowned the work was his own, and the branchlike arms played host to girls and boys, each wearing a different Highland plaid.

From behind the bed curtains, Gibby's grandmother emerged. She had white hair, yet her face bore fewer wrinkles than other women her age. "Oh, Revas," she cried. "'Tis sad work we've done this day. You've broken the lassie's heart."

And his own.

Oh, sweet charity, how would he rule without her? What had once loomed as a glorious future now yawned like captivity in a foreign land. How could he kneel in church and speak honestly to God with so much blackness in his soul? How could he be fair when nothing mattered?

For a day and a night, he pondered the question. Comfort came with the knowledge that she was well on her way to England by now. With Cutberth's army marching across Lord's Meadow, the battle would soon begin.

The landscape stretched before Meridene, but she noticed little of the Highland scenery. Her heart pounded like a drum, and with every mile they traveled, the beating grew stronger. The feeling was not new; she'd experienced it aboard the ship after Revas had taken her from the abbey. But she understood the source of her discomfort. The thrumming in her chest had been the Highlands calling her home. Now it wanted her back.

As if compelled, she looked over her shoulder. Once

she had condemned Scotland, but that was before—before she'd come to know the people of Elginshire, before she'd met Serena and Summerlad, the adorable Ellen, the quiet Lisabeth, and dear, sweet Gibby.

Or Revas. Her stomach bobbed like a cork, and not from the ride, for her mount was the best mare in Revas's stable.

Revas. Tears stung her eyes, but she willed them not to fall. A womanizer wasn't deserving of her love and devotion. But why had he taken up with that woman? What feminine aspect did Meridene lack that would drive him to seek companionship elsewhere?

Did the name Macduff's Halt have some base meaning? Yes, she thought. It was a halt to decency and a respite from his wedding vows. He was welcome to it, and she hoped the sin blackened his soul.

But a part of her could not condone that low opinion of him, because it did not fit. In the moments when her mind's vision was unclouded by the reasons that drove her away from him, she wondered if she hadn't imagined the lodge, the woman, and her unrepentant husband. That man was a stranger.

She had questioned Brodie, William, and the Forbesmen who served as her escort. With the twin towers of Auldcairn still within sight, she had interrogated them.

Brodie dismissed Revas's transgression with a mumbled "'Tis a wife's place to obey her husband."

Glennie Forbes had set his jaw and stared at the road ahead.

One of his kinsmen had declared, "A man has his needs." But he'd spoken with little conviction.

On reflection, she wished she had talked with Summerlad. Why had he been so sullen when they last spoke in the common room? Why had Sibeal simply glared at her husband, rather than interrupt and correct him as was her way? And why had Sim been so evasive and guilty?

And that had been the order of the day: guilt. She'd been so aggrieved at Revas, she hadn't stopped to say good-bye to any of her new friends. Lisabeth and Ellen deserved better from the Maiden of Inverness. Sim deserved a personal return of his father's sporran. Would Gibby remember Meridene as the cold step-mother who came and went in a few fleeting cycles of the moon?

What of that bright-eyed lad who'd presented Meridene with that precious wooden bowl on the day of her arrival? What story would Revas spread in explanation of his wife's hasty departure?

But it wasn't Meridene's fault. Revas had broken his vows. Revas planned to make war. Revas had sent his daughter away.

Why?

Like a wasting sickness, the word tormented her. *Why, why, why?* If Revas marched to Kilbarton Castle to face Cutberth, why send Gibby to a farm in the sleepy village of Aberhorn? She'd be safer behind the walls of Auldcairn.

Unless he planned to strike the battle elsewhere. A notion wiggled its way into the quandary, and Meridene guided her horse abreast of Brodie's mount.

"Revas is planning a siege of Kilbarton Castle. That's why he wanted me to leave, and the reason he sent Gibby away."

Brodie's hands grew slack on the reins, and the stallion sidestepped. "Nay, my lady. He'll not make war without me and the Forbesmen at his back. 'Twould be folly, and Revas is seldom foolish."

At this point, she didn't know Revas at all. At least not the Revas she left behind. Why hadn't he kept Gibby at the fortress? Why had he driven Meridene away?

Like a shower of sunshine after a raging storm, enlightenment rained over her. Revas *had* driven her away. He hadn't meant those hurtful words. "Damn his noble heart!" she cursed out loud, and pulled her horse to a stop. "I'm going back."

Brodie snatched her reins. "You cannot."

She looked to William, who looked away. And she knew that her brother had helped deceive her. Only Glennie Forbes met her gaze. Rash and eager, he was too young for noble thoughts. That was why Revas always gave Summerlad command of the Forbesmen. The Macqueen lad had stayed to fight, and he hadn't been able to look Meridene in the eye when last they met. Shame had caused him to twist his war bands rather than face Meridene and lie. Sim had shied from her. Conal had acted strangely bold. Sibeal had been angered by her husband's odd behavior.

Worse than all of their actions was Revas's treatment of Meridene. Oh, yes. He had thought to exclude her from the impending strife. Unfortunately for him, he had not considered that she, too, felt responsible for keeping the peace in the Highlands.

Her father had pledged to end the legend of the Maiden, and through his ill deeds, he had convinced Meridene, for a time, to do the same. But now she would preserve her heritage and honor the women who for centuries had sacrificed to keep peace in the Highlands.

"Glennie," she said. "Will you help me teach Revas Macduff that his wife is not a delicate flower?"

"I . . . ah." Completely ill at ease, he had to struggle to control his mount.

"Will you assist me in showing him that it's wrong to belittle the office of the Maiden of Inverness?" she demanded.

Suddenly he was a ready warrior. He rose in the saddle. "Aye, my lady. Stand back, Brodie! Forbesmen," he commanded, "to me!"

Surrounded by Glennie and his kinsmen, Brodie had no choice but to yield. "The sin falls upon your head, lad."

Glennie's chest swelled and his eyes narrowed with conviction. "'Twas wrong of Revas to drive her away. The Maiden belongs in Scotland."

William guided his mount close to Meridene's. "She must go back, Sheriff," he said thickly. Turning to Meridene, he said, "She's our only chance. Take heart, sister mine, and remember that you demand a crown from a monster who has ordered your death."

Yanking the reins, she wheeled her mount and headed home.

CHAPTER

17

❧

At sunset the next day, they crested the hill overlooking Auldcairn Castle. Below, the outer bailey teemed with a well-provisioned army. A pennon bearing her father's device told Meridene all she needed to know.

She called out for Brodie and explained what she must do.

"Oh, nay, my lady. 'Tis too dangerous. Should your father spy you—"

"I know the way to the postern gate, Brodie. I've used it before. I'll not fall prey to that monster again."

His eyes gleamed golden from the light of the setting sun. "Then take Glennie with you, or William."

Again, she knew only boldness would sway him. "Then I might as well bring a bannerman to announce my arrival."

"They'll think you a camp follower and behave accordingly."

She'd act the veriest wanton to gain access to her home. "Then I'll tell them I have the French pox!"

He looked away, but his mouth twitched with humor.

She grasped his forearm. "Worry not, Brodie. I'm the Maiden of Inverness. But give me your yellow sash to hide the color of my hair."

All grumbling dissent, he did as she asked. "Go safely, then, and quietly." He handed her a sheathed dirk. "Use it swiftly and strike here." He drew a line across his throat. "'Tis sharper than a razor."

She swallowed hard at the thought of taking another life, even in defense of her own. But she must ease the sheriff's mind. So she nodded and slipped the dirk inside her sleeve.

"And you must avoid the pond," he insisted, pointing to the spot where the goose girl and her flock should have been. "They'll water their horses there. Move in a wide circle to the south, and approach the wall from the east, but do not leave the shelter of the forest until night is full upon us."

With a last embrace for her brother and a silent prayer for God to keep William safe, Meridene covered her hair with the scarf. Then she pulled up the hood of her cloak, circled wide, and moved into the woods to wait for nightfall.

"Take this." Elizabeth Gordon, the herald of Robert Bruce, handed Revas a tankard. "'Tis the best brew o' the Highlands."

They stood atop the newest of Auldcairn's square towers. Tents and campfires dotted the outer bailey. The sheep and cattle now milled in the castle yard, and the village was filled with families from the small farms close by.

Turning his face in to the night wind, Revas surveyed the enemy. "You say that because Randolph brewed it."

"Be it trouble or ale, Randolph is a master at

brewing both." Her voice dropped. "Tell me what you are thinking."

Success hinged on the support of his allies. He'd sent messengers to Sutherland, to Macqueen, and to Bruce. Elizabeth Gordon had not gone to Calais as she'd said, but to Elgin's End, where she'd heard the news of Cutberth's march on Auldcairn Castle. She'd returned immediately, and since her arrival, had ferried messages between Revas and Cutberth.

"Revas?"

In complete honesty, he said, "We're outnumbered three to one. He hacks up my forest and builds siege engines before my eyes. The Davidsons hold the road to Elgin's End. Through you, Cutberth bids me to surrender. Through you, I tell him to rot in hell. My people sit like crippled field mice awaiting the hawk."

"But how do *you* fare?"

He knew what she meant, and even though he fought against it, he felt his guard drop. Meridene was gone, and he was an empty shell without her. "'Tis a miserable place for me, Elizabeth."

Tomorrow would bring a battle, and the fate of every man, woman, child, and beast within the walls of Auldcairn Castle now rested in God's hands. But Revas had thought and spoken of nothing else since Cutberth's arrival, and he was weary of the subject.

He picked an intriguing topic. "Will you wed Randolph when your service to the king ends?"

"Aye." She gave him a wry smile and said her good-nights.

Alone, Revas turned his attention back to the land. From the outer bailey came music from a harp and a flute and voices better suited to calling the swine. To the south of the merrymakers, the pond gleamed silver in the moonlight, and the warhorses of his enemies appeared as spiny black boulders. Past the pond and farther to the east, the archers camped in the shadow of the near-completed siege engines.

Movement caught his eye. Just beyond the firelight of the bowmen's camp, a whore strolled her territory. From Revas's vantage point, the woman appeared no bigger than a beetle. One of the archers left the warmth of the fire and approached her, but she ignored him, probably intent on peddling her wares among soldiers with larger purses.

Wenching and merrymaking were expected at battle's eve, especially among the army that was sure to prevail.

For the hundredth time, Revas cursed himself for not anticipating the siege. But he'd been preoccupied first with getting Meridene to accept her destiny, then later with having her throw it away.

In that, at least, he had prevailed. But as he made one last sweep of his defenses, he couldn't help wishing she were by his side. On that selfish thought, he returned to his quarters, but he could not get her out of his mind.

Sleep came grudgingly, but when it found him, he slept like the dead, which was fitting. When he awoke, his first thought was of Meridene, as if she'd been with him through the night.

He'd known this day would come, but he hadn't expected her to be involved. Challenging Cutberth and taking the sword of Chapling had always been in Revas's future. Except that now his heart ached with a pain that made trifling of the misery of slaying another man in battle.

He rose, and with Summerlad's help, donned his chain mail, his bracelets, and his war boots. When he reached for his broadsword, he found only a small scroll in the scabbard.

A better sword awaits you.

Inside a perfectly sketched cinquefoil was the letter *M*.

Sim burst into the room. As if setting up a cheer,

the steward said, "Lady Meridene goes to take the sword!"

Serena, Lisabeth, and Ellen led a throng of females. They poured through the gates and into the inner bailey. Mothers carried their infant daughters; grandmothers led toddlers by the hand. Arm in arm, girls of every age and complexion skipped happily toward the break in the curtain wall. It was as if they were hurrying to a fair, rather than to a camped army awaiting a battle.

Horses shied and dogs barked. Thunder rumbled in the northern sky. Armor rattled as knights shifted uncomfortably from foot to booted foot.

Then Revas saw her. From his post at the gatehouse, he saw her throw off her cloak and shake her glorious black hair. Upon it she wore a crown of rowans, and she'd donned the most elaborate dress in her wardrobe. The gown was bloodred and trimmed with gold, as described in the Covenant and worn by the first Maiden of Inverness.

Revas's heart leaped into his throat, and he flew down the steps and raced to catch her. Where were her guards, and how the devil had she managed to get inside Auldcairn Castle and put that note in his scabbard?

Summerlad came up beside him. Over the trill of feminine voices, the lad yelled, "Where's Brodie?"

Revas shrugged and tried to pry his way through the moving throng of women. But he was jostled and tripped and had to struggle to keep his balance. It was as if they intentionally blocked his way.

A cold chill slithered up Meridene's spine, and she walked on legs as stiff as sticks. When the march began, she'd searched out the pennons flying above her father's tent and set her feet in that direction. But with each step, her courage faltered.

She'd feared him all her life, and he above all others wanted her dead. Without her consuming love for Revas, not even her duties as the Maiden could force her wooden legs to propel her toward the man who'd made her life miserable.

The rowan leaves prickled her scalp, and the sea of soldiers nicked at her resolve. But then she heard the voices of the women behind her, and the joyous sound pushed her forward. She could not forestall her destiny.

The tent flap was thrown back, and with a sinking heart, she watched her father emerge. A figure towering above even that of her memory as a small child, he wore full Toledo armor and carried his helmet in the crook of his arm. The Highland crown, a heavy circle of gold bearing the thistles of Scotland, ringed his head. His hair was just above shoulder length, as she remembered, but age had dulled the blond color to pale brown.

A few more steps brought her close enough to read the expression of hatred on his face, yet even that bitterness could not thwart her resolve. Once and for all, she would dethrone this unworthy king who'd ruled her with the same wrath and vengeance that he governed her people. They deserved better, and she'd give it to them in the form of Revas Macduff. Her husband, a wise and loving man, who would bring peace and unity to the Highlands.

But somewhere inside, a little girl still cringed and begged her father not to send her away. Meridene stood tall. She was no longer that frightened child. Her parents had brought her into the world knowing this day would come to pass.

Just then her mother stepped from the tent, and Meridene felt new rage fuel her determination. Once so beautiful as to inspire bards, Eleanor now looked haggard. As always, she concealed her black hair beneath a coif, same as she obscured the tenets of the

Covenant, same as she closeted the symbols of the Maiden's might.

Compared to the images Meridene had conjured of her namesake, of Sorcha, and of Mary, this Eleanor made a poor showing for the women of their line. Seeing her mother thusly, Meridene cursed her father and made a solemn vow that her own daughter would carry the legend with dignity and pride into the future.

Revas would make it so, for he would love and cherish their daughter as he did Gibby. Was he watching now? Meridene wondered, and fought the urge to turn and scan the noisy crowd behind her.

But she could not afford the distraction the sight of him would bring; she had a mission to complete.

There would be no war here today, save a battle between daughter and sire. With that thought in mind, Meridene picked up her step and walked toward as cruel a man as ever breathed good Scottish air.

To her surprise, as she passed the soldiers wearing Macgillivray colors, one by one, the men stepped back, removed their helms, and bowed their heads. She glanced at her father.

Surprise, then something like awe, crossed his features. He'd sired her, beaten her, and tried to take her life many times. What could now make his eyes startle with fear, as if he'd met his own ghost?

His knees shook, and for a moment she thought he might kneel before her. But a more personal hate, one exclusively for a daughter who could destroy the dream of death he harbored, filled his eyes. Meridene realized his fleeting moment of weakness had been for the legend of the Maiden, for the office she must uphold—not for the woman who'd once been a small child under his control.

He, too, was stunned by the display of respect she commanded.

There would be no slaughter of women and children here today, only a celebration of the passing of the sword of Chapling. A queen taking her throne. A wife sustaining her husband.

Another soldier grasped her father's arm and captured his attention. Seeing them standing so close and watching their conversation, she knew with certainty the younger man was Robert, the older brother who was a shadow on the edge of her memory. He was unimportant now, an observer of a great moment.

Her brother stepped back. Meridene stopped and solemnly faced Cutberth Macgillivray. Her gaze never wavered.

In a clear and commanding voice, she said the words she had written. "As Meridene to Hacon, and then through the ages to Eleanor who gave to you, I declare before God that I am the Maiden of this time. I have spoken my wedding vows to Revas Macduff, and he to me. I take up the tenets of the Covenant, and by the authority begun with my namesake and upheld by the women of my line, I command you to yield the sword of Chapling and the crown and swear fealty to Revas Macduff, the new king of the Highlands."

A sneer curled her father's lip, but behind it, she saw the respect he didn't want to hold for the office he'd belittled in anticipation of this day.

Then he scanned his army and found them in submission. Resigned, he swept off the crown and pitched it to Meridene. She caught it, and watched him draw the sword of Chapling. His armor rattled as he took a step toward her. His eyes promised death, though he held the sword lightly.

Eleanor intercepted him and grasped the blade with a bare hand. "I gave the sword to you, husband mine, and now I take it back."

Meridene realized that her mother also anticipated her husband's intent and had finally found the courage to defy him.

If he moved, the blade would slice her hand to pieces.

A stunned Meridene saw her father yield, for the first time, to his wife. With her free hand, Eleanor grasped the hilt of the weapon and faced Meridene. She held the sword with a reverence she'd not shown for the other traditions of the office she'd been born to uphold. Like a waning moon, regret shimmered in her eyes.

Her face wet with tears, Eleanor held the sword in two leveled hands. "Rule long and well, Meridene, and if you can find it in your heart, please try to forgive us."

At the combined weight of the weapon and the sentiment in her mother's words, Meridene swayed. An arm circled her waist and held her steady. Revas. As always, her husband gave her strength and support.

Together they watched Cutberth escort Eleanor from the battlefield. No longer a king, he was now a soldier without an army. The little girl inside Meridene suddenly pitied them, but her forgiveness was better served elsewhere.

Looking up, she faced the new king of the Highlands, and she smiled. "I believe this sword is yours."

When he moved to take it, she said, "But you have much to answer for."

"That I do, Meridene, my beloved."

As he knelt before her, she remembered thinking once that a crown should adorn his glorious hair. She made it so, and when he gazed up at her, a circlet of golden thistles above his brow, she thought him the most handsome and able man in Christendom.

"I don't suppose," he said solemnly, "that you would see my actions as those of a weak man struck dumb by love?"

The crowd had begun to murmur. Over the din, she said, "Only if I were blind would I see your dreadful scheme that way."

He nodded, but there was mischief in his eyes. "Then could you perhaps view my sin as a *wee blunder* by a man struck dumb by love?"

Moving the sword aside, she bent over him and whispered, "Who was that woman in your bed?"

Embarrassment reddened his complexion. "'Twas Gibby's grandmother."

Meridene believed him and was so relieved, she had to lean on the sword. Oh, what a knave he was. But he was her knave.

"If you will forgive me, Meridene Macgillivray, I will spend the rest of my days making you happy. I love you more than this crown you have lovingly bestowed, better than any sword you could give me, more still than the next breath I take."

"And I love you, Revas Macduff."

She stepped back and shifted the sword so it lay across both her palms. With pride and love in her heart, she took up her duties as queen of the Highlands.

"Hark, people of Elginshire," she spoke into the respectful silence. "I, Meridene of this time, bestow the stewardship of our land and the governance of our people upon Revas Macduff, and I hereby name him our sovereign and lord of my heart."

A cheer went up. Caps and helms soared into the bright blue sky. When he'd taken the weapon from her, Meridene made her obeisance to him.

"Arise, my love." He lifted her and pulled her into arms that were strong and sure, arms that would shelter her in the days and nights to come.

Held securely in the warmth of his embrace, Meridene cast off the ghosts of the past and stood proudly beside the man who would rule this land with warmth and kindness, the man who had given her the love and courage to face her destiny.

EPILOGUE

I am the Maiden Meridene, the second of that name to wear the crown of rowans and the first to give birth to a prince of Inverness. We have named our lad Kenneth Alexander.

I am Revas Macduff, king of the Highlands and the bedeviled husband to the most stubborn of women, the Maiden Meridene. Archbishop Thomas has christened our wee prince Hacon of Inverness.

POCKET STAR BOOKS
PROUDLY ANNOUNCES

BETRAYED

ARNETTE LAMB

Coming from
Pocket Star Books
mid-October 1995

**The following is a preview of
Betrayed. . . .**

Rosshaven Castle
Scottish Highlands
February 1785

Sarah traced the wooden bindings on a set of children's stories and waited for her father to share his troubling thoughts. To her surprise, Lachlan MacKenzie, the duke of Ross and the once-notorious Highland rogue, fumbled as he filled his pipe. His hands were shaking so badly his signet ring winked in the lamplight. His beloved face, more ruggedly handsome with the passage of time, now mirrored the strife contained within his goodly heart.

Sadness had begun this winter day, and Sarah wanted desperately to help ease the burden of his loss.

She touched his arm. "Agnes and I used to fight for the privilege of doing that. Let me fill it for you."

His broad shoulders fell, and he blew out his breath. "I'm not your—" Halting, he gazed deeply at her. Affection, constant and warm, filled his eyes. "I'm not your father."

Although she knew she'd misunderstood, Sarah went still inside. He'd acted oddly five years ago when her half sister, Lottie, had married David Smithson. When another sister, Agnes, had left home on an unconventional quest, he'd tormented himself for months. The day Mary demanded her dowry so she could move to London to perfect her artistic skill with Sir Joshua Reynolds, Papa had ranted and raved until their stepmother, Juliet, had come to the rescue.

His vulnerability was born of his love for all of his children, especially the elders, his four, illegitimate daughters, Sarah, Lottie, Agnes, and Mary.

Now he was bothered by Sarah's upcoming marriage to Henry Elliot, the earl of Glenforth, a man whose husbandly abilities he questioned.

But Sarah had made her decision and countered Papa's every objection. "Just because I'm to wed Henry in the spring and move to Edinburgh doesn't mean I'll stop being your daughter."

His blue eyes brimmed with regret. "Name me the grandest coward o' the Highlands, but I'd sooner turn English than admit the truth of it. Oh, Sarah lass."

Sarah lass. It was his special name for her. His voice and those words were the first sounds she remembered— even from the cradle.

"Tell me what, Papa? That I cannot at once be daughter and wife, sister and mother? I'm not like Agnes. I will not forsake you. Yet, I want my own family."

Always a commanding man, both in stature and influence, Papa now seemed hesitant. He touched her cheek. "You were never truly my daughter—not in blood."

She stepped back. "That's a lie."

Unreality hung like a pall in the air between them. Of course he was her father. After her mother's death in childbirth, he'd taken Sarah from the church in Edinburgh and raised her with her half sisters. It was a tale as romantic as any bard could conjure. Those of noble blood were expected to leave the care of even their legitimate offspring to servants. Not Lachlan MacKenzie. He'd taken his four, bastard daughters under his wing and raised them himself.

A stronger denial perched on her lips.

He took her hand. His palm was damp. His endearing smile wavered. "'Tis God's own truth."

Words of protest fled. Sarah believed him.

Moved by a pain so fierce it robbed her of breath, she jerked free and fled to the shelter of the bookstand near the windows.

On the edge of her vision, she saw him touch a taper to the hearthfire and light his pipe. She felt frozen in place, a part of the room, as natural in this space as the books, the toys on the floor, the tapestry frame near the hearth. This was her place, her home. Her handprints had smudged these walls. Her shoes had worn the carpet.

Reprimands had been conducted here, followed by joyous forgiveness.

"You cannot think I do not love you as my own."

His own. And yet not. Bracing her fists on the open pages of the family Bible, she struggled to draw air into her lungs. The familiar aroma of his tobacco gave her courage. "How can you not be my father?"

"I said it poorly." He slammed the pipe onto the mantel and came toward her, his hands extended. "I am your father, in all that counts. You are my own, but"— his gaze slid to the Bible—"I did not sire you."

"Who did?" She heard herself speak the words, but felt apart from the conversation.

New sadness dulled his eyes. "Neville Smithson."

Neville Smithson. The sheriff of Tain, a man Sarah had known most of her life. He lived at the end of the street. She had taught his children to read. Absently, she touched the string of golden beads around her neck. Neville had given her the necklace for her twenty-first birthday. Lottie was married to Neville's son, David. Less than an hour ago, both families had stood in the cemetery and laid Neville Smithson to rest.

His heart, the doctors said. He'd been conducting assizes. He had died in Papa's arms. His unexpected death, which had come as a blow to every household in Ross and Cromarty, now took on a greater meaning to Sarah.

She was neither the love child of Lachlan MacKenzie nor one of his four bastard daughters. Their illegitimacy was common knowledge, always had been. But in his special way, Lachlan had presented his lassies, as he called them, to the world as cherished daughters, and pity anyone who questioned it.

Sarah thought of her half sisters. They all shared a birthday, yet different mothers. As a result, he boasted, of his first and only visit to court. "Did you sire Mary, Lottie, and Agnes?"

"Aye, but it changes nothing. In your heart you are their sister and my daughter."

At ten, Sarah had shot up in height. Although of an age with Lottie, Agnes, and Mary, Sarah stood taller than them. Other differences came to mind. Sarah had always been bookish and quiet. Lottie often swore that Sarah needn't come with them to court, for she'd sooner find merriment in the nearest library. Sarah had been a shy child. Later she held back, not for lack of gumption, but because her sisters were better leaders than she. They were gone now, each pursuing her own life. Soon she would do the same.

"Why did you wait until now to tell me?"

He folded his arms over his chest. "'Twas Neville's last wish. You were still in swaddling when I took you for my own. He didn't even know about you until you were six and we came here to live. When I told him, we agreed 'twas best you did not know."

"Why?"

"We feared your life might seem like a lie."

They could have been standing in the dungeon rather than this toasty warm sanctuary, so cold did Sarah feel. "'Tis one lie for another, Papa." The endearment died on her lips. He always praised her maturity, her sensible nature. But in his heart he did not believe his own opinion of her, for he hadn't trusted her with the truth. Not until now.

Sensible Sarah.

She didn't feel sensible in the least.

Betrayal fueled her anger. "Henceforth, how shall I address you? Your Grace?"

Misery wreathed his face, yet his will was as strong as always. "You canna be angry. Your best interests were at the heart of it."

"If a lie has a heart, it beats the devil's rhythm."

"Sarah lass . . ."

As if she could shove his words away, she held up her hand. "I'm not *your* Sarah. My father is—is dead." Anguish stole her breath. Neville Smithson had entrusted his children to her, yet he'd denied her the greatest bond of all: her own blood kin. And now it was too late to look him in the eye and ask why he had not claimed her.

Other ramifications were endless and baffling. "I stand as godmother to two of my own sisters."

"And a fine influence you are on Neville's younger children."

Neville's children. Her siblings. But Lachlan MacKenzie still thought of her as his daughter. She clung to the comfort. "But they don't know that I'm their sister."

"We'll tell them."

How? she wondered, her pride reeling. But there was no hurt in it for them. Was there? Neville's son, David, would surely rejoice and expect Sarah to take his side in his marital disputes with Lottie. What would the younger ones, her godchildren, say? Would they see her differently?

"Did Neville want you to tell them?" she asked.

"There wasn't time. God took him quickly. He spoke of his wife, then of you."

The information neither cheered nor saddened Sarah. She felt numb.

"You were always so different from my other lassies."

That was true, but Lachlan had given each of his children an equal share of his love. To Agnes and Mary, he exhibited great patience. To Lottie, he gave understanding. To Sarah, he lied. Worse, he was quick to swear that she was the image of his own mother, a MacKenzie. An impossibility.

Sarah marshaled her courage. "It was all lies. Did you also lie about my mother?"

"Nay. Your mother was Lilian White, sister to my beloved Juliet."

Sarah's stepmother was also her aunt, a situation that had always been the cause of great jealousy among her siblings. But all along, she had reason to envy them their blood ties to Lachlan MacKenzie.

"Neville loved you, too. He left you ten thousand pounds."

As a final blow, Lachlan MacKenzie, the only father she had ever known, thought her shallow enough to be bought. Something inside Sarah began to shrivel. She wanted to flee, to cower in the dark and cry until the pain ebbed.

But cowardice was not her way. She was three and twenty and would soon embark on a new life as the countess of Glenforth. Therein lay her salvation from the hurtful world this room, this moment, and this life had become.

You bear the mark of the MacKenzies, Sarah lass.

A lie. No MacKenzie blood flowed in her veins.

In reality, she'd been sired by a man who had toasted her every birthday and visited her when she was ill. A sheriff named Smithson, not a duke named MacKenzie. A man they had buried this morning. A man who sought to buy her forgiveness from the grave.

The cruelty cut her to the bone. "Neville Smithson left me guilt money."

"Nay. You are the same Sarah MacKenzie as you have always been. I would not have given you up."

Even if Neville had asked, she finished the thought. Neville Smithson hadn't wanted her. As a tutor for his children, she'd been acceptable, but not as a treasured daughter.

His fair face rose in her mind, an image as constant as any in her memory. Her father. Neville Smithson, a commoner.

"What are you thinking?"

The sound of Lachlan's voice drew her from the stupor her mind had become. "I'm thinking that I must go to Edinburgh and tell Henry." Yes, Henry and a new life.

"I'll go with you."

Denial came swiftly. "Nay. I'll take Rose." Her maid was company enough.

He sighed in resignation. "If Glenforth is unkind to you or judgmental, I'll make him wish he'd been born Cornish."

The remark was so typical, Sarah smiled. But her happiness was fleeting. Until this moment, it hadn't occurred to her that Henry would do anything other than accept the news with good grace. His mother, the Lady Emily, would not be so generous, but Henry always prevailed in their disputes.

Sarah would take only her MacKenzie dowry to Edinburgh. Lachlan had pledged the twenty thousand pounds months ago and put his seal to the formal betrothal. With Henry's help, she would heal the wounds Lachlan MacKenzie and Neville Smithson had dealt her.

Six Months Later
Edinburgh, Scotland

"Lady Sarah!"

Two of Sarah's pupils, William Picardy and the lad called Notch, dashed into the schoolroom.

Notch yanked off his cap, and the crisp air made his hair crackle and stand on end. "The king is dead!"

Sarah's own troubles fled. "Who says?"

Shoving the smaller William out of the way, Notch hurried to her side. "The Complement's just come off a warship. Everybody knows the Complement wouldn't come to Scotland for any less of a reason." His adolescent voice broke, and he cleared his throat. "I say the old Hanoverian's carved his last button and sent the Complement to give us the jolly news."

The King's Complement was an elite troop of horse soldiers, noblemen all. With great ceremony, the Complement had served English monarchs since the time of Henry VIII. The Hanoverian kings had relegated them to ceremony and foreign service, preferring a Hessian guard. The arrival of the Complement in Edinburgh certainly boded change, but did not harken the death of a king.

Notch's fanciful imagination, coupled with the need to rule the younger orphans, was likely at the heart of the rumor.

Sarah intended to get to the truth of the matter. "Did you hear them say the king is dead?" she asked. "You heard one of the soldiers speak the words?"

He slid her a measuring glance. One eye squinted with the effort. When she did not back down, he withdrew a little. "Didn't have to have it said to me like I was a short-witted babe."

She saw through his bravado. It was how he'd managed

alone since the age of six on the streets of Edinburgh. At eleven, he was as world-wise as a man double his years. But in many ways, he was still a boy. In all events, he deserved her respect and her guidance.

"No one expects you to predict the fate of kings, Notch. Even bishops cannot do that."

He stared stubbornly at the scuffed toes of his too large shoes.

The other children, five to date, preyed on Notch's every word. She hoped to make him understand the responsibility he undertook as their leader.

She leaned against one of the school desks. "But if you are speculating, and it proves wrong, you shouldn't feel a lesser man because you were merely voicing *your* opinion. You could even learn and discuss the views of others in the matter. Such as Master Picardy here."

Eight-year-old William Picardy clutched his frayed lapels and rocked back on his heels. His blunt cut brown hair framed a face of near-angelic beauty.

Wondering how anyone could have abandoned this precious child to the streets, Sarah said, "Why do you think the Complement has come?"

Eyes darting from the school desks to the standing globe to the hearth fire, William considered the question.

"What's it to be, Pic?" Notch teased and challenged at once.

"I believe—" William paused, obviously battling the force of Notch's will. Then he sighed and said, "The king's upped his pointy slippers."

"There it is." Notch basked in his conquest.

Sarah gave up the effort to teach them democracy and shared responsibility. Theirs was a precarious existence; safety lay in numbers for orphaned children.

"Have you ever seen the Complement?" William asked.

"Nay," she said. "They've been abroad for most of my life."

"She's from the Highlands," Notch reminded him, but in a mannerly tone. Then he held out his arm. "Come along, then, my lady. If we hurry we can find a place in the crowd."

Bowing from the waist, William swept a hand toward the door. "Even the gentlemen and ladies have turned out for the Complement. Do come with us, Lady Sarah."

Curious, she reached for her cloak. The weekly lesson had ended hours ago, and if she stayed here alone, she'd spend the afternoon pondering events beyond her control.

But as she followed Notch down the stairs and out of the church, she couldn't fend off thoughts about Henry and the odd turn her life had taken.

Upon arrival at Glenstone Manor in Edinburgh, Sarah had learned that Henry and his mother were on an extended holiday in London. Rather than stay in the family mansion, she'd leased a house in nearby Lawnmarket and awaited their return.

To ease the loneliness and fill her idle time, she'd begun teaching school in a converted storeroom at Saint Margaret's Church. Those who could not afford private tutors sent their children to Sarah.

But then Henry's mother had returned with news that Henry had been accused by the duke of Richmond of cheating at cards. The Lord Chancellor had thrown Henry in prison and demanded twenty thousand pounds for his release. The exact amount of Sarah's dowry —money Lachlan MacKenzie had worked hard to earn.

Now only the orphans attended Sarah's Sunday morning school.

"Look!" shouted William. "There they are!"

Over the noisy crowd lining both sides of High Street, Sarah heard the clip-clop of horses' hooves. An instant later, the first of the riders came into view. The gusting wind, as much a part of Edinburgh as the biting winter cold, ruffled the white plumes in his helmet.

He sat atop a magnificent crimson bay horse. Wearing the traditional uniform of blue tabard, white trunk hose, and a chain of office bearing the Tudor rose, he drew every eye.

George II had added knee boots to the uniform; George III had commissioned fur-lined, velvet capes.

The entire troop, thirteen strong, riding three abreast behind the commander, now filled the street.

Cheers rose from the crowd, but the leader did not take notice. With his chin up, his handsome features appeared carved in fine marble. Yet there was something warm and oddly familiar about him to Sarah.

Impossible, she silently scoffed. She was merely attracted to his rugged handsomeness and commanding air.

"Has the king tucked it in?" yelled Notch.

"Shush!" Sarah grasped the boy's arm.

The commander turned just enough to spy the lad, then look at Sarah. To her horror, she felt herself blush beneath his probing gaze. A slow, sly smile gave him a regal air.

A conceited rogue, she decided, and quelled her admiration. As leader of the most respected collection of horsemen in the British Isles, he was probably accustomed to having women fawn over him. Sarah MacKenzie had better things to do, such as convincing the mayor of Edinburgh to convert the abandoned Customs House into an orphanage.

But hours later when she answered the knock at her door, Sarah rethought her opinion of the commander of the King's Complement. She also knew why he'd looked familiar.

Poised on her threshold, he now wore a brown velvet coat over an Elliot tartan plaid, pleated and belted in kilt-fashion. Henry favored his mother. But this man bore the true face of the Elliots, the same features she'd seen in paintings in the family's portrait gallery.

He had to be Michael Elliot, Henry's younger brother.

Henry. Her pride rebelled at the thought of the scoundrel she'd almost married, and if this second son had returned home to attend her wedding to his brother, he'd wasted a journey.

"You're Michael Elliot."

He shrugged, drawing attention to the breath of his shoulders and his thickly muscled neck. "So my nanny told me."

An odd answer and much too personal to address. Besides, Sarah had had enough of the deceitful and greedy Elliots.

"Why have you come here?"

"For two reasons, actually." He lounged easily against the door frame. "I simply had to meet the woman who preferred to wed a toothless and blind draft horse rather than marry my brother."

Sarah had said that and other disparaging remarks to Henry's mother, but she did not regret her rudeness. The wicked Lady Emily had bullied and insulted Sarah until her patience fled. The woman had gotten precisely what she deserved.

"My sainted mother also said you were a trouble-maker, but she hesitated to mention how beautiful you are."

Was the sarcasm in his tone meant for his mother or for Sarah? Probably the latter, considering the poor manners of the rest of his family.

Bother the Elliots. Sarah was done with them. "You are too kind," she said, meaning nothing of the sort. "You said you came here for two reasons. Beyond repeating my wish to never set eyes on an Elliot again, what is your purpose?"

As bold as a rogue at court, he winked and marched into her home. "To change your mind, of course."

Look for
Betrayed
Wherever Paperback Books Are Sold
mid-October 1995